D0461379

Glass Soup

Also by Jonathan Carroll

The Land of Laughs
The Voice of Our Shadow
Bones of the Moon
Sleeping in Flame
A Child Across the Sky
Black Cocktail
Outside the Dog Museum
After Silence
From the Teeth of Angels
The Panic Hand
Kissing the Beehive
The Marriage of Sticks
The Wooden Sea
White Apples

Glass Soup

Jonathan Carroll

A Tom Doherty Associates Book
New York

This is a work of fiction. All the characters and events portrayed in this novel are either fictitious or are used fictitiously.

GLASS SOUP

The prologue, "Simon's House of Lipstick," was originally published as a short story in Conjunctions: 39 *The New Wave Fabulists* in Fall 2002.

This book is printed on acid-free paper.

Edited by Ellen Datlow

A Tor Book
Published by Tom Doherty Associates, LLC
175 Fifth Avenue
New York, NY 10010

www.tor.com

Tor® is a registered trademark of Tom Doherty Associates, LLC.

Library of Congress Cataloguing-in-Publication Data

Carroll, Jonathan, 1949–
Glass soup / Jonathan Carroll.—1st ed.
p. cm.
"A Tom Doherty Associates book."
ISBN 0-765-31179-8
EAN 978-0-765-31179-5
1. Fantasy fiction. American.

PS3553.A7646 G57 2005
813'.54—dc22

2005005327

First Edition: October 2005

Printed in the United States of America

0 9 8 7 6 5 4 3 2 1

To—
Jeffrey Capshew
Martina Darnell
Alice Kricheli

the most wonderful friends

Glass Soup

Prologue—Simon's House of Lipstick

Haden was in trouble again. Big surprise, huh? So what else was new, right? That man wouldn't have known he had a *pulse* unless the IRA was closing in, his ex-wife was circling his field with a squadron of divorce lawyers, or a rabid dog had just bitten him on the dick.

When he opened his eyes that morning this is what immediately filled his mind: he had no money to pay the bills on his desk. His car was dying of three different kinds of automotive cancer. He had to lead a city tour today and if he didn't do it well this time, he would likely be fired.

Earlier in his life it was okay when Haden lost a job because there was always another around somewhere. But now, like the last pair of socks in the drawer, there were no more left. He had to wear this one with the big hole in the toe or else go barefoot, and barefoot meant even more trouble.

Sighing, he threw off the thin purple blanket he'd bought at a Chinese discount store after his wife left him and took everything, including the blankets. But she was right to leave because he was a dog in every way except loyalty. No, that's not fair. To call Haden a dog was to insult canines. Call him a rat, a weasel; call him a disease with a head. Simon Haden was not a nice man, despite the fact he was a very handsome one.

His face had been the downfall of not only innumerable trusting women, but also onetime friends, used car dealers who gave him a better deal than they should have, and former bosses who were proud for a while to have such a handsome guy working for them.

Why do we always, *always* fall for good looks? Why are we never immune to them? Is it optimism or stupidity? Maybe it's just hope—you see someone pretty and the sight convinces you that if *they* can exist, then things are right in the world.

Uh huh.

Haden used to say women don't want to fuck me, they want to fuck my face and he was right. But that was history. Now few women wanted to fuck any part of him. Oh sure, sometimes one down at the end of a bar who'd had too much to drink and begun to see double saw two Hadens and thought he looked like a movie star whose name she couldn't remember at the moment. But that was rare. Now he usually drank alone and went home alone. He was a shallow, self-absorbed middle-aged man with a fading face and an empty bank account, who gave guided tours of a city that was no longer his friend.

Why a tour guide? Because it was mindless work once you got the hang of it. And the tourists he led were so interested in what he said. Haden never got over how grateful these people were. They made him feel like he was *giving* them his city rather than just pointing out its sites.

Once in a while a good-looking woman would be part of a tour group. They were like an extra tip dropped in Haden's hand. What a wonderful guide he was on those days! Witty and informative, he knew everything they wanted to know. And what he didn't know, he made up. That was simple because he had been doing that sort of thing his whole life. His audience never knew the difference. Besides, his lies were so imaginative and interesting. Years later while looking at snapshots of their trip, people would say "See the dog in that portrait? It lived to be twenty-eight years old and was so loved by the Duke that its gravestone is as big as his."

A lie of course, but an interesting one.

Maybe there would be a pretty woman today. Gripping the sink with both hands, Haden stared into the bathroom mirror and said a little prayer: Let there be a beautiful female face today in that crowd of blue hairs, hearing aids, and TV-sized eyeglasses. In his mind he saw them all—saw their cream-colored crepe-soled shoes the size of small hydrofoils, the permapressed leisure suits a thousand years out of fashion. He heard their loud voices full of whines and never-ending questions—where's the castle, the toilet, the restaurant, the bus? Was one beautiful face asking so much? A daughter along for the ride, a nubile granddaughter, someone's nurse, anything to spare him a day surrounded by the House of Lipstick. He said those words slowly into the mirror, as if he were an actor learning his lines. Today he was guiding a group of people from the House of Lipstick. What was that, a store that sold only lipstick? Or a business that manufactured it? He would know more when he opened the envelope given to him at work, detailing the job.

He smiled, imagining twenty old people with lipstick-smeared lips, all very attentive to what he was saying. Glistening red lips, the color of a clown's nose or a dog's rubber ball. Sighing, he picked up his toothbrush and began to prepare for the day.

Because Simon Haden was a very vain man, his small closet was bursting with the best clothes—Avon Celli cashmere sweaters, one-two-three-four Richard James suits, one-hundred-and-fifty-dollar belts. He certainly had good taste and style, but neither had helped him much over the years. Yes, they had enabled him to fool some of the people some of the time. But sooner or later everyone, even the dumbbells, figured Haden out and then invariably he *was* out: out of a job, out of a marriage, out of chances.

What's most interesting about people like him, even more than their pretty faces, is that they almost never understand why the world eventually ends up hating them. Haden had done terrible things to people. But for the life of him, he could not understand why he had ended up where he was now—living alone in a lousy cramped apartment, working a no-exit job, and spending far too much free time at the TV watching whatever was in front of his eyeballs. He knew which wrestlers were feuding with whom in professional wrestling. He had given serious consideration to buying those Japanese steak knives on the Shopping Channel. He carefully taped his favorite daytime soap operas if he had to miss an episode.

How did I end up like this?

If someone had told Simon Haden that he was a colossal prick and why, he would not have understood. He would not have denied it, he would not have *understood.* Because pretty people think the world should forgive whatever their sins are simply because they exist.

He finished in the bathroom and went to the bedroom. The envelope containing the day's instructions lay on the dresser. In his underpants and sheer black socks, he picked it up and tore it open.

A little man the size of a candy bar stepped out of the envelope into his hand.

"Haden, how you doin'?"

"Broximon! Long time no see. How are you?"

Broximon, dressed in a beautiful blue pinstriped suit, brushed off both arms as if being inside that envelope had dirtied them. "Can't complain, can't complain. How're you?"

Haden carefully put him down on the table and then pulled up a chair.

"Hey Simon, put some clothes on before we chat. I don't wanna be talkin' to a dude in his underpants."

Haden smiled and went off to choose an outfit for the day. While waiting for him, Broximon took out a tiny portable CD player and turned on some Luther Vandross.

With the music cooking in his ears, Broximon walked to the

edge of the table and sat down with his legs dangling over the side. Haden sure lived *low.* The man's apartment showed no signs of life. No texture, no soul, nothing there that made you go, whoa, that's cool. Broximon was a firm believer in "to each his own," but when you're in a man's home, you can't help looking around, right? And if you see that apartment ain't got nothing inside it but the heat, well then that's just the truth of the situation. You're not making any sort of value judgment; you're just reporting what you see. Which in this case wasn't much, that's for damned sure.

"So I'm showing around this House of Lipstick today, right?" Haden came in wearing a formal white shirt open at the neck and a sharp pair of black slacks that looked like they had cost serious money.

"That's right." Broximon reached into his pocket and pulled out a folded slip of paper. "A group of twelve. And the part you'll like is that they're almost all women, average age thirty."

Haden's face lit up. His prayer had been answered! He couldn't believe his luck. "What's the story with them?"

"Did you ever hear of Mallvelous in Secaucus, New Jersey?"

"No." Haden looked to see if Broximon was joking with that stupid name.

"Biggest shopping mall in the Tri-State area. Then someone started a fire in it and it became the biggest shopping mall fire ever in the Tri-State area."

Haden checked his pockets to make sure he had everything—keys, wallet. Then he asked without much interest, "How many died in the fire?"

"Twenty-one, over half of them in the House of Lipstick. The fire started right next to their shop and so they didn't have much chance of escaping."

"What was it, some kind of cosmetics store?"

"Yup. The guy who owned it—you'll meet him today—had himself a good little business because that's all he sold. Just about every brand of lipstick on the earth. You know how everybody's crazy for specialty shops these days. He had brands from the weirdest places, like Paraguay. You never think of women wearing lipstick in *Paraguay,* you know?"

Haden stopped walking around the room and stared at Broximon. "Why not?"

The little man was instantly embarrassed. "I don't know. Because it's—I don't know. Because it's fucking *Paraguay.*"

"So what?"

For want of anything better to do, Broximon stood and brushed off both sleeves again. In a cranky voice he asked "Are you ready to go or not?"

Haden stared at him a moment longer, his expression saying he thought the little man was an idiot. The message was conveyed loud and clear. Finally he nodded.

"Good! So let's go, huh?"

Haden picked up Broximon, placed him on his right shoulder, and left the apartment.

• • •

He always met the tour bus outside the café where he ate his breakfast. The bus driver was one of those saps taken in by Haden's good looks and sometimes-charm and was more than happy to detour a few blocks out of his way to pick up the tour guide.

The bus doors hissed open. Simon Haden charged up the steps, lit from within by two cups of strong cappuccino and the optimism that comes with knowing you are going to spend the day with a bunch of young women. The bus driver, Fleam Sule, waved one of its many tentacles in greeting at Simon. Then with another tentacle it pressed a button to close the door. Haden had always loved octopuses. Or was it octopi? He would have to ask Fleam Sule that some day, but not right now because Women Ahoy!

Winking at the octopus bus driver, Haden put on his best, most winning smile and turned to face the passengers.

Outside on the street, Broximon stood and watched as the bus pulled away from the curb. A maple leaf blown by the wind collided with him, hiding the tiny man completely from view for a second. He brusquely pushed it away and the leaf fled down the street. Shaking his head, Broximon reached into his pocket and took out a cell phone the size of a pencil eraser. Speed-dialing a number, he waited for it to connect.

"Hi there, it's Brox. Yes, I was just with him." Broximon listened while the other voice said something long and involved.

Down at the corner the traffic light turned green. The tour bus took a left and disappeared into the city.

Broximon started going up and down on his toes and looking at the sky as the other person talked on. Eventually he was able to interject "Look, Haden doesn't *get* it yet. It's as simple as that. He doesn't have the slightest clue. Do you understand what I'm saying? He's not even on the *map* yet." Broximon saw a bright red cookie wrapper skittering down the street toward him. He started moving out of its way long before it arrived. Seeing it pass reminded him that he hadn't had breakfast yet. That made him doubly impatient to get off the telephone and find a place to eat. "Look, Bob, I don't know how better to tell you—*he doesn't get it.* There is not one indication that Simple Simon sees the big picture."

Listening some more to the voice on the other end, Broximon was no longer paying much attention. To amuse himself, he stuck out his tongue and crossed his eyes. After holding that pose for a while, he couldn't take the other's verbal diarrhea anymore. So he said "What? Huh? What? I'm losing you. We're losing our connection here—" Then he pressed the disconnect button and turned off the phone altogether. "Enough. Breakfast time."

• • •

It took several seconds for Haden's eyes to adjust to the blue dark inside the bus. He was so eager to see the women that he squinted hard to distinguish who sat facing him. The first thing he saw was a cassowary in a green dress. Do you know what a cassowary is? Neither did Haden, nor did he remember the one time he had seen one at a zoo in Vienna. He had stopped to look at it, thinking once again how weird nature could be.

Seeing that giant bird staring at him now, his eyes narrowed in dismay. Oh no, they weren't going to do *this* to him again, were they? He remembered one tour he'd lead where—

"Excuse me?"

Trying to locate the face, he worked very hard to overcome his growing distrust. "Yes?" He hoped his voice sounded happy and helpful.

"Is there a lavatory on this bus?"

Lavatory. When was the last time he'd heard that ridiculous word used, fourth grade? Smirking a little, he looked toward the questioner. Seeing her, his smirk died and Haden almost yawped because she was absolutely hair-raisingly beautiful. And blind.

That's right—even in that shadowy space he could plainly see the woman's eyes were so deep set in her head that they could not possibly have been functional.

"Uh, yes, there's a, uh, lavatory at the back of the bus on the left side." Absurdly and without thinking he beamed his best, most winning smile at her.

Like a crazy young dog pulling on its leash, all Haden wanted to do then was race down the aisle to her side and ask everything. What was her name, why was she there, where had she come from . . . He held himself back though and tried to calm his mad-to-get there impulse. He silently chanted to himself slowly, slowly—do this right.

For the first time since being hired to do this miserable job, Simon Haden was glad to be a tour guide; glad that today's sightseeing would last for hours. It was the top dollar, see everything, fifteen stops, watch your step getting off the bus tour. Normally he loathed it. Today with this blind angel along for the ride, it would be bliss.

Not that it mattered now, but he looked over the rest of the passengers on the bus. There were a few people, a few animals, two cartoon characters, and an almost six foot tall bag of caramels. Nothing special, nothing new. If they had been his only customers that day, it would have taken a real effort to rise to their occasion. But with the angel sitting on the aisle in row seven, he was going to enchant them all.

He picked up the bus microphone and turned it on. Blowing into it once, he heard his short puff resound throughout the bus speakers, proof that the thing was working. Sometimes it didn't and to add insult to injury, he ended the day hoarse.

"Good morning and welcome on board!"

As one, the humans, animals, and cartoon characters smiled at him. But the giant transparent bag of beige candy shuffled impatiently in its seat. *Let's go,* it appeared to be saying. *Let's get this show on the road.*

Haden disliked caramels. He ate a lot of candy because he had a sweet tooth, but caramels were too much work and too much trouble. Invariably they stuck in his teeth like gluey pests and had once even pulled out an expensive filling when he ate one at his parents' house. But they were very much a part of his childhood memories because his father loved caramels and was always eating them. His mother stationed little plates of the golden squares all around the house for her man.

"Today we're going to try and give you a pretty good overview of the city. We'll be starting in the center naturally and then working our way out—"

"Excuse me?"

He recognized her voice immediately and with a dazzling smile that could have lit the inside of the bus like a thousand-watt lightbulb, he turned to the beautiful blind woman, ready to heed her every wish. "Yes?"

"Is there a lavatory on this bus?"

The only way to make beauty ugly is to show it's crazy. Like twisting the top off a jar of something wonderful to eat, the moment he's hit by the terrible smell of it gone bad, even the hungriest person will drop the jar in the trash without a second thought.

Haden took a short quick breath as if he'd been punched in the stomach. She had already asked that question one minute ago. Was she crazy? Was all that beauty wasted because she had scrambled eggs for brains? Or maybe she just hadn't heard his initial response. Was that possible? Maybe she'd been distracted or thinking about something else when he had specifically said—

He stared at her, not really knowing what to say now. And as he stared, something dawned on him. He *knew* this woman. We rarely forget great beauty but sometimes it does happen. He ignored her question now because something in him kept saying *I know her face.* But where did he know it from?

The bus suddenly jolted to an abrupt stop, knocking Haden way off balance. He turned to see what had made the driver slam on the brakes like that. Through the front windshield he saw a school class of young kids being shepherded across the street by a middle-aged black woman wearing a vibrantly colored dashiki and an Afro haircut that made her head look like a round, carefully trimmed hedge. When all of the kids had crossed the street and were safely on the other side, the woman raised a hand and wriggled her fingers in thanks to the bus driver for stopping. At first Haden didn't recognize the woman, her Afro hairdo or dashiki; it was her wriggle. He *knew* that wriggle. He had lived with it for almost a year at one time in his life. Seconds later he was absolutely sure of her. He knew the wriggle, knew the gesture, and now he knew the woman who made it.

Whipping his head around, he looked at the beautiful blind woman. He knew her too. What the hell was going on here? Why was the world too familiar to him all of a sudden?

Back a few rows in the bus, Donald Duck looked across the aisle at the cassowary and slowly raised an eyebrow. The cassowary saw it and shrugged.

"Mrs. Dugdale!" Her name fell on top of Haden's head like a brick dropped from the roof. "She was my teacher!"

The octopus bus driver looked at him. "Who was?"

Haden pointed excitedly through the windshield in the direction of where the children had just gone. "*Her*—the black woman who just passed with all those kids. That was my teacher in third grade!"

The driver looked in the rearview mirror a moment at the passengers. At least half of them had slid forward in their seats expectantly, as if waiting for something important to happen.

The driver feigned indifference. "Yeah? She was your teacher. So what? Too late for me to run over her now."

"Let me out. I've got to talk to her."

"You can't leave now, Simon. We just started a tour."

"Open the door, I gotta get out. Open the door!"

"They'll fire you, man. If you walk out like this on a tour, you're history. Don't do it."

"Fleam, we're not having a discussion here, okay? Just open the damned door." Haden was a big man with impressive muscles. Fleam Sule was only an octopus and wasn't about to argue. However he couldn't resist flinging a last warning at the other's back as Haden walked down the steps to the street: "You're in trouble now, Simon. As soon as I tell them about this back at the office, they're going to fire your ass."

Haden wasn't listening. He didn't even hear the door hiss shut behind him or the bus pull away from the crosswalk. He certainly did not see all of the passengers flock to one side of the bus to see what he was going to do next. Even the beautiful blind woman was there; her cheek pressed to the cold glass, listening intently as someone described to her what Simon Haden was doing at that very moment.

• • •

He hurried after Mrs. Dugdale and the children. It was amazing that he had abandoned the tour and even more, his chances with the gorgeous blind woman. But the moment he realized who was leading those kids across the street, Haden knew he had to talk to her.

Because her third grade class had been so important to him?

Hell no.

If he'd been forced on pain of death to remember one nice thing about that year in Mrs. Dugdale's class, all that he would have been able to come up with was she kept a goldfish in a large round bowl on her desk that was soothing to look at.

Then was it because Mrs. Dugdale herself was one of those memorable teachers who by example change our lives forever?

Nope.

The woman yelled at students or threw chalk at them whenever she felt their attention was wandering, which in her class was most of the time. Her idea of teaching was assigning individual oral reports on what was grown in Surinam. If you were bad (and most everything was bad to Mrs. Dugdale), she made you stand interminably in a corner against what she called "the Wall of Shame." In other words, she was like too many teachers you had in elementary school. Haden had endured her moods and mediocrity and morsels of knowledge for a year and then he moved up to fourth grade.

But there was one thing about her that he had never forgotten and it was why he was running after her now. In fact this one thing had played a significant role in forming him. It was one of those rare childhood moments that we can look back to and say without hesitation *right there*—that X marks the spot where something in me was changed forever.

When he was a boy, Haden had one great friend who happened to have the unfortunate name Clifford Snatzke. But Cliff was so utterly typical that he blended into life with only that unusual name to distinguish him from X zillion other boys. For a while, until girls eventually became both visible and scrumptious, the two boys were inseparable. In Mrs. Dugdale's class they sat next to each other which made the time with her slightly more pleasant.

Right before that school year ended and report cards were sent home, Cliff became frantic that he wasn't going to pass because he had failed too many spelling tests. He worried so much and so vocally about it that an exasperated Haden finally urged his friend to go see their teacher after class and just ask. After much hemming and hawing, Snatzke agreed to do it—*if* his friend would wait for him outside the school building. Although Haden had ten other things he wanted to do at that time, he agreed. What were friends for?

Not much in life bothered Clifford Snatzke and his face showed it. Usually he wore a slight smile or else a pleasant blankness that said he wasn't thinking about anything special and everything was okay.

But when he emerged from the school half an hour later, his cheeks were the red that accompanies great humiliation or a bad cry. Seeing him like that, Haden eagerly asked what had *happened* inside. At first Cliff wouldn't even make eye contact with his friend, much less tell the story. But eventually he did.

Mrs. Dugdale was sitting at her desk looking out the window when he entered her classroom. Always one to mind his manners, Cliff waited until he was noticed. When the teacher asked what he wanted, he told her in as few words as possible because all of her students knew that Mrs. Dugdale liked a person to get right to the point.

But instead of looking in her grade book or giving him a lecture on how to improve his spelling, his teacher asked what kind of name

Snatzke was. He didn't know what she was talking about but said only that he didn't know. She asked if he thought Snatzke was a very American name. He said he didn't know what she meant. She looked out the window again and didn't say anything for a long time. After a while he gently repeated his question about his grade in spelling.

Who knows why, who knows where such a thing came from in the woman, but Mrs. Dugdale then turned to this little boy and said "Get down on your knees and ask me, Clifford. Get on your knees and ask for your spelling grade."

Kids are dumb. They're trusting and they have faith in what adults tell them because adults are the only authorities they have ever known. But the moment he heard this order, even dumb Clifford Snatzke knew that what Mrs. Dugdale was telling him to do was both wrong and extraordinary. But he did it anyway. He got down on his knees as quickly as he could and just as quickly asked for his grade. His teacher looked at him for a few seconds and then told him to get out of her room.

That was the story. If Haden hadn't known his friend so well, he would have thought Snatzke made the whole thing up. But he hadn't. Before there was a chance to say or do anything, the front door of the school opened and Mrs. Dugdale emerged carrying her familiar brown leather briefcase. She saw the two students, gave them a fake smile and moved off.

Both boys stared at the ground for a long time. They couldn't look at each other until she was gone because of their shared knowledge of what she had just done.

Simon knew he had to act. Mrs. Dugdale had done a very bad thing to his friend. But Cliff would let it slide because he didn't have the guts to face her.

Haden *did* and for one of the only times in his life, he decided on the spot to do a genuinely selfless thing and right the wrong that had been done to his friend. Throwing Cliff a reassuring look, Simon trotted off in the direction of the faculty parking lot.

When he got there, Mrs. Dugdale was already in her beige Volkswagen and the engine was running. When she saw him coming toward her car she rolled the window down halfway. He would always remember that—the window went down only halfway; as if whatever *he* had to say was not important enough for her to make the effort to lower it further.

Moving toward the VW, he felt as confident as a god about to fling a flaming lightning bolt at a sinful mortal. He was going to let her have it because boy, did she deserve it.

"Yes, Simon? What do you want?"

He looked at her and panicked. Whatever godlike courage he had brought to that moment fled. He could almost see it running crazily away in a zigzag across the parking lot, its ass on fire like Wile E. Coyote in a Road Runner cartoon. Haden loved cartoons.

"Why—" he managed to squeeze out of his terrified lungs before starting to hyperventilate. He thought he was going to have a heart attack.

"Yes, Simon? Why what?" Her first two words were friendly; the second two were a steel trap snapping shut.

"Why—" He couldn't breathe. His tongue had turned to stone.

"Yes, Simon?" He saw her right hand release the emergency brake. Her mouth tightened and her eyes flared when she realized he wasn't going to say anything more and that he had delayed her unnecessarily. Desperate and terrified, he did the only thing his body could manage at that moment—he shrugged. Mrs. Dugdale would have said something nasty if she hadn't seen Clifford Snatzke walking toward them.

She didn't even bother to roll up the window. Putting the little car in gear, she shook her head and gunning the engine, pulled away from Haden.

• • •

On and off for the rest of his life he thought about that moment and what he *should* have said and done. It haunted him, as childhood memories so often do. He even dreamt about it at night sometimes. But always, even in those dreams when his big Cinerama, Dolby surround-sound moment came to be valiant, he chickened out.

Well not this time, by God! He had been having a rough go of it recently. Maybe seeing Mrs. Dugdale on the street now for the first time in thirty years was a test. If he passed it, things would take a turn for the better. Who knows? Life could be sneaky sometimes. The lessons it taught weren't always straightforward. Anyway, he'd like nothing more than to tell that bitch what he thought of her all these years later.

As he hurried after her now, a thought blazed up in his mind like a flame flaring in total darkness: maybe many of his failures in life had been due to her and that stinking incident so long ago. If she hadn't scared him into silence, the courage he'd had on the tip of his soul that afternoon would have emerged. For the rest of his life he would have known it was there in him and real and could be used any time he needed it.

Rather than a botched, half-assed, bill-laden, dead-end life full of microwave meals and lousy smells, Haden might have been a contender—if it hadn't been for Mrs. Dugdale. He picked up his pace.

A few moments after he caught sight of her, a car driving down the street lifted lazily off the pavement and took flight. It buzzed around overhead in a few circles before veering off out of sight behind an office building. Two large chimpanzees dressed like 1930s gangsters in double-breasted suits and black Borsalino hats came out of a nearby store smoking cigars, speaking Italian and walking on their hands. Haden saw these things but paid no attention. Because Dugdale was near.

As he closed in, he touched the tops of her students' heads as he went. Despite his preoccupation with wanting to reach his old teacher, he couldn't help noticing how warm the children's heads were under his hand. Like little coffeepots, all of them, percolating.

"Excuse me, Mrs. Dugdale?"

Her back to him, the woman turned slowly. When she saw the adult Simon Haden standing two feet away, her eyes did not ask *Who are you?* They said *I* know *who you are—so what?*

"Yes, Simon, what do you want?"

Aaaugh! The exact same words she had said to him thirty years ago in the elementary school parking lot. The same unsympathetic expression on her face. Nothing had changed. Not one thing. He was almost middle-aged but she was still looking at him as if he were a bad piece of fruit at the market.

Fuck that. His moment had come. Now was the time to act decisively. Now was the time to say something brilliant and important to show her who was boss.

Because he was in such a state of shock after hearing her familiar words, Haden did not realize that all of Mrs. Dugdale's students were frozen in place, staring at him with intense anticipation. Nor did he notice that essentially the whole world around him had come to a standstill because it too was waiting to see what he would do next. Oh sure, cars moved along the street and flies buzzed their mad circles in the air. But all of them—the flies, the drivers in the cars, the molecules in their lungs—everything and everyone had turned to Simon Haden to witness what he would do next.

He made to speak. We must give the man that. Stirring words came to him, perfectly right for the moment. The right words, the ideal tone of voice. He was all ready to go. He started to speak but then discovered he no longer had a mouth.

He worked his mouth up and down, or rather the skin on his face where a mouth had previously been. It stretched, it moved, but that was only because it was skin and he was working the muscles beneath it. Muscles that should have controlled a mouth but Haden did not have one of those anymore. He had only skin there—smooth flat skin like the long expanse on a cheek.

He put both hands up to touch it but that only confirmed what he already feared—no mouth. Unwilling to believe what they were feeling, his fingers kept groping around as if they were feeling for a light switch in the dark.

He glanced at Mrs. Dugdale. Her expression made that terrible moment worse. Scorn. The only thing on her face was scorn. Scorn for Haden, scorn for his cowardice, and scorn for whomever he was now in her eyes. He was reliving his thirty-year-old moment of truth with her in the school parking lot. And this time he *would* have prevailed—if he'd only had a mouth.

But he didn't. Frantically he slapped the space on his face where a mouth *should* have been. While doing that, he glared at the woman—this villain in an Afro who was winning again. The only weapon he had to use now was his eyes. But eyes are not meant for this kind of warfare. A dirty look doesn't have the firepower, the mega-tonnage a ripping good sentence does.

Somewhere in a far corner of his mind, Haden knew that he had been here before, right smack in the middle of this moment and same situation, mouthless. But his fury and exasperation combined brushed aside this déjà vu. So what if he had been here before—he still had to handle it now. Still had to find a way to defeat Dugdale and show her that he was not the fool her mocking eyes said he was.

Desperation growing, he looked around for something, anything that he could use. His eyes fell on a little girl. Her name was Nelly Weston and she was one of Mrs. Dugdale's students. The girl was tormented too often by the teacher for being too slow, too sloppy, too dreamy for Dugdale's liking.

Haden picked up Nelly and slid his hand under the back of her sweatshirt. It happened so fast that she didn't have a chance to protest. But when he touched her bare back she understood instantly what he was doing and smiled like she had never smiled before in her teacher's presence.

Nelly looked at Mrs. Dugdale and opened her mouth wide like the ventriloquist's dummy she had just become. It was all right though because she also knew what was about to happen. Out of her little girl's mouth came a man's deep voice—calm but a little threatening too—Simon Haden's voice.

"You mean old witch! You haven't changed at all in thirty years. I'm sure you're still torturing your students when no one is watching. When your door is closed and you think you're safe. Remember Clifford Snatzke, huh? Remember what you did to him? Well, surprise! You're not safe and some of us do know *exactly* what you've done, bully. Shithead."

Nelly mouthed his words perfectly. She could feel Haden's hand on her back manipulating her, but he didn't need to because the two of them were wholly in synch with the words. What he wanted to say she wanted to say, and she did.

When he was finished and staring triumphantly at Dugdale's stunned face, Haden barely heard a voice nearby say "Well, it's about time. Bravo for you."

He shifted his eyes over and down and to his real surprise, there was dapper little Broximon, hands on hips, a big smile on his face. Where had *he* suddenly come from?

A million or a billion synapses and connections and whatever else suddenly happened in Haden's brain. Something big was taking form in there, something was coming clear. He suddenly looked at life around him. At the street, the cars, the people, the sky, the world. And then an instant later, Simon Haden *understood.*

He gasped through a mouth that reappeared on his face the moment he made his discovery. He lowered Nelly Weston to the ground.

This city, this planet, this life around him was his own invention. He had created all of it. He knew that now. Where had he created it? In the dreams he had every night while he slept.

He looked at Mrs. Dugdale and was almost as surprised to see that she was smiling at him and nodding. So was Broximon. So was every person nearby. A small dog on a leash was staring and smiling at him too. He knew the dog's name—Kevin. He knew because he had created it one night. He had created this entire world.

Simon Haden finally realized that he was surrounded by a city, a life, a world that he had gradually made every night of his life in his dreams. Everything here was either fashioned by him, or taken from his conscious life and carried over into his dream world where he could play with it, fight against it, or try to resolve it in a place of his own.

At forty, Simon Haden had had more than fourteen thousand dreams. A lot of material there with which to build a world.

"I'm dead." He stated this—he did not ask it as a question. He looked at Broximon. The little man kept smiling but now he nodded too.

"*That's* what death is—everyone makes their own when they're alive. That's why we have dreams. When we die all of our dreams come together and form a place, a land. And that's where we go when we die, isn't it?" This time Haden looked at his old third-grade teacher for corroboration and she nodded too.

"Then you live in that dreamland you created until you recognize what it really is, Simon." She said it cheerfully, in the same tone of voice one would use to proclaim that it was a beautiful day.

Thoughts, images, and particularly memories shot back and forth across Haden's mind like tracer bullets in a night firefight. Octopus bus drivers, cars that flew, beautiful blind women—

"That blind woman—I remember her now. I remember the dream of mine she was in. She was always saying the same thing again and again. It drove me crazy. I had the dream right after I got married. I dreamt—"

Broximon waved the rest away. "It doesn't matter, Simon. So long as you realize what this is all about now, you can fit the individual pieces together later."

"But I definitely *am* dead?" For some reason, Haden looked at little Nelly Weston this time for the answer. She made a child's big up-and-down nod to make sure that he understood.

He gestured with both hands at the world around them. "And this is death?"

"*Your* death, yes" Broximon replied. "And you created all of what's around us at one time or another while you were alive. That is, except for Mrs. Dugdale and things like that giant bag of caramels on the bus. Remember how much your father loved caramels?"

Haden was petrified to ask the next question but knew that he must. In a low voice, almost a whisper, he asked "How long have I been here?"

Broximon looked at Dugdale who looked at Nelly who looked at Broximon. He sighed, puffed out his cheeks and said, "Let's just say you've had this meeting with Mrs. Dugdale pretty often. But before this, she's always won. You should be very proud of yourself, Simon."

"Answer me, Broximon. How long have I been here?"

"A long time, pal. A very, *very* long time."

Haden shuddered. "And I'm just realizing now what it's all about?"

"Who cares how long it's taken, Simon? You know now."

The woman and the girl nodded vigorously in agreement. Haden noticed that the rest of those around them were nodding too in much the same way. Even Kevin the dog was nodding—everyone clearly agreeing on this issue.

"Well, what am I supposed to *do* with it? What am I supposed to do now?"

Mrs. Dugdale crossed her arms over her chest and wore a very familiar expression on her face. Haden remembered it well. "Today you finally passed first grade, Simon. Now you move on to second."

An icy chill tiptoed up Simon Haden's spine. "Death is like *school*?"

Again, everyone and everything there grew the same smile and looked very pleased at his progress.

A Hot, Dark Yes

"If I were married to a woman who dressed like that, I'd murder her clothes and bury them *deep* in a forest in the middle of the night." Flora Vaughn said this too loudly about an overdressed woman who had just passed their table. Then Flora looked meaningfully at Leni Salomon. Both of them wore the same color of fingernail polish—matte brown.

Isabelle Neukor looked from one woman to the other and smiled. They were her best friends; they were all thirty-two and had grown up together. But her friends could not save her now. No one could.

Leni's cane leaned against her thigh like a silent devoted dog. She walked with a pronounced limp—her left leg was shorter than the right. She was also the best-looking of the three women but like most genuinely good-looking people, paid it little mind.

Leni Salomon and Flora Vaughn had husbands, Isabelle did not. Leni and Flora were not in love with their men, Isabelle was. Strange things had been happening to her lately; so strange that she could not believe some of them. Even after all that had happened in the last months, she could not believe these recent events had actually taken place. She had told no one about any of them, not even Vincent.

"Guess who died, like, a *year* ago but I just heard about it?" Flora sat back and dropped her large pink napkin dramatically onto her plate of half-eaten asparagus. She was given to stagy gestures—it was her way. She had a big man's laugh. She used a lot of body language when she spoke, as if trying to explain things to a deaf and dumb world. People had different opinions about her looks—some thought she was a knockout, others that she was creepy with her very long auburn hair and almost-Oriental eyes. Vincent liked her a lot. He called her "Big Red" after they met the first time and since hearing that, she often signed her notes to anyone "Red."

Leni made false teeth—gold teeth, bridges, false teeth. She was a dental technician, one of the best around. She loved the job, its intricacies and complications. She called it useful architecture. When anyone asked her a question, she held it up and turning it slowly, looked at it from every angle as if it were a tooth she was making. "Someone we know or someone famous?"

Flora looked at Leni and winked. Then her eyes moved over to Isabelle and she said in an oily way "Someone you and I once knew, Leni, but who *really* wanted to know Isabelle."

From a blank "Huh?" Isabelle's expression slid into a frown. A few beats passed until her eyes slowly began to widen in recognition. Aghast, she put a hand in front of her mouth. *"Simon?"*

Flora nodded. "Dead over a year ago."

Leni gasped. "Simon Haden died?"

Flora steepled her fingers and looked prayerfully toward heaven, like a saint on a kitsch Italian religious postcard.

As one, the three women burst out laughing at the fact of Simon Haden's death.

• • • • • •

Standing in a giant meadow next to an ugly black longhaired dog named Hietzl, Vincent Ettrich watched an airplane sail eight feet above their heads and crash nearby. Ettrich sighed. Hietzl would have sighed too if it had understood how much time and trouble its friend had put into building that plane. But the dog was so happy just to be out there alone with Vincent that its sigh wouldn't have lasted long.

Shaking his head, Ettrich walked to the wrecked model and squatted down next to it, hands on his knees. As was his style, he was dressed like a teenager—ancient washed-out jeans, gray and white skateboarder's sneakers, and a black T-shirt with a picture of John Lennon on it. Ettrich was young-looking anyway. Seeing him for the first time, you would have guessed he was in his thirties rather than the early forties he was.

Hietzl heard something and quickly turned its head to the left. Ettrich continued to stare at what was left of his model airplane and wonder what he had done wrong in assembling it. The dog began barking so furiously that Ettrich snapped out of his funk-trance and looked toward where his companion was pointing. Behind them was a giant stand of trees, their leaves blowing in the frisky warm wind. But Hietzl was pointing in the opposite direction—out toward the open field.

Puzzled, Ettrich looked down at Hietzl and asked "What? What's there?"

The dog ignored him and kept yapping.

That annoying rat-a-tat barking and the wind soughing through the trees around them was all there was. It was midsummer; a sky the color of shirt cardboard, the air heavy with humidity. No one else was around.

Ettrich came out here often with the dog to walk or lie on his back and look at the clouds. Since moving to Vienna, he had done little besides recover his strength and think about the child Isabelle was going to give birth to soon.

Ettrich had died but then been brought back to life by Isabelle. He had crossed and recrossed the great border. While on the other side he'd learned both the language and some of the requisite lessons of the dead. Alive again, he thought his mind had been wiped clean of what he had been exposed to in the short time he had been dead.

He was wrong. Ettrich retained everything he had experienced. But to access that room in his mind now, he needed a key to the door. Right now he did not have one.

As soon as it was possible for him to travel he and Isabelle had left America and flown to Vienna. Ettrich left his wife, two children, and a life he had once thoroughly enjoyed and felt content with. But he abandoned it all because he wanted to be with Isabelle Neukor. He was willing to throw everything aside so that he could spend the rest of his life with her and their child. Their doubts were over. They had crossed the great bridge between now and then.

Hietzl's barking took on a new tone: it was even more urgent, as if there was real danger nearby, or they were right on the brink of something. Ettrich looked again toward where the dog was pointing but saw nothing. Still, Hietzl's agitated tone made him uneasy. For some reason—who knows why?—he turned quickly and glanced back to the place on the ground where his model airplane had crashed a few minutes before. It was gone.

Ettrich did not appear surprised. His eyes flicked here and there around the area to make sure this was true. It was—the model had disappeared. Only then did a kind of alarm show on his face. The dog was right—real trouble *had* just arrived.

"Hietzl."

The dog stopped a moment, and then continued barking.

"Stop it! Come on, we've got to go right now." Ettrich touched the dog on top of its head. Then he began walking back toward his car as fast as he could manage. He had not healed completely so he couldn't run. But he would have.

• • •

Two hundred yards behind them among the thick stand of trees stood another man and his dog. This man's name was John Flannery. He was portly and rather short. He wore a trimmed salt-and-pepper beard. People sometimes remarked on the resemblance between him and photos of the older Ernest Hemingway. Flannery always liked hearing that. He'd never read Hemingway but liked who he was.

Today he wore a brand-new blue T-shirt that wasn't tucked into a pair of brand-new beige shorts covered with lots of pockets. Oddly, he was barefoot although he stood on a forest floor covered with a variety of sharp stabby things.

The dog, a Great Dane with black spots scattered across its white body like ink spilled on a blotter, was named Luba. It had blue eyes and stood unmoving by Flannery's side. The presence of these two had caused Ettrich's dog to start barking. Interestingly, Hietzl had sensed them but gotten their direction wrong. Ettrich saw nothing when he looked toward where Hietzl was yapping because nothing was there. Flannery and Luba stood far behind them, watching impassively, as the other two walked away and finally out of sight. Flannery held Ettrich's model plane in both of his hands. It was whole again and looked like it had just come new out of a box.

When the others were gone, Flannery turned toward the woods and lifted his arm high above his head. With a quick flick of the wrist, he threw the plane into the trees.

Defying all laws of logic and gravity, it stayed aloft for the next twenty minutes. Even when the wind around them died completely, the small plane continued flying through the forest—around trees, beneath and above and round and round long crooked grasping branches that normally never would have let it pass. The plane flew right by those branches. It taunted them with loop de loops and sudden swerves to avoid all kinds of collisions that should have happened but didn't.

After a while Flannery and Luba sat down on the forest floor to watch this performance. Now and then the man spoke to the dog in a relaxed companionable voice. It looked at him as if it understood every word.

At one point Flannery raised his left hand. The wooden plane instantly stopped and hung in the air fifteen feet up, next to a towering chestnut tree covered with flickering yellow-green leaves. A mile and a half away, Ettrich had started his car and was driving off. Flannery nodded and smiled for the first time, having waited for the sound of those tires crunching across the gravel of the parking lot. His hand dropped and the plane started flying again.

"Things *look* good, but we can't get excited yet. 'Thunder is not yet rain,' " John Flannery said out loud. He loved proverbs. He memorized whole books of them and always had one for any occasion. Suddenly another popped into his head. "Too large a morsel chokes the child." As he thought about it for a few moments, his face lit up in delight. He could use that. Damn right! He could use it this minute to make Vincent Ettrich's life a very, very uncomfortable place to be.

He raised his chin a bit toward where the plane was flying. It did a 180-degree turn toward him. As if waiting for instructions, it paused a second or two and then flew away. Out of the forest, away from the trees and Flannery and Luba the dog, the plane flew toward Ettrich and his dog and Isabelle Neukor and their child and the misery these people would soon know. Today was the first day of the end of their lives. Even John Flannery felt sort of sorry for these poor fuckers, if you can believe that.

• • • • • •

"So how did Haden die?"

Sitting back in the chair, Flora Vaughn crossed her arms over her chest. "How come I don't hear a lot of *regret* in your question, Leni?"

Leni rolled her eyes and proceeded to answer for all of them. "Because Simon told the women he wanted to fuck that he was dying so they'd feel sorry for him and go to bed with him. *I* did, and so did you. I don't care if he's dead."

Flora nodded and smiled. "Don't you love the way Leni phrases things so diplomatically? She should be an ambassador to some dangerous country—she'd start World War Three in half an hour. 'Mr. President, your foreign policy sucks. It's obvious you're either completely incompetent, or you've got a small cock and are compensating."

"We're not talking about me. *How did Simon die?*"

Flora took a drink of water and then pointed at the glass. "In a car wash."

Her answer was so unexpected that spontaneously the three of them broke out laughing again.

"No, really—how?"

"That's the truth. Sabine Baar-Baarenfels told me. He died in a car wash in Los Angeles. He had a heart attack while his car was being washed." Some answers in life are so weird yet satisfying that on hearing them, all that the mind can do is sit back and burp.

Simon Haden had enthusiastically pursued Isabelle for years, trying every method he knew to get her into bed. Usually he was very good at seduction, a real pro. He used dying, he used love, he used sneaky in numerous, original ways. To his great dismay, none of them worked on her. When they were together, Isabelle was charming and funny and great company, but she always, *always* knew what Haden was trying to do. Smiling, she invariably stopped him miles from any bedroom door. All of this flashed through her mind now as she stared at Flora Vaughn and digested the fact that Simon was dead.

"What was he doing in Los Angeles?" Leni's question broke the ice that had formed over the moment.

"Who cares? But you know what really annoys me? What really bugs me? Now that that *villain* is dead, I keep thinking sweet things about him. Like the time he brought me lilies, or the time we stayed in bed all morning and ate chocolates. It's not right, damn it. Simon does not *deserve* sweet thoughts, whether he's dead or alive. The man was a selfish pig who just happened to be handsome enough to be irresistible. But once you'd fallen for the temptation, he treated you like a piece of old gum on the bottom of his shoe."

Leni closed her eyes and nodded in agreement. "I felt more like an empty stained pastry box after he left me. But I agree. Who said you can't speak ill of the dead?"

Isabelle was only half listening to what her friends were saying. She was feeling sick again and was waiting to see if her stomach was going to hold down the meal she had just eaten or throw it back up. That was one of the only things about pregnancy that bothered her: she would suddenly feel horribly ill, or diarrhea would abruptly come hurtling down her guts like an avalanche. When these things happened she would have to drop everything and bolt for the nearest toilet. It was embarrassing and sometimes frightening to feel that you were not always in control of your own body and its most basic functions.

After a few seconds of waiting and listening to her body, Isabelle knew this was going to get worse so she stood up quickly. Both friends looked at her.

"I'm going to be sick."

Instantly concerned, Flora half rose from her chair and pointed across the restaurant toward the toilets. The room was large and Isabelle had a long way to go.

"Do you want me to come with you?"

Isabelle shook her head and started away from the table. Walking fast, she put a hand over her mouth.

Flora slowly sat back down but kept watching her friend cross the room. "Do you think I should go anyway? Maybe she needs someone to hold her head."

Leni moved her cane a few inches to the right. "Forget it. You know how embarrassing that stuff is. Who wants someone watching while you puke? I still can't believe that Simon is dead."

Two good-looking women at a chic restaurant, talking about a lover they'd once shared. Both of them had stories about Simon Haden that the other hadn't heard. Now that he was dead, they could tell them.

Time passed while they spoke and laughed. Isabelle did not return to the table. Flora and Leni were both aware of this but it didn't concern them at first. Isabelle was vain—it was not uncommon for her to take a while.

Eventually too much time passed and Leni mentioned it. Flora got up immediately and went to the ladies' room. Pushing the door open, she fully expected to see Isabelle standing at one of the mirrors over the sinks, primping and looking at her reflection. She wasn't.

"Isabelle?" She looked at the two toilet stalls. Both doors were closed. A toilet flushed with a hard *whoosh* and Flora was momentarily relieved. She was sure her friend was in there. But she wasn't. Instead, a nondescript middle-aged woman opened the stall door and glared at her as if she were doing something fishy. Flora ignored this and went up to the other stall door. The suspicious woman went to the sink and washed her hands. She kept a careful eye on this tall redhead who was now knocking on the stall door with a flat palm.

"Isabelle?"

"Excuse me—what are you *doing*?"

Flora looked at this woman for three seconds, and then turned back to the stall door. "Isabelle, are you in there?"

"Don't do that. What are you doing?"

Flora turned and looked witheringly at the woman. "Have you finished in here? Mind your own business and leave."

In true Viennese fashion, the woman huffed and puffed but then fled.

When she was gone, Flora knocked hard again on the stall door. This time the force of it pushed the door open. No one was inside.

Flora turned around and walked back into the restaurant. She could just make out across the dimly lit room that Leni was sitting at their table talking to someone. A man . . . Vincent Ettrich.

As was the case whenever she saw Vincent, Flora froze for a beat. Before he met Isabelle, Vincent and Flora had had a wonderful short affair that left her dizzy with surprise, desire, and longing. It had not gone the way she planned. For two years after it ended (her doing), Flora could not stop wondering in her secret heart if this was the man she had been waiting for her whole life. When it was happening, both of them had treated their relationship as something delightful but insubstantial—a classic fling. For a few days here and there together now and then, two married people being naughty away from the world among crumpled bedsheets and hotel room service.

When the end came, Flora was initially glad, then sad, and in due course dumbstruck by how much their affair had meant to her. A month after she had ended it, she saw Vincent again in New York. But she was so frightened of her feelings for him that she barely let him kiss her on both cheeks when they met for lunch. To her dismay, her aloofness didn't appear to bother him a bit. Naturally she'd had fantasies during their time apart. Some important part of her hoped he would have come to the same conclusions as she and run to her when they met, hope and gratitude flying off him like sparks. Instead Ettrich looked at her fondly, as if she were an old classmate he was pleased to see and shoot the breeze with about the good old days—but that was all.

Half a year later he came to Vienna for business and at a party they both attended, Flora introduced him to Isabelle. Later she swore to Leni that she knew the moment those two shook hands that that was *it;* Fate had just stepped onstage. But the truth was she introduced them because she was showing this man to Isabelle for her appraisal. She wanted her best friend to meet and talk to the guy so hopefully she'd have some new insight as to how Flora might win him back.

But part of her account to Leni was true—fifteen minutes after introducing Vincent to Isabelle, Flora Vaughn had seen enough to fade into the background. She turned quickly away with a gulp and a grimace when later she saw them leave the party together.

"Hi Vincent." She always worried about her voice when she was around him. Worried that it would betray her by going too high or low or crack or something that would tip him off as to how flustered she still was in his presence.

"Was she in there?"

The abruptness of his question took her off guard. Flora sat down. "No. I didn't see her leave, did you?"

Leni took out her cell phone and dialed Isabelle's number. "No, and you know she would have told us if she were going home."

Flora's eyes traveled back and forth between Leni and Ettrich.

Looking around the room, he slowly began to shake his head. "The whole thing is starting again." It appeared that he was talking to someone but it wasn't them.

Holding the phone to her ear, Leni looked at her friend to see if she understood what he was talking about. Flora caught the look and shrugged no. Then she gently asked Vincent what he meant.

Even if he had wanted to answer, there was no time. A giant, ear-splitting crash exploded from the front of the restaurant. People sitting at the tables there cried out and leapt from their places, glass shards and splinters splashing on and all around them. The wide front window of the restaurant had been destroyed. Half of it still sat in place, jagged and dangerous-looking. The other half, the top part, had burst across the tables and floors and customers seated nearby. It looked like a bomb had gone off.

There was such shouting, movement, and tumult that no one paid attention to what caused this. One minute the window was there, full of afternoon light, the next it exploded, showering a million sharp pieces of glass across the room. A woman stood frozen in place, her little round pocketbook held out in front of her like a shield to stop whatever came next. She jerked when another crash came a moment later—a waiter dropped the large metal tray he was carrying when he began to feel the glass shard wedged in his cheek. Part of the shard was black—a fragment of one of the letters spelling the name of the restaurant on the front window.

Leni had been trained in first aid and immediately went to help. Flora, not knowing what else to do, followed her.

Vincent's eyes darted all around, taking in the scene: paranoid, dubious, taking in everything. The room was chaos. No one else knew what he knew. What was worse—what had just happened, or knowing what he did?

He wanted to stop the world for just a moment before deciding what to do next. Despite what was happening around him, he dropped his head back and closed his eyes. No good—those few seconds in his own darkness brought nothing helpful—all he knew was that he had to find Isabelle immediately.

Head still tilted back, he opened his eyes. High above the table hung his model airplane. Motionless, it looked as if it were suspended there on wires. It was larger now, twice as large as the one he had built. But even at that distance there was no question that this was the same plane—same shape, same markings. Only now it was two feet long. Big enough to break through a thick window if it hit the glass with enough velocity and force.

The instant Vincent became aware of it, the model began falling toward the table. It dropped slowly, like a leaf drifting down from a tree on a windless day. A dip here, a twist, it descended like it had all the time in the world. When it landed on his table it gently knocked over a half-filled glass of red wine.

The plane lay so that Ettrich could see the cockpit. He had done a brilliant quick sketch there with a black felt-tip pen of Isabelle's head, as if she were the pilot. He had showed it to her as she was walking out the door to have lunch with her girlfriends. Stopping, she closely examined it and smiled. Without looking at him she asked "Am I the pilot of your plane?" He wrapped his arms around her big pregnant body from behind and growled "A hot dark yes to *that,* Cap."

Tunica Molesta

Isabelle Neukor was flying. Not only that, but she was doing it on her back. It was the most remarkable thing. She kept turning her head to look down at the sidewalk as she flew, sure that any second she would drop and really hurt herself, especially at that speed. But it didn't happen—she just zipped along. She was on her back two feet above the pavement, moving very fast toward who knows where. She was pumping her arms too, as if there were invisible oars in her hands and she was rowing a boat. Down to her knees, up to her chest, down to her knees . . . the faster she rowed, the faster she flew above the sidewalk.

No one around seemed surprised. She passed an old woman walking two little dogs. Then a mother pushing a baby carriage who glanced indifferently at her and then away. Not a word, not a raised eyebrow. Next, Isabelle passed a kid clicking along pretty fast in the same direction on a yellow skateboard. Then a well-dressed man in a Chesterfield coat standing in the middle of the sidewalk reading a newspaper. He looked down at her as she passed and impassively back at his paper. No one paid attention to Isabelle; no one gave her more than a cursory glance as she floated by, flat on her back, arms pumping.

If she needed to avoid anything she just stopped moving one hand and pulled hard with the other. That was how she steered left or right. It was exactly like rowing a boat.

Nor did anything seem strange about the world around her. She saw trees blowing in the wind, pedestrians, and a blue and orange hot dog stand with several workers lounging in front of it drinking beer. Nothing appeared different other than her mode of travel which, although strange, she was beginning to enjoy. She really had no idea where she was going, but for the moment that didn't matter. Because bizarre as it was, it had become one of the more exhilarating physical experiences she'd had.

This was the third time it had happened, so she was a little less shocked than before when the experience had been so new and disturbing. The first time she was brought here, she had been sitting on the couch in her apartment looking at a magazine. She was turning a page when suddenly—*poof*—she was in this place, this land, or whatever it was. For an hour or two she wandered around, scared out of her wits. But nothing happened. She wandered, looked at things, wondering and worrying all the time What is this? Where am I? Why am I here? Then just as suddenly, *poof*—she was back on the couch again.

The second time she was in the kitchen cooking an egg when, *poof*—she was back here. It appeared to be the same town but she didn't really get a chance to find out because her visit was very brief—only a few minutes. In fact that second time she was actually walking up to someone to ask them where she was when, *poof*.

This time the last thing she saw was her hand turning the silver lock on a gray toilet stall door. The next moment she was on her back flying above a sidewalk. It was that fast and simple.

Remembering something, Isabelle desperately dropped both hands to her stomach. Feeling the child inside her there, she let out her breath in a fast relieved *whoosh*. Now she was okay. She had always had the baby inside her when she was brought here before, but who knew how things worked in this mysterious place? She always had to check herself to see if she had brought Anjo with her.

For the first time since arriving, she looked down at her body and saw that she was wearing the same clothes she'd had on in the restaurant a few minutes before. That hadn't changed. Her mind was clear, her stomach swelled with the baby, her clothes were the same . . . it was as if she'd only walked from one room to another. But in this room she could fly—on her back.

She defined the experience to herself now as "blinking." Because that's exactly how it felt when it happened—one second you're *here,* then *blink,* and you're *there.*

This was the third time it had happened in a month. Isabelle had said nothing about it to anyone because she wasn't sure what she wanted to say yet.

If she had tried to describe the experience, she would have said From one moment to the next I leave here and appear there. It's completely out of my control how and when it happens. Sometimes it's strange and surreal there. I see things that are impossible to imagine or describe because no words do them justice. Other times when I'm there it is little different from real life. Nothing bad has ever happened. I am just taken there awhile and then I am returned to my life.

"Hello!"

Isabelle had been so lost in both her surroundings and thoughts about being here again that she hadn't noticed when the tiny man suddenly appeared on her stomach. About the size of a salt shaker, he nevertheless wore a fancy black suit, crisp white shirt, and black silk tie that reflected the passing light. Only his loud hello brought her back to the moment. Thirty inches down her body, he waved at her. He looked so happy and expectant that she felt compelled to say *something.*

"Hello. Who are you?"

Hitching up his trousers, he sat down on the high mound that was her tummy. But he did it so carefully that she barely felt the added weight. "My name is Broximon. How do you do?" He waved again.

"Excuse me? What did you say your name was?"

He smiled as if he'd heard that question before. "Broximon."

"Broximon." She had to say his name herself. It sounded familiar, but she was too preoccupied at the moment to figure out why. She did try his name out on her tongue as if it were some kind of new taste.

He crossed his arms over his chest. "That's right. And welcome to you, Isabelle. It's high time we met."

Because she hadn't moved her arms since noticing him, her body had begun to slow until it came to a complete stop in the air. Then it gently floated back down and landed on the sidewalk.

Bending forward and stretching his neck, Broximon looked over her stomach at the ground. "Don't worry—as soon as you'd like to move again you can. All you've got to do is pump your arms like you were doing before."

"You know who I am?"

"Of course, Isabelle. We all know who you are."

"You *all*? What does that mean, *all*?"

Broximon swept an arm out in a long slow 180-degree arc. "Everyone here."

Before she had a chance to ask where *here* was, he saw something off to the left and called out, "Jelden! Jelden, over here." He looked at her. "You've got to meet this guy. He's a real character."

This was nonsense. All of these things were coming at her at the same moment, but they were only more questions. She needed answers. Lifting Broximon off her stomach, she put him down on the ground and stood up. Only when she was fully erect did she look toward where he had pointed. Five feet away was a man made entirely of butter.

"Isabelle, I'd like you to meet Jelden Butter."

He was bright yellow. He wore matching blue jeans and a denim shirt. He wore a corny-looking straw hat with a hole in the brim and a dandelion slipped under the red bandanna sweatband. A long stalk of hay hung out of the left corner of his mouth.

"Howdy, Isabelle." He stuck out a hand for her to shake. But just as she reached for it, he jerked his away, thumb up, over his shoulder. Then he cackled. "Sucker! They fall for it every time."

Broximon rolled his eyes and patted Isabelle reassuringly on the shoe. "Don't mind him. He lives in a 1950s time warp. That's where all his jokes, no—that's where all his *life* comes from. Right, Jelden?"

Butter looked at the two of them and smirked.

"Did you eat Jelden butter when you were growing up, Isabelle?"

She was staring so intently at the yellow man that she didn't really hear the question. It was true—the closer she looked, the more obvious it was that he was made entirely of butter.

"What?"

"I asked if you ate Jelden butter when you were growing up."

"What's Jelden butter?"

Jelden Butter put a hand over his heart and said in a hurt tone of voice "*I* am. Weren't we just introduced?"

Isabelle looked from Butter to Broximon and then back at Butter.

Broximon saw her look of growing dismay and explained. "Jelden was a famous brand sold in California in the 1960s and seventies. They ran a bunch of television advertisements starring him." He pointed to the yellow man.

Jelden put his thumbs up into his armpits and sang very loudly,

"Jelden butter on your plate,
Helps to make the morning great!"

Broximon slapped his hands quickly over his ears. "No, Jelden! I swear to God, if you start singing those damned jingles again—"

Too late—the Butter Man was already singing his third jingle by the time Broximon dug in his pocket, withdrew a disposable lighter and flicked it into life. He stuck his arm out and walked toward the singer. Seeing that little flame, the fire that could melt him, Jelden shut up immediately.

All Isabelle could think was Why doesn't he just blow it out? But then she remembered where she was. Things were different here. Maybe in this world, people made of butter weren't able to blow out flames.

Taking a few quick steps back, Jelden said to Broximon "All right, all right, I'll stop. Put that away. I only came to tell you your friend is looking for you."

Isabelle didn't know what he was talking about. *What* friend? She looked down at Broximon, assuming he understood the statement.

Broximon asked "How do you know that? When did you see him?"

Jelden said petulantly "A few hours ago." He looked at Isabelle. "You don't know who I'm talking about, do you?"

She shook her head. "No."

"Simon? Simon Haden? You know him, right? You know that name."

"Simon is *here?*"

"This is his world. Welcome to Simon Haden land."

• • • • • •

When he was alive, if you had asked Haden how many times he'd dreamed about Isabelle Neukor since they first met, he would have been embarrassed to admit at least once a week. Women generally said yes to him because he was so handsome. If they said no he either dismissed them, or else became interested in finding a way into their hearts for the little while he needed to conquer them.

Isabelle said no to him often but so sweetly or wittily or sexily that his interest in her grew into a kind of low-grade obsession. And Haden had never been the obsessive type. Until a couple of years before he died, things had come easily to him. He'd had no need to obsess about anything because life was pretty much his for the asking. Not only that, but a great deal of what he wanted was offered to him.

Not Isabelle. After a while he didn't even know if she mattered to him—*getting* her mattered, fucking her mattered. Having her underneath him with her clothes off and his cock deep inside her mattered.

Haden ruined any chance he had when he brought her to a party where she met Vincent Ettrich. He had originally met Vincent in Los Angeles while there on business and liked him very much. Particularly because both men were unrepentant womanizers and had common ground on which to walk. Ettrich knew LA well and introduced Haden around to interesting people. The men had a good time together. A couple of years later when they bumped into each other at the Loos Bar in Vienna, Haden repaid the favor. When he heard that Vincent knew Flora Vaughn, he took him to a party where he knew Flora and Isabelle would be—and ended up regretting that invitation for the short rest of his life.

Within a week Ettrich had won Isabelle's heart, body, mind, and soul. Haden was appalled but what could he do? Worse, Ettrich was so grateful for the introduction to this phenomenal woman and the big magic that was happening between them, that all he could do was rhapsodize like a warbling bird about her when the two men met. Of course he didn't go into any kind of inappropriate *detail* because he respected her so much. But that's all Haden wanted to hear—her details. Where were her moles? Was she loud? Did she say no to anything in bed or was she shameless? From Ettrich's hints and smiling silences, Isabelle Neukor was a tiger, a whirlwind and a feast in every way. Haden thought his head would explode.

It was the beginning of the end for him although he didn't know that. Life, which had so mysteriously and unfairly favored him, turned against Haden with a twitch of its nervous tail and was never his friend again. Until his fatal heart attack less than two years later, he would only see its ass-end and never again the head.

Luckily business called him back to America and he was able to flee Vienna and the lovebirds he had so unwittingly helped to unite. However that didn't stop him from thinking and often dreaming about Isabelle. Sometimes it felt like his mind was a drafty room and she was the wind slipping in through too many cracks. No matter how much he tried to stop it, she always found a new way to sneak in and touch him.

Why her? Why *this* woman and not one of the countless others he had known? Who knows—ghosts choose us, not vice versa.

Two nights before Haden died he dreamed of her for the last time.

Once when they were having lunch together she described something she'd recently read that she couldn't get out of her mind. In the time of the Roman Empire, one of the favorite forms of execution was a horror called the *tunica molesta.* A shirt was dipped in pitch, naphtha, or something else highly flammable. The condemned was then forced to put the shirt on and it was set ablaze. Nero was especially fond of using it on Christians. Haden sort of knew who Nero was but was most impressed by the fact that Isabelle read about things like torture shirts.

In one of the last dreams he ever had, Simon Haden dreamt about a *tunica molesta.* Only here he was the victim and the "shirt" was Isabelle Neukor. He would have thought the idea of wearing Isabelle was great, asleep or awake, but his dream didn't agree.

In the middle of the night he woke curled in the fetal position, clutching a crunched-up pillow with two hot sweaty hands. In his dream she was all over him like fire—like napalm burning him everywhere. She crackled and spat, she *was* fire. His pain was so real and intense that Haden's cries would have awoken anyone sleeping nearby.

And while he burned she spoke to him. He could distinctly hear her voice somewhere, insistent beneath his screams. She was saying things as she killed him. How could these flames or torture shirt or whatever she was be a woman? But dreams have no rules—they make them up as they go along.

When he woke from this nightmare and knew at last that he was safely back in his world, his reality, he shivered down his whole body. What he had just experienced was pure terror. One of those dreams you remember a long time afterward and pray will never return.

He tried calling Isabelle in Vienna to chat and ask for her take on his dream, but no one answered. He'd had no contact with her since the night she met Vincent. After a third attempt with no luck, he realized she wasn't answering the phone because she was probably out somewhere with Ettrich. Haden's mouth tightened at that thought and he didn't try to call her again. A day later he was dead.

• • • • • •

"Would you like to see him?"

"Who, Simon?" Instinctively Isabelle slid both hands over her belly, as if to protect her unborn child from even the suggestion of meeting the dead.

Jelden Butter winked and removed the straw from his mouth. "He'd be easy to find."

Broximon had his hands in his pockets and was looking at the ground. "That is not a good idea."

"Why not?"

"Because I don't think she's ready for it yet, Jelden."

"But why not let her try, Brox? What could happen?"

Broximon made a sour face that clearly said the idea was ridiculous. "What could *happen?* Don't be stupid—you know exactly what could happen."

Listening to these men talking about her, Isabelle felt totally confused. "What are you two talking about?"

Jelden looked at her. "Do you want to see Simon, Isabelle?"

"No, not particularly."

Broximon clapped once. "Good—then that ends the discussion."

In a sincere quiet voice, Jelden Butter said "You should see Simon."

"Shut up, Jelden. Leave her alone."

"Really you should: if for no other reason then for your baby." The yellow man tipped his chin toward her stomach.

Isabelle stiffened on hearing that. She was about to ask *What do you mean?* when she blinked and was instantly back in the restaurant toilet in Vienna. She stood in the middle of the room, facing a bank of white sinks with silver mirrors above each. Reflected in all of them, she saw herself and the gray doors of the toilet stalls behind her. She could not catch up with what had just happened. Her mind was still back there, wherever Broximon and the Butter Man were. Looking at her reflection in one of the mirrors, she thought again about what Jelden had said—*if for no other reason then your baby.* What did he mean? Why would seeing Simon Haden again be important for her unborn child?

She continued looking in the mirror, no longer seeing herself there but replaying what had just happened to her.

"Hey you."

Isabelle turned slowly toward the sound of that well-known voice. Vincent Ettrich stood holding the bathroom door open with his left hand. He was the only person she wanted to see now but still couldn't bring herself completely back to the moment. "Hello."

"What's going on, Fizz?" From behind him came the sounds of loud disorder. As if something big had just happened in the restaurant and people were still buzzing from it.

The noise distracted her. She hesitated but knew sooner or later she would have to tell Vincent everything. "Did you know that Simon Haden died?"

He shook his head. "I don't care. I want to know what's going on with you."

She moved toward her lover. "You might *have* to care about Simon if you want to know what's going on with me."

• • • • • •

Jelden Butter and Broximon were arguing about Haden when they came upon him. Jelden wanted to tell Simon about meeting Isabelle,

Broximon did not. Both had good reasons for their positions and it would be interesting to see which one prevailed. Haden didn't like either man very much but after the episode with Mrs. Dugdale, he had finally learned to listen when spoken to by anyone here because sometimes it helped him to figure things out.

He was sitting at an outdoor café eating a large serving of chocolate pudding with walnuts (his favorite dessert—just the way his mother used to make it). Both of them waved at him and then glared at one another, knowing exactly what the other was thinking.

"I know what you want to do, Jelden, but don't."

"Why the hell not?"

"How many times do I have to repeat this? Because he's supposed to discover these things *himself*. That's the whole point of his being here."

"Yeah well, Isabelle is gone. How is he supposed to discover her if she's not around? Hmm?"

Jelden was six feet tall. Broximon was six inches. Yet somehow both of them felt a hand on their shoulder at exactly the same moment. They turned and there was John Flannery a foot away. Behind him was the giant black and white dog, Luba. It stared at Broximon a little too intently.

"Gentlemen." Flannery had his arms crossed over his chest. The same thought dashed through both men's minds: He just had his hand on my shoulder. But how could he do that with his arms crossed? Flannery saw Haden looking their way so he waved. Haden waved back with his spoon and returned to the pudding.

"You were discussing what to tell Simon?"

Who *was* this guy? How did he know what they were talking about? Neither had ever seen him before. But he radiated attitude like heat off a summer highway and that definitely meant something here.

At the moment Broximon was more worried about the Great Dane than Flannery. "Is that dog safe? Shouldn't it be on a leash or something?"

"Safe? No, Broximon, she is not. Luba would eat you in one second if I told her to. She's stupid but very obedient. The perfect combination." Having said this to the little man, Flannery slowly looked the yellow one up and down as if he were a desirable woman. " 'Jelden butter on your plate helps to make the morning great.' But you also smell, Jelden. Are you aware of that? If you put open butter in a frig, it absorbs the smell of everything in there. And that's you now—you smell of everything. It's not very nice.

"And you're not going to say a thing to Haden, Mr. Butter. Do you understand? Not a word about Isabelle, not a word about anything."

"Who *are* you?"

Flannery grinned. "You don't want to know who I am. Know what I mean?"

"Oh but I do. I really do want to know." Jelden said this in an unpleasant, challenging voice.

Despite the other's nasty tone, Flannery perked up as if he'd heard exactly what he wanted to hear. "Okay. I'm King of the Park."

Jelden paused to see if he was going to say more. Then he sniggered. "You're what?"

"I'm the new King of the Park. Does that help? Do you know what that is?"

"No. Am I supposed to?"

"Well, if you don't it means you're dumber than Luba here and that's saying a lot because she is very fucking dumb. But hey, that's okay. Broximon, do you know what it is?"

Brox put up both hands, palms out in total surrender. He didn't know what King of the Park was and he didn't *want* to know. The way Flannery said it in a deep, amused-in-a-scary-way tone of voice meant you didn't fuck around with the King of the Park. Broximon started to speak. Because he was frightened his words got faster and faster until he was almost unintelligible. "No, but that's okay. I mean I'm easy with this stuff. Really. Live and let live. King, queen, pawn . . . they're all fine with me, you know—"

Flannery slowly put an index finger to his lips to shut Brox up. He shut up. Jelden looked at the little coward with loathing. Broximon saw that and silently mouthed the words *Eat me.*

"I don't think I can trust you, Jelden. And that's the whole basis of a relationship. So it's time for you to die."

"Oh really? Well, uh, you can't die here, King. Because this *is* death, in case you didn't know."

"True, but *things* can die, Jelden. You're a thing. No problem with you. Watch this." He cupped a hand to the side of his mouth and called out to Haden sitting twenty feet away. "Hey Simon, no more butter, okay? It's gone."

Haden didn't even look up from his brown dessert. He only nodded and raised his spoon to indicate that he'd heard.

Jelden Butter disappeared. Broximon couldn't say how it happened beyond from one second to the next he was gone.

"Ho-lllllly shit—"

"Little Simon Haden put Jelden butter on his toast every morning when he was a boy because he loved their commercials on TV. He insisted his mother buy only that brand at the market. He'd sing those jingles to himself when he was alone. But no more. All he remembers now is margarine: how his Mom used margarine on everything because she read it was much healthier. No more Jelden butter," Flannery said.

Broximon looked like he was going to flee or pee any second. "You can do that? Even *here* you can erase his living memory? Even when he's dead?"

"I told you—I'm King of the Park."

"Holy shit."

"You already said that. Know what the Russians say? 'Every bastard meets his master.' Bye bye, Jelden. Come on; let's go talk to Mr. Haden." He picked up Broximon and put him on the dog's back. When Flannery moved toward the café, the Great Dane followed at a slow slink. Petrified, Broximon could only mutter "shit shit shit" under his breath and try to grab on to something fur to keep from falling off.

• • • • • •

As usual Hietzl sat on the backseat of the car intently watching the two humans in front of him. The Range Rover was parked at the top of the Vienna Woods on a turnoff near Cobenzl. It was one of their favorite spots because it offered a spectacular panoramic view of Vienna and the plains beyond leading all the way to Hungary. They especially liked it on clear summer nights when they brought a picnic along and sat in one of the huge rolling meadows up there, eating and talking and watching dusk fall while the city lights flickered on far below them.

Now both of them were quiet, facing forward. Isabelle had been talking for a long time. She had told Vincent everything about her three trips to the strange land. She described what she had seen and her feelings about what she'd experienced there. Most important she had told him about meeting Broximon and Jelden Butter. How Jelden had called the place "Simon Haden Land" and said how important it was for their son that she meet with the dead Simon.

When she had finished a tense silence followed, which was very rare for them. Vincent sat slumped in the passenger's seat, fingers laced behind his neck and one foot propped up on the dashboard. Whenever they were together Isabelle always drove because he loved the way she handled a car.

He turned to her. "Why did you think I wouldn't believe you?"

She took a deep breath and let it out as a slow, slow sigh. Tears came to her eyes but she held them in check. "All I want is for us to be together so we can raise this child."

"Agreed, but there's a lot more to it than just that."

"Yes, obviously, but why did they choose our child? Why did it have to be *Anjo,* Vincent?"

"Well, for one thing I'd still be dead if they hadn't chosen our child, sweetheart."

Despite herself, she chuckled. "That's true."

"Tell me again what they said about the place being 'Simon Haden Land.' "

While Isabelle repeated that part of her experience, Ettrich stared straight ahead and squinted. Narrowing his eyes always helped him concentrate. But soon after she'd begun her account, he began shaking his head as if something were wrong with it. He interrupted. "Okay, okay, I've got it. Was there anything else you saw when you were there? Anything that might be relevant? Not just this time either—any time that you 'blinked.' Tell me about the strangest things you saw."

She hesitated while running the experiences through her head, picking what was worth retelling. But then she surprised herself with what she said. "Do you know what was most strange; the most amazing thing? How it all fit together so seamlessly. Like today—I met a man made of *butter.* But after the first shock of seeing someone like that, two minutes later I was arguing with him. I wasn't thinking He's made of butter. I was only thinking This guy is an asshole."

Ettrich had died alone in an anonymous hospital room. No one he loved or even knew was there to say goodbye or sit and hold his hand through that final ordeal. His only company was doctors and nurses and the elderly man with whom he shared the room. Both patients had terrible, ruthless cancers that ate through their insides like salt on ice.

Ettrich's wife of many years knew he was dying but loathed him so much by then that she refused to come. Nor would she allow their young children to visit either. Because not long before being diagnosed with the terminal disease, Vincent Ettrich had abandoned his family to be with Isabelle Neukor. But in the cruelest irony of his life, she rejected him and he was left with nothing. Soon after he became ill.

"Vincent?"

"Yes?"

"Was it like that where you went when you died: the seamlessness of it?"

He was about to answer her question when he heard something outside which made him sit up fast. Throwing open the door, he got out of the car and walked a few steps away from it.

"Vincent?"

"Ssh." He put up a hand to silence her.

She had no idea what he was doing but still obeyed his brusque command.

His hand stayed frozen in the air, his head tilted slightly to one side as he listened hard to *something*. Opening her door carefully so as not to make noise, Isabelle stepped out of the car. She thought if she was outside then she might be able to hear whatever it was too.

It was summer and what she heard were everyday summer sounds—cicadas whirring, the snarl of a distant lawn mower, a child's voice shouting somewhere, and a truck going slowly up through its gears. Then after a pause she heard the noise of something skittering on metal. Turning, she saw their dog jump awkwardly down from the car. After stretching, Hietzl came over, sat down next to her, and looked at Ettrich.

"Do you hear that?" He spoke with his back to her.

"*What,* Vincent? What is it that you're hearing?"

"Listen carefully. You could miss it because it's very far away."

Setting her mind to it, Isabelle listened to everything around her as intently as she knew how. She tried to be totally in the moment, only listening, undistracted by thoughts or questions or other concerns. But to her dismay she heard only cicadas and the lawn mower which then suddenly stopped, leaving just the insect buzz.

"Fizz, you don't hear anything? You don't hear those insects?"

"Of course I hear *them*! Is that what I'm supposed to hear—bugs?"

The expression on Vincent's face changed dramatically. "You do hear them?"

"Sure. So what?" She thought he was joking—how could she not hear that close clamor?

"Tell me what you hear."

"Cicadas. You know—that high chirring sound they make."

Staring at her, his face said he didn't know if he believed her yet. "And it sounds far away?"

"No, right here around us. It's very loud."

"That's loud to you?"

"Yes." She didn't like the tone of his voice. "What, Vincent? What's going on?"

"Those aren't cicadas you're hearing—it's the dead. Some of the ones you brought back with you when you returned from there."

"How do you know that?"

He looked at her sadly. "Because I remember that sound from when I was dead. It's one of the few things I do remember about that time."

The Moon in the Man

"The moon in the man, eh?" was the first thing Vincent Ettrich ever heard Isabelle Neukor say. She said it to a woman she was talking with. Then she threw back her head and laughed with her mouth wide open. Vincent had been brought over to meet her by Flora Vaughn and Simon Haden. This Isabella had a face three or four years past beautiful. That was the first thing that came to mind when he saw her. After being introduced, he pointed to the heavy coat she was wearing and the first thing he ever said to *her* was, "Do you know what they call a coat like that in France?"

She smiled a little and turned to Simon and Flora to see if this was some kind of joke. Eventually she looked back at Vincent. "No, what would they call my coat?"

"A *houppelande.*" It cantered perfectly out of his mouth like a dancing horse. "Isn't that a great word? Hope-eh-lond."

Normally she didn't wear heavy coats but that night it was bitter cold outside. She had just arrived at the party and had not yet taken off her ankle-length gray loden cape. The hood on it was so long that it went halfway down her back. That coat along with her blonde hair, large blue eyes, and cheeks red from the cold made her look either like a fairy tale princess or a dancer in the Ice Capades.

"And what *is* a *houppelande?*"

"That kind of coat—big and dramatic."

"A Dracula coat?"

"I was thinking more like *Dr.Zhivago.*" He liked her already. Women who were quick, witty, and willing to laugh at themselves won him easily.

She began to unbutton the cape. "All right, then I've got one for you now." Her hands were numb and slow from the cold. She cupped them together and blew her hot breath over them before continuing. "Have you ever heard of the *tunica molesta?*"

"A torture shirt? Sure. Have you ever been to the torture museum in the Sixth District? All kinds of amazing things there: it's really worth a visit."

Isabelle looked quickly at Simon Haden, her eyes asking where had he found this guy? She'd never met anyone before who knew about the *tunica molesta.*

As the four chatted, it was obvious there was strong electricity going back and forth between Isabelle and Vincent. Flora and Simon saw that and it made both of them frantic. But there was nothing either could do about it.

Ettrich told a funny, surprisingly tender story about his father's prized accordion collection. And how as a boy, Vincent learned to play the instrument only because he fell in love with one model in the collection named the "Mount Everest."

"Can you really play the accordion?" Isabelle asked.

"Yes, I can. Even 'Flight of the Bumblebee.' "

She liked that very much, which showed both on her face and in her body language toward Vincent. Isabelle liked people who could do odd unnecessary things—ventriloquism, play the accordion, figure skate, or repair old wristwatches. She'd fallen in love with one man mainly because he taught her to tango.

On a table in her living room were a bunch of prized objects she'd made, found, or bought at various flea markets. None of these things had any real value, but Isabelle cherished them all because they were strange, unique, or memory incarnate to her.

For example there was a red rubber toy man from the 1920s that looked exactly like a figure in a Bruno Schulz drawing she loved. Next to it was a giant tooth from a favorite dog, long dead. A dented Viennese street sign for "Tolstoi Gasse," a figure of a frog dressed in a ballerina's tutu, and in an intarsia wood frame was part of a white blotter from her childhood desk. It was filled from edge to edge with a little girl's drawings, squiggles, cryptic notes to herself . . . a nine-year-old's world in her own words and illustrations. Looking at Vincent, this accordion player, this interesting man, she wanted to show him these things and hear what he had to say about them.

What clinched it though was the music. A few minutes later while they were talking, music suddenly came on in the room. Things quieted momentarily while the crowd absorbed it, then returned to their conversations. The song "These Foolish Things" sung by Peggy Lee began. Vincent raised his head and smiled as if recognizing an old friend. And it *was* an old friend—one of his all-time-favorite songs.

Without hesitating, he asked Isabelle if she would like to dance. She thought he was kidding but he wasn't. No one else in the room was dancing but he wanted to—right now with her to this song. Isabelle was a terrific dancer but had never been the first one out on a floor, never. She looked at her friend to see what she thought, but Flora Vaughn was fighting just to keep a straight face and not go hurrying from the room in tears. Haden knew about Flora and Ettrich's past affair and he would have been amused by his old lover's discomfort now if it hadn't been for his own utter lack of success with Isabelle Neukor. He knew for certain that if he had asked her to dance she would have dismissed the thought out of hand and said no to him immediately.

Ettrich put his hands up in the classic position, inviting her to join him. She felt like a young girl again—nervous and hesitant but excited too. *Thrilled*—that was the right word. She hadn't felt thrilled about anything in a long time but his request brought that emotion rushing back to her. Stepping forward, she matched her hands to his and they began. Flora and Simon moved back to give them more room.

People nearby looked over and smiled. Dancing—what a good ideal! But not until the song was almost over did anyone else join them. So this couple, these strangers, had the floor to themselves. Ettrich was careful not to hold her too close and she noticed that. To test or maybe to taunt him, she slowly pushed her body closer to his. Just as slowly he moved away so that little was touching between them besides their hands and arms. It reminded her of dancing school years ago, preparing for her first Viennese ball with a boy who was terrified of her.

Halfway through the song Vincent's mouth moved close to her ear and he spoke in a quiet clear voice. Not sexy but intimate, only to her. "My parents were the most romantic couple I've ever known. Whenever I hear this tune I think of them because they liked it so much. Both knew the lyric by heart."

She pulled back to look at him. "Really? I love it when people do that. Are your parents still alive?"

"No, they were killed in a car accident years ago." The way he said it chilled her more than the grisly fact. There was such sadness and loss in his voice.

Without hesitating she asked "What were they like?"

Now Ettrich pulled back and looked at Isabelle with surprise. "My parents? Do you really want to know?"

What touched her was again the tone of his voice: it was both eager and skeptical. He clearly wanted to answer her question; but he was also afraid of what she would do with it. His ambivalent tone asked *Can I trust you with this? I want to.*

Part of life is a quest to find that one essential person who will understand our story. But we choose wrongly so often. Over the ensuing years that person we thought understood us best ends up regarding us with pity, indifference, or active dislike.

Those who truly care can be divided into two categories: those who understand us, and those who forgive our worst sins. Rarely do we find someone capable of both.

Ettrich did not know this woman but her hand in his was firm and everything about her said *I am* here—*tell me whatever you want.*

In the meantime Flora and Simon had drifted off to the bar where they were both drinking big stiff ones and making forced, desultory conversation. Haden was the first to notice what was happening nearby but couldn't quite believe what he was seeing. "Look at them. Flora. You have to look, quickly!"

Flora had her glass tipped up and did not want to look at them, thank you. She had already seen more than enough. Simon was just being his normal shitty self and trying to make her suffer more. The next thing he'd probably do was suggest finding a room somewhere so they could have a quickie as a way of taking some of the sting away from their disappointment.

"Please, Flora, look."

She made an exasperated face, slapped her glass down on the bar and looked. The couple were close enough for her to see that Vincent Ettrich's cheeks were shiny with tears. He made no attempt to wipe them away. He only danced and stared at Isabelle as if she had just said something of the greatest importance.

"What the hell is going on with them?"

Flora continued to stare at the dancers while out of the side of her mouth she said "Look at them, Simon. What do you *think* is going on?"

He wasn't having it. "Oh come on. They met half an hour ago and now he's crying. Did she step on his foot?"

• • •

Isabelle kidnapped Vincent from the party. They danced on, oblivious to anything but each other. Flora and Haden stopped watching and went back to drinking. Then they began to argue about something stupid. But because both of them were inwardly fuming, ripe for a good fight, they really got into it. Later while she was speaking, Simon deliberately stuck out his arm and looked at his watch as obviously and rudely as possible to display how bored he was with this quarrel. Flora shifted her eyes to find the couple but by then they were gone. She brought this to Haden's attention, adding the soupçon that this whole damned thing was his fault for having brought Ettrich to the party in the first place. What the hell was he thinking?

CHOING! One could almost hear the bell ring for round two of their battle. Both came out swinging. When it comes to passion there is no substitute for sex, but anger is a pretty good one. Haden and Flora had been lovers a few years before but that only made them more formidable adversaries now. This time there was no coyness or reluctance in their verbal punches. No sexy hidden agendas or plans either. Because they had already gone through that stuff on their way to the bedroom and eventually out the other side way back when. As a result what ensued now was muddy, ugly, and true. They reached the low point of their relationship in no time at all and by unspoken mutual consent took it even lower.

• • • • • •

Two miles away Isabelle drove fast down the Linke Wienzeile, the dashboard lights of her car glowing in steady blue contrast to the neon and halogen city lights flashing by outside the car windows. An old Rolling Stones tape played quietly on the car stereo. She wanted to show Vincent something special; she wanted to show him her Kyselak. It would take ten minutes to get there. Neither of them had said anything for a while. It was enough to be together alone now, two people escaping into a glittering city, into an adventure, each of them nervously content, expectant and deeply surprised.

Vincent looked around, trying to do it as subtly as possible. He believed you could tell a lot about a person by what he kept around him—in his car, on his desk, in his pockets or her handbag. You are what you carry.

To his delight and secret relief, Isabelle's car that day was nice-messy. Lots of junk mail and colorful flyers—yellow! turquoise! orange!—spotted the floor. A recent *Time* magazine and a Viennese daily newspaper were down there too. He'd had to move a couple of tapes off the passenger's seat before he was able to sit down—Boris Bukowski and *Nighthawks at the Diner* by Tom Waits.

Ettrich envisioned her getting the mail on the way to her car. In too much of a hurry to throw these ads in the trash, she'd just dropped it all in here days ago and ignored it ever since. On the dashboard were a small black flashlight and a beautiful, deeply dented gold fountain pen next to an eight-inch-high rubber dancing Elvis figure stuck on with suction cups. Ettrich plunked a finger at Elvis who immediately shimmied and shook.

"My car's a mess—I know it. It's not normally this way. I saw you peeking." Isabelle didn't look over but she was grinning.

"This? This is nothing. I'll tell you a story that is absolutely true. Once a film company saw my car on the street and contacted me. They wanted to rent it for a movie they were making. Know why? Because in the movie there was a bum who lived in his car. They saw mine and paid five hundred dollars a day to rent it 'as is' because it was exactly as they'd imagined his."

"I don't believe that."

"I swear to God it's true. Hand up." He put up his hand as if he were swearing an oath in court.

"What was the name of the movie?"

"Angels at the Bar."

"I saw that! With Arlen Ford."

"That's the one. Then you saw my car."

Isabelle's mouth opened in awe. She slowly covered it with a hand while remembering something from the movie. "That scene where the police go to the guy's car and drag him out—"

"That was mine." Vincent reached out a finger and flicked Elvis again who quivered all over.

"—And they found all those *cats* living in there with him—"She started to laugh. "My God, that was really your car?"

Ettrich nodded "Without the cats, yes. I hate cats. But after the filming it smelled feline for weeks in there. I even took it to the car wash a couple of times and vacuumed the hell out of it but that did no good."

"For a guy who owns such a disgusting car, you don't look bad. And you smell really good. Great cologne. But are you dirty?"

Unfazed, Vincent answered mildly "No, just my automobile. I've always treated cars like the one drawer in a desk or dresser that I throw things into but never take out again. You know, like ticket stubs, single socks, old ice . . ."

"Old *ice*?" She knew she'd heard him right but the image was so silly and surreal that she wanted to hear it again.

"That's right."

The silence returned again but both of them were easy and comfortable inside it. Neither felt threatened. Things were just on "screen saver" between them for the moment.

Eventually Ettrich asked "Am I allowed to know where we're going?" But he didn't really care; he only wanted to hear her voice again.

"Do you really want me to tell you or should it be a surprise? Actually it's two things."

He thought about that and eventually said "Keep it a surprise. But I would really like it if you told me some more about yourself. You've said almost nothing, you know. Was that on purpose?"

She shrugged.

Vincent was not going to let her off with that. "Come on—you've got to tell me something."

"My father is a doctor."

He waited. After some more silent time passed she looked at him and raised her eyebrows. "That was something."

"Yes—your father's occupation. But what I want to know is about you."

"All right, here's something: When I was a girl I wanted to be a ballet dancer. I was very good back then and was accepted into the ballet school of the Vienna *Staatsoper.* That's where I met Flora. We were students there together.

"But I wasn't good enough and in dancing you know that by the time you're about fourteen or fifteen. I was good but not good enough. So I stopped and transferred to the American International School here because my parents wanted me to learn English.

"It's been that way with a lot in my life. I'm good at some things but never good enough. Never special." She said it without anger or regret. She was simply stating a fact. Vincent was touched by both her candor and the fact that she saw herself in this uncomplimentary light.

He knew women like she was describing, but none of them had ever admitted to what Isabelle just had. Because all of these others were attractive too, people gave them much more credit than they deserved for what they'd actually accomplished. Oh, such a pretty woman dances/paints/writes? Then her work *must* be good. But it wasn't. In truth it was rarely good. In truth, here was only another (good-looking) wannabe trying to be or create something interesting but failing.

Isabelle spoke again but he was still mulling over what she had said and missed it.

"Excuse me. What did you say?"

She downshifted and the car slowed perfectly. She was a wonderful driver. "I asked if you'd ever heard of an autographist."

"An *autographist*? No. That's a strange word."

"Actually there was only one of them. He created the term for himself. That's one of the things I want to show you."

Ettrich waited for her to continue. He'd already realized that Isabelle had a tendency to talk in spurts.

"At the beginning of the nineteenth century here, there was a man named Joseph Kyselak who worked as a clerk at the court registry office, whatever *that* was. Kyselak originally wanted to be a poet or an actor but wasn't any good. So instead what he did to get famous was paint his name all over the place. On anything you can imagine—buildings, bridges, furniture . . . Hundreds of Kyselaks everywhere. I heard he used some kind of stencil or template to do it. Or at least do it faster so that he could escape more quickly.

"Kyselak called himself an autographist. He even wrote a book that's still in print about a walking tour he made of the Alps where he wrote his name on top of every mountain he climbed. I have a copy of the book. It's called *Zu Fuss Durch Oesterreich*. He became so famous, or I guess notorious, for doing it everywhere that he was called in to the emperor's office for a royal reprimand. Can you imagine that, Vincent? The head of the whole Hapsburg Empire summoned this one little madman to tell him to stop writing his name on things!

"Apparently the autographist came in, got yelled at, and acted properly ashamed. But after he left the office, the emperor discovered that he had somehow managed to write 'J.Kyselak' across one of the reports lying on the desk." Isabelle constantly used her hands when she spoke. They made big circles or dove and swooped in the air like seagulls hunting over water. One or the other was constantly leaving the steering wheel to make or emphasize a point. Neither of them could stay put. Her face too was completely animated, completely alive. Reading it, it was easy to see which parts of a story delighted her and which were only a bridge to be crossed to the next really good part on the other side. Ettrich loved her manner and enthusiasm and couldn't get enough of either.

"What happened to him?"

"He died very young—I think he was only in his early thirties. And of course most of his autographs have disappeared over the years, but there are still some left, especially up in the Wienerwald written on trees and stones. It's the eeriest thing you can imagine to come across one out there in the middle of the Vienna Woods. I've heard there's a club of Kyselak fanatics who trade maps of where they've found his work.

"That's what I want to show you now—a real Kyselak. One I discovered a few years ago."

"How did you find out about this guy?"

"Petras Urbsys."

"Excuse me?"

She winked at him. "That's the second thing I want to show you tonight."

• • •

Isabelle's Kyselak was written low and at a peculiar angle on the wall of a baroque church deep in the heart of the Fifth District. They stood very close together on the sidewalk while she shone her flashlight back and forth across the wall down there, again and again lighting up the signature for Ettrich. Eventually she turned off the light and they stood together in the cold, looking toward the dark wall.

Ettrich said "Can you imagine how happy Kyselak would be to know that almost two hundred years after he did that, a pretty woman would be showing it off in the middle of the night as her treasure? That's pretty damned cool."

"Treasure? Yes, it's true. I like that, Vincent. I never thought of it that way, but it really is a treasure to me."

"Who else have you shown it to?"

She hesitated a moment before answering. "No one—only you."

He was startled by how much his happiness leapt up at that news. Just him—only him.

"Come on—I want to show you something else." She put her

gloved hand through the crook of his arm and gently pulled him forward. It was the first time they had touched since dancing together back at the party. She led them away from where her car was parked. Ettrich looked once over his shoulder toward it.

She noticed it. "Don't worry—this won't take long."

"I'm not worried. It's only that I left my gloves in the car and was wondering if I should go back and get them."

Without hesitating she slid her hand down his arm into the coat pocket and took his cold bare hand in her warm gloved one. What was most lovely about the gesture was that she made no big deal about it. She did it to warm his hand and nothing more. Only kindness, that rarest of things when it comes pure. With another woman in another circumstance it would have meant *a moment,* a decisive event happening between them. But instinctively he knew that wasn't the case here. Her simple thoughtfulness delighted him.

He looked toward their hands and then at her. "Where are we going?"

"I told you—to Petras Urbsys."

"I don't know if that sounds like a person or a Russian weapon. Maybe some new kind of amphibious tank."

She squeezed his hand. "It's a person, although he *is* Russian, or was, because he's Lithuanian."

"Petras—"

"—Urbsys."

"Urbsys." Ettrich waited a beat and then snuck in "Are you sure he's not a weapon *and* a Lithuanian?"

Isabelle squeezed his hand again but didn't appear to want to talk any more. They walked together through that nondescript working class district where the night air smelled of burning coal and wood, damp stone and winter. Cars passed, adding the acrid immediate stink of exhaust fumes. But it was late so there were not many. Once in a while a person appeared around a corner or walking toward them but these passersby kept their eyes averted. All of them were hurrying along to wherever they were going—home, or just out of that cold. It was a dull part of town in which to be taking a stroll. Other than row after row of dreary apartment buildings and the occasional run-down restaurant or *gasthaus,* there was nothing much to see. Ettrich wondered where they were heading.

Halfway down the next block he slowed when he saw something. When they reached the place he motioned for her to stop. They stood in front of a brightly lit store window. Almost every other display window they'd passed was either dark or too dimly lit to see much. It was late—at that hour who was around to buy what they were selling?

In contrast, this window glowed like Vienna needed what it had to offer day and night. That physical brightness was what had first caught his attention.

"Check out the stuff in this window. What the hell do they sell here?" Staring at the display, he was spellbound. Ettrich had a job in advertising. Most of his days were spent trying to convince people to buy products they either didn't know about or need. As a result, he loved to see how the rest of the world attempted to sell its products too.

In this store window ten Old Spice cologne bottles were lined up like oddly shaped bowling pins. Next to them were six thin men's ties in campy but now very "in" retro colors and geometric patterns. Ties from another era perfectly preserved. It was plain that they were originals. They all looked freshly cleaned and ironed; maybe they had never even been used. Dead stock. Ettrich remembered that term from the time as a boy he had worked in a stationery store. Products that were new but had never sold, so they were stored for a future time when they'd be brought out again and hopefully find a buyer.

Standing open behind the ties was a 33⅓ record album set of the recorded speeches of General Douglas MacArthur. Near that lying open was a large illustrated book about the sculptor William Edmondson. Beneath the book were eight square bars of soap with the words *White Floating* etched across their middles. A foot away was an old green crocodile purse in perfect condition. Vincent could tell at a glance that it was old by the striking shape—it was the sort of bag Lauren Bacall carried tucked up under her arm in a 1940s movie.

Scattered haphazardly between the objects in the window were black-and-white photographs from that era. Bending down for a better look, Ettrich saw that many of them featured one man. In about half of the photos he was dressed in a military uniform, but the outfit was unfamiliar. What army did it belong to?

In one of these pictures, the man sat among three nurses wearing high complicated hairdos. Another was taken in a bar, the man and another woman sitting close to each other on chrome stools, their glasses touching in a toast. In a third snapshot he was standing with this same woman, his arm around her, next to a small car, huge and beautiful snow-covered mountains looming in the background behind them.

"Vincent."

Ettrich could barely tear himself away from the window and trying to make sense of all this stuff, even when it was Isabelle Neukor calling. There was something about the things in the window and the way they had been arranged. Was it the strangeness of them placed together? Or the obvious care and thought that had gone into the display? The whole tableau reminded him of a very personal photo album, or a shelf in someone's living room where the most cherished, important keepsakes and talismans were kept.

"Look up."

"What?"

She lifted her arm and pointed to something high up. "Look there. Look over the door."

Not understanding why she wanted that, Ettrich nonetheless did what she said. Looking up, he saw a large black-and-white sign over the doorway that said only "PETRAS URBSYS."

He couldn't believe it. "*Here*? This is the place you were bringing me, Isabelle?"

"Yup. You can go back to looking in the window. It's great, isn't it? He changes it every week."

• • •

"He's selling his life." Isabelle licked her spoon.

Ettrich stared intently into his coffee cup as he listened to her speak. Otherwise if he looked at Isabelle he'd surely lose track of his thoughts. "Say again?"

They sat in the back of the smoky café Alt Wien, one of the few places in town that stays open very late. They'd gone there after Vincent had had his fill of staring in the window at Petras Urbsys.

Isabelle tapped the back of his hand with the spoon. "That's what he has in the store: everything from his life. Or a lot of it; the things that mattered enough to him to keep. And now he's selling all of it."

"How do you sell your life? And why would you?"

"Because he's an old man who wants to see *his* treasures go to good homes before he dies. It's not as crazy as it sounds. Most of what's for sale in his store are records and CDs. Petras is crazy for music—all kinds. I think he has something like five thousand records."

"Yes, but Isabelle, there were also old bars of soap in that window! Don't tell me he's selling the soap he's collected over the years too."

"Could be. It wouldn't surprise me. But think about it for a minute. You're old and lonely. No one cares about you anymore and no one wants to listen to you. Your stories, your complaints, whatever hopes and dreams you have left: no-one-cares. It's always like that with old people.

"But you've got some money saved, too much time on your hands, and a million memories you want to share. Can you think of anything better than to open a store and sell everything that matters to you to customers who will enjoy it as much as you did? *And* Petras wants to talk to you before he sells you anything. Because if he doesn't like the person, no sale. I've seen him refuse more than once.

"He said that most of the people who come into his store are lonely old ones like him who only want to chat, music fanatics with his kind of taste, or just interesting people who look in his window, get intrigued by what they see and can't resist going in."

Ettrich rubbed his forehead because he couldn't think of anything else to do. "And he has customers?"

"Oh yes, almost every time I go in there he's talking to someone. A lot of the time the people look lonely or ragged, or like they just stepped out of a UFO, but he's okay with that.

"You know that dancing Elvis on the dashboard of my car? One of his customers gave it to me—an Elvis fanatic. I was in the store the day Petras sold the guy a very rare live recording of Elvis in Las Vegas singing 'Ave Maria.' " Although Vincent and Isabelle both happened to be looking at their hands on the table when she said this, they cackled at almost the same time at the image of the King singing that most holy of songs. In Vegas.

When he spoke again his voice was as excited as a child's. "You've got to introduce me to this Petras. I've got to meet him."

Isabelle nodded "We can go there tomorrow if you like."

"Do you promise?"

It was such a funny thing for him to say, but somehow it made her very happy. "Vincent, I promise."

Petras

"What are you thinking about?"

Vincent spoke as he rubbed his eyes slowly with the heels of his hands: "That we should go talk to Petras about this."

They were again sitting in the car in the Wienerwald. Hietzl rested its head on Ettrich's shoulder. The windows were rolled down. Isabelle crossed her arms and, turning away from him, listened to the world outside. "How did you come to that conclusion?"

Reaching forward, he poked dancing Elvis on the dashboard. "I was thinking about the night we met and where you told me you got *him*." He gestured toward the small figure.

When she spoke her voice was wholly different. It came out high pitched, fast and querulous, like an angry child's. "I don't want to do that, Vincent. I really, really don't want to go to Petras for this."

"I understand. I'd feel the same way if I was you. But I think we have to unless you can come up with something else."

She knew he was right but that didn't make it any easier. Isabelle had known half an hour ago that it was her only course of action. The moment she'd learned what the cicada sound out there really was, the first thing that had come to mind was "Petras." And she hated that.

Now she looked again at Vincent, her eyes pleading.

He saw that desperation and took her hand. "Sweetheart, do whatever you think is best. You know I'll support you. If you don't want to deal with him, then don't. I just have no other idea of what to do."

"You haven't said yet what you think is happening to me, Vincent. You haven't said a word about it; except that I bring back the dead whenever I return from there."

She was being ingenuous. Sometimes she did that when she was trying to hide from the truth of a situation. It was an unattractive, weak ploy. But now he wasn't having it because this development was too big and dangerous. Isabelle had to face the truth and deal with it immediately.

His voice came out hard—harder than he would have liked. "What can I say that you don't already know, Fizz? You brought *me* back from the dead. To do that, you had to learn how to go there and Petras taught you. But remember, he told you back then what the consequences of doing it could be.

"You know the way into death but now someone is using it against you. They're pulling you back through that door whenever they want to, whether you like it or not. For some reason they've been taking you to Haden's death. I don't know why."

"I think they want our baby because Anjo's a danger to them. We've known that a long time."

"And why do you think I should see Petras?"

Irritated, Ettrich made a slow fist and lowered his chin to his chest. "Do you really need me to answer that question?"

Her mouth tightened "Don't talk like that, Vincent. Not now. I want you to help, not scold me. And yes, say why you think I should go see him."

Vincent's first impulse was to blurt out an emotional response. But he held himself back and instead reached over his shoulder and scratched the dog on the top of the head a while before speaking.

"After I died, you went to Petras and he showed you how to enter death and bring me back here. And he was right—it worked. I honestly think we need to talk to him now about all of this and hear what he has to say about it. There's no one else we can turn to, Isabelle. If anyone can give us advice on what to do with all this, it's him."

• • •

Vienna's Zentralfriedhof is one of the largest cemeteries in Europe. It is a gigantic, mostly beautiful, anti-Semitic place. Enter through the heroic main gates and one gets the impression that you are walking into a grand Elysian Fields–like resting place of the great and famous. You would not be surprised to see a grazing white unicorn there, or the contented ghost of Franz Schubert walk by, hands behind his back, deep in thought about his next work of genius. Mozart's grave is near the entrance and so is Beethoven's. Walk a little farther on and there are the final homes of more of the great and near-great: eminent writers, generals who fought and fell in celebrated battles, politicians, doctors, architects, and social reformers who made a real difference in their lifetimes. Farther along are the family plots—the huge Jugendstil or baroque whipped cream monuments of the rich, and the infinitely more dignified simple black stones/gold lettering of the *gut burgerlich* others.

But the dirty little secret of Vienna's main cemetery is the Jewish section. Many of the tombstones there have been vandalized or overturned and left that way. The entire section is indifferently tended by the cemetery's large grounds staff.

Isabelle and Ettrich had walked in the *friedhof* for almost fifteen minutes before reaching this area. Much of the time the only sound between them was that of their footsteps on the pavement and gravel. A thick hedge of misunderstanding and resentment had grown up between them since they sat in the car in the Vienna Woods trying to make some sense of all that had happened to them that day.

Isabelle knew where they were going here, Ettrich did not. He had visited this cemetery on several occasions but never this section, never for this purpose. Walking slightly behind her, he felt like a child that accompanies its parents on a Sunday to lay a wreath on Grandpa's grave.

She stopped, hesitated a moment as if to get her bearings, and then took a left down one of the rows.

"Fizz?"

Ignoring him, she kept moving.

Ettrich sped up, touched the back of her arm and hoped she would stop. She did.

But then he didn't know what to say. He'd said her name only to make her stop a moment and look at him. He loved her so much and knew that he had done everything wrong in the last hour. He was desperate to fix things between them, especially now when they needed each other so much.

"Yes?" Her voice and body language showed only impatience.

Vincent's mind ran all over the place looking to find something right to say, but finally he could only come up with "What . . . what are we looking for?"

"The ark. It's around here. We're close—I remember these surroundings from the last time I was here." She moved off without looking at him. Her tone of voice had been neutral, only informative.

"What ark?"

"The gravestone is a copy of William Edmondson's sculpture called 'Noah's Ark.' This one is just bigger than the original. There! Way down there—I see it."

He looked where she was pointing. Knowing nothing about either the Edmondson sculpture or the grave they sought, Ettrich logically scanned the many headstones around them for some kind of stone boat, some kind of "ark." He saw none but Isabelle kept walking determinedly in one direction so he dutifully followed.

A few minutes later she stopped in front of a brownish gray

headstone that was shaped like some sort of peculiar house. Or rather two houses because part of the peculiarity was that one rested on top of the other. The higher one was smaller and had the same shape as the plastic houses used in the game Monopoly. It had four sides, six windows, and a slanting gabled roof. There was absolutely nothing special about the building.

It rested in form-fitting niches on the flat "roof" of the larger house. That second one had four windows and at one end what Ettrich assumed were double doors. Both houses perched on top of two identically sized stone slabs. On one of them, PETRAS URBSYS was carved rather crudely and obviously by hand into the stone, along with the dates that he had lived.

"I thought you said Noah's Ark." Ettrich certainly did not want to cause any more trouble with her. But looking at this strange and mysterious monument marking Petras's grave, he was just too curious about it not to ask.

Stepping up to the headstone, Isabelle ran her fingertips over it. "This *is* a kind of ark. It's meant to be a church. But I've always imagined it as a church floating on a barge over some river or ocean.

"Edmondson was a very religious man. When he was young he had a vision where God spoke to him and said be a sculptor. He spent most of his life carving tombstones and religious figures. To him a church was an ark—a shelter from the outside world and all the evil in it."

Ettrich was moved both by the image and the concept. Despite the somberness of the moment, he smiled. "So the church is the ark and the world we live in is the flood?"

"Yes. Petras loved Edmondson's work. He said it was simple to the point of being divine. He spent hours and hours looking at pictures. They always made him smile." What she didn't add was that Petras was studying an Edmondson book the day she visited him to learn how to bring Vincent back from the dead.

Standing there watching Isabelle touch the gravestone with such tenderness, Ettrich couldn't resist touching it too. The moment he did, he found himself transported back to Petras Urbsys's store—the store that had closed months ago, after the death of its owner.

First he smelled the sandalwood incense burning. Petras loved the aroma of incense and there were always several joss sticks burning in ashtrays filled with sand placed around his store. Ettrich found himself sitting on a green velvet couch in the middle of the room. He had sat there often before when they'd visited the old man.

Now a very much alive Petras stood behind the counter, looking at what appeared to be a large coffee table book of photographs. He wore thick reading glasses which he kept adjusting on his nose as he slowly turned the pages. When the bell over the door clinged he looked up. Isabelle walked in. She was dressed completely differently and her hair was much shorter than it had been a moment ago at the cemetery.

"Isabelle, hello! Such a long time since we've seen you."

"We have to talk right now. Vincent is dead."

Petras's face showed no reaction to this news. He slowly closed the book and rested both hands palms down on it. Isabelle walked over to the counter and stopped directly across from him. "You have to help me now, Petras."

"I'm so sorry for you."

She nodded and continued to stare at him, her face blank.

"What are you going to do, Isabelle?"

She said nothing. She didn't need to. He knew why she was here. Eventually she looked down at the book he had been reading. "Edmondson. You really love his work, don't you?"

"Yes. He spoke to God with his hands."

"Petras, you know why I'm here."

"Yes, I do." He pushed the book to one side of the long counter but continued to look at it, as if it could somehow help him.

"Will you tell me now? You promised that you would if Vincent died."

"Yes, I did promise you." He removed the eyeglasses and slid them into his breast pocket. He appeared resigned, defeated somehow. "In Lithuania when I was a boy, I saw many things that were wonders. No one would believe me if I said them all what I saw, but that is all right. It doesn't matter because *I* saw them so I know that they are true. They are real.

"Many times when someone died, there would be things that were not fixed, not decided—" He appeared to be searching for the right word to use here.

"Unresolved?"

He pointed at her—one sharp jab in the air. "Yes, yes—unresolved. Like one dead man who did not tell anyone in his family where he hid his money, or who should receive a piece of his land. You know, things like that—sometimes they are big, sometimes small.

"No one wants to accept that they are going to some day die, so we try to ignore it. What happens then is we leave sometimes important things unclear after we're gone.

"Then it becomes very difficult for the ones who are still living. So sometimes it is necessary to talk with these dead ones and find the answers to our questions. It is not a big difficulty to talk to someone after they have died, but you must know how to do it—"

"I don't want to *talk* to Vincent, Petras. I want to bring him back here. I want to bring him back from the dead."

Petras nodded that he knew exactly what she wanted. He jabbed his finger into the air again. "I can show you how to do both, Isabelle. I could do this for you. But why? Why is it necessary to do this?"

"Because Anjo said I must. He told me that at the same time he told me that Vincent was dead."

Petras pointed to her large stomach. "The child still talks to you?"

"Oh yes. Since the first day he was conceived he's been talking to me."

"Show me this again, Isabelle."

She had already shown him twice in the past but today was different because now she desperately needed his help. She waited and listened. Petras and Ettrich watched her closely for a sign of something—contact, recognition. Nothing happened for a long time and slowly a palpable tension began to grow in the room. Isabelle continued to wait, unfazed. Eventually she straightened slightly and passed the back of her left hand across her mouth. She looked at Petras and said

" 'I saw in the east world,
I saw in the west world,
I saw the flood.' "

She had no idea of the meaning of what she had said so she asked "What does that mean? Do you know?"

The old man nodded and pointed to the Edmondson book on the corner of the counter. "It was how he described the time God spoke to him and what he was shown. That is what I was reading when you came in before. Exactly those words. Your child told this to you? Your Anjo?"

Impatiently she snapped "Of course, Petras. How else would I have known?"

"Yes, all right. Of course you are right—how else?

"So then I will show you. But first I must say something. There is one very great danger when you talk to the dead. It is the same for anyone: when you have learned how to go there, you will always remember the way. You will never forget. For some people this is a *Katastrophe.* Like the atomic bomb, you know? Once they discovered how to build it and then used it, they could not say *Oh that was a mistake—let's take it apart and put it all back in the ground again.*

"That is why old people were asked to do this when I was growing up. It doesn't matter if they know because they will die soon anyway."

"Have you ever done it?"

He waved a dismissive hand back and forth in front of his face. "No, I am a coward. The only brave things I have ever done in my life were accidental. I have never had a need to talk with the dead."

"But you know how to do it?"

"Yes."

"Then show me, Petras." She did not hesitate. Both men recognized that immediately and in their own ways, loved her for it. Ettrich particularly because he knew Isabelle intimately and knew she was not a courageous person.

"It is in your stomach—right here." He put his hand low on his stomach, about where his belt sat. She did the same thing—put her hand down there too.

"Yes, that's right—where your *bauchnabel* is. What is the word for that in English?"

"Belly button. What's there, Petras?"

"Your death—your life and death are in this same place. Here. Here was where you were joined to your mother once. That line was what kept you alive when you were inside her body. But when you were born they cut it so that you could be in this world. When you die you will have it again."

Incredulous, she could barely splutter "I'll be connected to my *mother* again after I die?"

"No, you will be connected in another way—but to everyone then, every *thing,* not only to your mother." He saw confusion narrow her face. "All of that is not important now, Isabelle. What you want to know is this and I will show you. Put both of your hands on your stomach again.

"Once in every person's life they dream of death."

She gave a small chuckle. "I dream of death all the time."

"No, this is different. One time in your life you dream exactly how you will die. And it is the truth. You see everything very clearly and every detail. Where, when, how—everything. All people have this happen to them. Everyone. But because we have so many dreams in life, we forget this one as quickly as we do the others. We don't even remember what we dreamed last night, right? How many dreams does a person remember?" Petras raised his index finger. "But *once* you dream the truth about the most important moment in your life. One time. You dream your death exactly as it will happen. For some people this is a nightmare, for others it is all right. For them it is quiet and peaceful.

"So, if you need to visit death or one of the dead while you are still alive, then you must find that one dream and enter from there."

On hearing this, Isabelle's head and heart warred furiously between skepticism and wonder. Could this really be true? "How do we know that we've even had the dream? Couldn't it happen sometime in our future? Isn't that possible? What about the people who don't have the dream until later in life?"

Petras shook his head. "Everyone has it before they are eleven years old."

"Eleven? Why eleven?"

"Pubertat."

"Puberty?"

"Yes. Everyone has their dream before they become an adult."

"Why? Why before?"

He started to answer but was interrupted by the sound of the bell ringing over the front door. Both of them turned toward it, annoyed at the interruption.

Ettrich watched all this from his perch on the couch. Obviously they were not aware of his presence there. Isabelle had never told him the details of how his resurrection had occurred. She'd said she was not permitted to. But now he was finding out exactly how she'd brought him back from the dead and he was fascinated. It was like watching a home movie of his life, but with the huge added advantage of being able to see what was going on simultaneously in the next room or in other people's heads. He remembered a line he'd once read to the effect that you never really know who you are until you learn what others think of you.

"Guten tag." A nondescript bald man wearing large brown glasses and holding a cheap brown plastic briefcase entered the store. He moved hesitantly, as if sensing from the first moment that he wasn't welcome here.

Petras said to him in German "I'm sorry, but the store is closed. Please come back another time."

The man appeared confused on hearing this, but then grew highly indignant. He brought the briefcase halfway up his chest and held it there with both arms crossed over it in an X. "What do you mean, closed? The door is open and the sign in the window says open."

"The store is closed. I'm the owner. When I say it's closed, then it is closed. If the door is open and I say it's closed, then it's closed. If the door is closed but I say it's open, then it's open. Should I continue or do you get the point yet?"

"But you have no right to do that. There are municipal laws involved here—"

"Are you Kifnitz or Mangold?"

The angry man was about to spew out some more but Petras's question stopped him cold. Closing his mouth, he licked his lips and looked apprehensively left and right like the walls were listening. "Mangold. But how do you know who I am?"

"That's not important. Just tell them that she must be told. Tell them the *child* says she must be told."

Mangold slowly lowered the briefcase. His voice was incredulous. "The child said that? Really?"

"Yes, the child. So go and tell them that and tell them to leave us alone."

"All right. Yes, all right." Mangold scurried away without saying another word.

Isabelle looked at the front door as it closed. Then she looked back at Petras. "Who was that? What were you saying to him?"

"What I'm telling you now is very dangerous, Isabelle. It has not been done for a very long time and there are many who think it should never be done again."

"But you just said that they did it all the time when you were young."

Instead of answering her, Petras crossed the room to one of the floor-to-ceiling bookcases. He stood in front of it for a while, obviously looking for something in particular. When he located it he pulled a book down from a high shelf and brought it back to the counter where he laid it in front of her. It was a faint mustard color, thick, and judging from its musty smell, rough-cut pages, and beat-up condition, quite old.

"This book is very rare and valuable, if you can even find a copy still. I do not think that there are many of them left. It was written by a distant relative of mine, a professor at one of the universities in Vilnius.

"He was the greatest scholar of his time in national folklore and myth. This man spent his whole life going around my country searching for every story that he could find. Then he would return to his home and add them to what he had already collected. This book is the result. Thirty years he worked on it." He slapped the book with his hand and paused both to let this information sink in and Isabelle to look at his treasure with new eyes.

"I have read the book several times. Some of it is very fascinating and of course some of it is boring. But you know what it is most of all? It is very sad. Why do I say that? Because it is all gone now, Isabelle. In Lithuania, Latvia, Finland, here in Austria . . . In all of the countries their magic has disappeared and will never return. The *stories* of the magic are still there, yes, but the truth of them is gone forever.

"If you go out into the country now anywhere, the people have no new stories like these because all of the magic has been stopped. Taken away forever. There is nothing mythic or magical on the earth anymore. Only the old stories have survived but without their beating hearts. Like the ruins of a great civilization that lived a thousand years ago.

"There are no more pigs that grant one important wish, or clouds that speak forgotten languages. No more trees that sing the end of the world . . . no more, Isabelle. They are all gone."

"It was real? Those stories are true?"

Petras roared "Of course they're true! No one could make all of those stories up—they are too deep and inspired. Do you know where most of them came from? Simple farmers and laborers, peasants mostly, country people. Do you really think those idiots had the kind of imagination to make them up? All hundreds and thousands of them? No, they didn't create these things, they *saw* them. They saw them, or their fathers or grandfathers did, and what they saw became part of the family history. Of course the stories were true."

"But then what happened? Why are they all gone?"

"Because man used them terribly and almost always for the wrong reasons. Think of the history of this century, Isabelle. Think of the way man has behaved and showed what he really is at heart: a selfish, dangerous monster that destroyed much more than he has created, and did so many more bad things than good.

"Do you really think people today can be trusted with magic and the power that comes with it? No, not at all. We cannot even be trusted to preserve ourselves. We cannot protect us from us! So that is the very good reason why they took it all away. And it is very sad because losing those things has made our world a smaller, less interesting place."

Petras broke eye contact with her and looking down, brushed dust off the thick book. "Somewhere in here is the story about entering death through that one dream we all have. Exactly like I told you. What is not here is the *knowledge* of how to do that. And you will not find it anywhere now because it has been removed. Why? Because it is too dangerous. It would be like giving snakes to babies to play with.

"All of it is gone now, Isabelle. The only thing left to see of that snake is its skin which are the sweet little myths and magic stories that we read to babies before they go to sleep. The skin is still very beautiful, but it is not the snake."

"Who did this? Who took them away?" She pointed toward the door. "Mangold? People like him?"

Petras shook his head. "He is only a messenger. But I cannot answer that question. It is something you must discover for yourself or not."

"All right, I accept that. But can you tell me this—was it God? Did God take this magic away?"

Petras hesitated, as if deciding whether or not to say anything. "God is not one thing."

Isabelle did not know how to react. She did not understand what he meant but knew that if she asked him to elaborate he would refuse. She did the only thing that came to mind. Putting both hands on her stomach, she asked "Then show me this. Show me how I can find Vincent."

• • • • • •

"Vincent?"

Vincent saw his hand on the tombstone, but his mind was still back in Petras's store with the old man and Isabelle. Trying to bring these two separate realities together was difficult for him. It was like staring straight ahead while slowly bringing your fingers in from the far left and right lines of vision toward the center.

"Vincent, nothing happened. It didn't work!"

He was again in the cemetery, again standing next to Isabelle alongside Petras's grave. He remained silent, still trying to grasp hold of where he really was and how much time had passed. She thought he was listening closely, waiting to hear what she would say next. In truth he was only stunned.

"I did exactly what Petras taught me but this time it didn't work.

Why? What does that mean, Vincent? Why didn't it work? Why couldn't I enter death?"

Ettrich noticed a bench nearby and led her over to it. After they'd sat down he slowly and in great detail described what had happened to him when he put his hand on Petras's gravestone. Isabelle did not interrupt. She sat with her chin down and arms crossed tightly over her chest. He didn't know what that body language signified but didn't waste time trying to figure it out. More important was to tell her everything about his experience so that she could know it all and process it.

She did not appear surprised by what had happened to him. When he was finished with his account she said nothing. Several times she almost spoke but didn't. She wasn't clear in her mind what she wanted to say. So her only obvious reaction was to nervously wiggle her outstretched foot back and forth. Both of them ended up looking at that foot as if it might know something they didn't.

"After you died, Vincent, Petras taught me how to go into death and bring you back. But this time I couldn't do it. That *possibility* is closed to me.

"Maybe I was allowed to go there only that one time. Whatever the case is, I can't do it now and ask Petras why these things are happening to me." She said all this to her wiggling foot. Only when she was finished did she look at Vincent.

He did not turn to her when he spoke. "True, but at the same time, I went into *your* past and saw how you learned to do it. Or almost—Petras was about to tell you how when you said my name and I was brought back here."

"What did you learn when you were dead, Vincent? That's what this is all about. What did you learn there that you might have brought back that will protect our son from them?"

Washing the Buffalo

Leni Salomon was in love and this time it was serious. After that bizarre luncheon with Isabelle and Flora, all that she wanted to do now was find him and go to bed for a couple of hours.

A month ago she would never have imagined thinking such things about this man. His name was John Flannery. Several times over the course of any day Leni found herself saying those names—*John Flannery*—just to have them on her tongue and then of course to think about him some more. She spent a lot of time, recently, thinking about that man.

To look at him, he was the most unlikely lover she could have imagined for herself. Physically, he was about a hundred miles away from her type. Much to her chagrin, Leni was a sucker for handsome clichés—the smoothies, elegantly dressed guys who were fluent in three languages, wore hair gel, and used those long elegant wallets that had slots for twelve credit cards and only fit in the breast pocket of a jacket.

But this Mr. John Flannery was shortish, roundish, and wore clothes that looked like they'd all just come out of a dryer without ever having said hello to an ironing board. He wore a salt-and-pepper beard and at fifty-four, bore a vague physical resemblance to Ernest Hemingway, of all people. She hated Hemingway's books.

And he was fifty-four—twenty-two years older than Leni. When she thought about the difference in their ages it almost made her blush. Nevertheless that's who he was and so be it. Leni Salomon was a pragmatist. She was handicapped. She was pretty. She had married the wrong man years ago but was not brave enough to leave him although she knew she would be much happier if she did. She recognized these things about herself and accepted them for no more or less than they were worth. Now she was in love with a man who already was a man on the day that she was born.

They met on a tram. He'd asked for directions to Sigmund Freud's apartment. By the time they came to her stop in front of town hall they were laughing. He had already asked her to join him for coffee and she'd said yes. She never did things like that although men tried to pick her up all the time. It was definitely not her style, but five minutes into their first conversation she knew that she must listen to this man some more.

Four years before he had seen the light. Or rather one afternoon at his big desk in Silicon Valley he'd realized that what he was doing was only earning lots of money so that one day he could be old with lots of money.

A week later he had quit his job, cashed in everything, and started traveling. He'd been around the world twice since then and didn't plan on stopping any time soon. He had seen the ghost of a Buddhist monk in Salyan, Nepal. Learned how to cook from a three-toque chef in Rome, trained a millionaire's horses in Northern Germany, and helped a woman he'd met in that cooking class build a stone house on the island of Sifnos in Greece. These were the sort of experiences he wanted to remember when he was old. One of the reasons why Flannery quit his job in the first place was the realization that despite having lived over half a century, he had very few great memories. A few perhaps, a small handful, but nowhere near enough to justify the half century he had existed.

When he saw that Leni was lame, John smiled. No one had ever reacted like that before. She was both taken aback and intrigued by his response. It turned out that his mother had had polio as a girl. As a result, she walked with the same difficulty as Leni. He grew up learning to walk slowly so as to keep pace with her. Children aren't used to walking slow. But early on it taught him patience and to pay more attention to his surroundings. He became much more observant and thus more appreciative of detail than most people he encountered.

Leni rarely talked about herself because she was shy, secretive, and at heart didn't think she was a particularly interesting person. But she talked about herself a lot that day to Flannery. She talked at the café and more when they were sitting in the *Volksgarten* afterward. He asked questions that were personal but never out of line or prying. Compelling questions, ones that made her consider carefully before answering, although they were about her and the way she felt or saw things. It felt as if she were looking at herself in a new kind of mirror—one that showed her angles she hadn't seen before. She told him things that day maybe she shouldn't have, but afterward she only felt good about their conversation and was eager to see and talk with him again.

At the end of their first meeting, Leni gave him her cell phone number rather than that of the phone at home. Writing it down, she knew she was giving the one and not the other because she did not want to chance John calling and having her husband answer. Naughty, naughty she thought as she handed the slip of paper to Ernest Hemingway.

For a long time she had no idea where their connection was going. Flannery was hugely entertaining, smart, and always insightful. He was bright-eyed alive, wide open to life and its possibilities, even at his age. So many things he said stuck in her mind. She found herself thinking about them throughout the day. Especially after listening to her husband crow or whine about his latest business, blah-blah.

The contrast between the two men was enormous. One was thirty-four, handsome, successful, and closed to just about anything outside his sphere of experience. The other was not, not, not, and definitely not.

Leni's husband also disliked dogs. One day John Flannery showed up at one of their meetings with Luba, his Great Dane that looked like a black and white Jackson Pollock painting in motion. Seeing the giant animal for the first time, Leni clapped her hands with joy. The dog was as calm as a pond. It looked at you with interest and if you were very lucky, rested its massive head on your lap and closed its eyes. The first time it did this to her, Leni laughed and said it felt like there was a watermelon on her lap.

"I always say I'm walking a jumbo jet."

"Yes, yes, that too! And you travel with her, this big thing?"

Flannery smiled and stroked Luba's back. "Sure, why not? They don't mind her on trains. As long as she's well behaved and I buy her a ticket."

"You've taken her around the world with you?"

"No, only Europe. I got her in Greece when I was there. She's been with me since then. Haven't I told you her story yet?"

Leni shook her head and almost purred with pleasure. She'd always assumed Flannery was Irish, with a name like that, and because he told stories like an Irishman did—riveting, funny, self-deprecating. She couldn't wait to hear him continue.

"Remember I told you that I went to Greece to help a friend build a house there? Her name was Helen Varcoe. We met in Rome in this cooking class we both took and became friends. What she didn't tell me till much later was that she was dying.

"There were only two things she wanted to do before she

died—learn how to cook a few great dishes from a master chef, and start building this house she'd been designing for years on a piece of land she owned in Sifnos.

"Luba was her dog." As he often did, Flannery suddenly broke off speaking and looked away into the distance. Over time Leni had learned not to say anything when that happened. She assumed a memory was washing over him, or something needed framing in his mind before he continued. She'd never asked what these abrupt pauses meant and eventually she even grew to like them, seeing them as only another facet of John's interesting and often unpredictable personality.

The truth was the only reason why Flannery made those pauses was for dramatic effect. He'd done it once the first day they were together and seen how she hung on the edge of her seat waiting for him to go on. So he added it to his repertoire.

"Where is this thing going?"

Taken off guard, she honestly didn't know what he was talking about. She said nothing for a moment—only blinked a few times and tried to guess his context. "Where is *what* going, John?"

He pointed to her and then to himself, to her, to himself. He looked straight at her but his eyes said nothing. "This. You and me, Leni. Where is this thing between us going?"

Through years of experience and honed method, she had her lie, fib, excuse, backup, detour, already ready on her tongue before she'd even finished digesting his question. Leni Salomon was so good at lying and avoiding, so adept. Secretive people usually are. She already knew to start her maneuvering with a verbal stall: she would ask *What do you mean by that, John? I don't know what you're talking about. What* thing *between us?* Next, she'd follow whatever he said with—

No.

Her heart stood up and said a loud *no*—not this time, not with this good man. No lies, no ingenuousness. A shouting match inside Leni exploded: Her heart yelled *Tell him the truth!* While the scared rest of her yelled back *Are you crazy?*

She was almost in love with Flannery. She already adored him. *That* was the truth. No doubt about it—a few more meetings and chats with him and she'd be in for both her penny and her pound. Was she supposed to tell him that? Yes, exactly that.

Looking at her now, he was as still as an owl. Once in a while his eyes blinked but not as often as she would have wished. He really did look like an owl sitting there, waiting for her to tell a truth that would cause trouble all over the place. Her bad leg began to ache which almost made her smile. Because that leg always seemed to start hurting whenever she got in trouble. She didn't know why, but it happened regularly; as if even her leg were saying *Don't try to deny it, you're in a fix.*

"What do *you* think, John?"

He answered immediately. "I was married once. I haven't told you about it, but I was. I was afraid to tell you because some women don't like to hear that. They think of it as some kind of black mark on your record if you're divorced. But it was a very good marriage and thinking back, I wouldn't change one thing about it even if I could."

Leni didn't know where he was going with this but chose not to interrupt. She'd always just assumed John had been married—maybe more than once.

"It ended after twelve years because we simply went in different directions—those things happen. Since then I've not been very . . . social in that way. That's why it was so easy for me to just pick up and leave America. I had no real ties, no obligations to anyone.

"But when I was in Greece with Helen working on her house, it was sort of like being married again and I liked it very much. That kind of close connection and communication you have with someone you really care for is a wonderful thing. It made me realize how much I had been missing, those years I was alone."

Leni couldn't resist asking "Were you together with Helen?"

He slowly shook his head. "No. Neither of us wanted that. We knew we were only meant to be friends but we were both very grateful for just that. It was more than enough.

"Vienna was only supposed to be a stopover for me. A few days here to look at the Klimt paintings, maybe see an opera, eat some *Sachertorte* . . . But then I met you and this thing started happening. Now I don't know what to do about it." For the first time in minutes he smiled, then patted his dog again. "I asked Luba what I should do, but she was no help."

Inside, Leni shuddered but couldn't tell if it was from joy or fear. She could think of nothing to say. She wanted to say something but nothing was in her head, *nothing,* other than the great hope that he would continue talking about his feelings.

"Do you know why I brought Luba today and not before? Two reasons—one was that I was afraid you weren't going to like dogs. Isn't that ridiculous? So what if you didn't? But silly or not, it was important to me.

"The other reason was when I woke up today, when I was lying in bed I thought, I'm going to bring the dog today. And if the two of them get along, then I'm going to tell Leni about being divorced. Even if it shocks her, it's time she knew.

"So it's all your fault and Luba's. If you two hadn't liked each other, you would never have heard this stuff."

Leni was tongue-tied. No, that wasn't it. Her thoughts, her words, her desire to tell John how she felt were all as lame as her bad leg now. In a flare of understanding she realized that her helplessness with him was due at least in part to inexperience. That's right—she simply wasn't used to being honest about how she really felt. Even with her husband who did not know her well enough and worse, didn't care.

With Flannery she had entered a foreign land where she knew perhaps ten words in the language and could barely decipher the street signs. The foreignness there was exhilarating and frightening in equal measure. Nothing between them had even happened yet, but still—

"Are you going to say anything?" His voice was soft and tentative, careful. Everything was up to Leni now. Both of them knew that. He had said his truth and it was time for hers. She knew that anything she said now would be accepted as the truth. She could tell a lie as big as the moon and he would believe it because that moment between them was so loaded.

A few days before, John had mentioned a quotation that he loved. On hearing it from him for the first time she did too—"Open your hands if you wish to be held."

She had no words now but did have her hands and arms. She used them to answer his question. Because she suddenly knew what to do, her face relaxed for the first time since their conversation began. Lifting her hands off the table, she slowly began to draw them apart, as if showing him the size of a big fish she'd caught. But then they spread beyond the size of a fish and went out as far as they could go. She was opening her hands because she wished to be held.

Flannery immediately understood her gesture and grinning, nodded his head eagerly. Seeing that, seeing that he understood what she meant so quickly, Leni had no more resistance to this man. Whatever came now would come. If in the end he hurt her then she accepted that. Like him, she wanted to have brilliant, wondrous memories of her life too. And one thing she had never really experienced was—

A strange look grew on her face. Flannery saw it and was about to ask *What's wrong?* but kept quiet instead. He could see that something was dawning on her, something crucial.

Leni brought her hand in and covered her mouth. First she'd thought, I've never really experienced a great love. But as that sentence, that realization crossed her mind, two different words jumped in front of them and took their place: *Real trust* replaced *a great love.* With a shudder she recognized she had never experienced real trust before. Seeing that was both enlightening and dreadful for her. More than any great love, Leni Salomon saw for the first time, she had never experienced real trust in her life.

If she trusted anyone, she *sort of* trusted them, whether it was her parents, her husband, or even her best friends Isabelle and Flora. She trusted her work only because it was so precise and relied entirely on her skills. But people, one single person? Had she ever felt 100 percent trust for even one single person? No. Hand still over her mouth, she looked at Flannery but didn't really see him. Her eyes filled with tears and she began to cry.

It was a curious picture: a lovely young woman sitting there with her hand over her mouth, eyes more startled than sad, tears spilling down her face. The middle-aged man sitting near her sees this but does nothing. He does not reach over and touch or speak or in any way try to comfort her. Nor does he get up and walk away because they are fighting. A huge Great Dane sleeps on the ground by the man's side, oblivious to all of this. If you were watching the couple from afar you'd have to wonder What the hell's going on? What's happened between them?

Because their tableau is so mysterious, you stare at them too long. Eventually the man's eyes slide over to you. Embarrassed, you look away, but not before a moment passes, a flash instant where you two connect. His eyes, his face or demeanor or simply something beyond words, scares the shit out of you. The sensation is so strong that you clumsily stand up, toss too much money on the table for your glass of wine, and hurry off without looking back. If you did, you would be even more disturbed because he is still staring at you, at your back now but just as attentively. It is as if he is memorizing you, writing down your license plate number for some time in the future when he will cross your path again, only then it will be on purpose.

• • •

Several weeks later, after that bizarre luncheon with her girlfriends, Leni stopped in the middle of the sidewalk and speed-dialed John's number on her cell phone. Smiling, she closed her eyes and thought about where he might be. She imagined him in his apartment, those two small but lovely sunlit rooms in the Second District near the Augarten Park. A friend who was working in the United States for half a year had lent it to him. Flannery seemed to have so many friends. He spoke about them with great affection, and judging by the fact that he had been given his apartment rent-free, his friends liked him too. She pictured him standing in the middle of that bright living room reaching into his pocket for the blue cell phone she'd given him half as a joke, half not.

Or he would be in the park with Luba, sitting on one of those green wooden benches in the *hundezone,* reading the newspaper while the dog sat at his feet contentedly watching the world go by. Leni loved to go to the park with them and watch how others—both canine and human—reacted to John's giant.

"Hello?"

Just hearing his voice instantly calmed her and closed all of her banging doors. He was exactly where she wanted to be.

"John, it's me, Leni."

"Hi, boss."

He always had a different name for her when they spoke, a different moniker—boss, sweetie, pal. The list went on and on. No one had ever addressed her like that. The names made her smile because they were very much a part of his manner.

"Where are you?"

He answered immediately. "On your tongue. In your hand."

The response was so unexpected and intimate that she almost swooned. "John, can I see you today?"

His voice changed tenor. When it came again it was concerned rather than teasing. "Of course. What's up? Is anything wrong, Leni?"

"No, no. Yes. I don't know. I just want to see you." Suddenly she felt like crying. Why?

"Sure you can. Where are you? I'm in the park with Luba."

Leni still felt like crying but at the same time broke out in a big smile. She loved hearing she had been correct about where he was. She loved being right about John. It made her feel like they were on the same page. "Where's Luba? Are you reading the newspaper?"

"She's by my foot watching a cocker spaniel piss on a bush, and yes, I'm reading the paper. Am I really that predictable? How depressing. What's up, my friend? You don't sound so good."

"I had a really strange lunch just now and I don't know, it just would be really, really nice to see you today, if that's okay."

"Yes, absolutely. Do you want to come over here or meet someplace else?"

I just want to fuck you is what she really wanted to say to him but could not. Leni had said and done things with Flannery that she never would have thought herself capable of before. But this line she simply couldn't say. She didn't have the courage yet. "Can we meet at your place? I'm in the First District now. I can take a taxi and be there in ten minutes."

"Can you make it an hour or so? Let me do two errands and then I'll meet you there. Is that okay?"

"Yes—an hour." Shoulders sagging in relief, she pictured the keys to his apartment in the inner pocket of her purse—their special home. The owner had given John two sets when he moved in. The first day Leni visited him there, the first time they'd gone to bed, he had given her one of these sets afterward. He said "Now if I lose my keys, you *have* to come over and let me in with yours." Sometimes when she was alone or unhappy, she got out these keys and simply held them in her hand. Everything was all right now. She clapped her telephone closed and took hold of the cane leaning against her leg.

She'd walk down Kartnerstrasse to clear her head and then catch a taxi over to his building. Everything was all right now.

• • •

A hundred feet away standing in the shadows of a doorway, Flannery watched Leni limp off in the opposite direction. Pressing the disconnect button on the blue phone, he dropped it back into his pocket. But as it touched bottom there it began to ring again. He was a popular boy today. He took the phone back out and answered. "Hello?"

"Where are you?"

He smirked at the demanding tone of the voice. This one didn't ask questions—she gave orders, even when ending her sentences with a question mark.

"I'm on your tongue. I'm in your ear."

*Tsk*ing her impatience, she snapped "Don't be an idiot. Where are you?"

"I'm washing the buffalo."

The weirdness of his remark stopped even her for a moment. "You're *what*?"

"I'm in Calcutta washing a water buffalo. I've become a Janist. This is one of our practices."

"A *what*?" She ran a hand impatiently through her long red hair.

"A Janist. The religion? It's based on the teachings of Mahavira, sixth century B.C.—"

"What the hell are you talking about?" But she was giggling now because he had gotten to her again. That was one of the things she loved about him. She could boss the world around but not this man. She pretended to hate how frustrating he could be. In truth she really liked how independent and unpredictable he was with everything, including her.

"Nothing. I am talking about absolutely nothing. I'm down at the Danube walking the dog." He said this while watching people pass by on Vienna's busiest walking street. The Danube was five miles away.

"Let's meet today. I'm dying to go to bed with you."

He watched a pretty woman with a perfect ass walk by. Her name was Ursula. He thought for a moment about whether he wanted to go to the trouble of entering her life. She liked the color periwinkle and to be fucked hard in funny locations—like on the kitchen table, or over the trunk of a car. He could not see into Ursula's future but he could see everything there was to see about her now.

"Hey Romeo, did you hear me? Do you want to go to bed with me or not?"

"Take it easy, willya? I was trying to work out whether it's possible for us to get together today, but I just can't do it. As soon as I get back to town I've got to go to a very important meeting that'll probably last a long time. Otherwise I'd happily peel grapes for you all afternoon, Mrs. Vaughn.

"How about tomorrow? I'll bring some Viagra so we can really have a *lonnnng* party." He knew she would say yes but only after pretending to think about it a moment or two. Because she didn't want him to think she was too easy. Women were so predictable.

"Can we go to a hotel? I love going to hotels with you. It makes it feel so much more dirty."

He decided to get off the phone now and find Ursula. Why did it seem like every other woman in Austria was named Ursula? Who would even consider naming a daughter that? He had about an hour before he had to meet Leni. More than enough time to make contact with *Urrrrsula.* Her ass was just too good to miss. Without missing a beat, speaking again into the telephone, his voice was a perfect mixture of sex, glee, and great good humor. "Flora Vaughn, we can go to any hotel you like."

Feed Me to Your Sister

"Just because I'm silent doesn't mean I have nothing to say."

"I understand that. Continue whenever you're ready."

"Just so we're eye to eye on that matter."

"Eye to eye. No problem."

Simon Haden looked at his seventeenth bowl of chocolate pudding and abruptly pushed it away.

Broximon waited politely for Haden to continue but he didn't. They were seated at a table with Volin Poiter, Seaburg Rasnic, Tyree Meza, Duryee Grenko, Mescue Rell, and Sneekab. Or rather, Haden was seated at the table, Broximon was sitting on the armrest of his chair, and the others were on the table because these others were houseflies. Once to amuse an eccentric woman he was trying to seduce, Haden had named every fly that landed on their table while the couple ate at an outdoor restaurant. Now these flies had returned to visit.

"The hell with her!" one said in fly-speak. But since this was his death, Haden was able to understand.

"That's right," said another fly with hearty gusto. "Who needs her?"

Haden dismissed the statement with a flick of his spoon. "That's easier said than done. Plus the fact there's obviously nothing I can do about it anyway, being dead and all."

The flies knew more about what was going on than Haden did, but weren't about to tell him anything. No way. They had trouble enough, just being dead flies. Instead, they turned their many eyes to Broximon who knew the secret too. They wanted to see if he would spill the beans.

Haden had called Broximon to say that he was stuck. The little man didn't know what Simon was talking about but nevertheless took his discomfort as a good sign. At least it meant Haden was thinking about things, which was a marked improvement. Brox could not believe that someone who'd experienced a breakthrough as big as Simon's could be so lethargic and unmotivated afterward. It was as if Haden was resting on his laurels and had no desire to move forward with his new knowledge and insight. But what laurels? He was only at the beginning and had such a long way to go.

"She haunts me, Broximon. How is that possible here? How can you be haunted when you're *dead*? Huh? And it's even more so now than when I was alive. She's completely under my skin. I don't understand that. It makes no sense."

Broximon looked at his highly buffed two-tone shoes. Pretty damned sharp shoes. "Have you seen her here?"

The flies buzzed a little louder. Things were getting interesting.

Haden was thinking too hard about her and didn't really hear the other's question. "What?"

"Have you seen Isabelle since you've been here?"

Something in the way the question was asked brought Haden to attention. "No. Why?"

Broximon reached down and brushed nonexistent dust off the tip of his shoe. "Well, you must have dreamed about her when you were alive, right?"

Haden spluttered "Uh yeah—about five thousand fucking times."

"Then there you go, Simon: she must be around here somewhere if you dreamt about her so often back then. This *is* your world—that's what it's all about."

"I've never seen her here," Haden said defensively, as if he'd been too dumb or unobservant to notice the obvious. But what Broximon said made real sense: some version of Isabelle had to be here because this *was* Haden's world. It was made up of bits and bytes that had stuck in his mind when he was alive. And Isabelle Neukor had certainly stuck in *his* mind.

"Maybe you should go looking for her, Simon."

Almost as one, the flies stopped buzzing for a moment when Broximon said that. Was he giving too much away?

Grudgingly, Haden asked "Yeah well, this is a big damned place, Brox. Even if you're right, where am I supposed to start looking for her, in the Yellow Pages?"

Broximon wanted to say *You really are an idiot, Simon* but that would have been counterproductive. Yet the longer he spent with this man the more he was convinced that Haden *was* an idiot.

He was spared having to say anything because just then Mrs. Dugdale came marching around the corner. She wore yet another appallingly colorful dashiki that looked like the result of an explosion in a crayon factory.

"Ah Simon, there you are!"

Despite his age and the fact that he was dead, Haden still reflexively sat up straight in his chair on seeing his old schoolteacher. And as if they all knew who the woman was, the flies fled.

"Hello Mrs. Dugdale."

Instead of answering, she looked at his half-eaten serving of chocolate pudding. Sitting down opposite him, she pursed her lips and pushed the bowl away from her to the very edge of the table with one finger. "You certainly do like your desserts, don't you, Simon?" Her voice was a thick semi-sweet scold.

Haden swallowed then swallowed again. "I don't have to worry about getting pimples here, Mrs. Dugdale."

Her look turned stern. "Don't be rude, mister. I was only making an observation."

Haden was tempted to grab his crotch and tell her to observe *this*. But he didn't.

"Hello Broximon."

"Hello Mrs. Dugdale."

"Those are very festive shoes you're wearing today."

All three of them looked at Brox's cream and brown two-tones.

"Yes well, thanks a lot. What's up, Mrs. D? We're sort of busy here, you know? We're having, like, a meeting."

The teacher was so unaccustomed to being addressed with such bald sass that she could only stare at this pushy little man sitting on the armrest in his pimpy shoes. Both of these people may have been parts of Haden's memory, but that didn't necessarily mean they had to like each other.

She crossed her arms over her breasts and gave him the ugly eye. "I'm very sorry to interrupt your *meeting,* Broximon. I'm only here because I've been sent to tell Simon something."

The men waited. Mrs. Dugdale glared. When she felt that they'd been glared at long enough, she continued in a slightly less aggrieved voice. "I've been sent to tell Simon that God wants to see him."

• • •

God's office was nothing special. By the way it was furnished it could just as easily have belonged to a North Dakota dentist or some comb-over in middle management. The secretary/receptionist was a forty-something nondescript who told Haden in a neutral voice to take a seat. "He'll be with you in a minute." Then she went back to typing—on a typewriter. God's secretary used a manual typewriter.

Haden sat down on a green chair and carefully looked around the room, trying to absorb every detail so that he would remember as much of it as possible afterward. God's office. You couldn't get much higher than that. He was sitting in God's office waiting for the man himself, who had personally summoned Haden to come by.

But for what? While waiting for the meeting, a realization began to dawn on him and it wasn't a pretty one: What if his Judgment Day had arrived? Instead of lightning bolts, crashing kettle drums and cymbals, it came via an old schoolteacher giving you the message that God wanted to see you? What if an hour from now Haden was standing waist-deep in a pot of boiling shit while being stabbed by legions of red devils with flaming pitchforks—?

"Next."

Panicking, he glanced toward the door to see if he could escape. He could try, but God's secretary was watching now and he was sure that if he made a break for it, she could stop him.

"I could. Now just behave yourself and go in there" the woman said to him in a harsh voice that sounded remarkably similar to Mrs. Dugdale's.

The day of reckoning had come. Haden sensed all along that this sweet kooky dreamworld/down-memory-lane afterlife had been too easy, too good to be true. *Now* came the fire and brimstone. The hot pitch and the cold sweats he'd always assumed would be waiting for him after he died. He felt like crying. He felt like running away but it was too late for that and besides, where could he go? The jig was up. *His* jig was up.

Utterly defeated and expecting only the worst, Haden stood and moved slowly toward the door. The image of that last bowl of delicious chocolate pudding crossed his mind and tormented him further. He'd left it half uneaten. Just like his mother used to make but he'd pushed it away. . . .

"It's not fair! You could have at least given me some kind of warning" he pouted out loud.

The secretary didn't even look up this time. She only wiggled a finger toward the door and said "Move."

He got as far as the door. Touching the knob, he let his hand drop, and then touched it again. Summoning the little courage he possessed, he turned the knob this time and the door swung open.

A giant white polar bear sat behind a giant black desk across the not so large office. The animal's size and that of its desk made the room appear much smaller. The bear was looking at a white paper on the desk. It wore rectangular black reading glasses perched on the end of its fat black nose.

The desk was empty except for that single sheet of paper and a copper-colored name plaque on the right front corner. The name engraved on the plaque was Bob.

God was a polar bear named Bob?

For the first time since entering the room, Haden realized there was no chair for him to sit in. There was the desk and the bear's chair but that was it. So he stood there uneasily and waited for whatever came next.

God was a polar bear?

Looking up, it saw him and the bear's features immediately softened. "Simon! Wow. Wow. Wow. It's been a *lonnng* time, eh?"

"Sir?"

"Bob" took off his glasses and with great delicacy lay them down on the desk. "Don't tell me you don't remember?"

Now it came clear—the whole thing was a trap. Throw him off with the polar bear, then when Haden answered its question wrong, a door beneath his feet would drop open and *zoop*—down he'd plummet right into hell. No wonder there was no chair for him to sit in: this wouldn't take long. One question, one wrong answer, and hello hell.

Now he really didn't know what to say. The bear appeared to be waiting for an answer but what could Haden say that wouldn't spell his doom?

"Uh—"

"Jesus, Simon, you're breaking my heart here. You don't remember anything?"

He looked at the bear and then straining, looked closer. He saw nothing but what was there. Finally when it reached the point where most bears would either have roared or eaten Haden, this one began to whistle. "Raindrops Keep Fallin' On My Head." It was a pretty good whistler too. Halfway through the song it stopped and looked at the man.

Thoroughly confused now but also somewhat encouraged because he hadn't been sent to Hell yet, Simon Haden looked back at the beast, trying with all of his mental might to use every brain cell to—

"Oh-my-God, *BOB*!"

The bear grinned now and slapped its knees. "Finally! Now get over here and give your old pal a hug."

It didn't need to say that because Haden was already bounding across the room to do exactly that. Embracing the enormous white animal which by then had stood up and come around the desk, Haden hugged it as tightly as he could. Tears were in his eyes. While being hugged, Bob started whistling the song again which only made Simon hug tighter.

Bob the polar bear was the first and probably greatest gift Simon Haden ever received. He was three years old when it was given to him. Both of his parents were odd people. Little more needs to be said about them other than neither believed a child under three years old understood or appreciated Christmas. Consequently there was no real point in celebrating the holiday in the Haden home before then.

Because his parents were also tightfisted crabby skinflint shitheads, they purchased for their little son's first Christmas: 1. a middle-sized tree that they left undecorated except for strung popcorn (homemade) because to them, ornaments were a needless frill, 2. a large stuffed animal that for some peculiar reason was being sold for very little at the gasoline station they frequented.

One December afternoon Mr. Haden came home with a fuzzy white polar bear under his arm. Around the animal's neck was a cardboard collar with BOB written on it in thick black letters. Thin Mrs. Haden stood in the doorway blocking the way until her husband had satisfactorily explained what he was carrying. He said it was a stuffed animal, a polar bear, which he thought was an ideal Christmas present for little Simon. Plus he had bought it for a very good price.

"How much?" Mrs. Haden asked as she strangled the hand towel she was holding.

"Eleven dollars down at the Shell station."

She didn't know if she was more impressed by the price, or the fact her normally unobservant husband had found their son's Christmas present at a gasoline station.

It was lub at first site. The little boy walked into the living room Christmas morning and saw the tree first but that made no impression on him. A tree inside the house, strung with popcorn: Who cares? Then he saw the white bear sitting on the chair next to the tree. Simon waddled over to that chair and simply stood there, captivated by this white apparition, this wonderful creature out of the blue sitting there in his house. It seemed as if it had been waiting all along for the boy.

"Hello."

The bear didn't answer but that was okay. Simon didn't know what to expect from the animal but so long as it stayed where it was and didn't leave, the child was content with its silence.

"I lub you."

Even flint-hearted Mrs. Haden melted on hearing her son say that to his new toy. Standing next to her husband, she took his hand in hers and squeezed it. A few minutes later while Simon was still getting acquainted with Bob, Mr. Haden put on a record. The room filled with B. J. Thomas singing the Hadens' favorite song, "Raindrops Keep Fallin' on My Head."

For the next nine years, that was the theme song of Simon and Bob the Bear. Sometimes when he was dreamy or scared or just happy, the boy would wrap his arms around the bear and sing the song to his most steadfast friend. He told Bob his secrets, his fears, his hatreds, and what he considered most important in the small world of Simon Haden. He told the stuffed animal about his friend Clifford Snatzke, a new very pretty girl in third grade, and tearily about being beaten up again and again in fifth grade by the class bully. Even when he was much too old to own a stuffed animal he kept Bob, although he relegated it now to a corner, where it lived sort of incommunicado until it literally came apart at its cheap seams. Over those years the bear served as friend, confidante, confessor, talisman, imagined protector, and finally as pillow. Always uncomplaining, always there to do whatever he could to make Simon Haden feel that there was at least one being in his world who could be counted on for everything.

A long time later in another world, Bob the Bear gently disengaged itself from Haden's embrace and stepped back to look at its old roommate.

Haden didn't resist. Wiping his eyes with the back of his hand, he let himself be examined from head to toe by the bear. While this happened, something dawned on him.

"Bob? They said I was coming here to see God." He quickly looked around to make sure God wasn't in the room with them.

"Mmh" Bob said, not yet having finished its examination. Needless to say, that response wasn't much help.

"But what—"

The bear held up a paw for Haden to be quiet while he was being appraised. When it was finished, the animal nodded to itself as if it had now correlated the data it needed on this man.

"I *was* your god, Simon. I was the only god you ever really believed in your whole life. Think about it: Who else in your life did you ever love so much? Who else did you trust with all your heart, confess to with complete confidence, or turn to for help in bad situations? Me.

"Your parents were weirdos; all of the women you had gave you some joy here and there, but never enough to make your heart peaceful. And you would never have dreamed of telling your men friends your secrets. Think about all of that and then you do the math."

Bob had exactly the kind of voice Haden had imagined when he had "conversations" with the bear years ago. Deep and sweet, it was a friendly voice that put its arm around your shoulder and pulled you in close. *Tell me everything,* it said. *You can trust me.* And little Simon Haden had trusted his stuffed bear in every possible way. Looking at it now, although the version in front of him was much larger than the original, a thousand childhood memories leapt across Haden's mind. He quickly realized that the animal was right: Bob the Bear *had* been his god. It had possessed every wonderful quality that we attribute to a benevolent deity, and then some. Best of all, it was a god that had always been right there for the boy, always a glance or an arm's length away, ready to be relied on, ready to be held, ready to be turned to when thunder, or his parents' loud arguing voices, or the monsters lurking under the bed threatened him. When any of these things attacked his world and sent little Simon Haden running for any kind of safety he could find, Bob was always there. Thank God for Bob. Thank God for God.

"I've gotta say, Simon, you don't look so good."

"Well maybe that's because I'm *dead,* Bob."

"No, it's not that." The bear walked in a large slow circle around the man. "Tired, that's what it is—you look tired. How come?"

Haden tipped one shoulder. "I don't sleep so well here."

"Is that right? Why's that?"

Haden slid his hands into his pockets and shrugged. "I don't know. Look, could you please tell me what I'm doing here? This whole thing makes me incredibly uptight, not knowing a thing. I think I'd feel a whole lot better if I knew what it was about."

"Isabelle Neukor."

Haden jerked to attention. "Who?"

"Your Isabelle. Don't play dumb now."

"Isabelle." Haden said the name like it was new to his tongue, like just saying it made everything a little bit better. "What about her?"

"She's in trouble and you've got to help her. That's why I'm here. That's why we're talking."

Haden now felt a tug of relief in one direction, alarm in another. This wasn't about him. It wasn't his fault, as had usually been the case throughout his life. But it *was* about Isabelle. She was in trouble. As a dead man what could he do for her?

"I'm dead—what can I do for her?"

"She's here, in your world, Simon. You've got to find her."

Haden's heart wrenched. "She's here? She died? Isabelle died?"

Bob shook its big white head. "No, she's still alive. But Chaos keeps bringing her here and now it thinks it has found a way of making her stay."

"I don't understand this. I don't know what you're talking about."

"Okay. Sit down, Simon." Haden gestured that there was no chair for him to sit on. Bob pointed to the one behind the desk. "Sit there—take mine."

Haden sat and Bob began. "I was sent here because this thing is a lot larger than you could grasp. It was thought that if it were explained to you by someone familiar—"

"Bob, I'm confused enough already. Just give me the facts."

"Okay, fair enough. Did you know that Isabelle is pregnant?"

Simon Haden died a little bit again then. No, he did not know Isabelle was pregnant. Nor was it news he wanted to ever hear, whether he was alive or dead. Not only had he lost Isabelle in life, but now as a dead man he learned that someone else had won her, hands-down, *finito-basta,* totally. Enough so that she was having his baby. Haden hated the thought. At that moment he hated it about as much as he hated being dead.

"No, I didn't know that. Who's child—Vincent Ettrich?"

"Yes, but there's much more to it than that." Bob continued talking but Haden tuned it out. Torturing himself, he pictured Isabelle and Ettrich rolling around everywhere—in a bed, in a car, on the ground, standing up . . . He tore himself apart fantasizing about Isabelle fucking, being fucked, moaning, moving, loving it, loving the person she had her beautiful long legs and heart wrapped around. Vincent Ettrich, that son of a bitch.

Another reason why this image tormented Haden was knowing that Ettrich had been as much of a shameless cocksman as he. Isabelle Neukor hadn't given her heart to some virtuous Galahad who kneeled before her altar and had never entertained a dirty thought in his life. Oh no, she was in love with Vincent Ettrich, who'd had more ass than a toilet seat.

"Simon, you're not listening to me."

Looking blankly at his oldest friend, Haden forgot where he was for a moment. When he remembered he felt like the naughty student caught dozing by the teacher in the middle of a lesson.

"I'm sorry, I'm sorry, Bob. Please excuse me. What were you saying?"

Caustically, the polar bear asked "Do you want to know the secret of the universe?"

Haden heard the question and it *did* register in him somewhere, but in a distant unused room way on the other side of his mental house.

"*What?* What did you say?"

"I asked if you want to know the secret of the universe."

"No!" Simon Haden answered immediately.

Bob was surprised. "Why not?"

Haden held up a hand traffic cop–style to stop any further discussion of the topic. "What would I do with it? Huh? Sell it on eBay?

Look, I'm confused enough in this place learning the basics, Bob. You know what I mean? Addition and subtraction—I don't know how to add two and two together. I don't even know what that *is* here. Broximon and the others keep showing me things and obviously they're as simple as pie to them, but not to me. No sir—I go home and stare at the wall, trying to put it all into focus and get some kind of big picture. But you know what? The only conclusion I ever come to is *Huh?* I—don't-understand. Basically nothing. Do you understand how depressing that is? Do you have any idea of how stupid it makes you feel?

"So thanks but no thanks, Bob. You can keep the *secret of the universe.* I'm confused enough as it is." Haden rubbed his mouth hard and then in frustration, slid his hand up over his face to the top of his head and rubbed it furiously, as if putting out a little fire up there.

The bear watched all this with calm equanimity. When Haden was done, it said "Too bad. You've *got* to know it so that you can save Isabelle." And with a small wave of its paw, Bob showed Haden the secret of the universe.

It took about the same amount of time as a hummingbird needs to flap its wings once. The secret of the universe is not a large thing nor is it particularly complex. That's man's problem—he keeps thinking it is and consequently looks for it in all the wrong places.

Haden emerged from his new knowledge the way a deep-earth miner emerges from the elevator that has lifted him back up to the surface: blinking against the bright sunlight, slightly dizzy, straining to find his correct mental and physical gravity. Because where he has just come from bears no resemblance to where he is now. It is both disorienting and breathtaking at the same time.

What Haden did not know was that what Bob had just done to him broke the most important rule of the afterlife. Literally, it had never been done before. Everything after death was intended to be deduced or discovered, deciphered, decoded or deconstructed by the individuals themselves. No being was ever to be taught the secrets of death by others. Rule number one. That's the way it had always been—until now.

Haden finally "saw" Bob and said without thinking "Karya buryamp."

Bob nodded and answered "Skeena haloop."

"Clapunda la me."

The polar bear heaved a sigh and commiserated "Gorpop."

"Let's speak English, Bob. I'm not used to those other words yet."

"Whatever you like."

"How am I going to do this? Where am I supposed to start?"

For the first time since their conversation began, the bear hesitated and looked away. Haden noticed and didn't like it. Knowing the secret of the universe had made him a little more sensitive to the moment. "What?"

The animal still wouldn't look at him. "Nothing."

"What, Bob? Eye contact, please. You're not looking at me. Yes, I noticed."

"Chaos wants to keep Isabelle here. That's why it keeps bringing her: it wants her to give birth to the baby here. If that happens, neither of them will ever be able to return to their world."

Because he was an irredeemably selfish person, despite knowing the secret of the universe, Haden didn't mind that idea; no, not at all. Granted, the child wasn't his, but the notion of having Isabelle around (and another chance at her) brought his thoughts to happy attention.

"That can't happen, Simon. Her child has to be born there and live its life there."

"Why?"

The polar bear roared. Not like a cuddly, pillow-talking polar bear might, but a full-throated, shit-your-pants/run-for-your-life wild animal roar. It was huge and deafening and froze Haden down to his cells.

"Stop thinking *alive,* Simon. Think dead, because *alive* is finished for you. You live some place else now. And here there are vastly more important matters to concern yourself with.

"No more pussy, Simon. Get it? No more double vodkas at the bar with a wide-screen TV and complimentary pretzels. Time's up, you stupid motherfucker."

"What—" Haden could barely squeak out that one small word. Fear had him by the throat and rightly so: the bear looked like it was on the brink of killing him, or worse. It was close enough to snatch him up in one enormous white paw and crunch him like a piece of lettuce. "What do you want me to do, Bob? I'll do anything."

"You have to go to Ropenfeld."

"I won't do it" Haden said without hesitation.

The bear roared again, even more furiously this time. But Simon Haden didn't even blink.

"No Ropenfeld. No way, no day" he said decisively. There was no give in his voice. Polar bear or no polar bear, this was a closed issue.

Seeing that he meant it, Bob decided to cool the roars and try a little diplomacy instead. "Isabelle is in Ropenfeld, Simon. That's where they keep taking her, although she hasn't met any of your nightmares there yet."

Just the thought of Ropenfeld sent a cold lizard scurrying up Haden's spine. Looking at Bob, he vividly remembered the night years and years ago that he dreamt, or rather nightmared, that he was being made to tear the bear apart and feed the pieces to his hateful little sister. Gouts of ropy blood spouted from the pieces as he pulled them off one by one. Blood ran down the corners of his sister's mouth as she happily, greedily devoured each and every scrap of Simon's adored stuffed animal. Even the eyes. All this happened in Ropenfeld. Dreams like that always took place in Ropenfeld.

It began when Haden was a child. His father's boss was named Ropenfeld. A man and thus a name despised in the Haden family for as long as Simon lived at home. According to his parents, Ropenfeld was evil and did everything he could to make poor Mr. Haden's life miserable.

One night little Simon had a nightmare that took place in a town he was told by one of its citizens was named Ropenfeld. When he said it for the first time, the man stretched out the name so that it sounded like something haunted. *Roooooopenfeld!* What followed was a lurid, horrific dream and the boy woke from it bleating like a lamb being slaughtered. When his parents eventually came in to check on their still-crying child, he told them all about it. Both of the adults smiled. Mr. Haden thought it very fitting and patriotic that his little son should have his first cry-himself-awake nightmare in a town called Ropenfeld. Mrs. Haden just thought Simon had an overactive imagination.

Oddly enough for such a mediocre unimaginative person, it didn't end there. For the rest of his life, many of Simon Haden's nightmares took place in Ropenfeld. He never understood why things happened there but eventually he came to accept it as part of his chemistry.

Sometimes he dreamed of drowning in Lake Ropenfeld. Sometimes he crashed in a plane that was about to land in the town. The pilot would make his announcement—"We're making our final approach to Ropenfeld airport." Then there would be the dire sound of a giant metal part breaking, the plane would lurch to one side, and they would fall into an endless nosedive. Haden had several plane-crash dreams and at the time took it to be a portent of how he *would* die eventually: in a flaming spin from five miles up. How dismayed he would have been to learn that in real life he would die of a heart attack while going through the last rinse cycle in a Los Angeles car wash.

Sometimes in his nightmares, a fifteen-year-old Haden walked naked down the halls of Ropenfeld high school carrying only his textbooks. Beautiful clothed classmates pointed at him and laughed hysterically. One time they laughed, then all of them pulled out switchblade knives and attacked him. In another dream, a car full of his mothers slammed on its brakes right next to him as he walked down Ropenfeld Street. Mom after mom jumped out, like a clown car in the circus. They kept coming and coming. All of his mothers screamed at him for not having done a hundred thises and disappointing them for another hundred thats.

The bear hesitated again, unsure whether what it was about to say was allowed. All of this was brand-new territory for Bob. It was new territory for all of them.

"I shouldn't tell you this."

"Tell me what?" Haden showed only irritation. He thought the bear was going to try a different way of persuading him.

"Sooner or later you'll have to go, Simon. That's how it works here: everyone who has died must return to their Ropenfeld and confront what happened there. Find out why you dreamt those things when you did. It's an essential part of understanding who you are through who you were. By returning to the nightmares you had and working through them bit by bit, you learn to understand certain important aspects of your life. That's part of the process here."

"Yeah? Well fuck it, Bob. I think I'll wait another thousand years or so before I tackle that *aspect* of my life. Just being here is enough of a nightmare for right now. My plate is full—I don't need a second helping."

"You can't wait; you have to go there now."

Before he had a chance to say no again (and again and again), Haden began to rise off the ground like a slowly filling hot air balloon. Instantly he knew what was happening. "No! You can't do this!"

"I'm sorry, but you have to go. You've got to try and save Isabelle."

Haden rose higher. He flailed his arms as if somehow that could stop or control what was happening to him. But it couldn't.

"This isn't fair. It's wrong."

"I know Simon, but it's necessary."

Haden wanted to answer but fury silenced him. When he'd risen about five feet above the ground, his body stopped and then began moving forward in one direction. He was being steered. The office window was wide open and he sailed through. It would have been a delightful sensation if he hadn't known where he was going—toward all those shitty, shitty things: the monsters seen through the 3-D eyes and imagination of a scared child. The terrors, the relentless moments of failure, humiliation, confusion, and worse that he had experienced in his many nightmares over the years. Haden was going toward all of them, toward Ropenfeld. There was nothing he could do to stop it. And for what, to save Isabelle Neukor? Save her from *what*? Yes, he knew the secret of the universe, but how did it apply here?

Celadon

John Flannery was late for his meeting with Leni because he was hit by a car. A brand-new Porsche Cayenne, no less. One of those four-wheel-drive, eighty-thousand-dollar Jeep-y testosterone-turbos that rich men drive to show the world they're larky, adventurous, but don't forget I'm rich too. A "Weekend Rambo" vehicle. This one was so clean and new that it had only two hundred and thirty-nine kilometers on the odometer when it blew through a red traffic light at Schwedenplatz and hit Flannery square on while he was in the middle of a pedestrian crossing. The car knocked him back onto the sidewalk into a huddle of shrubs.

A lot of people saw it happen. Some of them screamed. Others gaped, fascinated by this unexpected turn of events as they were walking across their day. A mother with two children turned around and ran in the other direction with them. The kids kept trying to look back over their shoulders to see if the guy was dead.

He certainly looked dead. Flannery lay unmoving, sprawled over the bush like some kind of lumpy tarpaulin. The driver of the Porsche panicked. For a split second he thought Floor the accelerator and get the hell out of here. Fortunately his good sense prevailed. After taking a few deep breaths, he slowly and carefully got out of his sleek new car that had just become a deadly weapon. Terrified, he walked toward the body. He felt as if his insides had turned liquid and he was going to shit them out any moment.

Until then his life had been golden. He had a successful business. His wife was beautiful *and* nice. He always drove through yellow lights turning to red. And why not? He was who he was. Life had always stepped back and let him go first.

To his horror and incredulous relief, the body on the bush moved. Someone choked out "He's alive!" A woman gasped and blurted so quickly that her three words became one "ohmyGod!" Then the body moved again—an arm raised, lowered, and rose again.

Seeing this slow-motion horror that he had caused, the driver once again had the wildly strong urge to run away. Leave his life, his wife, the car, leave everything and flee as fast as he could to anywhere. He forgot that a wallet containing all of his identification papers lay on the passenger's seat alongside his cell phone which contained an address book fifty-four numbers long in its memory. He forgot that there were license plates on the car that could trace him on a computer in two seconds. He forgot everything that minutes ago had comprised his life. All that filled his frightened head now was *Run—save yourself.*

Because even if the injured man survived, what followed would go on for years and ruin everything: the hospital, the recovery, the huge insurance claims, the lawsuits, the bad publicity, and yes, the money. Inside the now-screaming world of his dread he couldn't help thinking about the money too.

That's what went through his mind while standing there watching this body move so slowly, like a lobster or a crab that's been out of water too long. It was all his fault, everything. Good God, he'd be sued for millions. He had millions but would lose them now because—

The body slowly turned. It turned over completely so he could now see the victim's face for the first time. Someone said again "He's alive!" as if what they were seeing needed spoken verification again. But would the victim remain alive? How bad were his injuries?

The driver had to find out. He could not stand not knowing anymore. With his last drop of courage, he walked over to the man lying on his back now, staring up at the sky. Remarkably, there was no blood. How could that be? How could a person be hit square on by a very large car and knocked that far back without bleeding somewhere?

The victim slowly rolled his eyes away from the sky, over to the driver, and said "I want your car."

The driver jerked back in surprise. John Flannery had not only spoken clearly and directly to him, but in Flemish. How could he know that the driver was Belgian and Flemish was his mother tongue?

None of the other onlookers spoke that gluey, arcane language. They naturally thought the wounded man was out of his head with pain and speaking gibberish.

"Listen to me because I will only say this once. In a minute I'm going to speak German so everyone here will understand. I'm going to ask you to put me in your car and take me to the hospital. This has to be done fast because the police will be here soon and then everything gets official. If they come that's the worst thing that could happen to you."

The driver couldn't believe what he was hearing. He couldn't believe any of this was happening to him. But it *was* and there was nothing he could do to stop it.

"All right. Will you do it." Flannery said these things as statements, not the questions that they were. The driver mumbled yes.

When Flannery spoke again it was much louder and in perfect German. "I hurt. I hurt. I want to go to the hospital now. Right now. *Right now.*"

He kept saying that over and over like a keening lament. The bystanders told him to wait—surely an ambulance would come soon. Flannery's only mistake was standing up a little too quickly for someone who was supposed to be so badly injured. But he knew that the police were only eight minutes away. This had to be done right now. Staggering over to the Porsche, he opened the door and shouted "Take me now. Take me to the hospital! I can't wait. I hurt! I hurt!"

The driver watched this happen along with the others. He was a bystander too until someone said to him "Go, go ahead. We'll tell the police when they come. You go ahead. Take him to the hospital. We'll tell the police."

Bewildered and unsure, the driver got back into his car and put it in gear. Flannery was slumped against the passenger door looking waxy, in pain and very ill. When they had pulled away from the crowd, he spoke again in Flemish.

"I'll tell you where to go. When we get there give me all of the papers you have on the car, and then leave. Never report that it was stolen. Never make an insurance claim, and continue to pay the insurance on it for the next two years. After that you can stop. Do you understand? This is your lucky day if you're smart about it and do exactly what I told you."

"But how—"

"Shut up. Don't ask questions. If I want the ownership papers later, I'll contact you. But I probably won't need them. The car will never be used for anything bad so you don't have to worry about that. Give me the keys and the papers, get out when I tell you to, and disappear.

"Or you can take me to the hospital now. Then the police and everyone else will get involved and you'll lose everything. That's a guarantee. But if you give me the car and walk away clean, nothing else happens to you—all of it ends this minute. It's your choice. Can you trust me to keep my word? Yes."

The driver was trying to think fast, come up with all of the possible angles here, thinking what to do, what to do. But what *could* he do? All of it was his fault. That stupid red traffic light; this stupid new car. It made him feel bulletproof. *Had* made him feel bulletproof until now. And there had been so many witnesses. Some of them would surely come forward to testify against him. Everything was against him here. He was fucked any way he looked at it.

Out of the corner of his eye, John Flannery watched this moron melt down. The sight was beautiful. Flannery always loved these moments. He could easily have stolen a car off the street and saved himself the trouble and acting involved in the funny little ruse. But doing that was nowhere near as delightful as watching firsthand as Chaos devoured a person's life in a couple of bites. Especially because he knew a secret that the driver didn't, having done this sort of thing before, and that made it all the more delicious.

The secret was this was just the beginning. Flannery could have given this man a two-page printout of what was going to happen to him and when, give or take a few months. For example, today the driver would walk away from his brand-new car scared, unsure, ashamed of his behavior, and fundamentally overwhelmed. Even when he tried hard he wouldn't be able to think straight about any of it, and he wouldn't for a long time. Only his survival instinct would keep him going and moving away as far as he could get from the scene of his crime.

Eventually he would travel through resentment and worry, anger, helplessness, and even gratitude that he had been spared, like they were small-town railroad stations his express train passed by on its way to the capital city, Paranoia.

The driver was paranoid anyway—most successful people are. But after what had happened today, that paranoia would grow tenfold in his mind and heart, which was exactly what Flannery wanted. From now on, many times a day the driver would wonder Whatever happened to my car? Whatever happened to the man who took it? Should I be worried? Ashamed? What if the police knock on the door one day and say *Come with us. There's a problem.*

What if? What if? What if? For years the most innocent things, events and objects—a ringing telephone, a knock on the door, a strangely colored, formal-looking envelope in the mailbox, would all become dangerous, threats, things to worry about, enemies. New things that went bump in the night—and day. The man's life wouldn't be ruined by this event but it would be badly wounded and for years it would walk with a limp.

Flannery loved it. Four blocks from his apartment he told the driver to pull over and stop. They were on the Obere Donaustrasse, next to the Danube Canal. From where they were parked they could see the rushing water.

Flannery pointed. "Walk across that bridge. There's a taxi stand on the other side. Or you can take the subway home. Give me the keys and the papers now."

The driver reached to turn off the ignition but stopped. "How do I know—"

Flannery shook his head. "You *don't* know. You have to take my word that it ends right here. As soon as you get out of the car this whole thing is finished. Lucky you."

"But I don't know who you are. I don't even know your name." The man's voice sounded mournful, a sad soul asking for reassurance.

Flannery raised his head and spent time looking at the ceiling of the car. He considered admitting who he really was and then proving it to this fool. That would be exciting! But it wouldn't accomplish much. Or rather it wouldn't accomplish the kind of effect Flannery preferred: long slow never-ending woe.

"Do you like proverbs?" He continued looking at the ceiling. But out of the corner of his eye he saw the driver staring suspiciously at him, as if waiting for a nasty punch line.

"Proverbs? I don't know. What does that have to do with this?" His voice was the giveaway; its petulant, impatient tone told Flannery exactly what the guy was like. He had the voice of a spoiled brat, a bully whenever possible; a self-absorbed lightweight who'd had a lot of luck which he mistook for talent and canny insight. At all times he believed his priorities took precedence over anyone else's.

The only things of substance in his entire being at the moment were the coins he had in his pants pocket.

"Listen to this one—it's very appropriate: 'Whenever you take a mouthful of too-hot soup, the next thing you do will be wrong.' Isn't that brilliant?" Flannery's face lit up like a child's when its favorite television show came on.

The driver said nothing. His eyes said nothing.

It didn't matter. Flannery had an appointment to keep with Leni; enough of this. Reaching under his ass on the seat, he pulled out the driver's wallet and cell phone. The other man reached out to take them.

"No. Not yet." Flannery brought the phone close to his face and began to tap in numbers on it.

"What are you doing?"

"Calling the police. Do you know how much fun they're going to have with this? You ran a red light, hit a pedestrian in a crosswalk, then left the scene of the crime—*your* crime—with the victim. I'm going to tell them where we are and have them come get us. I HURT! I HAVE TO GO TO THE HOSPITAL! I HURT!"

There was a shocked silence when Flannery finished yelling. The telephone was close enough for the driver to hear someone on the other end of the line answer *"Polizei."*

Snatching the phone out of Flannery's hand and fumbling with the buttons, he managed to disconnect the call. "Give me my wallet." Taking it, he slid a transparent envelope out of an inner pocket. It contained the necessary papers to the Porsche. He wanted to ask more questions. He wanted reassurance again that this horror would go no further than today, right now. He wanted so many things but knew there was no way he could have them because . . . driving through that red light he had taken a mouthful of too-hot soup. He had caused this accident. What options did he have? Now he understood why the big man had recited that proverb—because it *was* totally appropriate.

He handed over his car papers and keys. Without looking, Flannery took them.

"And now I should just go?"

"Open the door and go. *C'est tout.*"

The driver clicked the handle and his door opened a crack. This car had cost almost one hundred thousand euros. He had had it six days. Street noise swept in. He looked through the window. It was sunny and clear out there. A delicious wisp of cool breeze blew in through the crack and across his face. He could almost taste its freshness. The green-brown water in the Danube canal over there moved by so easily and freely. More than anything else he wanted to be out there, away from this car, away from everything that had happened in the last half hour. He imagined walking over the bridge back into the center of town. He would do errands. That was good, a good diversion. He would do his errands and walk and walk. Eventually he would call his wife. No, not that. What could he say to her? He would have to create a perfect story about the car, a great alibi. One she would believe and accept without hesitation.

When his telephone rang these thoughts dissolved. He looked at the screen to see if he recognized the caller but it said only "Number withheld."

"Hello?"

"This is the police. You called before but then hung up."

When he responded his voice was cool and professional. He knew how to do this. He was in his element. "I'm sorry, but the call was a mistake. We thought we'd been robbed but then my wife discovered she'd simply misplaced her things. Sorry for the inconvenience."

The policeman on the other end asked a few more halfhearted questions and then rang off.

"That was impressive. You're very good at bullshitting. You won't have any trouble explaining what happened to your car."

The driver stared at Flannery who did look bad. "Are you really hurt? Or is all this just . . ."

Instead of answering the question, Flannery slowly slid his left trouser leg up. The leg was clearly broken in two places, one of them a savage compound fracture. "Wanna see more?"

One look at that hideous leg was enough for the driver. Recoiling, he stumbled getting out of the car and almost fell down.

"Hey" Flannery called out just as the guy was about to shut the door.

The driver looked at him in alarm. *God almighty, what next?* "Yes?"

" 'Beware of the silent dog.' "

Not sure he had heard right, the man leaned forward. "What did you say?"

" 'Beware of the silent dog.' "

"What? What do you mean?" All of these proverbs; why didn't the guy just say what he meant?

Flannery let go of his pant leg. The material slid back down halfway, covering only part of the wound. He licked his lips and smiled. "Woof."

The driver nodded his head fast too many times—yes, now he understood exactly what he was being told. Flannery watched him cross the street and walk double-time toward the bridge.

The interior of the car was black and silver, beautiful in its detail. "Beautifully appointed" Flannery said like a radio announcer, as if he were trying to sell the car to himself. He touched the steering wheel, the gearshift lever. Then he inhaled that indescribable sweet/sour smell of new car and new leather. Very nice. All of it was very nice. He had chosen well.

But what color was the car exactly? He had forgotten to ask. It was a kind of grayish yellow-green. No, it was more than that. He closed his eyes a moment and searching, found the word—*celadon.* He had never heard of the word before but that's what color this car was—a celadon Porsche.

"Okey dokey." He slid both hands slowly down either side of his broken left leg, as if the whole thing were wet and he was squeezing water out of it. On reaching the ankle, he pulled up the pants to look. His leg was whole again—unbroken and unmarked.

He had a date in a few minutes. He needed to look presentable for it and not like a man who had just been struck by a car. Running his hands over his whole body, the torn and dirty clothes he wore disappeared and transformed into what he had been wearing an hour before—a new white T-shirt and beige shorts. He moved his hands up over his neck and face. All of the smudges and scratches from the accident disappeared as soon as they were touched. Now his beard was carefully trimmed and the smell of Gray Flannel cologne filled the car. He reached over and turned the rearview mirror toward him. Looking at his reflection, what he saw there was okay. Time for Leni.

• • • • • •

"Celadon." Ettrich said the unfamiliar word with surprise. It had just popped up on his tongue like an egg.

Isabelle looked at him, waiting for more. They sat in a tram holding hands while riding back into town from the Central Cemetery. Nothing had been accomplished there by visiting Petras Urbsys's grave. Both of them were depressed and at a complete loss for what to do next.

Ettrich shook his head. "I have no idea what that word means."

"Then why did you say it?"

"I don't know. It came out of nowhere."

She gave him a So what? look. But Ettrich shook his head because there was more to this. "No, you don't understand."

"Then tell me, Vincent."

He paused to think and then looked at her hand in his. Removing his, he opened her fingers and laid his flat palm on top of hers. She felt something—a tickle, a thin but persistent heat. He lifted his hand. Written in the middle of her palm was the word *celadon* in neat block letters the exact color of the word. She gasped, closed her hand into a fist.

Ettrich began to smile. "That's it. It means that color."

"What does?"

"Celadon. It's the color of those letters." He pointed to her hand. His smile was twice as big as before.

"How do you know that, Vincent? You just said—"

"I know, I know. Hold on a minute, Fizz. I have to think this through."

Frustrated by what had already happened that day, she was now almost angry at him for pulling this bizarre stunt and then not explaining it to her. In her irritation, Isabelle could think of nothing else to do at the moment but look again at her palm and the unfamiliar green word that had appeared there. Celadon. She wanted to rub her hand on her pants and get it off.

Vincent was silent a long time. She kept looking at him both directly and sneaking peeks to see if he was ready to say anything yet. But he continued staring out the window and didn't look at her once.

Isabelle grew increasingly more fidgety and exasperated as the minutes passed. Her temperature rose but so did her curiosity. What was going on? She looked at the word on her palm, she looked at Vincent, she looked out the window. She did not have a clue about what was happening. But neither did she have a clue about how they were going to get out of this fix. Perhaps Vincent did know, or *would* when he emerged from his silence. Maybe he was really onto something that might help.

Reaching into his pocket, he took out his wallet. He removed a scrap of paper from inside. She saw a list of single words written on the paper.

"What's that?"

"Give me your hand again."

She frowned but did it. He looked at her and after glancing at his piece of paper, asked "Do you know what the word *hermeneutics* means?"

"Herman what?"

"Perfect." He put his open hand over hers. Again she felt that heat or tremble or whatever it was there. Nothing to make you jump or get scared, but something definitely felt.

Ettrich smiled and said "It means interpretive, explanatory."

"Huh?"

"Look at your hand."

Written where *celadon* had been a moment ago was now *hermeneutics* in celadon-colored block letters. She snatched her hand back and pressed it to her chest.

Ettrich pointed to the paper. "Whenever I'm reading and come across a word I don't know, I jot it down. When I have a chance, I look them up in a dictionary. Sometimes there's a whole bunch of them."

Isabelle looked at his list and saw that *hermeneutics* was the first word on it. "You didn't know what it meant till you did that hand thing with me just now?"

"Exactly." Ettrich said it encouragingly, hoping she would understand without being told what was becoming clear to him now.

"And you didn't know what *celadon* meant either?"

This time he said nothing, letting her go with it, letting her think it through out loud.

"So it's *us,* Vincent? Us together—not you alone, or me. Answers come when we're together, when we're connected?"

"Yes, I think that's exactly what it is, Fizz."

"Do it again. Try another." She took the vocabulary list out of his hand and slowly read the funny-sounding second word on it. " 'Borborygmus.' " She stuck out her hand palm up and wiggled her fingers at him. "Come on, take it—try again."

Ettrich took her hand and said the word. And then he laughed. "It means stomach gas. It means when your stomach rumbles because you haven't eaten, or because it's upset."

"Stomach gas?" Pulling her hand away, she covered her mouth with it because she was giggling now too. When she got around to thinking about it, she took her hand from her mouth and looked at it. Written in celadon in the middle of her palm was *borborygmus.*

"Let me try. Let me try." She grabbed Vincent's hand and said *"Hudna."* Her eyes were all expectation.

He didn't hesitate. "It's an Arabic word. It means a temporary ceasefire. Where did that come from?"

"In an article on Israel and Palestine I read yesterday. I love that word; love the way it sounds. I kept saying it to myself—*hudna, hudna.*"

"But so you knew what it meant already?"

"Yes Vincent, but *you* didn't. Let me do another. I love this. *Anak.*"

Ettrich laughed again. "*Shit.* It means *shit* in Eskimo."

"Right!" She looked at her hand and written there was that Eskimo word for shit. "No more, that's it. I want to keep this one." Like a little girl, she stuck her palm in his face so he could see *anak* there too. He took her hand and kissed the palm.

"This is beginning to make sense to me now. Remember back at the cemetery when I saw you and Petras in his store the day he taught you how to come and get me after I died? Do you remember how that happened?"

Isabelle said "I touched his gravestone—"

"No honey, we both touched his gravestone at the same time. Do you remember? *At the same time.* That's what this is all about. Together. Two. You and me and not each of us separately."

"But I didn't do anything, Vincent. I didn't do anything to make it happen. Did you? It's not like we waved our magic wands together and things started happening. We weren't in control of anything."

The truth of her statement took some wind out of his sails. "You're right, you're right . . . But put that aside for a minute and only think about this: together somehow, we make these things happen. I lived for a while in your past today—I was actually there. I saw every detail and heard every word of your conversation with

Petras. Then there were the definitions to those silly vocabulary words that neither of us knew before. They came as soon as I touched your hand—as soon as we were joined. Get it? When the two of us become one, things happen. Things we can't do alone. I bet—I'm *sure*—it goes much farther than that."

And it did go much farther than that, but they had to wait till later in the day to experience it. When Isabelle opened the door to their apartment, Hietzl the dog looked over from its chair across the room but didn't get up to greet them as usual. It was angry at having been left at home when they went to the cemetery. Ettrich had explained to Hietzl that dogs weren't allowed in cemeteries because they pissed on the gravestones and shit where they shouldn't. Who wants a steaming pile on their final resting place? But despite the explanation, the dog only stared dolefully up at him from its place on the floor.

As they were going out earlier, Isabelle had hoisted her purse on to her shoulder and said "It's my fault, Hietzl. I don't want to drive out there, so you can't wait for us in the car. We're taking the tram."

Now that they had returned, the animal was giving them the cold shoulder. Not that they really noticed it because both of their minds were full of Vincent's theory. They could talk of nothing else.

Isabelle sat at the kitchen table while Vincent prepared coffee and put the cups and cream in front of her. "Where did *celadon* come from? Why did you just suddenly say that word out loud?"

He turned from searching a cupboard for sugar and shook a finger at her. "Good question. I was trying to figure it out before. But you know what? Out of nowhere."

"But you must have seen it before. Maybe you read it somewhere. How else could you have thought that word up?"

"I don't know, Fizz. As far as I can remember, it really is the first time I've ever heard of celadon. The idea about you and I combined creating a third . . . *something* that knows much more than either of us alone, came when the word did.

"Look—when we touched that gravestone at the same time suddenly I was living in your past. Then later came *celadon*. What's that? The minute I took your hand I knew what it was. *And* at the same moment, this 'you-and-me-makes-three' theory came into my head. It's not the first time I've had the idea. And I'm not just talking about our child either. What is it? What's the third thing? I don't know. But today we've had pretty good proof of it."

They were silent awhile, until Ettrich brought the coffee to the table and poured some for each of them.

"There's something else. Please don't get pissed off."

"Pissed off at what?" She had the cup to her mouth so that when she spoke, her breath over the hot liquid pushed smoke in front of her lips.

"At the question I'm going to ask. Tell me about Frank Obermars."

She lowered the coffee to the table without taking a sip. Months ago when they had gotten back together, one of the first things they swore to each other was to tell the truth about everything, no matter what. Since then they'd had some difficult wrenching discussions and full-blown arguments. But she had always kept her word and told him the complete truth.

Now she was tempted to lie. She was tempted to ask "*Who's Frank Obermars?*" because he wasn't important. No, he *was* important in a historical sense, but not to them, not now, not anymore. Frank was over. Frank was the past. Frank was what she did when she left Ettrich and swore she would never see him again although she knew by then that she was pregnant with his child. Leaving Ettrich was the cause, Obermars was the effect.

He was a good-looking smart Dutchman who worked for Philips Electronics in Vienna. Another time they might have had a rewarding relationship. But there are people we meet in life that miss being important to us by inches, days, or heartbeats. Another place or time or emotional frame of mind and we would willingly fall into their arms; gladly take up their challenge or invitation. But as it is, we encounter them when we are discontent or content and they are not. Whatever serious chemistry might have been possible if, isn't.

Isabelle initially reasoned that having a fast electric fling with someone clever and sexy would lessen the pain of losing Vincent. So she said yes to an invitation from Frank and went away with him for a long weekend to a beautiful lakeside village near Salzburg. Everything there was perfect. It was an enchanting place that the Dutchman had chosen carefully.

At the end of their first day there, he made love to her for three hours. Never once did a cheerless, detached look leave her face. He tried every trick and tactic he knew to please her. He had a lot of them. He was used to satisfying his lovers because he knew what women liked and he genuinely reveled in sex. But not once, not for a second, did he feel that Isabelle was there with him sharing this experience, much less enjoying it. Obermars would later remember their encounter as similar to making love to an adept prostitute. A woman who knew the right moves but if you saw her face when she didn't know she was being watched, you'd see only a blankness there that would chill your heart.

He tried and tried until Isabelle became almost still. As soon as he stopped she rolled onto her side away from him. He thought she was going to cry but she only remained silent, which was even worse.

He asked if she was all right. She said yes. The word came out a stone. He asked if there was anything he could do. She said no, but that she wanted to return to Vienna in the morning. He could not imagine spending an entire night with her and her silence, so he offered to drive back immediately.

She turned then and looked at him. "Yes, that would be better. You're a good guy, Frank." She said it in English for some reason. It was the first time she had ever spoken to him in that language although she knew that he was fluent. Maybe it was because they had entered another country of the heart now. German was spoken in their Before, English in this After.

Obermars smirked and bent down to the floor to retrieve his clothes. He didn't want to look at her because right then she was lovelier than he had ever seen her. He didn't know if that was because she was naked or because he knew there was no chance with her. This was the one and only time he would ever see her this way. His longing and sense of utter defeat were equal. Her face glowed in the soft light of the room, the whiteness of the rumpled sheets contrasting with her tan skin.

"You look like a piece of toast" he said, looking for his second sock. He had nothing else to lose. He could say whatever he wanted now.

"Like *what?*" She slowly sat up but did nothing to hide her body. He thought she would cover it after what had just happened between them and her wish to leave.

"Like a piece of toast. Your skin against those sheets. You look like a piece of golden toast on a white plate."

She remembered that image and the look on Frank's face when he said it. She saw the unhappiness there, the way his spirit was already moving away from her out of that lovely room, into the car, onto the road, back to Vienna where their lives would never intersect again. She didn't care. She only wanted to go home and try to figure out a way to live the rest of her life.

• • •

"Fizz?"

She came out of her memory tunnel blinking several times at the sound of Ettrich's voice. After a few seconds pause she asked "What do you want to know, Vincent? How do you know about Frank?"

He pushed the sugar bowl across the table to her. "It came before, when you asked for the meaning of *anak*. A picture of you and him came to me at the same time as the definition of the word."

"Oh. What picture of us?" She turned her hand over but *anak* was no longer written there on her skin.

"At the rest stop on the autobahn—when you had him pull over so that you could throw up."

She put her hand over the top of the cup and instantly felt heat lick the middle of her palm. She assumed by his tone of voice that Vincent knew everything that had happened between her and Obermars. "I said I had to go to the toilet and would he please pull over. But what I really needed to do was puke." Her voice suddenly rose almost into anger. "I had to get *away* from you, Vincent. My head, my body, all of it had to break away. You were over. We were over. I had to clean you out of my system or else I couldn't have survived. So there was Frank. And I tried with him but it was a disaster. Does that make sense? Do you understand?"

"Yup. Drink your coffee."

She looked at him suspiciously, not believing the calm and even tone of his voice. "Do we talk about Frank now or can we talk about something else? Because I want to know something, Vincent: two times today you've gone into my life like you were just entering a room—it was that simple. How did you do that? It's like you just turned some doorknob and walked right in. How does it happen?"

He looked away and then turned toward her. "By talking to time."

"Say that again."

"You talk to time. Because it's organic; it *understands.*

"Look Fizz, you asked before what I learned when I was dead. I said I didn't know. I don't remember much about being dead except for little pieces; fragments and fuzzy snapshots of mysterious things, images that have no meaning to me.

"But today I discovered something at the cemetery. I realized something, or understood it, or whatever, and goddamn if it didn't work. Do you know about Lomo photography?"

"*Lomo?* No, what's that?"

"Interesting stuff. We used it very successfully in an advertising campaign at our agency once. Years ago in Russia, before the Iron Curtain came down, they sold this cheap little camera there called the Lomo. I think that's the name of the company that makes them. It cost almost nothing and was really primitive. You have to wind the film advance with your thumb and I don't think that you can even adjust the focus on it. Back in those days in Russia what could you expect? But it made it possible for everyone there who wanted one to have a camera.

"Eventually some smart guy came along with the idea of using the camera's limitations as advantages. They began taking pictures with a Lomo without looking or framing the shot. Or they didn't aim. They didn't even look through the viewfinder. They took pictures from the hip, over the shoulder, or holding the camera behind their backs and snapping whatever was there, off to the side . . . it didn't matter. Spontaneous, accidental, whatever way you want to do it—just shoot and shoot in every way and direction you can think of. That way, chance decides whether the pictures will be any good or not.

"And you know what? Some were. Some of them were fan-tastic. Today it's huge—there are Lomo exhibits all over the world: Lomo galleries, clubs, websites . . . It's become very popular because it works. Ninety-nine-point-nine percent of the pictures are awful—lousy, out of focus, dull. But one in a million is totally brilliant.

"My memories of being dead are like a big batch of Lomo photographs piled on a table. Ninety-nine-point-nine percent of them are bad, out-of-focus crap. You can't even tell what's pictured in most of them. But today when we touched Petras's gravestone together I found one picture in the pile that's not only clear but beautiful."

"Tell me."

His eyes shifted to her hand still resting on top of the coffee cup. "I'll show you instead."

Isabelle didn't know where to look then because Vincent avoided her eyes. Instead he continued staring at her coffee cup, so eventually she looked at it too.

Over the top of the cup now was a small hand, a child's hand. On the fourth finger was a cheap plastic ring shaped like a sunflower. Isabelle had owned an identical ring when she was eight years old. She'd found it on the ground in the Stadtpark when she went walking there with her family one Sunday morning. Because sunflowers were her favorite flower, she'd assumed finding the ring was a magical sign; it would bring her luck. So she wore it religiously for two years, rarely taking it off.

An eight-year-old's hand wearing that ring was at the end of her wrist on top of the cup now. The hand was small, the fingernails short to the nub, bitten away by a nervous mouth. Isabelle's mouth when she was a girl and edgy about everything. Those nails, that hand, that very ring.

She was almost as surprised by her calm acceptance of knowing for certain that she was looking at her own eight-year-old hand as she was by the fact that that's what it was.

And then it changed.

The hand got bigger while the fingernails grew longer and sprouted color—glaring green. A horrible, funny color she remembered well from a day when she was twenty. Flora had bought a bottle of psychedelic-green fingernail polish as a joke gift for Leni. Then the three friends ended up painting their nails and toenails with it that afternoon because they were completely bored and looking for anything to do. Flora's mother took a picture of them showing off their green hands and toes. Isabelle had the photograph framed and still kept it on her desk.

"What are you doing, Vincent? Why is this happening?" She did not take her eyes off her hand.

"I talked to time. I asked it to do something. It understands what you say if you ask it correctly."

“What did you ask it to do?”

“To show you your hand past, present, and future. Do you recognize them? Are they you?”

She looked at him blankly.

Ettrich said “When a person’s alive they think time’s only what’s on a clock—hours, minutes, and days. But they’re wrong; I learned *that* when I was dead. Time’s also—” While he spoke her hand started to change again. In a moment what it became silenced him.

The green nail polish disappeared, replaced by a delicate silver and jasper-stone ring that Vincent had given her the week before. A thick small scar, the result of scraping her hand against a wall just after they returned from America, blossomed across the back of her thumb. At a glance it was clear this was Isabelle’s hand today. Except that one of her fingers was now missing.

Knee-Deep in Sunday Suits

"This is where I leave you."

"What?" Haden barely heard Bob the polar bear because the animal was so far in front of him. It had been that way for miles. They had walked and walked across the city, Haden's dream city, for most of the morning. But because the bear did not respond to his questions, the man had no idea where they were going except toward his nightmares.

"I *said* this is where I leave you, Simon."

"What does that mean? Will you stop walking for a minute, please? Just stop for one fucking minute."

Bob stopped but did not turn around. Haden looked at that huge white back in front of him and waited. Nothing happened so he used this stop time to catch his breath. When he had but the bear still hadn't turned to face him, Haden looked around. He had never been in this part of the city. Or if he had, none of it was familiar. He knew that this place and everything in it came from his own memory and imagination. But one of the things he had learned here was that most of what a person does, thinks, and creates in a lifetime is forgotten. What remains in our memory, or in others' hearts, or on the earth after we are gone is often a surprise.

A woman wearing a radiant blue "spinning Bobo" funeral mask from Burkina Faso walked by and said jovially "Hi Simon!" Haden was used to this sort of loony event here by now and only acknowledged her greeting with a half wave.

"Follow her, Simon."

Thinking about something else, Haden didn't really register what Bob had said. "What?"

"Follow her—the one in the mask."

"No Bob, I won't follow her." The bear still hadn't turned around and frankly at that point Haden didn't give a shit if it ever turned around again. The goddamned bear—who did it think it was, bossing him around like that? "What's going on here anyway, huh? Where are we? *What is this?*"

The masked woman disappeared into a doorway down the block. For a moment Haden wondered who she was and where she was going.

Then something dawned on him—something big. Without another word, he dashed off down the street toward the woman who had disappeared.

Bob crossed its giant paws and *tsk*ed its tongue like a disapproving auntie. It was about time! From having lived with Simon Haden all through those little-boy years, Bob knew that he was dumb. But to have grown up and remained as dumb was both disheartening and impressive. Instead of his life experiences soaking down into him like water into porous stone, thereby making him weightier and more substantial, Haden seemed like glass when water is poured over it—nothing stays. Well maybe a little, but only in the remote corners and definitely not much.

The woman in the blue mask had been just about the last rabbit Bob had left to pull out of its hat. If Simon had not reacted after seeing her, the bear really would have been stumped as to what to do next. It'd led Simon through the man's own city, past clues and signs anyone with half a brain in his head would have recognized. To no avail. Five, ten times during their walk Bob had wanted to stop, point directly at specific things, and say *Look at that, Simon!* Or *There—don't you recognize it?* But they had told the bear to avoid "point and tell" as much as possible so it didn't. Eventually in the end Haden *had* reacted to something, thank God.

"I think you're wrong about Simon. I used to think the same thing as you, but I realized something today about the guy: he's really not so dumb. He's just got a bad attitude. He'd look angry eating an ice cream cone."

Bob heard the voice but looking around, could not locate the source of it. Eventually he did look down low enough to see Broximon standing nearby, nattily dressed as always. Today he was wearing argyle and looked like a 1930s golf pro.

"Well, hello Broximon."

"Hey Big Bob. Have you got time to go get something to drink?"

"I'll tell you, I've got such *shpilkes* from going around in circles with Simon Haden that about the only thing my stomach could handle now is cold milk."

"Then cold milk it is, pal. There must be some place around here we can go."

Bob looked left and right. "Do you even know where we are? I'm sort of at a loss here. I know nothing about this part of town."

"Me neither. But there's gotta be a diner nearby. Simon loves diners and must have put one up around here somewhere. There are about a thousand of them in this town. They all serve that same kind of disgusting chocolate pudding with nuts he likes. Come on, we'll find a place to go." They started walking, Broximon moving as fast as he could just to keep up with the bear.

"Listen, Bob, I need to ask you something. Have you ever heard of John Flannery? Do you know him?"

"Who?"

"John Flannery. Big guy with a beard, sort of fat?" Broximon stroked an imaginary beard on his chin. "Goes around with a humungous Great Dane named Luba?"

"Nope, never heard of the guy. And the only Great Dane I know is named Spot. Maybe I will have something to drink."

• • • • • •

Suzy Nichols. That was her name. Suzy Nichols was the girl beneath the blue mask who had greeted him on the street minutes before. Haden had loved her a lot earlier in his life. Maybe as much as any woman in his life, but that was because he was thirteen when he knew her and everyone knows that young love is as purple and electric as a summer thunderstorm.

What was Suzy doing wearing a spinning Bobo funeral mask on the street of Simon Haden's dream city? Because of the dance, of course—the seventh- and eighth-grade Halloween dance.

Remember junior high school dances? Where most of the girls spent most of the time running in and out of the toilet to talk with each other about the evening's latest developments. Where most of the boys slouched cool against various walls to show these girls that they didn't give a damn about anything, most especially these girls.

And there was *always* at least one girl over in a far corner crying, inconsolable about something that had just happened, surrounded by her sympathetic, clucking, consoling friends. A few geeks and losers usually showed up, making sure to stick close to each other. They did little else besides guard the shadows and stare at the goings-on. Farther down on the prestige ladder a weirdo or two was there too, which made people who noticed wonder for a second what the hell motivated *them* to come tonight?

Possibility, that's what. Kids believe with all their hearts that anything can happen at school dances. Magically enough, now and then it does. The most unlikely kids pair up, things are said beneath the pound of the music that changes everything, secrets are shared amid the open, stirring hope that tags along to any gathering like this. Things could happen here tonight; sometimes they do.

Following the girl in the mask, Haden opened the door to the building and walked straight into the seventh- and eighth-grade Halloween dance at his school's gymnasium. He was surrounded by kids in costume and the instant-nostalgia sound of Barry White singing. He immediately knew where he was and did not hesitate. Suzy would most likely be across the room at the punch bowl with the rest of the girls, or having a summit meeting in the toilet with her best friend Melinda Szep.

He remembered this night and the dance but not the dream both lived in. That was not surprising though because Haden had had over fourteen thousand dreams in his life. In his stocking feet he walked across the gym (it was a sock hop—you took off your shoes at the door so as not to mark up the wooden floor). He gradually realized that many of the dancers were looking at him. It was disconcerting but he had other things on his mind. Anyway, so what if a bunch of twelve-year-olds stared?

There was Suzy. Her blue mask lay facedown on the refreshments table. She was talking animatedly to Melinda and holding a paper cup in her hand. She was so pretty—tall and pretty. That's why he hadn't recognized her when he saw her before out on the street—he'd mistaken her for a woman. Even in eighth grade Suzy Nichols was tall and had a full enough figure to be mistaken for someone much older; especially when her young face was covered by a mask. Now Haden remembered that that belonged to her older brother who had served in the Peace Corps in Burkina Faso. He had gotten the crazy-looking thing there. And Suzy *had* worn the mask to their junior high Halloween dance, shocking those who knew her. Normally she was not the kind of girl who called attention to herself. Yet for some elusive reason, that night she went to the dance (something she almost never did anyway) wearing a spinning Bobo.

Melinda Szep was the first to see Haden. Eyes widening comically, she quickly looked down and put a hand across her eyebrows to prevent herself from looking again. She must have said something about it to Suzy though because the tall girl stopped speaking and looked straight at Simon.

Her face showed shock and wonder in equal amounts at what she saw. Her expression said she could have been looking at a nine-foot-tall Martian or ocelots having sex. Haden remembered how much he wanted her to like him. But now her face said the only reason she was looking at him was the wrong reason. He remembered that others in the room had stared at him too as he crossed the floor. So he looked down.

Males often look down at the front of their trousers when they see people staring at them. Because they're sure their fly is open and that's why people are staring. Or there's a suspicious obvious wet spot down there. Or . . . something. For boys and young men especially, everything down there is essential, magical, and sometimes devastatingly embarrassing to them and who they want to be in the eyes of the world.

Not much embarrassed Haden anymore; especially now that he was dead. But when he looked down at the front of his pants and saw what was there, he was not only embarrassed but amazed. His penis, or someone's penis (because it sure as hell wasn't his—the thing was longer than any dick he had ever seen before), stuck straight out of his fly like a wooden stick. It must have been thirteen inches long. It looked like Pinocchio's nose. Pinocchio porn. And sitting on this thing, this dick-stick, was a large parrot.

"Ahoy matey!" the bird squawked. It raised both wings and fluttered them vigorously a few moments before settling back down on its perch. Haden felt its claws gripping his dick. It didn't exactly hurt but didn't feel terrific either.

Mouth open in awe, he slowly raised his eyes and saw Suzy Nichols staring. She wasn't staring at his face.

"What-the-fuck—?"

Hearing that word, she looked up at him but her eyes weren't focused.

He had wanted to tell her things. He had to tell her some things. That's why he had run in here after her.

"Wait a minute, it's a dream! *That's* all this is! It's a nightmare I must have had when I was a kid." The realization stung him like a wasp. Of course! Bob the Bear said it before—Haden had to go and face his nightmares. That's what this whole thing was, although he remembered none of it. But for God's sake, he must have had the dream, what, twenty-seven years before?

All the touchstones of a nightmare were there too—love interest, school dance—and at the moment of truth, his dick exposed for the entire world to see. *Voilà!* You didn't need a cookbook to whip those ingredients into a big fat juicy nightmare; especially when you were thirteen years old. What was worse to a kid than horrible death? Horrible embarrassment, by a mile. Because kids don't really believe they'll die. That's why they're so fearless. Everyone else will die, just not them. But when you're young, embarrassment lurks around every corner. As a result, their antennae are hyper-tuned to it. Some people dreamt of walking down the street naked. Haden dreamt (apparently) of having a foot-long wooden erection with a parrot sitting on it in full view of Suzy Nichols and other schoolmates.

He found that he couldn't move. Frozen to the spot now, he stood there helpless and outraged that he couldn't simply reach down, knock the preposterous bird away, and put his Pinocchio penis back in his pants. But the rules of this dream apparently wouldn't permit it. He tried lifting his arms—first the right, then the left. He couldn't move them away from his body. It was as if he were underwater. No—as if he were encased in tree sap or school glue, something claustrophobically thick, viscid, and unwilling to let him budge and do what he wanted with his own body. He tried to turn this way and that but to no avail.

Suzy watched it all, her face going through a whole alphabet of emotions. When Haden knew he wasn't going to succeed in freeing his body, he tried to say something to her, he didn't even know what. Something, anything so that he could connect with her some way. To say he was sorry, to tell her to wait until he was free of this and then they could talk, to tell her it was all ridiculous but—

Nothing. He couldn't speak—again. He remembered the time he lost his mouth when confronting Mrs. Dugdale. Now he couldn't tell if he even had a mouth because he couldn't get a hand free to touch his face and feel for it there.

Kids began to come up, to sidle up, to edge closer to him. Close but not too close. They wanted to see. To them Haden was a live volcano that they wanted to get as close to the edge of without actually falling in or getting cooked by molten lava. He had whipped out his weenie at a school dance. Wow! What would he do next?

Out of the corner of his eye, Haden saw Mr. Nabisco coming over. Mr. Nabisco? Who was that? How did he know the man's name? He'd never seen the guy before in his life. Then again, Simon wasn't living his life right now—he was living in his dreams.

Nabisco was the name of the company that made the cookies and biscuits he'd liked so much as a boy: Oreo, fig Newtons, and Triscuit . . . And now he remembered! This man had been the Spanish teacher in junior high school.

"Just what the heck do you think you're doin' there, fella?"

Mr. Nabisco was chubby, wore a white dress shirt that was perma-pressed and shiny, carried four identical ballpoint pens in his breast pocket, and had a kind of Beatles/Merseybeat haircut that didn't help his look much. "I asked what you're doing." He pointed to Haden's still-erect penis. "You come with me, mister."

"No, he ain't going anywhere, *mister*. And what are you supposed to be, the fucking fifth Beatle?"

Haden heard this but because he was unable to move, he couldn't turn around and see who'd said it. The voice came from somewhere behind him.

Mr. Nabisco looked toward the speaker. Seeing who it was, his mouth set hard. "Do I know you? Do you go to this school?" He waited, hands on his hips, for an answer that did not come.

The school gymnasium, that giant echoing room full of the ghosts of ten thousand past games, wooden everything, and kids in stocking feet, had grown quiet. No music played now, very few voices spoke.

Something brushed by Haden's paralyzed body. Seeing what it was turned his angry blood to ice water. It also set him free. As soon as it touched him Haden was no longer encased in whatever, unable to move. He could move everything again. The first thing he did with his everything was look frantically around for the nearest exit.

Because Sunday Suits was here. It had said those rude things to Mr. Nabisco and was now moving toward him. Haden hadn't been so frightened since dying. He didn't remember his dreams and he didn't remember his nightmares but he sure remembered Sunday Suits.

Ironically, it was one of the last nightmares Simon Haden ever had as an adult. Horrific, bloody, and believable, it was so right-in-his-face *there,* inescapable and pitiless, that it woke him at 3:37 one morning, his mouth locked open in a silent scream.

At the terrifying center of that last nightmare was Sunday Suits. Haden had no idea where its strange name came from. But here it was again, gliding past him toward Mr. Nabisco.

"Wuzzup, Haden? Got a little business to take care of here." Its voice was low and seductive, confident. "Stick around though—I want to talk to you after I'm done."

I want to talk to you. . . . The phrase was like a finger jabbed in his eye.

The monster moved on to Mr. Nabisco and without pausing, wrapped itself entirely around him and began to squeeze. The man didn't even have a chance to run. A snake coils around its prey. Sunday Suits, Haden's last dream beast, was much worse than any snake.

The teacher's Beatles hair whipped back and forth as he tried frantically to free himself to breathe, to get air into his lungs. A strangled dry cry sounding more birdlike than human scratched its way out of his throat.

Responding to this cry, the students attacked Sunday Suits. From everywhere in the gym they came running. Those closest leapt straight onto it, only to be swatted off as if they were gnats. Fearless, they got up and went right after it again. The ones farther away raced toward the creature with no hesitation. All of this happened so fast that Haden forgot running away and stared, awestruck.

Kids large and small swarmed the thing, tearing at it, pulling, biting, punching and clawing. Some of them made noise while they did it. One girl kept screaming "Mama!" over and over again in a high mad whine as she stood knee-deep in Sunday Suits, trying like the others to kill it.

Some were silent, but all of them fought in a violent frenzy to stop it, to destroy it. When the monster realized that they weren't afraid, weren't going to give up, and that more and more of them kept coming, it dropped the limp teacher on the ground and turned full force on its attackers.

There were sixty-two students at the dance. No matter how fearsome Haden's nightmare creature was, being attacked by sixty-two enraged, fearless, sugar-stoked, adrenaline-pumped twelve- and thirteen-year-olds was a challenge.

The fight was fierce but astoundingly even. So many kids ganged up on Sunday Suits at once that it couldn't focus on any of them and was thrown totally off guard. It was like being attacked by a swarm of five-foot-tall bees. Almost the only effective thing it could do in response was twist and turn and swing its limbs around, trying to knock as many of them away as it could. The problem was for every one that fell, four pounced.

There were blood and screams. Those it hit or grabbed were doomed, but there were so many of them that it almost didn't matter. Sixty-two children wanted to slaughter it. Sixty-two children were trying.

Haden watched as if a brutal car wreck were happening right in front of him. Then he saw the blue mask. The fight was fantastically colorful because most of the kids wore Halloween costumes. There were bursts of jungle green and saffron, silver . . . all in motion, all at once. But the African mask was such a singular brilliant blue that his eye saw it immediately when it fell. Next he saw Suzy Nichols lifted into the air and snapped back and forth like a flag at the finish line.

Thirteen-year-old Haden who worshiped Suzy Nichols and was totally unafraid of this creature awoke in him and moved to save her.

Forty-year-old Haden, terrified of Sunday Suits and so much else, froze.

He could feel both of his selves pulling powerfully in opposite directions.

The man knew so much. The boy knew no fear.

When he felt the other's scared resistance, the boy stepped out of the man he would some day be and went to save Suzy by himself. But of course that wasn't possible. Two steps away, energy poured out of him like blood from an artery. He was barely able to turn to the older Haden and wheeze "Help me!"

The man saw his younger self being brave and magnificent and foolish. But that boy wasn't him anymore, those qualities were long gone. How many years had passed since he'd been courageous?

Then he watched as the boy staggered and called for his help. Haden knew he must try and save him. He had to save that brave and hopeful heart.

While he tried to figure out how to do it, Haden stiffened. Out of the blue he suddenly grasped that the boy and Sunday Suits were here *together* now. His past self and present nightmare stood together in front of him at the same moment. Forty-year-old Haden was a few feet away from thirteen-year-old Suzy, their eighth-grade classmates, et cetera. All of them were here together—now.

Haden the man had dreamt about Sunday Suits. Haden the boy had dreamt about being exposed in front of Suzy Nichols. Each of them thought the other's nightmare was ridiculous. The boy had no fear of Sunday Suits because such a being frightened only adults. And the man thought that a dream about his penis sticking out with a parrot sitting on it like a perch at a school dance was goofy, not shameful.

"There's no time here. Everything is right now."

At last he understood that in death, time as he had always known and lived it was gone. Beginning, middle, and end were finished. There was only now, but a now comprising every second he had lived. So Haden the man and the boy coexisted now. All the Hadens who had ever been since the moment he was born—their experiences, knowledge, strengths and weaknesses—all of them existed *now.*

Without hesitating, Haden willed the boy everything that he was. He gave up owning the moment and handed it freely to his thirteen-year-old self. At once the energy that had bled out of the boy flooded back in. He rose from the floor and with only the briefest look back, moved to join the fight against Sunday Suits.

It ended very soon after that because none of the children had any fear of this adult nightmare. Grown-ups forget what it is like to have no fear.

A monster is not a monster if it does not scare you.

• • •

Broximon and Bob the polar bear were sitting in a diner having strawberry frappés when Haden sauntered by outside. Broximon saw him first and slowly slid the straw out of his mouth. Bob saw the surprised look on the little man's face (Brox stood on the table so that he could drink from the glass which was taller than him, and look at the bear while they talked).

"What's the matter?"

"Check out on the street." He gestured with his head.

Bob looked and saw Haden who was wearing an expression that said he'd just won a jackpot. Both silently watched him pass.

"That was *fast*."

"I told you the man wasn't dumb."

"Yeah, but come on, Brox, that was way too fast. I mean, really . . ."

"Sometimes it happens that way, Bob." He snapped his fingers. "Just like that."

"From what I know of Simon Haden, boy *and* man, he is not a 'just like that' guy. It's more like he needs a road map to find his shoelaces most of the time. How old was he just now? I couldn't tell."

Broximon smiled. "Me neither, but that's no surprise. He's probably trying on all his ages again—like they were different clothes. Mix and match."

Both of them looked out at the empty street. A round cartoony automobile with fat black balloon tires, like a vehicle R. Crumb would draw, toodled past. It was filled with large palm trees sticking out of every window.

Bob shook its head. "They have to be helping him. Simon couldn't have worked it out by himself so quickly—it's just too difficult. They need him now, so they fixed it so that he would understand. There's no other way he could have figured out the time thing so fast."

Broximon had known Bob for years. The two of them had first appeared together in a Haden dream when Haden was thirty-eight. They'd always gotten along well. Broximon instinctively felt he could trust the bear. "Bob, I know we're never supposed to ask each other about these things, but I'm going to do it anyway because I am fed up with being in the dark.

"Do *you* know what's going on here? Because I don't. I know this much." It held up his little finger.

Bob answered without hesitation. "Chaos has become conscious. It's learned how to think and knows what it wants. What it's trying to do now is take over." He picked up his glass and looked into it, thinking about what to say next. "Always before, chaos just *was,* like a stone or a wave. But somewhere along the way it grew a brain and learned how to use it. Now it wants to be the boss."

"But what about this—" Broximon gestured at the world around them. "Isn't this chaos? You and me drinking strawberry frappés and having this conversation, a car full of palm trees?"

"No, *that* is imagination, not chaos. Human imagination can be chaotic, but most of the time it's man's only constant proof of God.

"If Chaos wins and takes over, then you and I will disappear. That's a given. Simon and his imagination, which created us, will get sucked into its whirl and crushed up together with everything else in there. You've seen what's left after a tornado moves through a town."

Broximon was appalled but not surprised. He'd had inklings and connected some of the dots between things he'd heard and recent events. It had all pointed vaguely in this direction, but hearing it explained now put everything into clear, ugly focus with a thick black frame of dread around it.

"What's being done to stop it? *Can* it be stopped?" Halfway through the two questions, Broximon heard his voice become plaintive. It sounded like a scared child's asking a parent for reassurance.

"There's a woman named Isabelle Neukor—"

"I know Isabelle. We met. I was told to keep her away from Haden because he's supposed to find *her*. That's all. That's all I was told."

"Then you know she's pregnant. They believe her child will be able to help fight Chaos if it's given the proper education."

"It's *Haden's* kid? They didn't tell me that."

"No, it's another man's. The father died but was brought back to life to help teach this child."

Broximon touched his forehead in disbelief. "*What?* That breaks every rule in the book."

Bob smiled for half a second. "There is no rule book anymore. Only survival of the fittest and no more rules. Chaos saw to that. It's why I'm telling you these things; I never would have been allowed to before. You know how the system worked. But now all bets are off and whatever help they can get, they'll take."

Broximon moved his index finger back and forth as if it were a windshield wiper. "Okay, there's Haden and pregnant Isabelle: What's their big connection?"

"Simon often dreamt about Isabelle when he was alive, so Chaos keeps bringing her here into his dreamworld. It's trying to figure out how to force her to stay and have the baby."

"Bob, that's not possible. She can't give birth here—this is *death*. The child would be born dead."

"That's exactly what Chaos wants."

"Whoa! And how does Haden figure into this?"

"This world is his creation. He's the only one who can keep her out of it."

A Paper Trumpet

None of the people who knew him now were aware of the fact that not long before, John Flannery had been one of the richest men in America. You had to look hard to see any remnants of that wealth, but some were still there. He wore a plain-looking George Daniels watch that had cost $107,000 at a Christie's auction. A Creditanstalt bank book taped to the bottom of a dresser drawer carried a balance in his name of 839,133 euros. One of his dog's eyes was false. The substitute was an ingenious feat of American bio engineering and one of a kind. Flannery was an exceptional cook who had once made a simple meal for Flora using ingredients that were obscenely expensive. Not that she knew it. Her only comment was that everything in it tasted almost as good as sex. He served the leftovers cold to Leni the next day.

He enjoyed doing that sort of thing; liked tickling people's noses with a secret feather only he knew existed. Once after they had made love, Leni picked up his watch from the bedside night table and examined it closely for the first time. He could see appreciation rising in her eyes and that made him happy. She wasn't a total loss.

"This is a beautiful watch, John. I mean it's *really* beautiful."

"Thank you. It belonged to my father." He slipped it gently out of her hand. He did not want her to notice or remember the name of the maker. If she became too curious about it, she only had to look up the brand name on the Internet to discover some eye-opening information about Daniels watches, not least of which was how much they cost. Then Flannery would have real trouble explaining to her how he could own one of the most highly treasured watches in the world. You could never be too careful about these details, no matter how stupid humans were. Strapping it on, he looked at it fondly. He knew exactly what to say to get her mind off the thing. "Did I ever tell you about my father?"

Her eyes left his wrist and moved to his face. He had never said anything to her about his family. This was a first. She was definitely intrigued. "No, never. Tell me."

Opening the door to his apartment today, Flannery called out her name and was somewhat surprised when she didn't answer. She wasn't here? He looked at his watch. Two hours had passed since they spoke on the phone and agreed to meet here in one. Hmm. Leni was never late. Something serious must have happened. She was such a good little Girl Scout. He was sure she would either show up at his door with an excuse in her hands like a trembling bouquet, or call as soon as she could to explain why she was late. In the meantime, he decided to celebrate his new car with a small glass of whiskey.

He'd ordered a new Porsche Cayenne right before being reassigned by Chaos to Vincent and Isabelle. It was one of the few things he regretted about leaving his previous post. The vast money and power he'd left behind were no more than a shrug to Flannery. But he *had* wanted to see how well Porsche made its first four-wheel-drive car, and was vaguely sorry at the time that he had to forego the chance. Now he would know. Celadon was a bad color choice that made him wince a bit when he pictured it. But the car was new and he would be using it only a short while.

He was thinking about the Porsche and a glass of good whiskey when he turned the corner to the kitchen and saw Leni sitting at the table. She was staring directly at him. Luba the Great Dane was asleep at her feet.

"Hey there. How come you didn't answer when I called?" He started for the cupboard and the unopened bottle of 1967 Glenlivet. Halfway there he stopped on realizing that she still hadn't said anything. "What's the matter?"

Leni lifted one of her hands off the table. Beneath it was a four-inch-long toy miniature of the automobile John Flannery had just stolen. It was even painted celadon. The color more than the toy beneath her hand told him what was going on.

Chaos was here in a whole new form. Somehow, somewhere, Flannery had made a serious mistake without knowing it and it had come to straighten him out. Or worse. He fell to his knees and stretched his arms above his head, prostrating himself in front of this Leni Salomon replica. He was not afraid because fear is a combination of what is and what could be. Chaos is not a combination of anything—it simply *is*. Flannery was only angry at himself for having unwittingly done something wrong. He was usually so good at his job. It had often commended him.

• • •

When the real Leni figured she had waited a long enough time, she opened the bathroom door as quietly as she could, thrilled to have pulled off her surprise. She'd heard John come in and call her name. Like a little girl, she had put both hands tightly over her mouth and tittered.

She wore the sheer white cotton robe that she'd just bought and nothing else beneath it. John had often joked about her one day greeting him at the door wearing a drink and nothing else. Well, today his fantasy was going to come true. It had taken longer to buy the robe than she had planned because the saleswoman at the Hanro store kept showing her one more beautiful, sexy piece after the other and it had been so hard to decide. White finally won over black, but it was an erotic white, almost entirely transparent. If they'd had to give that color a name they should have called it "who are you kidding white." Leni was also a few days away from having her period, so her breasts were heavy and full which looked great beneath the tease of white in the robe.

She was at first disappointed when she arrived at his apartment and discovered John wasn't there. But then she realized it was good because it would give her time to prepare. If Flannery came in while she was getting ready then he would just have to wait. It would be worth it. Today Leni felt like eating him with a spoon.

She went into his bathroom and took off her clothes. Naked, she looked in the mirror and pretended to give herself a wolf whistle. Next, she ran her fingers over his colognes on the shelf above the sink and wondered if she should put one of them on. But John often said that he loved the smell of her body and that it turned him on. He asked her not to use deodorant or bathe right before coming to meet him. I want to smell you, not Éstée Lauder. When he had first said that it made her uncomfortable and embarrassed, but later the thought was incredibly alluring. No man had ever said anything like that to her. It made her feel secretly wicked, as well as much more sensual and feminine. Sometimes when they were in bed he would run his tongue all the way up her hip and side to her armpit. There he would stop and she could feel him, hear him, breathing her in.

Now standing in the doorway to the kitchen, ready to give him everything, Leni finally saw John. Back to her, his face was down on the floor as he appeared to be worshiping . . . her. An identical Leni Salomon was sitting across the room at the table, dressed in exactly the same clothes as she had worn earlier.

Now that it was capable of thought, Chaos fancied itself witty and very amusing. Usually it visited Flannery in its own skin. But this time it decided to do something different and funny. Flannery was fucking this crippled woman? Well then, today the cripple would fuck him.

So it sought out Leni and found her in the lingerie shop. It watched her confusion as she tried to decide which robe to buy. With that impression of her fresh in mind, it went to Flannery's apartment and re-created the Leni Salomon it had just witnessed. On entering the kitchen, John saw Chaos living in the confused body of his lover. Without hesitating he fell to his knees and bowed to his creator.

But it had made a mistake. Chaos recognized only itself in people. It dismissed all other human qualities as either useless or flaws. Chaos understood the chaos of love, but not the bond. The anarchy of art but not the harmony or communication it creates. It knew that sometimes it was color blind to certain human qualities but it didn't care. It could not see them because they were off the scale of its perception. Like high whistles only dogs can hear. That's why from time to time it made someone like John Flannery and sent him into the world awhile. There *were* certain errands, certain tasks that needed to be done by a real live human being. "People things" that could only be accomplished by people.

Here's the irony—Leni was brilliant in any crisis. Flora frequently joked that she wanted her best friend nearby when World War Three started. Because Leni would be the calmest person around and know exactly what to do while the earth melted around them.

Looking into the kitchen and seeing John kneeling in front of an exact replica of herself, Leni thought calmly This is a joke, a trick; John arranged this scene to freak me out.

Across the room her other self spoke. This woman, this copy, wearing the same outfit she'd taken off and hung on the back of the bathroom door minutes before, now spoke to Flannery. What it said was impossible to understand. The imposter's language was unlike anything Leni had ever heard before. The quick dissonant jangle of sounds spilling out was eerie. High and melodious, they sounded almost like a kind of birdsong. There was real music in it, but something was wrong with this music. It sounded sort of pleasant but mostly *off*—as if it were being played on false instruments like a paper trumpet or a violin made of cloth. John replied at length in the same language. Then there was a rapid-fire back-and-forth between the two of them. They *conversed.*

In the middle of it, the other woman abruptly stopped speaking and looked straight at Leni. But it did not see her because unlike their first encounter hours before, there was no chaos in Leni now. She was composed and still. She saw something bizarre happening and understood that John was part of it. That's all. As usual in an urgent situation, she did not allow her mind to go beyond those facts. The other woman broke eye contact and started speaking again to John in their private mad language.

Leni took two slow steps back from the doorway, a hand behind her to touch anything back there that might be in her way. She was naked beneath the robe and wore only a pair of cheap red rubber sandals that she kept at John's place. How happy she had been the day she bought those silly things, knowing what she was going to do with them. How exciting it was later to tell John that she was leaving them in his apartment because it was more convenient. Both of them knew however that it had nothing to do with convenience. The sandals staying there was her way of staking a small claim to both his property and his life, which at the time appeared fine with John.

His back still to her, his full attention was on the other woman. Leni knew that as soon as John became aware of the fact that she was there, she was lost. She had to get to the front door, open it silently, and then run. She stepped slowly backward, carefully and as quietly as she could. But her bad leg kept making trouble for her balance. It was Leni's worst enemy now, messing up every move. For years she'd thought of that leg as her retarded sister, the one who never left her alone and ruined or broke everything it touched. Her constant companion, the leg forever demanded her attention but gave back only discomfort and embarrassing situations. She hated it and herself for never having grown enough to ignore its drag on her soul.

While John and the other woman talked, it was easier to move toward the door. Leni could not do it soundlessly; that would have been impossible for anyone. But the noise of their conversation made hers less. Taking a quick look over her shoulder, she was elated to see how close she was to the exit.

Something John said appeared to anger the woman. Her voice rose to a scald and the strange-sounding words flew. Flannery looked up for the first time, but the women screeched and his head quickly dropped down again.

What was she saying? How could he understand it? Who was this imposter? Who *was* this man? Almost at the door, almost free, Leni's heart and mind staggered at that thought, that question: Who was John? What was happening here when everything was supposed to be so different today? Love, passion, but now also the *confusion* that she felt about him welled up inside Leni and overflowed her banks. There was nothing she could do to stop it even though she knew she must escape.

The dog opened its eyes. Raising its giant head, it did not turn and look at the woman sitting nearby at the table. It did not look at John Flannery. The Great Dane opened its eyes and stared directly at Leni.

In her purse on the bathroom floor were treats for the dog. She brought it something to eat or play with every time she came to visit. One of her favorite things in their relationship was to accompany John when he took Luba for a walk along the Danube Canal. Because of her bad leg they could never go far. But the dog seemed perfectly happy to lie at their feet while they sat on a bench, the three contentedly watching the river and the world pass by.

"Is your leg bothering you again?"

Leni froze. At first she didn't recognize the voice although it was clearly addressing her. It wasn't John's voice nor was it the other woman's. But it was very familiar; her memory knew it although she hadn't heard it in a long time. She turned just as a hand touched her shoulder, making her flinch.

Her father stood nearby wearing his beloved Brooklyn Dodgers baseball cap, work shirt, and faded khakis. The clothes he always changed into when he came home from the office. The clothes he had been buried in after he died four years before.

"Papa?" He was so real, so very there next to her that she forgot where she was and her predicament.

But by then Leni Salomon was already two minutes dead. Seeing her father was the beginning of her own afterlife. How did she die? She was killed by Flannery, or the Great Dane, or the other Leni Salomon. Which one was actually responsible for the act doesn't matter. The moment the dog opened its eyes and saw her, confused by her great love for John, she was murdered before she even had a chance to be afraid.

She was found later slumped on a park bench by the Danube. According to the police, she'd had an aneurysm and died instantly. Her mind had popped.

• • • • • •

Isabelle's watch stopped working in the middle of Leni's funeral. She looked down at her wrist because she couldn't bear to look straight ahead one second more. Straight ahead was the coffin of Leni Salomon, about to be lowered into the ground forever. Just that thought was unbearable, much less the visual confirmation. Looking at the amber-colored wooden box and knowing what lay inside it was unbearable.

Vincent stood on one side of Isabelle while Flora stood on the other. Flora had not let go of her hand once during the ceremony. Oddly enough, neither woman had cried. Vincent noticed this but was not about to ask why. He knew how much they had adored their dead friend. If their grief for her was silent, then so be it.

He also knew that wherever Leni was now, she was all right. Like an amnesiac slowly regaining his memory after a traumatic blow to the head, Ettrich had begun to remember bits and pieces of what death was like. As he had said to Isabelle, most of these memories came to him like bad, out-of-focus photographs. He would stare at them, turn them this way and that in his bafflement, wonder what they were, what they meant, where they were taken. But a few of the pictures were clear and distinct. Ettrich had begun carrying a small notebook in his pocket in which he wrote down things he thought relevant to these memories; or associations between them and his hunches.

What he didn't grasp was that one small part of his mind worked light-years faster than the rest now, accelerated even more so when he was in physical contact with Isabelle. This part of him had recognized important details in these "photos" and gone on to make fundamental connections. Racing ahead of the rest of his conscious mind—seeing, analyzing, and filing—this super-perceptive sense was one of several things he had unknowingly brought back with him from death. Right now however it did him almost no good because he was only beginning to recognize it and its messages.

For example on the first page of his notebook, amid an array of memory fragments, lists, and free-association doodles, he had written *Flannery*. But when he wrote it, a name that had come to him out of nowhere, Ettrich thought it referred to Flannery O'Connor whose short stories he had loved as a student. On the seventh page of the notebook in a corner he had drawn a first-rate cartoon of a Great Dane.

This highly developed part of his mind knew that he and Isabelle were in danger and even where the danger came from. But no matter how brilliant or informed it was, it had no way of conveying the warning to him directly. This was not death where a Broximon or Bob the Bear could break the rules to help. Ettrich was alive again and here he would have to discover things on his own.

Nevertheless he was the first one to see John Flannery at the funeral that day. It was held in Weidling, a village about five miles from Vienna. The bucolic crowded graveyard was at the edge of town alongside a narrow curving road that led into the Wienerwald. Leni's family had a plot there.

Cars were parked haphazardly all up and down the road because there was no cemetery parking lot. As a result, the only space Ettrich found was far away. They'd had to walk back quite a distance, arriving just in time for the beginning of the ceremony. Along the way they passed a celadon-colored Porsche Cayenne. Vincent recognized the color and smiled briefly. He was about to mention it to Isabelle but remembering the solemnity of the occasion, said nothing. He looked back at the car twice though as they walked on, both times saying the word *celadon* to himself.

Ettrich had never liked Leni Salomon and vice versa. So he felt vaguely guilty going to her funeral while feeling little more than the conventional sadness for someone who dies unexpectedly and much too early. Leni had always been aloof and curt toward him as long as he knew her. The first time they met, he felt disapproval coming off of her like waves of cold off someone who has just come inside from a February day. Things never got any warmer between them either. He knew she was aware of his affair with Flora, and that Flora had subsequently introduced him to Isabelle. Did Leni dislike him because he had gone from one of her best friends to the other? Had Flora said nasty things about him after their relationship ended? Or was there some other reason why Leni had never made any attempt to disguise her dislike for Vincent?

As he walked down a short hill into the cemetery with Isabelle, he remembered the summer night a whole bunch of people had gone to a *heurigen* in Sievering to drink new wine and eat the delicious fried chicken served there. It was a happy gathering and the wine made things even nicer. Halfway through the evening Ettrich found himself sitting next to Leni. They had a spirited interesting conversation about their favorite books. It was the first time he had ever felt the slightest glimmer of interest from her. At one point he lightly touched her elbow with two fingers to emphasize an idea he was expressing. The moment contact was made, she snatched her arm back while a look of such dislike flashed across her face that he was both stunned and deeply hurt.

It was the last time they ever spoke at length. After that, he heard about Leni and her life from Isabelle who frequently spoke of her friend with the greatest love and respect. Ettrich listened as neutrally as he could to these stories and anecdotes but in the end he still didn't think much of the lame pretty woman.

They walked across the graveyard toward a sizable crowd gathered at the door of a small open chapel. When they were almost there, Flora came out of the crowd and over to Isabelle who she embraced for a long time with her eyes closed. Ettrich felt awkward and uncomfortable in their intensely emotional presence. He didn't know what he should do or say. He and Flora had made their separate peace long ago. Still, whenever they met he often saw her face tighten and her smiles turn into the patently fake ones politicians wear.

He thought it best to give the women room to talk and console each other. He slowly moved away from them, always checking Isabelle's face and body language in case she suddenly signaled for him to return. He drifted to the back of the crowd, just close enough so that anyone observing would know that he was here for this funeral. He watched as the two women walked hand in hand to the coffin and each in turn bent down to kiss it. Although it was done in public, Ettrich had the feeling that there was no one else out there then but the three friends having their final conversation. Even this far away he felt like he was eavesdropping.

Turning around, he looked out at the rest of the cemetery. Scanning the tombstones, one eventually caused him to squint and move his head forward to see it better. When he was sure what he'd read was correct, he walked over to the stone and stared at it with a combination of respect and sadness. It marked the grave of Arlen Ford, the American film actress. Earlier when they were driving here, Isabelle had mentioned that the movie star was buried in this cemetery.

Ettrich wasn't aware that she had died. A wave of nostalgia hit him while he went through a fast mind-shuffle of the films Arlen Ford had made and how much he had enjoyed her in them. They had even used his car in one of her films.

On the gravestone beneath the dates of her birth and death was a quotation in English. He read it several times and liked it but had no idea what it meant.

"I'LL COOK YOU SOUP AND HOLD YOUR HAND."

He assumed it must have been a famous line from one of her films.

Sighing, he lifted his eyes from the grave toward the sidewalk and street beyond it. Standing up there was a big bearded man. No, he wasn't big—he was fat. Well, not really fat. He was . . . it was hard to say what he was from that distance. The man appeared to be watching Ettrich and smiling. Or maybe it just looked like that. He wore a black suit and a white dress shirt but no tie. The outfit made Vincent think he had come to attend the funeral. But the guy didn't move at all—just stood there and smiled. He appeared to be waiting for something. Maybe he was someone's driver. That made sense. Maybe he was someone's chauffeur. Whoever he was, it wasn't polite to stare at him and really there was no reason to. Ettrich turned away and walked back to the funeral.

Seeing this, John Flannery frowned. He was genuinely disappointed that Vincent Ettrich didn't do something, anything, to demonstrate some sign of recognition or unease. Flannery had wanted a more concrete, more delicious frisson from their first face-to-face. Instead, he had only gotten a couple of long looks and then Ettrich walked away. What kind of bullshit showdown was *that*? Shrugging it off, Flannery reached into his pocket, pulled out a fresh horsemeat sandwich, and bit into it contentedly while watching his lover's funeral begin.

He liked the taste of horsemeat; something he had acquired while living in Vienna. It was sweet and strong and vaguely disgusting. Knowing how much Leni loved horses, he had once cooked her a meal using a big filet of horsemeat as the centerpiece of the recipe. She tucked right into it, had a second helping, and never once asked what kind of meat she was eating. Flannery had enjoyed doing things like that to her. He would persuade Leni to tell him her secrets, dreams, and fears. Then without her ever knowing it, he would take these intimate fragile things and shove them back up her ass in furtive and creative ways. He would have done the same to Flora, but all that cow ever seemed to want to do was fuck.

He liked a dab of sweet *Kremser* mustard on his *pferde leberkase*; a fresh roll, tangy mustard, and a nice thick chunk of boiled horse. When he had finished the sandwich and licked the remnants off his shiny fingers, he entered the graveyard and walked over to the funeral. He knew Flora's husband was here today. But Flannery wanted her to see that he was there, or that "Kyle Pegg" was there, so that she would be touched by his secret support in her time of sadness and need. He'd learned that about her from Leni: Flora Vaughn was bad in emotional situations. She had a tendency to break down and lose control. It was useful information to know. And vice versa naturally—From Flora he learned many handy tidbits about Leni. Best of all, from both women he learned most about Isabelle Neukor and Vincent Ettrich, which was the whole point of course.

Flannery enjoyed cemeteries. He relished their tidiness and artificial beauty because he knew both were the result of fear and dread. Not the love people felt for their deceased. To him cemeteries represented the useless pathetic gestures and shrines human beings made to try and ward off the big bad wolf of death. Fat chance of that happening. It's gonna *git* you, kiddo, no matter how many calla lilies you lay on Mom's grave this time, next time, or any other time.

It was not really death people feared, but the unimaginable chaos it might bring. He could smell that fear, the longing for order forever, but most of all the desperation people brought to any cemetery whenever they came to visit.

It was always the same: first they laid their wreaths or bouquets on the grave, thought awhile about dead Dad, wept some, and then the good stuff started. *One day I'll be in a place like this too.* They would look around at the peaceful surroundings as if seeing them for the first time, trying to imagine that fateful day, all the while knowing full well that wherever they went after they died wasn't going to be a cemetery. Next came the inevitable predictable questions like what is death? What if it *is* horrible chaos? What if there really is a Hell? All those endlessly delicious clichés that stirred people up into a tizzy or down into a black funk by the time they left here for home after their little visit.

Especially the old people—they were the best. Walking toward the crowd, Flannery looked for any oldies because they were invariably the most fun to watch at a funeral. Won't be long now, eh, Grandma? Are you really weeping for the dead or for your own skinny, unnoticed, wasted life now that it is five minutes from finished? The proof is right there in front of you, darling. Can't do much carpe dieming when you know that every tomorrow is iffy for you. Typically, the old people either cried bitterly or else their faces were the most expressionless as they listened to the priest talk about the world to come.

And how did the priest know? Had this man recently died and then come back to regale the crowd with what he saw on the other side? As that thought crossed his mind, Flannery recognized Ettrich and Flora standing on either side of Isabelle. Both women looked especially good today. Black clothes really did highlight the female figure. He looked them up and down slowly with great lascivious appreciation. Flora had better breasts, but Isabelle had those long shapely legs Flannery preferred on a woman. He wondered what Isabelle was like in bed. It would be so much simpler if he could just kill her and her boyfriend and then go home. Unfortunately however she was pregnant with *that* child, that supremely dangerous child, and Ettrich was the father. Plus unlike the priest at the funeral nattering on about the hereafter, Ettrich really had returned from the dead which made him dangerous in his own right.

No, Flannery couldn't kill either of them. But he could make their every day misery and eventually drive Isabelle mad. Then she would run from her cursed life and enter the other dominion without hesitating. That was the plan and it cheered him. Raising his chin high, he moved toward the mourners.

Looking at Flora, he thought of their relationship and how they had met. Or rather, how he'd arranged their meeting. Like many rich aimless women, Flora Vaughn considered herself to be very spiritual. She had originally tried reading the likes of Thomas Merton, P. D. Ouspensky, and Krishnamurti but her flitty, forever distracted attention span found them all much too dense and difficult to grasp. So she settled for the kinds of books and thinking that were accessible, blandly inspirational, and appeasing at the same time. The sort of New Age/self-help bunk that said *You* are a terrific person even though you think you're a piece of worthless shit. But guess what? You can be even better if you follow these easy steps.

They met at a Rick Chaeff lecture. Chaeff was the author of the bestselling book *An Open Place* and was touring Europe at the time to promote various translations of his work. Flora had arrived at the venue early so as to find a good place to sit for the lecture. She loved *An Open Place* and often carried a copy of it in her purse. The large room filled quickly.

Eventually a big burly guy with a beard sat down next to her. He was holding a copy of the book. When she glanced over, she noticed that it was full of yellow Post-it notes marking different passages throughout. Flora grinned because her other copy at home looked exactly like that, only her Post-its were blue and not yellow.

"You've been doing your homework, huh?" She pointed to his book. She spoke in English because the man next to her looked either English or American. He had the sort of hearty outgoing aura that announced *Hiya, how're you doing?*

He looked at her, perplexed a moment, then down at his book and slowly began to smile. "Do you know today was the first time I found out where the title of this book comes from? I never knew it before and I must have read the damned thing four times already." She didn't recognize it, but he spoke with an Australian accent.

Intrigued, Flora smiled. She was wearing an anthracite-blue silk dress with a high neckline that clung to her in a nice way. It made her look both sexy and serious. "Really? Where does it come from?"

The big man tapped the book. "The Bible; the lines are from Psalms:

> " 'He brought me out into an open place; he
> rescued me because he delighted in me.' "

Flora sat back and crossed her arms, very impressed. "Wow! That's exactly the whole point of the book."

"That's right. But why didn't Chaeff say in the book where the title came from? I learned something else too—"

He was interrupted by a woman standing at the front of the room tapping the microphone with a pencil to get people's attention. Obviously things were about to begin, but Flora was distracted now and wanted to hear the rest from this guy. Bending closer to him, she whispered "What else did you learn?"

"How to read in the dark."

She was flabbergasted and her face showed it. "Reading in the dark" was an essential metaphor at the heart of *An Open Place.* It had to do with learning to merge the human spirit with the five senses and thereby enhance their power immeasurably. Author Chaeff repeatedly stressed that accomplishing it was crucial to the spirit's growth and a goal he had worked toward but never once achieved.

"No! Is that true? You really did it?"

Flannery nodded and slowly raised his right hand, palm out, like a witness swearing to the truth in court.

He introduced himself as Kyle Pegg. She thought it an odd name but when he said he was Australian, it somehow seemed more acceptable. Plus she was curious. "Do you really know how to read in the dark?"

"Yes, I do now. And you know what? It's not that hard to learn."

What Flora and the rest of the world didn't know was Rick Chaeff and most other self-help gurus floating around out there in gullible land were all creations of Chaos, as was Kyle Pegg/John Flannery. It was a minor but interesting way to fuck people up that worked surprisingly well. All you had to do was make them aware of their shortcomings, which wasn't hard in this age of guilt and doubt. Next, convince them that they were nevertheless close to "the Answer," the key to happiness, the end of the rainbow, Nirvana . . . whatever. Only a few baby steps more and you'll be there *if* you follow my instructions.

Except there was no *there* there because people were constantly changing and so were their needs and desires. They could never land on one spot and stay—sure that this was their happiness forever. Because mankind had the attention span of a housefly. How many houseflies do you know that have found their bliss and stay at home evenings?

Of course Kyle Pegg knew how to "read in the dark." It was no more than a parlor trick, a bad magician's sleight of hand. He could teach it to anyone in fifteen seconds.

• • •

For Flora, the Chaeff lecture turned out to be okay but nothing special. Perhaps she would have liked it more if she hadn't met Kyle Pegg and he'd set her mind spinning before the talk began.

The question-and-answer session at the end was interminable. Flora's hands were crossed but she wasn't aware that she was nervously jiggling her sunglasses up and down until Kyle looked over, distracted by the commotion. He looked at the sunglasses, then at her and raised his eyebrows as if to ask if anything was wrong with her.

She made an exasperated face and hissed "These questions are so stupid. If they'd read his book they'd know all this stuff."

"Do you want to go have a cup of coffee?"

She was surprised that he was willing to just stand up and walk out on the spur of the moment. She liked that kind of courage and spontaneity. Although tempted by his offer, she shook her head. "We can't go now—it'd be rude in front of all these people. We'll go after."

He didn't argue. He knew she would say no but wanted her to think he was game for anything when it came to making her happy.

• • •

Afterward they sat in the Café Schwarzenberg eating pieces of chocolate and marzipan cake the size of small pianos. Kyle had two. Flora was tickled both by his gluttony and his obvious enthusiasm for her. Flora was a drama queen. She demanded the limelight. If you were willing to accept those two qualities, then she was your best friend forever, and she was a very good friend indeed.

Her husband and children adored her but like everyone else in her circle, they danced to her tune and knew when to run from her temper. She was not content with one lover, so she usually had two. Every one of her men was completely different from the other. She told her boyfriends point-blank that she couldn't imagine being monogamous, and that included them too. Take it or leave it. Sometimes people did leave. A lover walked out, friends got fed up with her vain nonsense and said no more. Flora Vaughn was hurt by these people but not for long. She was Italian. She was impatient. Life was opera. It was too interesting to her to get stuck on any one thing or person. She knew there were many others she could love and like and get along with, so it was rarely a big loss when someone did say *basta* to her.

What Flannery/Pegg found most interesting about Flora was her uncanny ability to bring out qualities in people they never knew they possessed. For example from the beginning, she saw him as a sexy guy and took him to bed every chance she got. Big fat John Flannery. He thought it was funny because that went completely against the game plan he had devised to win her heart. But he had to give her credit—she was such a passionate and wanton lover that he had a really good time. Plus she taught him an array of sexual tricks that he immediately put to good use with her friend Leni.

When they first met, Flora's husband was a brilliant, sweet, dull industrialist who derived great pleasure from ironing his own three-hundred-dollar shirts while listening to obscure Sibelius symphonies. She rolled up her sleeves and tunneled beneath his ironed layers into some undiscovered part of his soul. There she found a suppressed weekend Rambo who, at her encouragement, took up archery and twice bungee-jumped off the eight-hundred-foot-high *Donauturm*. She was an interesting contradiction, especially for someone as self-absorbed as she was. But Flora was genuinely empathetic and understanding much of the time. It was one of the reasons why her good friends loved her.

Still, there were limits. Leni never trusted Flora enough to tell her about John Flannery. She never told Isabelle either, although she had planned to. The problem with Flora was too often she took off in the worst possible direction with any new piece of information. Told it to the wrong people, or blabbed about it to others when it should have remained secret. She did this only because she was so happy and excited for you, but too often her enthusiasm had caused big problems. Or she would ask intimate embarrassing questions, the answers to which were either none of her business or ones you weren't ready to give yet.

Soon after they met, Kyle Pegg asked Flora not to tell anyone about him or their relationship. When she indignantly asked why not, he said the perfect thing to shut her up forever: "Because INTERPOL is looking for me. If they find me, I'm cooked." That was all. His admission was so unexpected and exciting that she locked it inside her heart and never told a soul. Kyle said almost nothing more about it in all the time they spent together. Once he alluded to his "problem" having to do with counterfeiting American dollars in Syria, but no more. She wanted to know everything but the only other bit he admitted to was the fact that his name wasn't Kyle Pegg, which was sort of the truth anyway. When she asked what his real name was, he hesitated and looked at her appraisingly. In a grave voice he said "Maybe I'll tell you when I believe I can trust you."

It was thrilling. She had never been with a criminal before. And a counterfeiter wasn't a killer or anything. What was the term for it—victimless crime? She was involved with a man on the lam from the law who read Rick Chaeff books and treated her like a queen. Flannery cooked dazzling meals for Flora. He told her stories of his life and exploits in places like Samarqand and Aleppo. This man *knew* things. Strange, marvelous bits of trivia spilled out of him in a continuous entertaining flow. "Did you know the woodcock shits before it flies, so when you cook the bird you can eat all of it—the guts, everything." "Historians say the first bread was probably made by accident about eight thousand years ago." His conversation was peppered with wonderfully appropriate proverbs that made her laugh out loud. "When luck gets tired, it'll even sit down on a dumb cow." And sometimes his insights about life made her look at her life with startlingly new perspective.

While making a shopping list one morning, Flora began daydreaming about Kyle Pegg and unconsciously wrote the word *fireplace* on the piece of paper. Because that's what her newest lover was for her—a large, crackling fireplace that you wanted to sit by and watch for hours. It radiated warmth and comfort, but don't ever forget the fire inside. Kyle *was* a criminal but that made him even more appealing to her.

• • •

Flora's criminal stopped now at the rear of the crowd to survey the faces and postures of the mourners who had gathered to pay their last respects to Leni Salomon. There was her husband. Flannery knew Michael Salomon because he had studied the man for some time to see if he could use him in any way. He was a handsome fellow, but those good looks were really his only high point. From certain angles he vaguely resembled Simon Haden. It made sense that Leni had slept with both men.

Michael was a dentist and an oral surgeon. Leni made false teeth. They met when he visited her office one day to supervise work on a very complicated bridge for a child who had lost most of his teeth in a horrendous accident. Leni made the bridge and it was perfect, more than perfect. Sitting at her workbench, she held it out to the handsome dentist on her open palm and said "Here you go—false teeth for mice." They started dating. He was able to convince her that he was more interesting than he really was. Months later when he proposed marriage she said yes because something about him made her feel safe and protected. He secretly loved the fact she was both fine-looking and lame. There was something poignant about that, a kind of cosmic balance. He was fluent in English which was a real plus because she loved speaking that language. He owned a Laverda motorcycle for a while and looked heroic on it. She liked to ride with him, her cheek pressed to his back, arms wrapped tightly around his waist. Michael treated her like a lady and his absolute equal. They lived well. She owned two horses. He made a lot of money even though he was only an average oral surgeon. But he had trained in America which gave him a certain prestige with the Viennese. Both of them liked grilled salmon, ambient music, and contemporary fiction. He was a bore; she was a bit of a scold and at times a malcontent. They got along if they weren't around each other too much.

Now Leni was dead and he was bereft. How could this happen? Dentists plan. They map things out before they begin. He'd had the rest of their life together altogether in his head. Next year he would try and convince her to have a child. He wanted to build a house on a lake and fish there with his son.

Flannery watched all this chaos, loss, and confusion twirl around now in Michael Salomon's eyes, like a car careening on black ice, that great phrase for those insidious patches of hidden ice that catch drivers unaware in winter and from one second to the next send their cars flying off the road or into deadly spins. Dr. Salomon had been on black ice since hearing that his wife was dead. The horror was not only the total loss of control but the fact he could not get off this ice. Every way he turned in his life now there was only more confusion, more facets of loss. He had genuinely loved her, he had, but she had been just one element of his busy successful life. Only when she was gone did he realize what weight and importance Leni had carried.

Now Michael looked from her coffin to the ground, the damp brown-black earth that would first hold his wife's small body, then her bare bones, then whatever was left—a few teeth, a rotted shoe curled like a potato chip by dampness, and whatever crumbling faded cloth that managed to survive the long journey beneath the earth down the years.

It was at that moment, this obscene moment between recognition and closure for Michael Salomon, when Leni's ghost appeared to him and all the people attending her burial that morning, including John Flannery.

Forty-one people had come. Some of them had known the deceased woman well, some barely at all. Some had been invited to the ceremony; some had heard about it from others or read the public announcement in the newspapers. Two of her former boyfriends were there. One of them still vaguely loved her. An old university classmate showed up who had hated Leni and vice versa. The only reason why this woman came was to gloat. A couple of children came; one because he was the dead woman's nephew, the other because her parents could not find a babysitter in time. There was a seventy-nine-year-old pensioner who had not known the deceased, but stopped by on his morning walk simply because he enjoyed the communal feeling of funerals. About half of the people had eaten breakfast. Some hadn't, and some could not because they knew that later they would be going to a burial.

At precisely 11:17 the same image appeared in the minds of every single person in attendance: Leni sat at the kitchen table in her apartment, facing forward as if she were a television news broadcaster facing the camera. She wore the black dress she was buried in. The expression on her face was calm and purposeful—nothing more. She held up a white piece of paper in front of her. Written on it in thick black, hand drawn letters were the words *Glass Soup*.

Staring straight ahead, she raised this paper in front of her face to give a better view to what was written there. A moment later she lowered it and mouthed the two words. *Glass Soup*. Then she nodded as if to say Yes, you heard me right—*Glass Soup*.

The children were the first to react to this vision of the dead woman. The little girl, who had come because there was no babysitter for her, immediately closed her eyes and made a wish. At just that moment she had been thinking about fairies, so she presumed quite reasonably that what she saw was a fairy in black who appeared because she'd been summoned. The little girl wished for an elephant; but only a small blue one that could get into bed with her at night and keep her company.

The little boy knew that the woman he saw was his aunt Leni. But he had only the vaguest idea of what dead meant, so he sniggered. He was just beginning to learn how to read, but only in German. He did not know what the English words *glass soup* meant. So he sniggered at her and the stupid words she was showing that he did not understand. He would ask Aunt Leni what they meant when he saw her again.

The adults had a wide range of reactions to the vision. Their faces showed surprise, consternation, some were distraught, and some were delighted because they believed in various gods and were sure that this vision of a living Leni Salomon at her own funeral was a sign from above. But none of these people, not one, not even John Flannery, thought that what they had just witnessed had also been seen by others. That is the wonder.

Some of them looked around guiltily, as if the other mourners could see into their heads and the weird vision they'd just had. But for the time being no one at the funeral thought or imagined that *What I just saw he just saw too.* People looked down or away in embarrassment, at the sky to clear their eyes of tears, or even at the coffin to reaffirm it was still there.

But what was Glass Soup?

The Dinosaur Prayer

John Flannery knew what *Glass Soup* meant. The moment he saw Leni hold up her sign, he turned right around and hurried away. He looked like a man who urgently needed to find a toilet. His eyes were too wide; his hands kept opening and closing into fists. When he reached his car he had trouble fitting the key into the door lock. He eventually remembered that it could be opened remotely by simply pressing a button on the ignition key.

The first thing he did after getting into the car and sitting down was to fart. Flannery had never farted before but this one was a real toupee lifter. It happened because he had nervously swallowed so much air walking from the cemetery to the car that his alarmed body had to get rid of it somehow. Startled, he turned in the seat and looked down at his ass like dogs sometimes do when they fart; as if what just happened had nothing to do with *them*. They're just as surprised by the noise as you.

The smells of fresh fart, new car, and expensive leather filled the space around him. Flannery sat staring straight ahead, knowing he should get moving, but stunned still by what had happened. The rules had just been broken by the other side. Some kind of immense new dynamic was at hand. If he had known that every single person at the cemetery saw what he had seen, he would have been genuinely frightened.

As a human being, John Flannery had never farted and had never been afraid. Afraid of what? What was here that could frighten a being like him? He did not eat unless he needed to fool people into believing he was human. His heart did not beat unless it was necessary for that same reason. He breathed only because if someone were to notice he *didn't* breathe, then there could be trouble. He was here to do a job and the body he wore was the required uniform. Until now he had been very good at this job. But in all of his many incarnations as a human being, nothing like this had ever happened. It shook him profoundly.

The living have their world, the dead have theirs. The borders between the two are strictly defined and *never* crossed. Once that was sacrosanct and inviolable to all but Chaos. It recognizes no boundaries or laws and never has. Chaos does what it wants and that is why Flannery could flit back and forth between life and death with no hesitation. But then Isabelle Neukor and Vincent Ettrich made the crossing. Much more dangerously though, Leni Salomon had crossed too and then sent a clear message from one world to the other. To those who understood her message, it divulged a fundamental fact that mankind had sought to know for as long as it existed.

Since Flannery was unaware that others had witnessed Leni showing her message, he didn't know that what those people saw were the English words *Glass Soup* and nothing more. Leni had spoken to the living in the language of the dead. But it did not translate. As a result, the living saw two words they understood but which made no sense other than as a surreal image signifying nothing.

That's why there was no noticeable reaction in that crowd to the vision at the time it happened. The majority of them thought it was only creepy nonsense, as meaningless as Leni's message. A dead woman held up a sign that read GLASS SOUP. So what? Were they supposed to turn to their husband or neighbor in the middle of this funeral and exclaim *I just had a vision of dead Leni! She showed me a sign that made no sense.* That would have been a big hit with the other mourners; it would have added a lot to the solemnity of the occasion. Even her best friends Isabelle and Flora remained silent about it, although both were immediately convinced that their visions meant something significant.

In fact Isabelle was so caught up thinking about what she'd just seen that she didn't realize for quite a while that her Vincent was no longer standing nearby. On discovering his absence though she wasn't particularly surprised. It was just his way—Mr. Fidgety. Vincent could never stand in one place too long. He called himself KADD—the King of Attention Deficit Disorder. She assumed he was somewhere nearby.

He wasn't. Because like John Flannery, Vincent Ettrich also knew what *Glass Soup* meant. When Leni held up her handwritten sign, he read the two words on it and his eyes widened slightly. Ettrich felt neither panic nor joy. He did not feel like running off in all directions at once. In the language of the dead, *Glass Soup* described and explained the mosaic, and the mosaic was God. One of the first lessons a person learned after dying—what it was and what it meant.

Walking away from the funeral, his mind was in the afterlife, looking slowly around at all that it held. Passing through the cemetery gates, Ettrich realized he knew how to do so much now; so much more than before.

• • • • • •

"Shit."

Both Simon Haden and Leni Salomon looked at Bob the Bear.

"What's the matter?"

"It didn't work."

"What do you mean?"

"How do you know?"

The bear rubbed its head and said angrily "Shit shit shit. It didn't work, do you understand? It's my job to know these things. It didn't work."

Haden and Leni glanced at each other at the same moment with the same question in their eyes—how can it be sure?

Haden looked away, muttering his own curses. It had been so difficult to reach Leni in the first place. Find Leni and her dream-world in the limitless regions of death. And if you do that, then you must figure out how to enter that world and find *her* in it.

But Haden had done all of that. What's more, he did it alone. No help from Bob or any others. His search for Leni Salomon had been tedious, then frightening and grueling. Full of wrong turns and false hopes, eventually he had done it. He had no idea how long it took in life-time—a thousand years or ten minutes? This was death and the clocks here were different. Haden was so proud of himself, prouder of this than anything he had ever done. Prouder even than the bravery he had displayed toward Mrs. Dugdale and later against Sunday Suits back in the school gymnasium.

He would not forget the expression on Leni's face when he walked up to her on the bench while she was feeding the dinosaur. He didn't know that as a girl, Leni had dreamt of dinosaurs night after night after night. Maybe it was because of the contrast—she was a small child with a bad leg and dinosaurs were so very huge and powerful. Or maybe she just liked them. Even with a little girl's tongue she could perfectly pronounce their polysyllabic names as if they were the players on her favorite team, or the words of a much loved children's prayer.

When Haden finally located her in death, adult Leni was sitting on a green park bench near the banks of the Danube River, about four miles away from where she had been buried. It had been one of her favorite places to sit when she was alive, so naturally she carried it with her into death.

At her feet was a large brown wicker basket filled with cooked hamburgers. Sitting obsequiously on its hind legs nearby was a nine-foot-long Troodon, once known as the Stenonychosaurus. The smallish dinosaur took each burger it was offered with the most careful, delicate gesture and then put them into its mouth with a paw and claws that looked like they could have torn a hole in concrete if this monster got pissed off.

"Hey there" Haden said from a reasonable distance, not sure if he wanted to get any closer to this burger-vore, dream creature or not.

Dead Leni turned to him and recognizing her onetime lover, smiled at Haden but not very warmly. "Hello Simon." Her voice was flat. She appeared neither happy nor surprised to see him here.

He crossed his arms and tried to find a comfortable standing position. But every time he looked at Leni's friend the dinosaur, Haden went up on his toes, ready to run at its slightest suspicious twitch or flick.

She reached into the basket, brought out another burger, and handed it to the creature. It gently hooked the meat with one huge claw and brought it to its mouth. "I'll give you one of these hamburgers, Simon, if you can tell me what its name is."

Haden only smiled and shrugged. He didn't know anything about it and didn't want to know. "Donald?"

"It's called a Troodon. The name means 'wounding tooth.' This used to be my favorite dinosaur when I was a girl because it's relatively small. My family once took a trip to London and I made them all go to the Victoria and Albert Museum just so I could see the bones of one they have there.

"The greatest gift I ever received was Isabelle Neukor found a Troodon tooth for sale in an auction catalog somewhere and got it for me."

Haden tried to look interested but was not. He just wanted to make sure that fucking mega-lizard wasn't going to eat him.

"What are you doing here, Simon?"

"I came to see you."

"Obviously, but why?"

He didn't know exactly what to say next. It was a precarious moment: he was strictly forbidden to tell her anything he had learned about death. That was taboo, off limits, no way. All of it had to come from her. He had to find out how much Leni knew and then he could proceed from there.

"Will Mr. Jurassic Park mind if I sit down?" He pointed to the dinosaur which was now looking at him with cold-eyed interest. Haden tried to make his question come out sounding light and funny. It didn't.

"Troodons were carnivores. They only ate meat" she said while reaching down for another burger. Haden thought it best to remain standing.

They'd had their affair. It had been a good one too for the short while it lasted and that's what made Leni angry, even now. She'd gone into it knowing full well that Simon was a Casanova and wouldn't stick around long. Fair enough—she knew that but said yes anyway because an affair was exactly what she wanted at the time.

The problem was Simon Haden possessed a quality few males do. It was an instinctive thing that most of the men who had it didn't even know was there. Yet it was the most formidable part of their arsenal: they made you feel totally comfortable when you were together with them. On the street, in bed, having lunch, having sex, having a laugh, a walk or whatever—it didn't matter. You breathed normally with them. You didn't feel any need to put on airs or puff out your chest or pretend to be someone you weren't. Yes, this fellow wanted to be in your pants, but he also wanted to be in your head and hang around together sharing the day. You felt that whenever you were with him. You were certain that you were exactly where he wanted to be at that moment. The things you said or did genuinely interested him.

That's why Leni so disliked Vincent Ettrich—because he possessed that same uncommon quality. Every time she was around Vincent, she remembered the fiasco with Simon and it rubbed her wounds. Because just when she'd gotten comfortable and content in the space she'd created with Haden, he walked out on her. Now here he was again, the first time she'd seen him since he left.

"You didn't answer me—why are you here?"

He thought Here we are and we're both dead and she's feeding a dinosaur and I just crossed a universe to reach her but now I don't know how to begin to say what I came for.

"What was it like for you?"

He looked at her, not understanding the context of her question. "Hmm? what do you mean?"

"When you died, Simon. What was it like for you? I was murdered." She said it quietly, not showing any of the rage, the confusion, or the helplessness that had constantly roiled inside her since the moment she understood she was dead. Right now she wanted to grab Haden and shake him, shouting *It isn't fair! It isn't right! It has to be put right again. This isn't possible. It can't be possible.* But Haden saw none of that because showing her emotions had never been Leni's way, not before, not now.

Her dinosaur made a kind of whinny like a horse. It wanted some more meat.

Haden couldn't stop himself—in a haze he walked over to her bench and sat down heavily on the corner farthest away from the beast. "You *know* you're dead?"

She pointed her little finger at the Troodon. "You can't feed hamburgers to dinosaurs in the real world, Simon. Yes, I've known for quite a while."

"You figured it out that quickly?"

She said nothing, but the hint of a sly smile floated somewhere near her lips.

He saw it and couldn't let the subject go. "Leni, you really figured it out that quickly?"

"It took about half a day after I got here. When I saw the second

Troodon I knew. When I was a little girl I dreamt of them all the time." She couldn't resist telling him the truth.

"Damn!" Haden threw up a hand and blew through his lips in disgust. The sense of great pride and achievement he'd felt at having found Leni Salomon suddenly melted inside him now like an ice cube inside a microwave oven. How long had it taken him to realize that he was dead? Forever? Half of forever?

"I don't want you here, Simon. I want you to leave." She closed her eyes and dropped her head. All he could think to do then was stare at the Troodon.

When she opened her eyes a moment later and saw him, she appeared surprised. "You're still here. Why are you still here?" Her voice was a demand.

"Leni, we've got things to talk about—important things."

"I don't want to talk to you, Simon. I want you to go away. Why haven't you disappeared?"

The creature looked unhappy at the stridency in her voice. Haden wondered if a dinosaur could be trained to attack, like a dog.

"Why are you still here?"

Testily he said "Because I *want* to be here, Leni."

Her voice took on even more of an edge than his. "That's not how it works here. This is my world, these are my dreams. If I don't want something to be here, I say that and it disappears." To prove her point she turned to the dinosaur and said "Go away." The creature literally evaporated. Without giving him a chance to digest that astonishing vision, she looked at Haden and said to him in exactly the same tone of voice "Go away."

"Forget it, Leni. I'm real, not part of your dream."

"You can't be real, Simon—you're dead."

"Both of us are and that's why I'm here, not because you dreamed me."

Each struggled to process their different information. But it was like trying to eat a whole loaf of bread as fast as you could. No matter how quickly you chewed, your cheeks stayed full, your throat grew dry, and your jaw got tired. But still there was so much more left to eat.

Rational even in death, Leni wasn't having it. She did not believe or accept what Haden had just told her—that he was not part of her dreamworld. Having learned to conjure here, that's what she did now. She conjured the Simon Haden she remembered and been together with in life. The lover who treated her well for a while but also the bad guy he later became when he jumped ship.

Leni's conjured Haden materialized standing where the Troodon had been minutes before. This second Simon was dressed beautifully. His shirt was the thick lustrous white of milk fresh out of a bottle. His fingernails shone from a recent perfect manicure. He smiled and his teeth looked like old turnips and uprooted gravestones. They looked like they hadn't been brushed or worked on by a dentist since the invention of the drill.

"Damn!" the real Haden said for a second time. He knew what she had just done but seeing his face on another man didn't bother him. Seeing a brown graveyard in "his" mouth did. "What happened to my teeth? They don't look like that." He wished he had a hand mirror right then so he could check them. Surely they weren't so ugly.

Haden #2 said nothing and only continued smiling, unfortunately. He slipped his hands into his pockets and tipped his head jauntily to the side in a Gene Kelly/Hollywood way that said *I can wait all day—I know who I am.*

"You have terrible teeth, Simon. I kept telling you that."

"Yes, okay, but not that bad. Jesus, Leni, do you really remember me that way?"

She would not look at him; only at her imagined Haden. Her brain was working fast. In this place there could be two of anything if that's what you wanted. She could have created five Simon Hadens in five different colors if that had been her wish. So two of them in front of her was okay. But what she couldn't understand was #1 not disappearing when she told him to. It was as if one of her dreams had a mind of its own. *That* was disturbing. Until now, death had not been a hard place for Leni to figure out. This was the first time she had hit a speed bump here and banged her head hard on the roof. Was this a test?

The real Haden walked over to #2 and examined him carefully. "What's that cologne you're wearing?"

"Sandalwood" #2 said in a voice slightly deeper than the original.

"*Sandalwood?* I never used sandalwood cologne in my life."

Leni sat back on the bench, her elbows out to either side to support her. "*I* like sandalwood on a man, if you don't mind. Is it all right with you if he wears cologne that I like?"

The real Haden would have protested if he were somewhere else. To him, cologne was like a person's signature; one of the ways of telling the world who you were. Wearing disgusting sandalwood cologne was like signing your name with the wrong hand.

Number Two was a few inches shorter than him too, but Haden did not bring that discrepancy to Leni's attention. He just kept looking at his clone that was not a clone but close enough so that most people would have had a tough time telling them apart. The real Haden had no such trouble. Those vile teeth, the nose-wilting cologne, the wrong height . . . He noticed more and more details that were wrong about this imposter and they made him mad. Leni's imagined version of him was simply not him.

His frustration spilled over when #2 asked for something to eat—maybe an avocado? Haden loathed avocados. Those strange green things that always reminded him of legless frogs . . .

"I hate avocados! I would never ask for one."

When he said that, Leni looked at him with outraged, hurt eyes and immediately began to cry. Why? What had he said?

She put her head in her hands and wept. Haden's clone looked at him and *tsk-tsk*ed its disapproval.

"What? What'd I say?"

"You fucked up now, brother. Look what you did to her."

"All I said was I don't like avocados."

Leni looked up from the wet bowl of her hands. Her eyes were shiny. "You bastard. You told me you loved avocados. That was one of the nicest afternoons I can remember. Now it turns out you were lying. Thank you very much, Simon. You are a bastard."

"What the hell are you talking about, Leni?"

She wouldn't answer him, so the other Haden did.

"Don't you remember the day you two went shopping together and you stole her avocados?"

Flummoxed, Haden looked at the ground and tried to match these words to a memory. Shopping? Stolen avocados? When she was sure he wasn't looking, Leni peeked up to see if his expression showed any kind of recognition. He dug deep in his memory but that first attempt came up with nothing. Digging deeper he saw something but it was vague and amorphous—a ghost of a memory, ectoplasmic at best. Leni watched him trying to remember but finding nothing. Tears welled in her eyes again.

One of life's (and death's) nastier lessons: what's important to us is not necessarily important to others, no matter how close we are to them. What we love or hate, they don't. What we hold to be true is not often their truth. How could Simon forget? How could a day that lovely have slid through his memory like water and fallen away forever?

Leni's husband was out of town for a weekend conference. She went to meet Haden at a café. He needed groceries for his apartment so they went shopping at an outdoor market nearby. The sun was out for the first time in a week; the sky was the blue of a baby's room. He bought this and that while she tagged comfortably along. It amused her to think strangers imagined them as a couple: this handsome man and his handicapped wife.

At one stand she noticed two beautiful fat avocados and on a happy whim, bought them. When she got home later they were gone from her bag, replaced by a note that said if she wanted to see her avocados alive again, she had to go to this address at a certain hour later that day. It was Simon's address.

When she arrived, his living room table was laid with a bowl of bad lumpy guacamole surrounded by potato chips and other simple finger food she realized he had bought earlier when they were shopping. They drank two bottles of Barolo wine and never touched each other. She stayed till late in the afternoon. The sky outside was falling into deeper and deeper purple. She hadn't slept with him yet but that day decided it for her. She wasn't used to surprises. This experience reminded her of how much she enjoyed them.

Meanwhile, #2 only had to say two or three sentences about their avocado day to jog Haden's memory. "Ohhh yes, I remember that day." He was smiling now. "You choked on a carrot stick."

She stood up. "You bastard. You son of a bitch."

"What? Why are you so upset, Leni? What's the big deal?"

Again she patted herself on the chest, only this time hard enough so that both men heard the hollow thump each time she hit it. "Because it was *my* memory and *my* life. Now you've changed it and there's nothing I can do about it, you bastard! Now it will always be the day I choked on a carrot stick and you hate avocados. Not the day you stole them from me and made us guacamole. Thank you—you've completely ruined a memory, and it was one of my favorites.

"You ended our thing badly, Simon. But you were also the avocado thief and that always made me smile when I thought of you, even afterwards. That day, that *memory* mattered. You were sweet and thoughtful and we had such fun. After our relationship was finished, when you ruined it by leaving for no good reason, something in me, in here, still treasured that avocado day. It was good—it was almost worth everything else."

What Leni left out was that experience was also one of the main reasons why she later fell for John Flannery. With seemingly innocuous questions their first time together, he learned how much she enjoyed being surprised by a man, thrown off balance and, well, swept off her feet by imagination and thoughtfulness. Once Flannery had that piece of information, winning her was very simple.

"All right, Leni, fine. So now it's my turn: Petras. Hmm? Did you get that? I'll say it again for you—Petras." Haden spoke in a challenging petulant voice.

She stopped and frowned. "What are you talking about?"

"Petras Urbsys."

Despite the strangeness of the name, it was familiar to her. As if he might be able to help, she turned briefly to her imagined Haden and threw him an inquiring look. He held up both hands as if to say *I know nothing. Remember, I came out of your head.*

She didn't like this turn of events. She didn't like the way Simon had turned this event. It felt like he was doing it to avoid blame. She would humor him for another thirty seconds and then get back to the avocados. "I don't know what you're talking about. Should I?"

"Petras Urbsys was the man who owned that great strange store I took you to one day in Vienna. Don't you remember? The guy who was selling his whole life in there? All of his possessions were for sale. I loved that store. I loved it so much that I took you and Isabelle to see it. I even introduced you to Petras. But you don't remember it, do you, Leni?"

"No."

"Exactly. So we're even. I don't remember your avocados and you don't remember Petras Urbsys."

This was wrong—Simon was hijacking this. What he said wasn't really correct, but then again it was. He'd outmaneuvered her, checkmated her using the same moves. Leni was abruptly left with a mouthful of nothing to say and feathers.

"May I add something to this conversation?" Haden #2 asked sweetly.

Haden and Leni had momentarily forgotten about #2 in the

heat of their battle. Now they both looked at him, annoyed at his interruption.

"No!"

"Go away" she said and like the Troodon before him, #2 evaporated.

"Leni, no matter what you think of me, this isn't about me. That's not why I'm here. It's about Isabelle Neukor."

Leni had so much resentment in her heart and so many questions in her head. All of them vanished when he said her friend's name. She immediately asked "Isabelle's dead?"

"Worse."

"What is it, Simon?"

"Come with me and I'll show you."

• • •

"What *is* this?"

At that moment Haden was too busy to answer her. Whipping his head back and forth, he kept looking for a break that they might scamper through in the insane traffic rocketing by. He had never seen traffic like this before. It literally never appeared to slow or stop. It reminded him of documentaries he had seen on television showing blood cells rushing through veins. These cars were going by so fast that none of them had real shape—they were all just large colored blurs to his eye.

"What are we doing here?" Leni stood behind him with her hands on her hips. She sensed what he had in mind, but there was no way she was going to try and cross that whizzing flow. With her bad leg? Was he crazy? For what purpose?

To make matters worse, Simon hadn't said a thing to her about any of it. They'd taken an elevated train to a forlorn edge of the city that bordered this busy highway. It looked to her like the main road out to the airport. On the ride over, he wouldn't tell her anything about where they were going or why. The reason being that he was afraid she would turn around and leave if she knew. Instead he made vacuous small talk that bored both of them right up until they got off the train and, leaving the station, walked to the edge of this road.

Zoom zoom zoom—the flow of traffic never stopped or lessened, not for a second. "Simon, I came this far with you, but I swear that if you don't tell me right now why we're here, I'm leaving."

Resigned to the worst, he sighed and asked "What was your favorite song as a kid?"

Leni almost physically recoiled at the strangeness of the question. *"What?"*

He raised his voice. "I'm answering your question. What song did you, Isabelle, and Flora play all the time when you were girls, especially when you were together?"

Exasperated, she snapped "What does that have to do with this?" She pointed to the traffic. A long and loud horn blatted by them and on down the road.

Haden waited till it was gone to answer. "Leni, you asked me a question. I'm giving you the answer. How many times do I have to say that? What was your favorite song when you were fifteen?"

All right, all right—she'd go along with this and see where he was going with it. She squinted, trying to find the answer to his question in her attic of memories. Her favorite song? What grade was she in at fifteen, tenth?

Haden didn't wait. "If you can't remember that, who was your favorite rock group back then?"

A picture entered her mind: the three teenaged girls standing shoulder to shoulder in Flora's living room. All of them were wearing huge, helmety horrible hairdos and identical black T-shirts that announced in yellow letters AC/DC, the heavy-metal rock group.

She smirked at the image and that memory, remembering the day and the mood: how cool they thought they were in those haircuts and shirts. "AC/DC. We all loved AC/DC."

"Right. And what song of AC/DC was your theme song?"

She didn't hesitate. " 'Highway to Hell.' "

Haden threw a thumb over his shoulder to indicate the busy road behind him.

She looked toward it and then back at him. "What? What are you saying?"

"There it is—your Highway to Hell."

"I don't understand, Simon." Disturbed, she glanced again at the road. It was only a road, as far as she could see; just a road with lots of cars on it.

"This is your dreamworld, Leni. You made all of this and that's part of it. You loved that song when you were young, so somewhere in your teenage dreams you made up a real Highway to Hell and this is it. Our problem is that we have to get across it now because what I need to show you is on the other side."

"You mean all of these cars are driving to Hell?" The moment she said the word she became scared. "You mean there *is* a Hell?"

Haden could have answered that question and wanted to, but knew he wasn't permitted. Restraining himself he said only "We have to get across that road."

"Wait a minute. Simon, those cars are going in both directions. How can they be going to Hell if they're going in opposite directions?"

He looked at the ground, unwilling to make eye contact with her.

"Simon?"

A half-filled paper cup of Coca-Cola was tossed out the window of a passing car. It hit the ground near them and splashed across their legs. Leni screeched and was about to yell at whoever threw it, but saw something that stopped her. A few feet away the cup lay rocking back and forth on its side. She could see inside it. Three yellow somethings lay in there. Peering closer she realized they were three slices of lemon. Chin tipped up, she looked toward where the car had been seconds before, then back to the cup. Something was dawning on her; not fast but gradually. Leni looked at Simon Haden; she looked at the road, the cup, the road.

Taking several cautious steps forward, she tried to see into the passing cars to catch glimpses of the passengers. It was difficult because they moved by so quickly. But Leni had a powerful hunch now and wasn't going to be deterred. While this happened, the song "Highway to Hell" played over and over in her head for the first time in years. It had been their anthem and rallying cry as teenagers. With their big hair and dreams of spectacular futures, the girls played the tune constantly, especially whenever they were together.

She knew her hunch was correct when she saw the hand. A car sped by. Sticking out of the passenger's window was a bare arm, the fingers of the hand open and playing with the wind. For an instant she saw the fingernails—they were all painted green. She didn't see who the hand belonged to, but the green fingernails were enough.

One day when they were twenty, Flora had given her a bottle of green fingernail polish as a joke. Because they were bored, the three friends had painted their fingers and toes with it. They'd even had a picture taken. Wanting to be certain though before asking Haden, she continued staring at the highway. In time Leni noticed something else which turned out to be the convincer.

All of the cars were the same. Seven different makes and models passed in both directions again and again and again. Car after car, always the same seven. Their colors never varied either. The Opel was always navy blue, the Volkswagen bus beige; every Mercedes-Benz station wagon that passed was white. Once she recognized this fact about the seven cars, she understood why their colors never changed. She checked every passing Mercedes after that just to make sure. On the rear window of each in exactly the same place was a decal of the cartoon character Asterix and his big friend Obelix. Leni recognized the decal because she had put it on the car window herself when she was twelve and had read every Asterix comic book numerous times.

Every one of the vehicles on *this* particular Highway to Hell were the cars Leni Salomon had had in her lifetime. The Opel Kadett, Volkswagen, and Mercedes were her parents' cars; the ones she had grown up with until she was old enough to have her own. Those later cars were here too—the yellow VW bug she'd gotten as a high school graduation present, the black BMW 320 with the "Rapid" soccer club decal on one of the rear windows. She'd had sex in the backseat of that car with Simon Haden. She wondered if he remembered that. A gray Lancia she'd once owned and wrecked when she was going through her phase of driving too fast. And her red Honda Civic. The car she owned when she died.

"It's me in there, isn't it? In every one of those cars it's me. I always drank Coke with three slices of lemon. And the green fingernails—"

"You're warm."

"What do you mean *warm,* Simon? Is it or isn't it me in there?"

"You're warm, you're close. Keep going."

"*Close?* This isn't a game."

More to himself than to her he said "No, it's your Ropenfeld."

"What? What did you say?" Another horn honked nearby.

"Nothing, Leni. You're really close now. Look again. You'll get it."

She wanted to ask him what *Ropenfeld* meant but this was more important. Now that she had an idea of what was going on, she watched the scene with different eyes. But squinting and concentrating as hard as she could, she still failed to see anything concrete inside those cars—only forms. No matter how hard she tried to shape them into a person or a face, she could not. This world around them, although entirely her creation, was indifferent to her. When she went into her deepest heart and asked for help, it offered none.

A smell shoved its way between everything else and up to the front of her mind. Leni didn't notice certain of her senses when she was concentrating on others. Staring hard at something, she would forget or take no notice of the smells in the air, the sounds all around, her cold feet, or a sour metallic taste in her mouth. But this smell was so pervasive now that it refused to be ignored. It hung around until she became fully conscious of it.

A wet dog—it was the smell of wet dog. Animal, thick, not nasty but not nice either. When she came around and focused her attention on it, she recognized what it was. She knew what it was and it both surprised and shamed her.

It was the smell her body had given off all of her life whenever she was very afraid. It had followed her into death. As fastidious as she was, she nonetheless exuded this odor in varying degrees whenever she had been genuinely frightened. One doctor she consulted said it was only a minor hormonal aberration she could not change. Besides, it was only body odor that disappeared whenever the threat disappeared. He said a surprisingly large number of people had the same problem. Unsatisfied with that prognosis, she visited two highly esteemed endocrinologists who told her essentially the same thing. The irony was that in most difficult situations Leni was the calmest, most reliable person around. But whenever this singular odor began to rise off her skin, she knew it was her body's way of saying *Run away!*

The smell was unmistakable now, but there was something wrong this time because she wasn't afraid. Curious, yes. On edge and wary of what was happening . . . But not the kind of frightened that in her past had always caused the smell.

It grew stronger but that was because she was fully aware of it now. The cars flew past a few feet away. Standing nearby, Simon Haden remained silent.

The answer came when those lemon slices in the cup led her to suddenly remember a name—Henry County. He was the boy Leni had dated on and off throughout high school. He was American, wickedly clever, and manic-depressive. She never knew whether she really liked him or was just sort of spellbound by his erratic character. But he did have his own odd compelling gravity that kept pulling her back to him for a while.

Once toward the end of their relationship he'd gotten angry at her while driving them to a movie. She was drinking Coke out of a paper cup. He snatched the cup from her hand and threw it out the window. A Coke with three slices of lemon in it. The speed and wildness of his gesture frightened her and the smell came right away.

The day she had painted her fingernails green with Flora and Isabelle, a man followed her home afterward. He sat across the aisle on the 35A bus but moved over and sat down next to her. He started a conversation by asking too many questions about her "interesting" fingernails. She stopped answering them after the fourth and pretended to look out the window, trying to ignore him. He would not be ignored. Fortunately they arrived at her stop and she got off the bus. But he got off too and followed. When she paid no attention to him, he tried to touch her arm.

"Get away! *Don't touch me,*" She spoke in a strong angry voice. He hesitated, thinking she was bluffing. When he realized she wasn't and could make real trouble for him, he took two giant steps back and smiled. Leni didn't look at him again as she walked the remaining blocks to her house. Fearful that he might still be somewhere near, she could smell herself as she limped along. She hated the man for frightening her and hated her body for its betrayal.

"It *is* me in all those cars—every one of them." She said it evenly now while watching the traffic. Despite the noise, Haden was pretty sure he'd heard her correctly. When she spoke again he was eager to hear how she worked her way through this.

"But fear is driving the cars, not me. I'm just the passenger. Back and forth, it doesn't matter where they're going. Every single one. *That's* why it smells so much around here—every car is full of me and my fears." She swept an arm from left to right, taking in the scene. At the end of that arc her arm remained in the air for a few more seconds, pointing forward. Eventually it dropped slowly to her side, brought back to earth by this sad realization. Then to Haden's surprise, she appeared to chuckle. "You were right, Simon—it really is a Highway to Hell. Mine."

Her back to him, she closed her eyes tightly and sucked in her lips, as if fighting back tears. Perhaps she was.

"He went to Harvard. He was the only person I ever actually knew who went there. I never heard from him again after he left Vienna." She was talking about Henry County but Haden didn't know that. He thought it prudent to remain quiet and let her talk.

But Leni had nothing more to say. Instead she took a deep breath and walked straight toward the highway and its monster traffic. Cars raced back and forth in an endless stream. The two of them were already near enough to the traffic to feel its strong gusts of wind. The closer she got to the road, the more fascinating it was for Haden to see what she was actually going to do. It looked like she was going to walk right into that traffic. Was it possible? Would she really do that?

Stepping onto the road, she reached forward with both hands and quickly pulled them apart, like she was opening a pair of curtains. Without a sound the scene in front of them tore in two like a piece of ripped cloth, revealing pitch blackness behind.

It was as if all that they had been seeing was really only a picture projected on a mammoth movie screen Leni had ruined by tearing it in two. The road, the cars, the sky, the horizon . . . Where she stood now there was a large opening in the center of the world. It went up toward the sky and down to the ground. Solid black peeked at them through the crack. Without hesitating she walked through the tear she'd made and disappeared.

"How did she know? How could she have figured it out so fast?" Haden asked, looking around for someone who could answer his questions. But he was alone out there by the side of a busy road. Alone and frustrated. "I feel like a fucking retard. Damn!" He walked hurriedly over to the long tear in Leni's dreamworld, pulled the two dangling flaps apart, and followed her into the darkness. *"Damn!"*

• • •

"You create most of your own fears in life. That's what keeps you busy: something to worry about at every turn. But when you're dead, there's no reason to be afraid of those things anymore." Leni said all this and then looked at Bob to see if it was correct. The animal remained silent, but nodded its great ursine head in slow, complete agreement.

Simon Haden said nothing. He only sat there and stewed. Occasionally he shifted his unhappy eyes to Bob the Bear, which was looking at Leni with warmth and complete approval in its eyes. The three of them sat on chrome bar stools in the middle of an empty stage. Haden was so resentful of what had been going on that he even began hoping his old friend Bob would fall off. The polar bear kept scrooching around on the unstable stool, making it wobble and teeter. It was so goddamned big and so was its ass. How could it remain balanced on such a small seat? It must have been like sitting on a 25-cent piece.

"Go on" Bob said, eyes still on Leni.

She rubbed her hands together as if she were warming up. "I saw those three slices of lemon in the cup, and then that hand with the green fingernail polish. Both images brought me back to moments where I was petrified with fear. It suddenly dawned on me that I'd carried those fears over here with me from life.

"But that's ridiculous; why do that? When you're dead, life's experiences have no importance anymore. Or they *shouldn't*. I won't see Henry County ever again unless I conjure him. And I'll never bring back that creep on the bus. So why am I letting those fears drive on my highway still?" She shook her head at the idiocy of the idea. "It's like you move from Finland to Brazil, but insist on bringing your warmest parka along. Why? It's always hot in Brazil. You never need a parka there.

"When I was alive the worst fear I had was of dying. Well, I'm dead. All the *crap* that frightened me before is over. It's finished because I'm here now."

Both Bob and Haden lifted their heads when she said the word *crap* so vehemently.

"Simon, thank you" she said to him and smiled.

Caught off guard, it took some seconds for his brain to shift from rat-brown jealousy to surprise and then halfway back to skepticism. "Thanks for what?"

"I'm not sure yet. I haven't figured it out, but for now just thank you.

"Bob, where are we? What is this place?"

"It's a theater."

They waited for more but no more came.

"Bob, we can see *that*."

The bear squirmed some more on its bar stool. "I'm sure you could, Simon. But I was answering Leni's question."

"The dead put on plays?"

"They only rehearse here. No plays, just rehearsals."

"Rehearse what?"

"Specific dreams that you had at night when you were alive. This place was Leni's theater. You had one too, Simon. Certain crucial dreams were carefully planned and choreographed here. This stage is where particular elements of Leni's dreams rehearsed their roles."

Haden asked the question first that was simultaneously on Leni's mind. "*Every dream* we had meant something? Every one of them? The dream where I went into the kitchen and made a grilled cheese sandwich with a banjo instead of a frying pan? That *meant* something?"

"No, only some dreams; maybe ten or twelve over the course of your lifetime. For example both of you dreamt this meeting when you were alive, in your own separate ways. Leni dreamt it when she was twenty-five, Simon when you were nine. Both of you dreamt it exactly as it is now—this stage, the three of us talking, the works."

Now it was Haden's turn to squirm on his bar stool. "I dreamt of Leni when I was nine?" He sounded incredulous.

"Yes, but you quickly forgot about it the next morning. The only thing you remembered was a big version of me," Bob scolded.

"Why do we have those dreams? What good does it do to see the future if you have no context?"

For the bear it was a relief talking to Leni Salomon. She was so much more rational and easy to deal with than Haden. She didn't explode in anger or tiresome, self-pitying rants like Simon so frequently did. A no-nonsense pragmatist, Leni asked pertinent questions and then moved on after getting the answers, whether she liked them or not.

"Remember those tests where they showed you ten or twenty different photographs very quickly and then afterwards questioned what you remembered?"

"When they asked for details in the pictures?"

"Exactly."

Haden and Leni nodded as one—they remembered.

Bob went on. "There was a time when you would have remembered everything in every photograph. You could have said how many blades of grass there were. Or how many clouds were in the sky and described each of their shapes, everything. But I'm not really talking about photographs now—I'm talking about your dreams.

"At the beginning, mankind had two minds. One you could call his day mind, the other the night mind. They complemented each other perfectly and were meant to work in concert. When a problem arose in your daily life that you were unable to solve, normally all you needed to do was go to sleep. Then the night mind, with its different way of perceiving things, would take over and help figure it out. Not always, but much of the time. Using these two together like that kept you more balanced, open to other possibilities and approaches."

"It sounds like that right and left brain theory. You know the one that says each hemisphere of our brain has its specific purpose. One is creative, the other is analytical—"

Bob dismissed her statement with a wave of its big white paw. "No, Leni, it's very different from that. The reason why people have such difficulty understanding life is because it is meant to be comprehended on both a conscious and unconscious level. Imagine your life as a piece of meat that can only be properly eaten if you have both an upper and lower set of teeth to chew it." To demonstrate this, the bear placed its paws together one on top of the other. It flapped them open and closed a few times like a masticating jaw.

Haden wasn't having it. "Most of my dreams are ridiculous. The rest are forgettable."

"You're right—*now* they are, but not in the past."

"How come our two brains don't work together anymore?"

"Chaos." Bob said the word calmly and evenly.

"Explain." Haden looked at Leni to see if she was paying attention. Then he slowly crinkled his nose, narrowed his eyes, and held up a finger for the others to wait a sec while his body decided whether or not it wanted to sneeze. It did. He was one of those sneezers who are so violently loud that they can drown out any sound in a room when they let fly. Leni saw it coming on his face and turned quickly away—she had already experienced Simon's blasts when they were alive.

Turning her head, she happened to look toward a far corner of the stage and saw something that caught her eye. Haden sneezed again. Very curious, Leni got off her stool and limped over to what she had seen. Bending down, she picked a bright yellow rectangular flashlight off the floor. The kind with a handle across the top and which throws a very powerful beam across any darkness. Stuck all over it were decals of Walt Disney characters.

"My God, this *is* it." Cradling the flashlight in both hands she looked at it as if it were a holy object. She was so overwhelmed with emotion that she brought it to her lips and kissed it.

"What is that? What have you got there?" Simon asked in between sniffs.

She held up the flashlight so he could see it and said happily "I haven't seen this for twenty-five years. It saved my life when I was a kid. Is this the one, Bob, the real one?"

"Yes."

"That's so wonderful. I am really glad." She returned to her stool, put the light in her lap, and covered it with both hands.

"What's the big deal about a flashlight, Leni?"

"I was very afraid of the dark when I was a girl. My parents put night-lights in my room, left the door to the hallway open. I slept in their bed with them when things got bad, but nothing really worked.

"One summer I went away to camp. While I was gone my father painted the ceiling of my room a brilliant shade of turquoise and covered it with hundreds of gold stars all about this big." She held up her thumb and index finger to demonstrate that the stars had been about the size of a large coin. "But best of all, he gave me this." She patted the light as if it were a beloved pet. "He told me that whenever I got scared at night, I could turn this flashlight on and point it at that blue sky above me. Then I would see that the only things up there in the dark were gold stars and all of them were my friends.

"Do you know how many times I turned this on to look at those stars when I was little? Probably every night for years, and almost every time it worked. All those perfectly shaped stars. They were my friends and protected me from the dark. I rolled over and went back to sleep."

"Try it now."

Leni could barely contain herself. "Should I?"

"Sure—turn it on and shine it up at the ceiling." Bob's voice and its tone said nothing more than that—*give it a try.*

"Okay." Her thumb slid to the on-off button.

"What about chaos, Bob? I thought you were going to explain that."

"I will in a minute. Go ahead, Leni—do it."

She switched the light on. Its beam leapt across the stage and made a vivid white circle on a far wall. She moved the beam up toward the ceiling.

"My God!"

What first crossed her mind when she saw the scene above them was one of those plastic domes you shake to make a little snowstorm swirl inside. These snowflakes are usually white, but once in a while they're gold or silver. Now Leni felt as if she were inside a snow dome. Because her flashlight lit up a storm of a million different-colored flickers and flakes falling slowly to earth in the air everywhere above them. Astounded, she moved the light beam from here to there, back and forth, left to right across the ceiling above the stage. Everywhere the whole sky was full of glittering shining flakes.

On closer examination, however, she realized something even more wonderful—although they were the size of snowflakes, each one was actually a tiny different Victorian Christmas tree ornament. She knew that on sight because she had been a passionate collector of these ornaments for years and now recognized many as they drifted past.

On impulse she dropped her glance to Bob. The bear stared straight at her, ignoring the storm. The multicolored blizzard of ornament/flakes fell slowly down around them onto the floor. Leni and Haden kept looking back and forth between this dazzle and Bob. But the bear said nothing—it only watched their reactions.

"Put out your hands."

When they did what immediately caught their attention was that none of the flakes that fell on their bodies remained. Any that made contact with them passed straight through their hands, knees, shoulders . . . and kept falling until they reached the floor. They watched these colorful ornaments fall and saw some of them touch but pass right through their bodies as if they were made of air themselves. This delighted Leni. She grinned at her empty open palm, wriggled the fingers, and said "I guess we really are ghosts."

For a while after she spoke it was as silent in that theater as it is on any empty street at 3 A.M. in the middle of a great snowstorm.

In time Bob spoke again. "This is how it began. Don't ask when that was because I don't know. Eight zillion years ago. Five trillion millenniums. Whenever. There *was* a big bang. In fact there have been several big bangs, but I'll get to that in a while.

"Before it blew apart, that was God."

"*What* was God?"

"Everything joined together in one grand design. That was God. But God blew apart, scattering his bits and pieces to every corner of every universe. His bits and pieces *made up* universes." The bear stopped to let the image sink in before continuing. Leni found herself looking closely at the snowstorm falling all around; as if it meant more now because she knew how important a part it played in this story.

"Now imagine every one of those snowflakes is an individual life. That one is a tree and that one is a bug, that one is a person . . . every single flake is a distinct life. Some of these living things are intelligent, some aren't. The bug is smarter than the tree. But that has never mattered until recently. Every thing lives its life, has its experiences, and dies."

"Then what?" Leni spat out.

Haden was surprised by the terse way she asked the question. "Then we all come here, obviously."

"You be quiet. Bob, then what?"

Miffed by her rudeness and the way she had dismissed him, Haden shot back "Look at your feet."

Until then Leni had been so captivated by the snowstorm and watching the polar bear explain God that she had not thought to look down. She did now and what she saw on the floor was startling.

The snowflakes that had fallen had formed and were continuing to form a beautiful abstract design. She had never seen anything like it before, but there was a grace and harmony to the design that was profoundly affecting. Seeing it for the first time was like coming upon an abstract painting in a museum and being so struck by its combination of balance and colors, shapes and emotional weight, that you're held fast and stare at it in a kind of trance.

Almost as amazing was imagining that each flake of the falling snow was a life and appeared to know exactly where to go when it fell toward the floor. The white ones dropped in among the other whites, the blues into the blues, and so on. As the two people stared the layers grew thicker, the colors more vivid and complex.

"What is it?" she asked in a low, reverent voice.

"The mosaic."

"And what is the mosaic?" She addressed Haden now because he had told her to look down and then the name of the miraculous thing at their feet. Obviously he knew what was going on. "How do you know these things, Simon?"

"Because Bob explained it to me before you and I met up. That's why I came to find you."

"What is the mosaic?"

"God reassembled." He glanced at Bob to see if that was a proper way of putting it. The bear nodded its approval.

Holding on to the sides of the stool with her hands, Leni pointed at the mosaic with her foot. "*That's* God?"

Haden started to answer but Bob talked over him. "With the big bang theory scientists say that the universe will continue expanding outward to a certain point. But eventually it will slow, stop, and then begin to return to its source. Eventually it will all coalesce again. The same is true with this.

"There are really two mosaics, Leni: the one that is your life and the larger one that is God. How they happen is similar. When you were born your being exploded out into this new life in every direction. All the experiences you had, all the choices you made, all the different things that went into creating the person you were before you died—"

"I was murdered." Leni paused and then because she couldn't hold it back, she hissed through gritted teeth "I was *murdered!*"

Bob looked away. Even he couldn't take the intensity of her glare then. "Yes, I'm sorry—before you were murdered. However long a person lives, they create a mosaic with their lives like this one on the floor. A singular design that only they could have produced. When you die the first purpose of the afterlife is to learn how to add your unique mosaic, the one you made of your life, to the greater one that is God.

"Put out your hand again and watch it." Leni did as she was told and waited. After a short time a lime green ornament snowflake landed on her outstretched palm and remained. All of the others that touched her continued to pass through her body on their way down. This green flake stayed.

"That one is you," Bob said.

She was inordinately pleased to hear it and found herself grinning at the small green multifaceted object on her hand. She shifted her eyes to the design on the floor. Thinking about what Bob had just said, she wondered where hers belonged in it.

"Look closely at the mosaic now. Do you see the gaps in it—the black spaces sprinkled all over?"

Yes she saw them. More important, once her attention was directed there, Leni noticed something intriguing about these small black gaps scattered around the mosaic: any snow that fell on them melted immediately and disappeared as soon as it touched the blackness. All of these spaces remained empty despite the heavily falling snow.

Bob repeated himself now to make sure she had understood everything. "From time to time a big bang takes place and all of the pieces fly out, but then eventually return. When they come back, they form a different mosaic."

"They're forming a different God?"

"That's right. The distances they've traveled, what's happened to them on their voyages out and back—it changes them. When they do return to form a mosaic, they're different. Your green snowflake might have been white at the beginning of its journey. Like you, Leni—you weren't the same person as a child that you were when you died. So your changed shape and color altered the final design of both you and the greater mosaic."

"God is constantly changing? *God*?" The concept was equally ominous and enthralling to her.

"Yes. Because you change, so does God."

"What happens when all the pieces return and a new mosaic is completed?"

"There will be another big bang and the process starts over again."

It was so complicated yet so simple. Leni could only stare at the remarkable design at her feet while considering what she had heard.

"But there's one more thing and it changes everything."

She forced her eyes from the mosaic to look at Bob. She had not digested the information. It ricocheted wildly around her past and present. Her mind kept applying it to this and this and this, things that had mattered when she was alive. Mysteries that once compelled or puzzled her, significant events that had taken place, experiences that began making sense now because she understood their context.

"For the first time ever, Chaos has become conscious in this mosaic—it is able to think. Chaos was part of every mosaic, but only as a force before, like the weather. But imagine how different life would be if the weather could think."

"What does it mean, Chaos can think? How does that apply to us?"

Tipping his head back, Haden opened his mouth wide. For a few seconds he tried to catch snowflakes on his tongue. In time he turned to her and said, "Imagine what it would be like if lightning didn't *like* you."

"So what?"

"Well Leni, if it didn't, it would come looking for you and hurt you every chance it got. Like those poor people who actually do get hit by lightning six times in their lives. Why is that? Why them? Maybe the real reason is because lightning doesn't *like* them and that's why it keeps striking them again and again."

She looked to see if Bob agreed with this. The bear stared back but said nothing. It wanted her to work through as much of this on her own as possible. If she asked her own questions, came to her own connections and conclusions, then things would proceed much faster.

"All right, forget the weather—what about Chaos?"

"Chaos doesn't want a new mosaic formed because it likes this one; it likes being able to think. So it's doing everything it can to stop a new mosaic from being formed. That's why there are so many empty places in the design down there—because it has already found ways to disrupt the process."

"How?"

Haden chuckled because it was exactly the same one-word question he had asked in the same belligerent tone of voice after hearing the explanation.

Bob said the same thing to her that it had said to Simon. "The simple answer is people. Every individual has their precise place in the mosaic. But if Chaos can transform people into Chaos, then they abandon that place and it remains empty because nothing else fits there."

"Did John Flannery kill me?"

"Chaos killed you and Flannery is part of Chaos."

"If it's so powerful, why doesn't it just change everything to the way it wants?"

"Because it's neither strong enough yet nor is it fully aware of what it's capable of doing. But as it has grown smarter and savvier, it's made people more chaotic. It's made the *world* more chaotic. Soon the balance will tip."

"And what does this have to do with me?"

"You were one of the first people it actively interfered with and changed your fate. Before now it was more indirect; it convinced people to do its bidding, but never actually caused things to happen."

"Why did it choose me?"

Haden said "Because your best friend is Isabelle Neukor."

"What does it have to do with Isabelle?"

"Her child. The baby she's going to have could help stop Chaos. We have to tell her that, and we have to tell her how to do it before it's too late."

"How can you reach her?"

Bob said "Only you can do it. You're going to tell her."

"*Me?* I'm dead."

"True, but there's a way."

Zi Cong Baby Palace

Isabelle didn't know whether to be concerned or annoyed. She and Flora were walking out of the cemetery together. Ettrich was still nowhere to be seen. "Have you seen Vincent?"

"No."

"Neither have I. Not since halfway through the funeral. I have no idea where he went."

Flora didn't care where Vincent went. All she wanted to do was get Isabelle alone so she could describe the vision she'd had earlier of Leni holding up a sign that said GLASS SOUP. It had to mean something.

"That is just strange. Vincent doesn't disappear like that; especially not today."

Flora had told her husband that she was returning to town with Isabelle, but not before stopping off to get something to eat and have a long talk. He squeezed both her shoulders and said he would see her at home. Don't worry about the kids—he'd take care of them. He was such a good man. Times like these, she was reminded again that his greatest quality was he always made her feel loved. Flora wished she loved him more than she did.

The two women left the cemetery and walked down the narrow road back toward Isabelle's car. Where had Vincent gone? Isabelle had forgotten her cell phone at home and was still so distraught by the burial and Vincent's disappearance that she didn't think to borrow Flora's. She wanted to call him right now and give him a blast—*Where are you?*

Flora was wondering whether it would be better to describe her vision of Leni while they were riding in the car and she had Isabelle's undivided attention, or wait until they got to the restaurant and drank a couple of glasses of wine first to settle them down.

Maybe today was also the day to talk about her new lover Kyle Pegg. Just tell her best friend in the world everything about the affair and wait to hear what she had to say about it. Leni's death had suddenly made life feel so urgent; so right-this-moment because there might not be another.

How touching and considerate of Kyle to come to the funeral. She saw him right away but made no sign because her husband was standing nearby. But Flora was deeply grateful for his thoughtfulness and presence. It helped make the burden a little lighter. She honestly never expected Kyle Pegg to show up there. Flora felt his concern and support embrace her. How lucky she was to have two such stand-up guys in her life.

By the time they reached Isabelle's car, Flora still hadn't decided whether or not to spill the beans about him. She couldn't read her friend's face which was only blank and drawn. Flora knew that Isabelle had been closer to Leni than to her. She knew too that although both friends loved her, they thought she was over the top, too much, too often without perspective or clarity on too many matters.

Isabelle rounded the car and stood by the driver's side door, looking at her keys but not really focusing on them. What should she do now? And where was Vincent, damn it? She had no desire to go anywhere now and certainly not to some *Gasthaüs* to listen to Flora prattle on about Leni or her latest personal crisis. Flora was a gem, but there were times like right now when she wanted to be on the opposite side of town from her.

As Isabelle inserted the key into the lock, she looked inside the car. Broximon was sitting on the edge of the backseat. He raised his eyes from the magazine he was reading and waved at her. He closed and then slid his small reading material into an inside pocket because it was a bondage magazine. Better she didn't see that. He had been studying the pictures in an illustrated article titled "Eat, Drink, and Beat Mary."

"Grüss gott, meine damen" he said.

Isabelle said quietly "You're bigger than the last time I saw you."

Flora looked across the roof of the car at Isabelle and frowned. "What did you say? What do you mean, bigger?"

Broximon crossed one leg over the other. "True. They made me a little bigger for this trip."

"And you're *here.* How can you be here, Broximon; how is that possible?"

He ignored the question. "How are you, Isabelle? How was the ceremony?"

"It was all right. How did you get here?"

"By plane."

"By *plane*? You flew here?"

"Yes, there's one flight a week."

"Isabelle, what are you talking about? Who are you talking to?" Flora's voice was high and concerned. She really didn't know what to make of this.

"Flora, could you excuse me for a few moments?"

Flora crossed her arms and then uncrossed them. She looked down to the left, and tapped her foot. What the hell was going on? Why was Isabelle talking to herself? Slowly Flora walked three meters away and pretended to look back toward the cemetery.

"You did not fly here in a plane."

"Yes I did, and you're going to fly back with me"—he shot his cuff and looked at his wristwatch—"in two hours."

"Two hours, really? I'm going to get on a plane and fly away with you—*there?*"

"You must, Isabelle."

"Leave everything and just fly off?"

"You must."

"Why?"

"Because of Anjo. You have to go with me to save your son Anjo."

• • •

Vienna airport is a half-hour ride from the city. Isabelle drove down the autobahn at slightly under the speed limit, her hands unmoving at three and nine o'clock on the steering wheel. Staring straight ahead, she had not said a word the whole trip. Flora sat next to her in the passenger's seat, scared stiff of what to do or say. The only thing she wanted was to get out her phone, call Vincent Ettrich and tell him to come get Isabelle before it was too late. What would happen if she couldn't reach him in time?

Isabelle had been so matter-of-fact about everything. They walked to her car after the funeral, no problem. But the moment she opened the door, she suddenly started talking to someone who wasn't there. Initially Flora thought it was some kind of badly timed joke, a weird diversion intended to take their minds off what they'd just endured and the crushing weight of Leni's loss. However when it became clear that it was not a joke and Isabelle was really talking to ghosts, it was frightening. Flora had never heard the name "Broximon" which Isabelle kept using, but knew very well the equally peculiar "Anjo." It was the name Isabelle and Vincent had chosen for their child.

An even worse moment came when Isabelle asked her to move away from the car so that she could speak to this Broximon phantom alone. Flora walked a few meters and then turned to look back at the cemetery, wondering the whole time how best to contact Vincent without being seen.

Soon Isabelle waved her back over and announced that she must go to the airport right now because she had to catch a plane. Would Flora mind riding out there with her and then driving her car back to town because Isabelle didn't know when she would return?

One of Flora's two best friends was dead and the other was going insane before her eyes.

They were now passing the Schwechat oil refinery, six or seven minutes away from the airport, and then what? *Have a nice trip, Isabelle; see you when you get back from madness?* What was going to happen next kept whizzing around in Flora's head like a spun ball about to drop in a roulette wheel.

All right, yes, Isabelle *had* been acting a little strangely in the last weeks; long before the unexpected horror of Leni's death. But so what? Flora had known Isabelle Neukor for twenty-five years and she *was* an eccentric woman. Of their trio, Leni had always been the rock the other two leaned on, Flora was the diva, and Isabelle the creative but unsteady one. She was not especially fragile and always chose to present herself to the world as a tough guy. But Isabelle was tough only when it was easy and there was no danger. When faced with real difficulties she couldn't take any kind of punch without falling down or running away. Her two friends had felt responsible, always on the lookout for people and situations that might cause her trouble. It was another reason why Flora didn't like the fact that Isabelle and Vincent Ettrich were together now. From her experience Vincent was not a steadfast soul, although in fairness to him she had to admit that since returning to Vienna he had been a model partner. But all of that aside, right now she needed his help no matter how she felt about the man.

Isabelle said just loudly enough to be heard "I can't get over that they actually have a flight from here to there."

Instead of blurting out *What the* fuck *are you talking about?* Flora looked at the chipped fingernail polish on her thumb and mentally counted to ten before responding to Isabelle's weird non sequitur. Before she had a chance to say anything though, the phone rang in her purse.

She stuck a hand into the bag and rummaged around until she found it and lifted it out. "Hello? Oh my God, Vincent! Hi!"

"It's Vincent? Let me talk to him." Isabelle took a hand off the wheel and wiggled her fingers for the phone. "Come on, let me talk." She thrust her arm out impatiently and tried to take it without looking. Because she still had her eyes on the road, she only managed to knock the phone out of Flora's hand onto the floor. It hit and bounced under the passenger's seat.

"Shit! Great. Will you please just drive, Isabelle? Try not to kill us. I'll give it to you in a minute if it isn't broken now." Flora slid forward and reaching under the seat, tried to fish the phone out without looking.

Behind them on the backseat, Broximon had been sitting silently the whole trip keeping an eye on Isabelle. When he heard who was calling he started to move forward. But he had no time to act before the phone flew out of Flora's hand and ended up under her seat.

• • •

Brox was the size of a small dog now. He landed on his feet but the jump down from the seat was farther than he had judged. On landing he winced, feeling the shock all the way up his legs. But he had to get to that phone before Flora did. Dropping to his hands and knees, he scuttled under the seat toward her silver Nokia. He watched as Flora's hand danced around on the floor, her long fingers searching for it here and there. Because he was so close, Broximon heard Ettrich's voice coming out of the small speaker. What was he saying? Could Flora or Isabelle hear it?

• • • • • •

The boys had bought their lunches minutes before and were walking home with them. Those clean white cardboard boxes were still warm in their hands. One of the pizzas had slices of pineapple, goat cheese, and onion spread thickly across the top of it. The restaurant called it their pizza #7, "Hawaii Surprise." It looked disgusting and smelled suspiciously like room freshener, especially after it had cooled awhile. But the kid who bought it loved #7—it was his all-time favorite.

They were in the middle of the pedestrian bridge that crossed over the autobahn. One of them, always the idiot, stretched his arm over his head. The pizza box rested on top of his fingertips like some kind of fancy tray a waiter brought to the table with a flourish. He planned on doing a few show-off things with it up there to impress his sidekick. Unfortunately he quickly lost the balance of the box and in a heartbeat it slid off his fingers and over the side of the bridge into the traffic below.

Flabbergasted by the mad coolness of the gesture, his friend threw *his* pizza box over the side too without a moment's hesitation. But he launched his overhand, as if throwing a shot put.

The two mates looked at each other across an overjoyed split second and then took off running as fast as they could, laughing like loons at the total Dada awesomeness of what they had just done. Nonetheless they weren't about to be caught and punished for the act. Only for the fleetingest of instants did either wonder what would happen when his large lunch landed on a vehicle speeding by on the road below.

Just over the edge of the bridge a lively gust of wind yanked open the first box and then flipped it aside, as if anxious to get to the food. But any pizza dropped from a great height holds together for only so long—sticky cheese or not. On #7, the yellow pineapple pieces were the first to pull off and fall alone. They were big chunks so they dropped pretty fast.

A few seconds later four of them hit the windshield of Isabelle's Land Rover. Each one made a loud hard *splat* before exploding into strings and bits of yellow goo across the safety glass. What little was left slid leisurely down toward where the windshield wipers slept.

An even louder explosion went off above them when the twenty-inch body of the first pizza landed on the rear of the car's metal roof. Isabelle was an excellent driver, steady and focused. But who can be expected to remain steady when attacked from above by plunging pizza and pineapple pieces?

Luckily the car was in the slow lane of the highway. When she veered hard to the right after the first hits no other vehicle was nearby. Even though her seat belt was fastened, Flora's head snapped viciously to one side and then back against the headrest. She yelped from fear and outrage against everything that was happening. But her cry was cut off by the much larger punch of pizza body hitting the roof.

Skittering across the carpeted floor, Flora's cell phone banged into one of her seat's metal struts, bounced, and, small miracle, slid forward until it was directly in front of her right foot. She didn't see it. But Broximon did. He had just gotten back up onto all fours after having been painfully thrown into the seat frame when the car veered to one side. Different parts of his body hurt now but he had to get to that phone. As he moved toward it, Isabelle slammed on the brakes and they stopped abruptly with a jerk and a screech. The phone jumped farther away.

Flora couldn't get out of the car fast enough. The moment it came to a stop she unclipped her seat belt and flinging the door open, swiveled and moved. Her foot kicked the phone aside. Hyper-alert because of their near-accident, Isabelle heard the sound and looked down. There was the phone! Vincent was on that phone. She bent over and grabbed it up ahead of the now forgotten Broximon. There was only chaos around her but just having that phone in her hand, having *him* in her hand, made things better.

"Vincent? Vincent, are you still there?" Phone pressed to her ear, she opened the door and climbed out.

"Yes Iz, I'm here. What's happening? What's going on, are you okay?"

"I don't know." She saw and slowly recognized the pineapple on the windshield. She reached out to touch it to make sure those thick smears were what she thought, but changed her mind and dropped her hand. Looking next at the roof, she saw the pizza mess up there.

"My God."

"What's going on?" His voice was shrill.

"Something just hit my car. I think it was a *pineapple.*" She choked out a bewildered giggle.

"Isabelle, listen to me. Who's in the car with you?"

"Flora."

"Besides Flora—is there anyone else?"

She hesitated.

"Is Broximon with you?"

"Yes. I think he's still here. But how did you know that, Vincent? Do you know him too?"

"It's *not* Broximon. Do you hear me? Get away from him, Isabelle. Get away from the car."

Ten feet away Flora paced back and forth, looking from Isabelle to the traffic speeding by. Their car stood at a strange urgent angle on the shoulder of the autobahn. It looked either like it had been carjacked or for some mysterious reason the driver had pulled over in a hurry, jumped out, and fled.

"What should I do, Vincent?"

"Where are you now? Where's Broximon?"

"I'm standing out on the road. He's still in the car I think. I was driving to the airport. That's what he told me to do. Broximon said—"

Ettrich cut her off. "Forget that. Here's what you do."

When Isabelle disappeared Flora was not facing her. Who knows how that flighty woman would have reacted if she'd actually seen her friend walk a few steps with the phone still pressed to her ear, and then from one instant to the next vanish?

When Flora did turn around to face Isabelle it was to announce *Okay, that's enough, I want to go home now. We can talk about things tomorrow or over the phone or at another time. But right now—*

But right now Isabelle was gone. After Flora saw and absorbed that fact, she called out to her friend first tentatively, then louder. For a while she was certain that Isabelle was still somewhere nearby only just not immediately visible. Like when you take the dog for a walk; look away a moment, it invariably disappears over a hill or around a corner and has to be yelled back. But here they were on a flat stretch of autobahn with no hills or corners to disappear *behind.* No matter how stubbornly she denied it, eventually Flora had to accept the fact Isabelle was gone.

• • •

By the time a taxi pulled off the highway and right up behind the Range Rover eight minutes later, Flora was gone too. In her high heels, silk stockings, and formal dress she had nevertheless managed to climb over a waist-high concrete safety barrier and down across a muddy ditch toward civilization.

Vincent Ettrich got out of the cab and walked straight to Isabelle's car. His taxi pulled away and back into traffic. Opening the door to the Rover, he saw Broximon sitting on top of the dashboard, back to the windshield. He acknowledged Ettrich by giving a half-hearted salute with two fingers to his forehead. "Hey Vincent. Do you know who I am?"

Ettrich nodded. He had been told in great detail about Broximon.

"You're late."

"She's gone?"

Brox shifted his ass to a more comfortable position. "She's gone. Both women are gone. I didn't think Flora had it in her but by God, she just climbed right over that wall and kept on moving. I assume she's going home."

Furious, Ettrich slapped his hand down on the roof of the car. "Damn it! If I'd just had a few more minutes . . . I would have gotten here and this wouldn't have happened. I would have stopped her."

"I don't think so, Vincent. It was done too fast. They knew exactly what they were doing. As soon as Flora's telephone rang I knew it was them. And I knew they'd try some kind of trick, but I never imagined they'd use your voice as bait. That was genius. Of course she went when she heard *you*. She got out of the car with the phone, took a few steps and zip—she was gone. They tricked her into choosing to go there. She couldn't have done it on her own because Isabelle doesn't have that power anymore. They told her she was in danger and the only safe place to hide was over there. She said I want to go and that was it—her choice. She probably thought you were helping her. And I was fooled because I thought once I got her out of town she'd be safe."

Ettrich sighed, and stared into the distance. "Maybe. Maybe you're right, but I would like to have tried, damn it. What could they have said to her to get her to go over there so fast?"

"I don't know."

"What happens to you now, Broximon?"

The little man carefully brushed nothing off his knee. "What happens to me? Nothing. I stay here now. I can't go back. They told me that when I volunteered to do this. I'm stuck here for good. Your world is my new home whether I like it or not. Do you know of any nice apartments for rent?" Brox tried to keep the irony and sadness out of his voice but Vincent heard both. He knew what a great sacrifice it had been for Broximon to come over here to try and save Isabelle. It must be especially miserable for him now that he had failed and knowing there was no going home.

Ettrich sat down in the driver's seat and pulled the door closed.

After it slammed shut he took a deep breath and let it out long and loudly.

Broximon studied his expression and guessed correctly what he was thinking. "You can't follow her there, Vincent, so don't even think about doing that. Isabelle *chose* to go over. The living can visit death as often as they like if they know how. The dead can't, and you know that."

Ettrich slid a hand into his breast pocket, took out a pair of black eyeglasses, and put them on. Reaching for the keys still dangling from the ignition, he started the motor. "I can't just sit here and wait for her to come back; *hope* that she'll find a way to come back. I can't do that, Brox. If I do I'll go crazy."

"If you go there now, Vincent, you can't return. Isabelle brought you back from the dead once. But if you go there now then you'll have to stay. That won't help anything—not you, not her, and not your child."

"Well what am I supposed to do?"

Broximon was encouraged that Vincent had at least asked the question. "For now? Just wait. Wait and see what develops. There were three people at that funeral who understood what glass soup really meant: you, Isabelle, and the guy who calls himself either John Flannery or Kyle Pegg, depending on who he's with. You know who Flannery is now, don't you?"

Ettrich nodded. "Yes, I found out back there." He gestured with a finger toward the direction he had just come from.

"Right—because you had to know.

"The three of you have experienced life after death. But you and Flannery know more about it than she does. It will take time for her to understand it more completely."

"She knows about the mosaic, Broximon. We've talked about it a lot. And she has experienced death; at least *my* death."

"But not her own and that's the difference. It's a whole other thing. Right now she's in Simon Haden's after-death world. Before, she was in yours. Both times for her it's been like going into someone else's house and not knowing where anything is—not the bathroom or the kitchen. . . ." Broximon looked at Ettrich and saw that nothing he'd said so far had helped. "But there's good news too, Vincent; something incredibly important. Isabelle *saw* me. Flora didn't. No one else at that funeral would have either, even though they all saw Leni holding up that sign.

"But Isabelle saw me and talked to me, which means—"

Ettrich finished Broximon's sentence "—she can see in both worlds now and they overlap for her."

"Exactly, and that is a *huge* advantage for her. Chaos has to hate it particularly because it means things are more equal now. It will have to play on a much more even field with her. Isabelle may not realize it for a while, but she's become a redoubtable opponent, Vincent. You can be sure that she makes them nervous."

Ettrich pulled his ear. "Redoubtable. What does that mean?"

"It means kick ass, my friend. It means your woman has got game now."

• • • • • •

"You take off clothes. Lie down on table."

Unpleasant music played while Isabelle undressed. It was the kind of kitschy, cloying Muzak one invariably hears playing in the background at Chinese restaurants. High-pitched, single-stringed twinging and twanging.

"Take off everything? Even my underwear?"

"No, no—keep underpant on. Underpant and bra." The doctor spoke impatiently, not once looking up from the notes she was writing on her clipboard. Whenever this small thin woman spoke it sounded like a command. Isabelle was cowed but intrigued at the same time.

When she had undressed, she lay down bit by bit on the white examining table. Although it was covered with a cotton sheet, the table was chilly. Cold enough to make her shiver.

The doctor finished writing and put the clipboard down silently on the desk. That was another thing Isabelle had noticed about this woman: when she spoke it was to command, but everything else she did silently. The contrast between the two traits was disconcerting. "Now we look at Zi Cong Baby Palace, huh?"

Isabelle lifted her head off the table and looked at the doctor. "What did you say?"

To her surprise, the doctor reached down and put a small warm hand on her stomach and gently patted it. "This is your Zi Cong Baby Palace. That's what we call it in Chinese medicine. You call it wum."

"Wum?" Unconsciously Isabelle began to smile. She couldn't help it. What was a wum?

The doctor saw nothing funny in this and patted her stomach again. "Wum. You-tore-us."

"Uterus. Oh yes, the *womb!*"

"Yes—wum."

This memory of her initial visit to the Chinese doctor in Vienna lifted Isabelle's spirits and made her feel better for the first time since arriving here. *Arrive* was not really the accurate word though. *Appeared* was better, or *materialized.* As had happened every time in the past, she moved from her world and reality to this one with the ease of turning her head from left to right. One moment she was standing next to the autobahn near Schwechat, talking on a cell phone to Vincent. A blink later she was sitting at a large outdoor sidewalk café eating a bowl of lousy chocolate pudding with nuts and thinking about her baby palace. She stared across the street at a storefront that had a sign above the door announcing: TRADITIONAL CHINESE MEDICINE. Seeing that sign had handed her a lovely bouquet of memories of the first days of her pregnancy. She reveled in them.

She said the word *wum* now under her breath and then spooned up some more of the chocolate pudding. She did not like chocolate pudding and this bowl of it was bad. Too thin and watery, it had the consistency of a sluggish milk shake and with the added insult of nuts mixed in. On the other hand, pregnancy had given Isabelle a sweet tooth the likes of which she had never experienced before and any kind of sugar these days was okay with her.

Wedged between the salt and pepper shakers in the middle of the table was a menu. She reached over and picked it up. Perhaps there was something a bit more appetizing to eat at this place. Still, judging from the tasteless pudding, eating here was dubious. The menu was black with neat white script lettering. Opening it, she was more than surprised to see that it offered only two things—chocolate pudding and lima bean soup.

Lima bean *soup?*

Isabelle put the menu back in its place and looked again at the Chinese medicine building across the street. As far as she knew, there was nothing else to do here now, so she allowed her mind to slip back into daydreaming about her first visit to the Chinese doctor.

Petras Urbsys had recommended the acupuncture treatments. He gave her the name of his doctor after hearing that she felt listless and tired much of the time. She was not usually an alarmist but had begun to wonder if this lethargy was due to her pregnancy. Isabelle had never done anything like acupuncture before so she was hesitant to go at first but later grew to enjoy it. For three or four days after each treatment she felt revitalized and vibrant with residual energy. The doctor was a stern no-nonsense woman who clearly knew her business and made Isabelle feel like she was in safe hands.

Across the street the front door of the building she had been watching swung open and a woman walked out. Nondescript, middle-aged, dressed in beige, there was not one reason to notice her. Isabelle didn't for several seconds while continuing to daydream about her acupuncture treatments. Finally some part of her brain shook her and said *Look who's there.* She straightened and focused her attention on this anonymous woman who was already halfway down the block.

Realizing who it was, Isabelle stood and hurried after her because she had to talk to that woman. For the first time in Simon Haden's dreamworld she had recognized someone she knew! It was astounding, and even more so considering whom that person was.

As she was about to step down off the curb into the street, a white bull terrier with one black ear pedaled by on a small red tricycle. Isabelle guessed who it was too because Simon had once told her at mind-numbing length about his beloved boyhood bull terrier Floyd. At any other time she would have called out the dog's name and tried to stop it. Maybe in this strange place dogs talked and she could find out valuable things. But at the moment she couldn't let that woman escape. After the dog had pedaled past, she rushed across the street.

Simon Haden was unquestionably a selfish, immoral man. Yet he had once done something wholly out of character that Isabelle always liked him for very much. One Saturday morning several years before, her phone had rung and out of the blue it turned out to be Simon. He was in town for two days with his mother. Isabelle thought he was joking but he wasn't. He wanted her to meet his mom and asked if she would join them for coffee and cake at Café Demel on the Kohlmarkt.

Arriving there an hour later, she saw Simon talking animatedly to an unfriendly looking sourpuss of a woman dressed in clothes so uniformly beige and nondescript that she almost faded into the background of that sumptuously ornate café.

When Simon saw Isabelle coming, he stood up and with great enthusiasm and fanfare, introduced her to his mother. Beth Haden took Isabelle's hand and looked at her as uninterestedly as one would look at a choice of brooms in a market. The next hour with mother and son was both a bore and a surprising testament to filial love.

Beth Haden had been widowed five months before. She was living alone now in a retirement community in North Carolina. She liked nothing. She had no friends, no hobbies, and no ambitions. Everything in her life was either flawed, flat, suspect, or not worth the effort. She inherited some money when her husband died but had no plans for spending it. What for? She didn't need anything and there was nothing she wanted.

At which point Simon interrupted her and said sweetly "That isn't true, Mom. There was something you wanted and now that you're actually here, you have it: Europe." All her life Mrs. Haden had dreamed of going to Europe after having read the Lanny Budd books of Upton Sinclair when she was a girl. Throughout their marriage she had periodically and pointedly told that wish to her husband who either ignored it or said don't be ridiculous.

At his father's funeral, Simon put his arm around her and said "Ma, let's go to Europe together for a few weeks—just you and me. There's nothing stopping you now. We'll go anywhere you want. I'll be your traveling companion." His mother looked at him like *he* was being ridiculous now, but in due course she agreed.

When Isabelle met them in the café that day, they had been in Europe for two weeks and Mrs. Haden hated it. Everything was too expensive. The food was too hot or too cold, unsalted, unsavory, or untrustworthy. In Greece she had seen things hanging in butcher shop windows that would give her nightmares for the rest of her life. European beds were lumpy, drivers were insane, the toilet paper felt like tree bark, and everyone smoked everywhere. There was no escaping it. She said all of this in a monotone of relentless woe that soon had Isabelle fighting back laughter. It was the first time in her life that she had ever encountered a true misanthrope. Most people liked something, but apparently not Simon's mom. Feeling reckless and naughty, Isabelle asked Beth how she'd liked the Louvre (too crowded), the Spanish Steps (crawling with hippies on drugs), the Parthenon (not much there left to see), and the Viennese opera? It was a bore.

As a final experiment, Isabelle ordered a slice of her favorite cake in the world which by nice coincidence was a Demel exclusive and served only there. All her life she'd eaten that cake and if it didn't belong on God's table in Heaven then no food did. Yes, it was that sublime. When the cake arrived she slid it across the table to Mrs. Haden and said she must try it. Beth did not hesitate reaching forward with a fork and gouging off a hefty piece. Isabelle caught Simon's eye and gave him an assured thumbs-up.

After swallowing her piece of the greatest cake in the universe, Mrs. Haden lay the fork down just so next to her plate. "It's flavorsome. But I'm no great fan of hazelnuts."

• • •

Add to that she walked like a fast duck. Hurrying to catch her now, Isabelle watched Beth Haden move up the street in a kind of determined waddle. Well maybe not a waddle, but her feet pointed out to the sides whenever they landed, giving her a marked side-to-side gait.

When close enough to be heard, Isabelle called out "Mrs. Haden? Beth? Wait, Mrs. Haden. Please."

The woman stopped but did not turn around. Isabelle caught up with her and walked a few steps farther so that without turning Beth could see who was calling her name.

"Mrs. Haden, do you remember me? My name is Isabelle Neukor. We met a few years ago in Vienna when you were there with your son. I'm a friend of Simon."

Beth Haden said nothing. She was waiting to hear more.

"We all had coffee together in Vienna at the Café Demel when the two of you were traveling in Europe."

Mrs. Haden's face relaxed. "Oh yes, Isabelle! You're the one who had the delicious cake. Now I remember you. And do I ever remember that cake! Mmm. What was it called again?"

"You mean the marzipan *nusstorte?*"

"Yes, *nusstorte.* That's right. It was the most delectable sweet I ever had in my entire life. I'm so grateful you made me taste it. I've always remembered that bite."

Right off the bat Isabelle was nonplussed. Even the word *delectable* sounded wrong. Grumpy people find nothing in the world delectable. Judging by their previous meeting, Beth Haden was 101 percent grump.

"What are you doing here, Isabelle? Are you looking for Simon? He's coming to lunch today. Why don't you come too? I'm making my lima bean soup which is his favorite meal on this planet. Lima bean soup for lunch, chocolate pudding for dessert." Mrs. Haden laughed. It was a delightful laugh—light and full of happiness.

Isabelle became even more bewildered. She felt the urge to step closer to this woman to see if she was an imposter, a fake Beth Haden who now laughed freely like a cheerful girl and remembered tasting another's "delectable" cake years later.

"Come on, you can help me make the soup. Have you ever tasted lima bean soup, Isabelle? It's really very good."

• • •

They didn't have far to walk. Four blocks down, a left and a right and they were standing in front of a nice split-level house on a large plot of land.

Curious, Isabelle asked "Is this where Simon grew up?" She remembered hearing that Mrs. Haden had sold the house and moved to a retirement condo in North Carolina.

Beth shifted her purse from one hand to the other so that she could unlock the front door. "Yes, it is. Would you like to see his room?"

Simon did not come for lunch that day but it didn't appear to bother his mother very much. She rolled her eyes and said she was used to it—no big deal. The two women made the soup together, set the table, then sat down and talked while they waited for him.

Unlike the first time they'd met when she'd only reeled off that cranky harangue about Europe and then fallen silent, today Beth Haden was a charming chatterbox. She talked about her life, her acupuncture treatments, her garden, and the new grocer at the market she was convinced was making eyes at her. She spoke nonstop, in striking contrast to the last time they had met. Most of what she said was entertaining even if 99 percent of it was about herself. Now and then Isabelle threw in a question or comment, but it wasn't necessary because Simon's mother had so much to say and a willing listener.

Eventually she got around to asking "Why are you here, Isabelle? Don't you live in Vienna?"

"I do, but I'm looking for your son. I need to talk to him."

Beth glanced at her wristwatch and shook her head. "I don't think he's coming. And I was sure we'd fixed it for today. But this isn't the first time Simon has skipped one of our dates. You know kids; sometimes they forget or have other things to do. . . ." It was a rebuke but much more love and forgiveness were in her voice than scold. She adored her son—that was very evident.

Something was wrong here but only after Beth had spoken did Isabelle grasp what it was. In Vienna that day at the café after having finished every last crumb of his cake, Simon had pointedly said to Beth "Look, Ma, I cleaned my plate."

Crabby Mrs. Haden glanced at it, gave a small *humph,* and lifted one shoulder in dismissal. Simon smirked and said to Isabelle "Its an in-joke between us. When I was a kid there were two absolute laws in our house that could not be broken: I had to come for a meal as soon as I was called, and I had to eat everything on my plate or else I was slapped."

"Slapped?" Isabelle had never heard of any parent doing such a thing to a child.

"That is correct. My mother gave me exactly seven minutes to get to the table. She would even time it. I could be playing ball a mile away, but if I wasn't at the table in seven minutes—wham-o. Then I had to eat everything that was on my plate and there were no exceptions. Even if it was brussels sprouts in hot vinegar, if I didn't eat it all—"

Mrs. Haden smiled slightly and said "You were slapped."

"That's right, Ma, and it happened more than once, remember? You guys were pretty tough on your son." He patted her arm.

Irate, Isabelle snapped "That's nuts!"

"No, that's the way to teach a child respect."

"No, Mrs. Haden, that's nuts. You should be ashamed of yourself. Will you excuse me?" Isabelle got up and marched off to the toilet without being excused.

Today this same child-slapping, disagreeable woman was as sweet and fluffy as cotton candy and sounded only wistful that her son had once again been rude enough to stand her up for lunch. Something was too wrong with this picture. Yet Isabelle knew from her previous visits that there were no rules in this place and looking for them or any logic at all was useless.

Lacking for something to say, she thoughtlessly scratched with her index finger at a black spot on the white kitchen table. It looked like a bit of old food. The black came away easily, as if she were scratching away a makeup smudge. Beneath it was a grass-green color. As she kept scratching, more of that green appeared. What was this? Why did the paint come off so easily?

Slightly more curious, Isabelle scraped a larger and larger area, first with her index finger and then growing more industrious, with her thumb. Green.

Flattening her hand on the table, she vigorously rubbed her palm in a large circle. In seconds the white was gone and there was only that green beneath it. Looking over at Beth for an explanation, she was startled to see tears glistening on the other's cheeks.

"Green was the real color of this table, not white. It was never white. This kitchen was never white. Simon changed almost the whole house. There's so little left of what it was really like when we lived here. It's almost unrecognizable."

"I don't understand." Isabelle sat back.

"Me, his father, even the color of this table . . . Simon changed everything when he reimagined his life after he died: us, the colors, the furniture. Nothing is the way it really was. He must have hated everything, Isabelle. There's so little left of the real us and the life we lived together. Simon changed it all when he died and created this world from his memories.

"In this world we're the way he always *wanted* us to be, but not the way we were. Like this table—it was never white, it was green. Our kitchen table was green. I even remember the day we bought it on sale."

"Why are you allowed to tell me this?"

Beth shrugged one shoulder exactly the same way she had in Vienna that day. "Because you're not Simon. Every one of his creations here knows the truth. He's the only one who doesn't. This place is full of lies and illusions and tricks and mirages . . . but they're all Simon's illusions. Until he realizes that, he stays trapped here."

Isabelle had nothing to lose so she said exactly what she'd been thinking to Beth. "If you were a terrible mother, then Simon has every right to change you here. It's almost a compliment—he still wants you in his thoughts. But not the woman who hit him when he didn't come to dinner on time. I'd change you too if I were him. Sometimes lies save us."

Instead of answering or defending herself, Simon's mother only stared at Isabelle and after a while slowly nodded.

• • • • • •

When Vincent Ettrich rang Flora's doorbell two hours after the funeral, she was alone in her living room sitting on the couch in brand-new La Perla silk underwear and listening to Otis Redding sing "I've Been Loving You Too Long." Flora had several ways of ridding herself of tension and these happened to be two of them. She loved expensive underwear. She loved the feel of it, the naughtiness that went along with buying some when she knew a new lover's eyes were going to see her in it, the sheer sinful indulgence of spending a preposterous amount of money for something that weighed as much as a sparrow and took up about as much space in the universe. In most other aspects of her life she was unexpectedly practical and thrifty, but not when it came to her underwear, especially "stress underwear" as she referred to it. Sometimes when she was in a good mood she would even buy some and store it away for a bad day. Like today: the first thing she had done on returning to her empty house was take off her clothes and change into the unworn lingerie she had bought in Rome three months before. "Whenever I feel a nervous breakdown coming on, I buy lingerie," she had said many times. This retail therapy must have worked because Flora had many bras and panties but not one nervous breakdown.

And listening to the music of Otis Redding was like an antibiotic for her soul. She felt her problems were a joke when compared to those of anyone who was singing that sadly. Invariably after listening to one or two of his albums she felt the clouds lift from her heart.

Flora was the kind of uninhibited woman who had no compunction about answering the door in her underwear and that's exactly what she did now. When she saw who was there she made a face but felt no embarrassment about her exposed body. God knows, Ettrich had seen her in less. "Vincent."

"Hi. Nice underwear. I used to know a woman who owned a lingerie store. Can I come in?"

"It's really not a good day for a visit, Vincent. I'm sure you understand with the funeral and everything."

He looked at her coldly and gently pushing Flora out of his way, stepped into her house. "We have to talk about your friend Kyle Pegg."

• • •

When Ettrich left the cemetery that morning he knew what *glass soup* meant, but did not know where he was going. He would insist on that later when asked to recount exactly what had happened. He saw Leni hold up the sign with those two words on it and immediately knew that he must leave the cemetery. He could not say why; he only knew that he had to go.

But what about Isabelle, what was she going to think about his abandoning her in the middle of the funeral? That was a problem but there were other, more pressing concerns that needed to be handled first. She would just have to trust that he'd left for a good reason.

On reaching their car he took out the keys but while unlocking the door he stopped, frowned, and raised his head. From afar it looked like someone had called his name and he was reacting—except for the fact his eyes were closed. Ettrich had heard a voice inside himself distinctly say *Go into the woods.* Nothing more. When he opened his eyes it was to look at the forest directly across the road.

The village of Weidling is at the very beginning of the Wienerwald, the Vienna Woods. To this day they are fairy tale woods—dark, deep, and endless. They cover five times more land than the combined boroughs of Manhattan. It is easy to get lost in them despite the fact they are only a half-hour drive from downtown Vienna. Both Vincent and Isabelle loved walking there together and often did. The starkness that the shadows and silence of the forest evoked was a perfect contrast to walking there with someone you loved.

Ettrich did not question why he heard this voice now or the order it gave. He dropped the car keys back in his pocket, crossed the narrow country road, and walked toward the woods.

More than ever before, he had grown to trust this inner voice as well as his instincts and hunches. He had been brought back from the dead by Isabelle. Why? Because of their unborn son Anjo. Perhaps it was Anjo who was talking to him now, telling him what to do. Perhaps Anjo was behind all of the otherness Ettrich had been experiencing recently; even Leni Salomon's message to him from Death. *Glass soup.*

Vincent entered the woods and the temperature immediately

dropped to a coolness that felt like fall. Air that only a moment before had smelled of dry earth and high summer was now damp, thick, and fecund.

Hands on hips, he did what he always did on entering a forest—craned his head back and looked straight up. He loved watching sunlight flicker through the leaves of the trees. Whatever he was meant to do could wait a minute while he watched the play of light and dappling of colors high overhead.

He began walking. He had no idea where he was going or what he was supposed to do here but walking felt right. Although he didn't know it then, while Vincent moved deeper and deeper into the forest, Leni Salomon's funeral ended. Her two best friends walked back to the car where Broximon waited for Isabelle.

Ettrich walked for about an hour before stopping to look around. There was still no sign or indication of why he had been told to come in here, but he was all right with that. There had to be a reason, he was convinced, and eventually it would reveal itself to him. A distant bird sang and the sun, flirting down through the trees, lit the ground here and there.

He had passed only one other person as he walked deeper into the forest—an old man who smiled warmly and tipped his Tyrolean hat at Ettrich.

He had no idea where he was. Mounted on individual trees throughout the forest were markers from the Austrian Hiking Club that said things like FROM THIS POINT, IT IS A THREE-HOUR WALK TO THE ALMHUTTE. But that did Vincent no good because he had no idea where the Almhutte was or any of the other posted destinations in relation to Weidling or Vienna. From Ettrich's perspective the signs might just as well have said THREE HOURS TO ZANZIBAR.

A few times frantic thoughts stampeded through his mind like What the fuck *am* I doing here? But he pushed them all away by constantly reminding himself he had heard the voice.

KYSELAK was written on a tree several feet in front of him. Ettrich's mind was so full of the surroundings that it took time to register what he was seeing. When it did, what first crossed his mind was What kind of fool would go to the trouble of carving his name on a tree this deep in the woods? Who was ever going to see it? That's what the conscious part of his mind thought. The unconscious part, which was awakened by the glass soup sign, declared without hesitation: I know that name. Where do I know it from?

He walked over to the tree and stopping in front of it, tried to fish up where he had seen this strange name before. KYSELAK. Carved in crude block letters, almost childlike in their earnest simplicity, the name had to have been done long ago because the letters were very faded and the bark had grown up around them. A few more years and the letters would be absorbed back into the texture of the tree. This man-made scar would have healed and become nearly invisible.

Kyselak. The autographist. The signature on the wall in Vienna that Isabelle had been so eager to show him the first night they met. The eccentric who wrote his name on everything and got into trouble with the emperor as a result. Ettrich had inadvertently found an original Kyselak!

He turned his head from side to side, thrilled and grinning, wanting to share this with someone. But there were only the trees, the sunlight and shadows, and they were all indifferent. How happy Isabelle would have been to make this marvelous discovery with him. Vincent missed her terribly then.

To compensate for being alone, he reached forward and slid his left hand over the tree, then the signature. He ran his fingers over and around, then down into the carving. Like a blind man reading braille, Ettrich felt the seven letters of the other man's name on his skin. A line from a television commercial he had watched as a boy came to him: "Let your fingers do the walking through the Yellow Pages." He let his fingers walk across Kyselak's autograph. They said to it *How do you do?*

To amuse himself and fill the silence that surrounded him, Vincent said out loud "How do you do?"

"Quite well, thank you" Joseph Kyselak answered. He was sitting on the same rock Ettrich had used moments ago while resting. Kyselak wore the style of clothes and long fanciful sideburns that men favored in early nineteenth-century Vienna.

"We were worried that you wouldn't find us, Vincent."

"Were you the one back there who told me to walk into these woods?"

Kyselak smiled. "No. They've been giving you instructions for ages but you've never heard them. Today was the first time. Congratulations."

"It was probably because of Leni. Seeing her message." Ettrich pointed toward the cemetery.

"*Everything* has been a message to you since you were brought back to life, Vincent. The food you ate, the color of the clouds, my autograph on that tree . . . The list is very long."

"I didn't know."

"That's all right, because now you do." Kyselak's voice was jovial and unconcerned.

Ettrich lifted his chin toward the name on the tree. "Did I find this just now or did it find me? I mean, did someone steer me here or did I find it on my own?"

Kyselak crossed his legs. "Totally on your own. That's what they wanted to find out—whether you are really awake now. It's clear by this that you are."

Vincent's nose itched. He took his hand off the tree to scratch it. The moment he did, Kyselak disappeared. Like *that* he was gone. Ettrich's reaction on seeing this was no different from Flora's out on the autobahn when she saw that Isabelle was gone. The difference between them was Ettrich, unlike Flora, knew exactly what to do in response. He put his hand back on the tree and Kyselak promptly reappeared, still sitting on his rock.

"Very good, Vincent. Very, very good."

Ettrich looked at his hand against the tree. He understood that by making contact with it, he touched the tree's entire history. He had brought it all into this moment to see, including Kyselak who had carved his name into it so long ago.

Ettrich tried something like this earlier when he showed Isabelle her hand's past, present, and supposed future. But now that he understood how to do it properly, he knew it was not possible to show the future because it doesn't exist yet, not even in time. Isabelle's missing finger was only one of many future possibilities for her.

What a person *could* do was see the past and present at the same moment if he knew how to perceive time the correct way. Ettrich was doing it right now: here he was, talking to a man who had cut his name into this tree almost two centuries ago.

"Can you do it to yourself now?"

"I don't understand."

Kyselak stretched his arms behind him on the stone and leaned back on them. "What you're doing with the tree—experiencing its whole history, seeing everything about it. Can you do that to yourself?"

The question frightened Vincent. "I think I can but to tell you the truth, the thought scares the shit out of me."

"You don't want to see what made you what you are? You don't want to see your life as it really was, or is?"

Despite his anxiety, Ettrich half smiled when he remembered something. "The truth mirror."

"What's that?"

"I had a teacher in high school who used to talk about a truth mirror. He told us to imagine a mirror that when you look in it, it shows you the absolute truth about who you are—both the good and the bad. It was like God—it knew everything about you and wouldn't lie. We talked about it a lot in class. Then he asked how many of us would want to try it. Not many raised their hands."

"Did you, Vincent?"

"No."

"Ramses the Great of Egypt had a tame lion named Slayer of His Foes. Did you know that?"

Ettrich was taken aback. He had no idea what Kyselak was talking about. Ramses the Great? A tame lion?

"No. Uh no, I didn't know that."

"He did and so do you. You have a Slayer of Your Foes too. A very powerful one."

Ettrich spoke carefully. "I'm not getting this. I don't really understand."

"You have a lion too, Vincent; it's in you and part of you. A Slayer of Your Foes. That lion led you to this place in the forest. It told you to touch my autograph on the tree and then how to summon me. It can do miraculous things if you learn what else it is capable of doing; if you learn what *you're* capable of doing. Bringing me back now is only a sample of that.

"But your lion doesn't come when you call. It's not tame yet. To make that happen, you have to look in your truth mirror and see who you really are. There's no other way, Vincent.

"You can't know what you're capable of if you don't know who you are. You know what life is and you know what death is. You even know what *Glass Soup* means. It's time to learn what else Vincent Ettrich knows in every corner of his soul. Get past the good and evil in you. That's the small stuff. Find the immortal parts."

• • •

It didn't take long. It took no time at all to do what Kyselak recommended. A short while later Vincent Ettrich walked out of the forest near where he had entered it. He saw that his car was gone but that didn't disturb him. He knew Isabelle was with Broximon and that she was safe for the moment.

He walked onto the road and turned right in the direction of

Weidling. It would take him about fifteen minutes to walk into town but that was good. It would allow him time to organize his thoughts and hopefully figure some things out now that he saw the world and his life with new eyes.

He walked on the shoulder of the road with his head down while the occasional car drove past nearby. He did not notice the lovely small *Jugendstil* villas tucked away among the trees, or the centuries-old wood-and-stone farmhouses that were a reminder that these surroundings had once been rural countryside, easily a day's journey from Vienna. If he had wanted to, Ettrich could have stopped at any of those buildings and by touching a wall seen what life had once been like there.

In the courtyard of one small farmhouse, he could have witnessed the winter day in 1945 when invading Russian troops shot the thin family horse and then feasted on its steaming body. Or several houses down, Franz Schubert sitting in the lush garden on a sunny day, feeling peaceful and well for the first time in months. Ettrich was able to see such things now but knew he must concentrate on how best to save Isabelle and Anjo from Chaos.

A taxi driver who lived on that road was just beginning his shift and driving to Vienna. He was surprised to see a man in a dark suit waving him down. People who lived out here didn't often wear suits or use taxis. They either had their own cars, bicycled, or walked. The driver was delighted when this customer with the American accent said in good German that he wanted to go to the airport. A long ride from there, it meant a fat fee. This was a nice way to start off the day.

The driver, whose name was Roman Palmsting, would begin to regret this ride about halfway through it. As they passed the Urania Theater in downtown Vienna on the way to the airport, the passenger began talking to himself.

Palmsting had lousy hearing because he spent too much time listening to loud vintage heavy-metal music on a cheap Walkman.

When he first heard the man behind him mumbling, he thought he was being given instructions. The driver resented it when a fare did that. Because he prided himself on being honest. Never once in a fifteen-year career had he taken the long or wrong route anywhere just to make a little more money on a fare.

"Excuse me?" he asked, glancing in the rearview mirror. The passenger was looking out the window and saying something. Palmsting raised his eyebrows and looked back at the road. He assumed that if this guy really wanted to get his attention then he would repeat what he'd said.

Until two minutes ago Ettrich had forgotten about the set of keys Isabelle had given him to her apartment and car. Because they were the only thing of hers he carried with him, he took them out of his pocket and held them in his hand like a good luck charm while he looked out the window.

Almost immediately information came to him like signals on a radio so powerful that it receives too many stations at once. It sounds like gobbledygook until you fine-tune it. Ettrich realized that when he took the keys in hand, he was wondering where Isabelle was and what she was doing. He was finding out now, but there was so much Isabelle coming in that he could only decipher a fraction of it.

All of this was so new to him. It would take time to learn all that he was capable of doing now. He wanted things to stop or at least slow down so that he could get his bearings. But from all indications it appeared that it went at its own speed and too bad if you couldn't keep up.

Something came to him that was so strange he had to say it out loud just to hear it. "Zi Cong Baby Palace." Ettrich enunciated each word slowly and crisply. Then he said them again, this time as a question. "Zi Cong Baby Palace? What the hell is that?"

The taxi driver looked at him for a long time in the rearview mirror.

Images rushed through Ettrich's mind in the course of a few seconds: a small hand patting a bare stomach. An Oriental woman in a white doctor's lab coat. Some other Caucasian woman dressed in beige. A hand on a white table. A vivid shade of green. A photograph of Simon Haden. The woman in beige again, only now she was crying.

"I don't get it. I don't get it." Ettrich raised a helpless hand to the car window, as if gesturing to someone on the other side of the glass to wait a minute.

Roman Palmsting looked in the rearview again and pursed his lips. He began figuring out what to do if this passenger was crazy and started acting weird or dangerous or worse. A traffic light ahead turned from green to yellow and he shifted his attention back to the street. He didn't see Ettrich's mouth drop open and then the man slump back against the seat, defeated. But Palmsting did hear the other squawk in dismay "No! She didn't go there; she can't."

Several minutes later Ettrich told the driver to pull off the autobahn behind a Range Rover that was parked at a strange angle on the shoulder of the road. Palmsting was happy to oblige and once paid, happy to drive away. The last picture he had of this strange passenger was of the man in a suit leaning on the open door of the Range Rover, talking to someone inside. But from what Palmsting could see, there was no one inside that car. This lunatic was just talking to himself again. Naturally the taxi driver could not see the very small man sitting on the dashboard of that car, listening intently to Vincent Ettrich.

• • • • • •

John Flannery was writing in his journal when the doorbell rang. He stopped, capped the silver fountain pen, and read what he had just written: *Up close, most women's pussies look like a piece of chewed gum.*

Flannery liked keeping a daily journal and had been doing it for years. He saw himself as a flaneur, a boulevardier, a keen observer and appreciator of life on earth and mankind in particular. He liked people, he really did. He had no hesitation killing any of them or making their lives miserable, but generally he got a big kick out of mankind and had no complaints about working with them.

Behind him he heard the Great Dane walk to the door and wait there as it always did when someone rang the bell. Flannery despised that dog more every day but there was nothing he could do about it. When he'd been assigned here, Luba had been sent to accompany him as a so-called partner. It meant that they still didn't trust him fully although he had never done anything to merit their distrust. He was a good soldier—followed orders and never complained. But what was his reward? A dog the size of an aircraft carrier that watched Flannery's every move and tattled on him at least once a month. Luckily Flora Vaughn detested dogs so she'd never seen this one when she came over.

John Flannery kept two apartments in Vienna: the small place near the Danube Canal where Leni visited him. And this one, in a different district three miles away, which was leased to Kyle Pegg. Pegg's place was much nicer and he spent most of this time here. It was on the top floor of a nineteenth-century building with a wide view of the eastern part of the city. He had arranged his desk so that it faced that panoramic view. He often just sat there with a glass of whiskey looking out the window, a perfectly contented man.

Standing up now to answer the door, he wondered who was there. Flannery couldn't think of anyone in particular. Leni didn't know about this apartment and besides, she was dead. Flora was at home. It was too late in the day for the postman to be delivering the mail. Maybe it was religious fanatics going from door to door selling their always engaging version of God. He always enjoyed zealots.

The dog was blocking enough of the door so that there was no way Flannery could open it. This had happened before. It was almost like the animal was mocking him with its size. He longed to kick the damned beast in the ass to get it to move out of the way but knew if he did, that juicy piece of information would get back to his boss and only cause more trouble.

"Could you move?"

They locked eyes but the dog did not move.

"Please?"

Luba moved just enough inches for him to maneuver.

"Thank you." He opened the door. Vincent Ettrich was standing in the hall. Still dressed in his funeral suit and tie, he could easily have been mistaken for one of those religious nuts. Flannery was genuinely startled.

"Mr. Flannery or Mr. Pegg—which would you prefer I call you?" Vincent's voice was relaxed and secure, not the slightest trace of fear in it.

A big smile grew on John Flannery's face. What an impressive opening line! He had never imagined Vincent Ettrich would be so collected when they first met, but bravo. It made things much more engaging than if this man had only been a cowering little mouse.

"I prefer Flannery, if you don't mind. Will you come in?"

Ettrich strode into the apartment, took one look at the large black and white dog, and kept moving into the living room. Flannery was again surprised. When most people saw Luba for the first time they either hesitated or grinned uncertainly at the behemoth. Ettrich did neither. He looked at the dog as if it were a side table and walked past it.

In the living room he went to one of the windows and stared out at the impressive view. Flannery came in and stood behind him but said nothing. He was fascinated to see how Ettrich was going to play this one. If he knew that John Flannery and Kyle Pegg were the same person then Ettrich knew a great deal, yet he showed no fear.

"Did you get my address from Flora?"

"Yes. I just spoke with her," Ettrich said without turning around.

Which was seriously rude. Flannery's smile fell. He didn't like that. Ettrich should have turned and faced him, answered his question, and then turned back to the nice view. This *was* Flannery's home and Vincent Ettrich was an uninvited guest.

"Did Leni ever come here, Mr. Flannery?"

"No."

"Only Flora?"

"Yes."

Ettrich reached forward and with two fingers touched the brass turn on the window. For a moment Flannery thought that he was going to open it.

"You killed Leni." It was a statement, not a question.

There was no reason for Flannery to lie or be evasive. "Yes. I suppose you could say I did. Yes."

"Would you have killed Flora too to make Isabelle go over there?"

Flannery answered cheerfully "Maybe, but I never really thought about it."

Luba walked into the room and over to a large foam-rubber bed made up for it on the floor below one of the windows.

"Do you mind if I sit down?" Ettrich's voice was still easy and conversational. There was no anxiety in it, no desperation.

"Not at all. Would you like something to drink? Coffee?"

"No thank you. I'd just like to sit." Vincent moved from the window over to a slinky black leather couch Flannery loved. It was one of the only pieces of furniture in the room. He had searched for months and only found what he wanted at a showroom in Udine, Italy. It had cost seven thousand dollars. It was beautiful and sexy and comfortable and perfect. He almost hit Luba the day he came home and found the dog stretched out asleep on it. When he pushed it off, there were white spots on the couch from its dried drool and (he assumed) urine that had to be carefully scrubbed off.

Sitting down on it now, Ettrich said "I want to talk about cancer."

The statement was so bizarrely out of context that Flannery stopped and stood there, thoroughly confounded. "*Cancer?*"

"Yes." Vincent put both hands flat on the couch.

This was getting more interesting by the moment. Flannery sat down on the other end.

Ettrich continued "Tell me something. You should know about this; it's right up your alley."

Their first meeting wasn't turning out the way Flannery had planned, but it certainly was different.

"I don't understand cancer."

Flannery looked to see if Ettrich was putting him on. Was there a catch in his voice or a smile in his eye to indicate he was bullshitting?

"What's not to understand?" Flannery tried to modulate his voice so that it sounded serious but not too serious, just in case.

"Whenever cancer destroys a body it also destroys itself."

Flannery nodded.

"Which means that cancer is either suicidal or suicidally stupid. Because the result is the same—it dies when the body it attacks dies." Ettrich's voice rose in annoyance.

"I never thought of it that way but you're right, Vincent."

Luba came over to the men and laid its big head on Ettrich's lap. He didn't appear to mind. But did he know this dog was cognizant? Did he know it understood everything he said? Flannery looked at Ettrich and wondered just how much he *did* know and why he'd really come here today.

"Chaos is like cancer, isn't it, John?"

Head still on Ettrich's lap, Luba shifted its eyes to Flannery.

"Why do you say that?" John's voice remained neutral.

"Because whenever chaos comes, it destroys and then disappears too. It doesn't have much of a half-life. Disease, asteroids hitting the earth, plane crashes . . . You kill things and then you die, or whatever happens to chaos after it's finished. Like cancer."

Flannery shook his head. "Those were the old days, Vincent. Things have changed. We're very aware of what we do now. Chaos doesn't come at random anymore—there's always a reason. Using your analogy, it's as if cancer specifically chooses its victims."

Ettrich petted the dog. "But you haven't mentioned one important thing."

"What's that?"

"Your history, what Chaos used to be like. Back in the bad old days when you *didn't* have brains and just destroyed things. That part is still in you, John. You can't get rid of it, anymore than I can get rid of my gene sequence. The problem with being conscious is your past always lives on somewhere inside of you. Take a dog—if you corner it and it gets scared, it reverts back to being a wolf and bites you."

Ettrich drew a folding knife out of his pocket and opened it. With a quick vicious thrust, he stabbed it into the fine leather sofa.

Flannery froze "Hey! What are you doing?"

Something welled up out of the gash in the leather. Translucent white and gelatinous, it looked like some kind of hair gel. About six inches long, it skimmed very fast up the side of Ettrich's leg, across his arm, hand, and then onto the Great Dane's face. The dog pulled its head back but the thing was already sliding into its eye socket. It felt nothing.

Chaos entered the dog's eye. The first chaos that had been Luba at the dog's beginning; a pure form that once was and still was immutably part of it.

When he touched the place on the couch where the dog had once lain, Ettrich found Luba in the same way he had found Kyselak when he touched the tree in the forest. Only this time he did it consciously. Then he had gone all the way back to the dog's beginning when Luba was just-created, pristine chaos. That's what emerged from the couch now and reentered Luba. No thought, no sophistication. Like cancer, this simple chaos only knew how to do one thing—multiply.

Chaos evolved was no match for chaos in its first and purest form.

Ettrich did not see its effect on Luba because he was watching Flannery. The dog was dead the moment chaos entered its eye. A living body is an ordered thing. All those cells and complex structures work together in harmony for a common cause. Drop frenzy and disarray into the center of it and that fragile sophisticated engine breaks immediately.

Flannery watched Luba die. Because they were made of the same stuff, he saw and understood exactly what happened next. The chaos that had been summoned continued to work. When the dog was dead, it moved into what the animal had previously been and began to destroy that too.

Everything that Luba had ever been was first infected and then wiped out. Life after life, incarnation after incarnation, disappeared before Flannery's eyes. He could not stop watching. Never before in all of his many lives on earth and elsewhere had he seen anything like this. It was so hypnotic that he did not notice when Ettrich reached over and gently touched him on the knee. He did not see Ettrich close his eyes, turn his head away, and then turn back. He did not see that Ettrich's eyes were confident when he opened them again, as if something significant and final had been decided. Flannery could only watch in awe at the ongoing sight of every trace of Luba being erased.

"John." Ettrich waited and then eventually said much louder. *"John."*

The expression on Flannery's face was that of a child encountering a twenty-foot-long feeding python—mesmerized and appalled.

"Do you see that, John? I did it. Do you hear? It was me who did that to her."

Stunned by everything, Flannery could only nod slowly. Yes he heard. Yes he understood.

"And now I'm going to do it to you. For what you did to Leni, for everything that you've done here. Everything you've hurt and destroyed; you and your dog. You and all your dogs." Ettrich spoke quietly but with a cold rage in his voice that Flannery heard and couldn't resist answering.

"Hey well, fuck you, *Vince.* Your Isabelle's right where we want her now. Nothing you can do about that, is there?"

"Nope. But I can send a message, John, and you're gonna be it." Ettrich stood up and without looking back walked toward the door.

Flannery watched him leave. He also kept glancing at the gash in the couch, fully expecting something else to emerge from there any second. Nothing would though because Ettrich had already found Flannery's first chaos and set it loose when he touched John's knee.

The front door clicked close. Soon after, John Flannery felt the beginnings of a faint tingling throughout his body, like the prickly sensations up and down a leg when it falls asleep. Or when you drink ginger ale and the bubbles fly up your nose. It was a funny feeling, strange but almost pleasant.

For a little while.

Drownstairs

"Where *are* we?"

They were running, that was for sure. The three people were running as fast as they possibly could because they were being chased by a space alien, a Komodo dragon, and George W. Bush.

Before this, it had all been going so well. It had been going spectacularly. They'd found Isabelle. Simon and Leni had put their heads together and came up with a plan to find her in Haden's afterworld. It didn't work. But then purely by coincidence they had bumped into Haden's childhood dog Floyd the bull terrier which told them it had seen Isabelle and Simon's mother walking down the street together. They rushed over to Simon's house and found the two women sitting on the porch, talking about Chinese medicine.

To celebrate the reunion, they'd taken Isabelle to eat at a *heurigen* they all knew well and liked. When he was alive, Haden had gone there often on his trips to Vienna so he had dreamt about the place four times. That was why they could visit it here and now.

A wine garden/restaurant in Salmannsdorf, it sat on the edge of a picturesque hilly vineyard. When they arrived that afternoon, the air was redolent with grilling chicken and ripe grapes. Perfect late-summer weather welcomed them to an outside table. The surroundings were still and almost silent. They were alone there in the garden except for a man Haden used to know who was sitting by himself in a far corner reading a newspaper.

They ordered wine and chicken because it smelled so good that it was irresistible. Then they sat back into happiness for a few minutes before talking about any next step. Isabelle was impatient to hear how they'd found her, but Leni and Simon looked so proud and jubilant that she thought it best to wait and let them bask in their triumph awhile before asking questions.

They didn't get to bask for long. To their dismay and then annoyance, a radio somewhere started blaring. The peace and quiet was broken by the staccato sludge of a pop song. Leni looked at Isabelle and grimaced. Haden turned quickly this way and that, trying to locate the source of the jarring music so he could at least try and get someone to turn it down.

No luck. The obnoxious wail continued to fill the air and coat their good moods tongue-sick-yellow. Worse, when the song finally ended, another, even more egregious one immediately followed. It was the song by the rap group Drownstairs that had been so wildly popular a year or two before. The summer it came out, every time you turned on a radio it seemed that one was playing. There was no escaping it for a while.

"God, I hate this song." Leni fanned a hand in front of her face. Not because it was hot but more like she wanted to get the tune away from her, as if it were an irritating mosquito buzzing around her head.

Haden said "I hate this fucking song."

Leni gave him a scornful look. "Simon, I just *said* that."

He ignored her comment. "I just remembered that it was playing on the radio in the car when I died."

"Whoa. You remember that?"

"Yes. I'm remembering more and more things now. Some of them aren't so nice."

That silenced them all for a while.

In spite of herself, Isabelle started humming the tune. She couldn't help it.

Haden jolted everyone by suddenly shouting "Will someone please turn off this fucking song, please?"

Whether he was heard and obeyed, or because this was Haden's world and he was boss, the music stopped abruptly. Simon bowed his thanks and continued. "Not only is that song stupid, but did you ever see the video of it? The group gets chased across the desert by a big lizard and a guy in a silver space suit."

"And George Bush. Don't forget him."

"That's right, Bush was chasing them too. And do you remember what happens at the end of the video? Bush catches the group and eats them."

"*Eat?*" Isabelle didn't watch television so she hadn't seen the video.

"Yup—President Bush eats black rappers. Eats them without taking off their wrappers."

The waitress brought their drinks and said the chicken would be ready in a few minutes. After she was gone, Isabelle asked. "Then what happens?"

"Where?"

"In the video. If Bush eats the singers then that sort of ends the song, doesn't it?"

Leni snorted. "You would think so, but unfortunately it goes on."

The women continued talking. Haden tuned them out to think some more about the video and song. More precisely, to think about the last time he'd heard it, moments before dying. He was sitting in that car wash on La Cienega Boulevard in Los Angeles. Three days earlier he had been fired from his job. A month before that, the woman he had been living with had asked him to move out of her house. He remembered all of these things now, down to the smallest detail. When he first came here, he didn't even know that he had died.

"Simon."

Leni's voice reached him, but just barely. He tried to ignore it. Only recently had he begun to see the events of his finished life with clarity and real understanding. This was the first time that penultimate moment had come back to him in full and he wanted to examine it to see if—

"Simon!"

"What, Leni?"

"What are you doing?"

"Why?"

"Because look around us! What are you doing?"

When he focused back in on the moment, he saw that everything was gone—the restaurant, the vineyards, everything but the three of them standing together in the middle of nowhere.

"What happened?"

Leni grabbed his shoulder. "That's what I was asking. What were you just doing?"

"Thinking about when I died."

"What else?"

"Nothing, Leni, only that."

"Then what's happened here?"

He shook his head. "I don't know."

They would have said more and probably ended up arguing if the four members of Drownstairs, dressed in identical white jogging outfits and askew white baseball caps, hadn't come sprinting out of nowhere and blown past them without saying a word. The only sounds they made were the swish of their clothes, the pounding of feet, and the loud labored breathing of four scared men running hard.

A few feet past them, the last man in white—the slowest of the bunch—stopped and turned to Haden. "You'd better get moving, man. Your girlfriend here just screwed up by humming our song." He pointed to Isabelle. "Chaos heard her. It's got out an all-points bulletin on her and it's been *listening*. But *you're* the one it wants to eat. We're only the hors d'oeuvres. Know what I'm sayin'?"

Haden took a quick look at the women, then back again at this guy in white. "Why me?"

"Because everything in this world comes from your memory. It wants all of it *gone*."

Without hesitation Haden said "Isabelle, Leni, run."

The women didn't ask why because his face told them plenty. It said *Trust me, we're in danger, I'm scared and you should be too.*

They ran. The man in white ran in front of them and they followed him. But the surroundings had disappeared. They ran across nothing toward nothing.

"Where *are* we?"

Haden didn't know where they were but he knew exactly what was happening. Chaos was coming after them. If it succeeded now, it would erase the world Simon Haden had created from his life's experiences and memories. We are the days of our lives, the experiences we have and what we remember of them. Erase those things and what is left of us? If Chaos destroyed his world, it would destroy the world Isabelle had fled to for refuge with her unborn child.

They could hear it coming now. Like the sound of a summer storm rolling in, they heard it coming toward them.

Haden reached out and grabbed Leni's arm while they were running. "Remember before when you conjured that version of me? That guy you remembered me as being?"

"Yes, Simon."

He stopped them. "Do it again, Leni. Do it right now. Conjure every version of me that you can think of; every me you can remember."

She did not ask why. She did not have time.

In seconds she surrounded them with Haden after Haden, tens

of them and then a hundred at least, all summoned from Leni Salomon's memories of the time she'd spent together with Simon when they were both alive.

Kind, well dressed, funny and charming Haden. Scruffy, hungover, selfish and bad-tempered Haden. Scared and vulnerable, surprised and childlike, mean and manipulative. Short hair, long hair, dirty hands, just-manicured ones, suit, pajamas . . . One after the other these Hadens flooded out of her mind and memory, surrounding the three people like a rush-hour crowd at a big-city railroad station. They emerged from the ethers fully realized. Since they were different versions of the same man however, they immediately began talking to each other and comparing notes. Leni, Isabelle, and Simon watched it happen.

"Why did you want this, Simon?" Leni asked.

"Because Chaos is trying to destroy my memories. If it does that, then it destroys my world—this world." He looked at Isabelle. "And then she won't be able to survive. That's why they tricked her into coming here on her own. She'll be stuck here in whatever's left. I don't even know what that would be, some kind of limbo."

"But why them?" Isabelle gestured toward the hoard of Hadens around them.

"Because they all have memories, but they remember things differently. When I'm pissed off I remember things differently than when I'm in a good mood. When Chaos meets these guys it's going to have to sort through all of it, all of them, to find out what's true before it can erase things. That will give you some time to get away. You two have to go now; right this second."

"Go *where*? And what are you going to do?"

Haden smiled. Neither woman had ever seen that expression on his face. "Now it's my turn. I'm going to stay here and use this"—he touched his temple—"to make more me's—lots and lots of them. As many as I can before it arrives. Then I'll just sort of lose myself in the crowd and hope that it doesn't find me for a while. But you have to leave now. No more talking."

"Where, Simon? Where *can* we go?"

He nodded at Leni's question. He had expected it, thought about it, and knew the answer already. "If I do this right, Chaos will have to stop here for a long time and work through all of these guys and their memories. It will have to figure out which are Leni's people and which are mine. *Then* which memories are real and which aren't.

"That should give you enough time to get some place in this world that still exists. After that I don't know, Leni. You two are going to have to figure it out later. Right now you've just got to get Isabelle out of here."

Moved, Isabelle protested "But what about you?"

He gestured around them with both hands. "I'll be fine. I'm here in good company. I know these guys." He took Isabelle's right hand, squeezed it and dropped it. "Go now. I'll be fine. I'll see you." He motioned for them to leave.

"Wow, Simon. Wow. Thank you."

"You are welcome. And good luck with the baby."

"Simon?" Leni pointed to the growing crush of Hadens around them. "I just thought of another Simon to add to this group. He's a good man after all. And he just surprised the hell out me."

Hearing her compliment, Haden's tense face relaxed a moment. He saluted them and walked straight out into the crowd. It quickly grew and grew as he moved until the women couldn't tell which one was the real Simon anymore.

"Let's go."

• • •

To their very great relief, the women did not have far to travel before coming to a recognizable place. At first they hadn't known what to expect, so they were suspicious of everything. There was still nothing around them; it was as if Simon's world had been swept clean or they were at the beginning of a new one. It reminded Leni of being inside an airplane as it came in to land on a completely overcast day. The only thing around them was various shades of shifting gray, like thick clouds outside a plane window.

It lasted only a few miles. As they walked, this gray began to evaporate and what appeared to be some kind of border crossing loomed in front of them. They saw that they were now walking on a primitive, badly paved road. It led to a small booth and the kind of moveable gate you see at rural railroad crossings. What was absurd was that all one had to do was step off the road a few feet, walk around this booth/gate, and you would cross over to the other side of the border unhindered. There were no other fences or barriers to keep you in or out.

The surrounding landscape was brown, barren, and rocky. Off in the distance loomed a high and dramatic mountain range with jagged snow-covered peaks. The steel blue and white of those mountains contrasted dramatically with the brown everywhere around them.

Astonished by this utterly unexpected sight after emerging from the suffocating grays, the women stopped for a better look around. Before either had a chance to comment, a bell's thin *ching-ching* came from close behind them. Turning, they saw a red-faced man on a bicycle that was loaded down with far too many things. It looked like he had loaded his whole life onto that bike. He was pedaling as hard as he could but the great weight on the bicycle made it slow going for him. He huffed and puffed slowly past, ignoring them.

They watched as he pedaled toward the crossing. About twenty feet from it he got off the bike and pushed it the rest of the way. Two men in gray camouflage military uniforms came out of the booth to meet him. The three appeared to know each other. Their conversation was brief and full of smiles. One guard patted the man on the back while the other went over to the gate and raised it for him. He waved at the guards and pushed his bike over the border into the other land.

"Where are we?"

"I have no idea. Let's ask them."

"Do you think they speak German or English?"

"We'll find out right now." Isabelle walked toward the crossing. Leni peered over both shoulders to make sure that no one else was creeping up on them.

While walking, Isabelle asked herself what the air smelled like. There were the odors of dryness and dust and earth but something else too. A spice of some sort—cumin or sage? Definitely a cooking smell. Way out here in the middle of this desolate, moon-landscaped nowhere, a very spicy and delicious smell hung in the air.

Watching her approach, the guards' faces said nothing. Isabelle took a deep breath and readied her hands to do a lot of gesturing in case she couldn't communicate with these men through words. She thought she'd try first with English.

"Hello! Do you speak English? *Oder Deutsch??*"

"Both, missus. English and German—whichever you would prefer." He had an authoritative deep voice and a slight accent she could not place.

"That's wonderful. Can you tell me where we are?"

The man pointed at his feet. "We are in death. Over there is life." He pointed across the border.

Leni had caught up and stood next to Isabelle. "Can we go over there? Is it permitted?"

"Yes missus, of course."

Leni looked at her friend and opened her mouth to say something but Isabelle put up a hand to stop her. "*Both* of us can go over there?"

"Yes missus."

"But I'm still alive and she's dead."

"We know that. We can see your hearts—yours is beating and hers is not."

"But still we can both go over there?"

"Yes, it is not a problem," the other guard said.

The women exchanged a look. They were confused by this simple yes—why wasn't there a problem?

"Who was that man who went through here before?" Leni pointed toward the other side of the border.

"A dead man, like you. He is going to visit his mother who is still alive. He comes through here twice a week."

"What were all those things on his bicycle?"

"He uses them to try and communicate with her. He is an imaginative fellow but none of his ideas ever work. No, that's unfair to say—sometimes they work, but very, very rarely." This time the guard smiled broadly at his partner who chuckled and coughed into his hand. "Both of you can go over there to life, but you will not be back *in* life. Do you understand?"

When the women said nothing, the other guard added "It will be like going to the aquarium. You will be next to the fishes but there is a very thick glass between you and them." He spread his hands apart ten inches, as if demonstrating the thickness of the glass.

Isabelle was too excited by their proximity to life to really register the importance of what he said. She managed to keep a neutral expression on her face, heard the references to the aquarium and thick glass, but none of it made much of an impression. She was bursting with impatience. *Life* was just over there, which meant Vincent and home and her life again. She didn't know how long she had been in Simon Haden's dreamworld since being lured here. It didn't matter though because life was again so near that she could take fifty steps over to it.

"Come on, Leni, let's go."

One of the guards went to the gate and raised it for them. The women walked across the border and kept going toward the distant mountains. The guards looked at each other. One of them shook his hand slowly and exaggeratedly to affirm those were two good-looking chicks and he wouldn't mind diddling either of them. His colleague nodded in agreement but that was the end of it. This was a busy outpost. People passed through it all the time. These men had often seen odd things go by here. Two pretty women was a nice distraction but not all that special. Besides, back in the guard booth a very nice lentil stew was cooking and both men were hungry. The recipe had called for a variety of spices and their pungent smells perfumed the air, a harbinger of good things to eat. The guards preferred to think about their upcoming meal.

• • •

The women walked on, expecting anything, everything, and nothing. The barren landscape around them did not change. Life appeared to be the same as death. When they first crossed the border, both of them had assumed something dramatic was imminent: they would be magically transported to a familiar place or meet up with people they knew in life, but nothing like that happened. They walked beneath the raised gate back into life and down a poorly maintained road full of potholes and large stones. The delicious spicy smell that had accompanied them faded as they walked on and in a little while was gone altogether. Isabelle missed it.

After they had been going for more than an hour she finally said "I don't get it."

Leni knew exactly what she meant. "Me neither."

"I thought—"

"Me too." Feeling sorry for her, and sharing her deep sense of disappointment that nothing had changed, Leni reached over and took Isabelle's hand. It was unexpected but the perfect thing to do. The two friends had often held hands. They had been doing it along with Flora since they were kids.

When Isabelle looked over, she saw that Leni was crying.

"Hey, what's up?"

Leni impatiently pushed her free hand across her wet eyes to wipe the tears away. "Nothing. I was just hoping you'd be able to go home now. That's all." She let go of Isabelle's hand. For want of something to do, she bent down and picked a stone up off the road. Feeling its heft, she tossed it up and down while she spoke. "I want you to go back home and have your baby and live happily ever after." Angrily, with all of her might she flung the rock away. "Tell me about the greatest time you ever had with Vincent. Tell me about the time you loved him most."

Isabelle did not hesitate. As they began walking again, she recounted the night she met Vincent and how they had visited both the Kyselak signature and Petras Urbsys's store. Both of them had their eyes down while she spoke. It was a nice story and they concentrated their full attention on it.

Leni was the first one to look up, but did so only because she heard something impossible three separate times and that third was just too much to resist. She had to take a look because damn it, she was certain she heard a seagull. In the middle of this wherever-they-were desolate landlocked countryside, Leni heard a seagull call out. She knew the sound well because her parents' apartment was near the river in Vienna. She had grown up hearing gulls squawk and talk to each other.

When she looked up now, she saw that they were passing the bench next to the Danube Canal where she had been found dead. They were back in Vienna. A large seagull was flying directly overhead. She said quietly "Isabelle, look up."

She did and her first reaction was to reach for Leni's hand. "What happened?"

"I do not know, but we're here."

"I want to go to our apartment. I want to see Vincent."

"That's fine, but I think we'd better walk there. Who knows how things work here for us and I would truly hate to get stuck on the subway for all eternity."

The city was at its most beautiful. Summer afternoon sunlight poured across the buildings, illuminating the gargoyles, busts, and stone wreaths on their facades. They were among many details, many visual treasures one didn't notice normally but couldn't miss on this sublimely sunny, clear day. It reminded them once again of how generous much of the Viennese architecture was; it offered so much to see and take in.

The outdoor cafés they passed were full of tanned bare skin, extravagant cakes with *schlag* and everyone wearing sunglasses. Horse-drawn carriages clopped slowly around the Ringstrasse, indifferent to the cars whizzing by them. In the Burggarten families ambled around eating ice cream cones. Lovers lay sleeping on the grass in each other's arms. At a sidewalk fruit stand peaches the size of grapefruits were for sale.

The women met the first dead person they knew at the corner of the Getreidemarkt and Mariahilferstrasse. One of their high school classmates, Uschi Stein, had died in an airplane crash the year after they graduated. When Isabelle and Leni reached a busy intersection just a few blocks from the Secession Museum, they saw her walking toward them and smiling.

"Uschi?"

"Hey you two. Where's Flora?" She looked exactly as she had in high school; exactly as she had the day she died.

Trying to keep her voice under control, Isabelle asked her "What are you doing here?"

"Looking for my stupid mother; she's never on time for anything. We had a date for lunch. You'd think it would be easy to find your own mother when you'd arranged a time to meet, but not today."

Uschi had been dead fifteen years.

"Look, I've got to go find my mom. I'll see you guys around, huh? Let's have coffee or something." She walked toward Mariahilferstrasse without looking back.

When she was far enough away, Isabelle murmured "She doesn't know! She doesn't know she's dead."

Unfazed, Leni agreed. "No, and she never will. She's a ghost; ghosts never know they're dead. They're only confused forever. That's why she's still hanging around here looking for her mother."

"But what about you and Simon? Why aren't you like her?"

"Because Chaos got to her first after she died. We were lucky. Chaos creates ghosts; that's where they come from. One of its more modern and clever inventions; only a few thousand years old. If you totally confuse a soul, it'll never be able to find its way to the mosaic."

Walking down through the Naschmarkt on their way to Isabelle's apartment, they passed eleven more ghosts. Among them was a transvestite, an old woman sitting by a window in an apartment house directly across from the open market, a bum who somehow managed to stay drunk even in death, and a Turkish child who had died a week before of encephalitis. These dead and more were part of the crowd they passed. Leni could distinguish them from the living, Isabelle could not. The only Vienna the friends could see now was the Vienna they had experienced together.

They were talking about coffee when the accident occurred almost directly in front of them. They had just walked past the Café Odeon. Leni saw the place and mentioned the night the three of them had ended up there very late after a party. They drank one Irish coffee after another and talked talked talked until the place closed.

"I had so much caffeine that night; I don't think I slept for a week."

There was a high screech of brakes and then that horrifying, instantly recognizable sound of something being hit by a car.

It came from in front of them on the busy Linke Wienzeile. A man in a hurry and absorbed in a conversation on his cell phone stepped out between parked cars without looking and was immediately struck by a gigantic yellow moving van from Holland. He was hit a glancing blow and might even have survived had he not been knocked back into a thick tree that was planted between the sidewalk and the street. The back of his head smacked into the tree first and that was it. He was dead before the rest of his body dropped to the ground.

The women were hurrying toward him by the time his soul began to rise out of the top of his head like smoke. Both of them saw this; Leni because she was dead, Isabelle because she existed now in this no-man's-land between life and death where souls are visible when exposed.

It was white. The dead man's soul was white as are all souls, contrary to what many people believe. The crows saw it too. Chaos likes birds. It likes their nervousness and paranoia, their incessant shrieking, their uselessness, and the way they shit on everything. Because birds are everywhere on earth, save the middle of the oceans and deserts, Chaos often uses them to do small errands. One is to snatch the souls from the dead before they get away to the mosaic. Sometimes a soul does not leave a body for a long time because it is lost and cannot find the proper way out. That is why vultures can be so effective in certain situations. Because they are the only bird that knows patience; they know how to wait.

The crows in Vienna come from Russia. Normally they arrive around the end of October, spend the winter, and then return home at the beginning of spring. But there are always some lazy ones, a few that don't want to make the long flight east again. Or those that find the temperate Austrian climate suits them. Every year a handful stick around. They're noticeable because as the weather turns warmer, the color of their feathers changes from slick shiny black to a mixture of matte black and dirty gray, sort of like bum penguins.

Three of them flew in and landed on a telephone wire nearby immediately after the accident. Crows are not quiet birds. They are forever fussing loudly; they like the world to know they are there. But these three silently watched the man die. After a short time Leni noticed them and she knew why they were near. She was unable to do anything about it however because the dead cannot interfere. She thought about asking Isabelle to try but that was too risky; who knows what it might have brought? Isabelle's only task now, and it was an urgent one, was to find a way back to her life.

The dead man's soul had separated completely from his body and hung unmoving in the air above it. This was always the crucial stage; this was when a soul was most vulnerable. One of the crows flapped its wings several times but did not move off the wire. The birds were watching to see what happened next. They were impatient but they were careful. They had done this many times before.

People—the living—the helpful, the curious, and the dismayed, began to move toward the slumped body to see if there was anything they could do, or just to stare. The driver of the truck had stopped the vehicle and thrown open the door, but he did not move from his seat in the high cab. Terrified, the little-boy part of him still living somewhere inside thought If I don't move, this will go away. If I stay up here in my safe place it will stop.

The first crow jumped off the wire and dropped toward the floating soul. Unexpectedly when it was very close, the big bird stopped its dive and, cawing raucously, veered off and flew away.

"Did you see that? Did you see that big crow? What was it doing?"

"Checking. Testing to see if the coast is clear."

"To see if *what* coast is clear? Leni, what are you talking about?"

From a distance they heard the sound of a siren approaching. Slowly the soul began to rise. The women watched it and the crows watched it. People had gathered around the body, close but not too close. Some squatted down on their haunches, others stood with grim faces and arms crossed. A young mother gripped too hard the handle of the blue and brown baby carriage she was pushing. Another woman had found the dead man's cell phone and laid it gently on the ground beside the body. In a while it began to ring. People jerked as if the phone were the dead man suddenly come back to life. Others cringed at the absolute wrongness of that familiar sound now.

"Is that his soul in the air, Leni?"

"Yes."

The second crow dropped off the telephone wire and swooped down toward the soul. The baby in the carriage began to cry and then to scream. It was so immediately loud and distraught that one would have thought something was hurting it. The crow squawked, outraged, but flew away.

"Good!" Leni made a triumphant fist and pressed it to her side. "Chaos sent those crows to steal the soul. But see—the baby's cries keep them away."

"Why? How?" Isabelle's thoughts went to her own unborn child.

Leni shrugged. "I don't really know; maybe because babies are innocent and so new to life. Their pureness reminds a soul what it's really here for and where it's supposed to go when it's finished. But I'm only guessing."

The mother took the infant out of the carriage, hefted it over her shoulder, and patted its back the way mothers do. From where they were standing, the baby was only a small bundle of pink although its cries were surprisingly loud. The last crow walked back and forth on the telephone wire dipping its head forward and back, opening and closing its beak again and again but no sound came out of it.

"How long does a soul have to wait before it's safe?"

Leni did not look at Isabelle when she answered. "That depends on the life the person led."

Soothed now, the baby stopped crying. The soul began to rise again. At the same time it also began to very slowly disperse like water vapor. From out of nowhere, the first or second crow came sweeping back in, snatched up the fragile white soul in its open beak like a rag, and flew off with it. The crow still on the telephone wire dipped its head up and down, up and down, up and down, cawing like crazy.

Because the two women were watching all this, rapt, they did not see the immaculately dressed little man emerge from inside the baby carriage, climb over the edge of it, and drop to the ground. No one saw this happen because those who *could* see him were watching the soul snatcher, and those that couldn't were looking at the dead body sprawled against the base of the tree.

The little man spent time brushing himself off and straightening his beige drape-cut suit. When he was satisfied with his appearance, he walked over to Isabelle and Leni.

"Hello ladies."

"Broximon!"

Leni looked down at him and then over at Isabelle. "You *know* this man?"

"I do. What are you doing here?"

Broximon hiked a thumb over his shoulder. "Pinching that baby. But it didn't do much good. The crow still got the soul, huh? I couldn't see from in there."

"You were the one making the baby cry?"

"Yup. Sometimes one good pinch will make them cry for half an hour. Half an hour usually does the trick. Chaos doesn't have the patience to wait around longer than that. But sometimes these babies shut right up even after you've given them a hell of a pinch. Then there's not much else you can do. Did either of you know the dead guy?"

Isabelle looked at Leni. "No. But what are you doing here?"

"I came to help you get out of here."

"By pinching little babies?" Leni demanded.

Broximon stayed cool. "If needs be, yes. Babies recover—souls don't."

The siren they heard belonged to a police car. It pulled up behind the moving van, blue lights flashing. Two cops got out, a man and a woman. The woman walked right over to the body and looked at it coolly and appraisingly. Her partner talked to different people in the crowd who were only too happy to fill the police in on what had happened.

"Vincent is here."

Isabelle froze. "Vincent? How can he be *here*?"

"Anyone can be. The problem is getting back to his side of here."

"Where is he?"

"At your apartment. That's where you were going anyway, wasn't it?"

Isabelle started to say yes but to her real surprise, Leni interrupted her and said loudly "No."

"No?"

"No."

"Then where were you going?"

"That's none of your business."

"Leni!"

"Isabelle, he isn't real; he's Chaos. He's your own chaos."

The idea was so unexpected that it stopped Isabelle. "What do you mean?"

"He's from Simon's world, right? That's where you know him from?"

"Yes." Isabelle said it hesitantly, the one word sounding like a question.

Leni shook her head. "You fished him out of your memory of Simon's world to save you now. It won't work."

"But I saw him in the other world too, Leni, the real world. After your funeral in Weidling."

"Yes, you told me. But was he able to stop you from coming here?"

"No."

"Exactly. And he can't save you now either. You can re-create him and make him damn real, but he's only a delusion. Most of our lives we create our own chaos, Isabelle. We don't need much of it from the outside because we're so good at making it ourselves.

"We do it because we believe, we honestly do believe that it'll help us or save us . . . but it's usually what ruins us.

"Nobody can help you get out of here now but yourself. Not Vincent, not your fake little magic man, no ruby slippers. Not me or Simon—only you. Only you can do it."

"But what about that whole scene with the soul we just saw; the crow stealing it and the crying baby? Were they real?"

"Yes, but this guy is not. Not some little leprechaun who pinches babies. He's your creation. You made him out of your memories because you hoped he'd help get you out of here. He won't. He can't."

• • •

To make matters worse, afterward this false Broximon wouldn't go away. When they started walking again toward Isabelle's apartment he followed them without asking permission. Fifty steps on, Leni made a disgusted sound and stopped. Turning to him, she asked/accused "What do you think you're doing?"

"Walking."

"Walking where?"

"That's none of your beeswax," he said nonchalantly.

"Oh really? That's interesting." But Leni was at a loss for something else to say in response, so she started walking again albeit more quickly.

Broximon walked a few feet behind them. He frequently interrupted their conversation by asking what this or that was along the way, as if they were tour guides. It quickly became both exasperating and annoying. When he wasn't asking questions, he whistled that moronic song from the group Drownstairs neither of them liked.

"Broximon, will you please stop that? If you're going to follow us, at least just shut up. Don't ask any more questions and stop whistling."

"Why?"

Isabelle held up a rigid fist at him to be quiet now—or else.

"Leni, why is he still here if what you said is true?"

"I don't know—ask him."

Isabelle asked.

To their surprise he answered. "Because you brought me here. You're the only one who can make me go away."

"How?"

"I don't know—I didn't make me. Ask yourself."

Isabelle asked herself but didn't have the faintest idea. Leni didn't have the faintest idea either.

Brogsma

The three of them stood there looking into the front window of a vacant store. False Broximon was behind the women and off to one side. He had continued talking, asking irrelevant questions and whistling the Drownstairs tune on and off all the way over here. The women wanted to strangle him. He was like the awful little brother you had while growing up who seemed to make it his goal in life to infuriate you with everything he did.

"Why are we looking into an empty store?"

They pointedly ignored him, but the truth was Leni would like to have known the answer to that question too.

Isabelle remained silent and stared. It had been her desire to come here. While walking toward her apartment, she had unexpectedly veered off onto a side street without any explanation. For the next ten minutes she said nothing while leading them here.

The empty storefront looked vaguely familiar to Leni. But she had lived in Vienna all of her life so much of it appeared familiar, no matter where she was in the city.

"Why are we looking into an empty store window?"

"We heard you the first time you asked that question."

Broximon's voice went up a half octave "Yes, but you didn't answer me the first time, so I'm asking again."

Ignoring both of them, Isabelle continued to look intently into the empty window as if there really was something in there only she could see.

"Isabelle, why *are* we here?"

"This was Petras Urbsys's store, don't you remember?"

"Ah, that's right!" Leni remembered Simon Haden scolding her for forgetting the time he brought her and Isabelle here and introduced them to Urbsys.

"I want to go inside. Can I do that?"

"Sure, but why?"

"I just want to go inside, that's all. How do I do it, Leni?"

"Push the door open and walk in" Broximon said.

Isabelle checked Leni who nodded that this was true.

She gave the door a push. It didn't budge. She immediately thought It won't let me do this, it won't let me go in there. But a moment later the door yielded to the pressure of her pushing hand and slid open. Isabelle walked in.

Leni remained outside with Broximon, assuming her friend would be inside only a short while. Plus she had no desire to go in anyway. The only things she remembered about Petras was that he talked too much and he smelled. Go into his funky old empty store now? No thanks. Broximon did not go in either. He stood nearby whistling. Leni was sure he did it only to irritate her.

"Petras? Are you in here?"

The empty store remained silent. Did Isabelle seriously believe he would be in there? Yes, some optimistic part of her believed exactly that. She said his name again, only this time with no question mark at the end.

It smelled of mildew, old air, dust, and wood in the store. It smelled of emptiness and long neglect. It had once been such a vital unusual place. A compelling man had passed his last days in here. Old Petras knew that his life would soon be over. While he still had time though he wanted to share his stories with people who would appreciate them and cherish the objects that had helped populate them. Isabelle walked aimlessly around that large, shadowy, empty room searching for anything that would bring back even a trace of Petras Urbsys.

On the floor in a corner of the room was an old disconnected telephone. Clam gray, it had one of those rotary dials she hadn't seen for a long time. Squatting down beside it, Isabelle slid a finger into one of the holes and slowly dialed her own number at home. She left the receiver in its cradle. For a fine few seconds she envisioned the black telephone ringing in her apartment. She saw it on the small redwood table next to the couch in the living room. Then she pictured Vincent entering the room and walking toward the phone to answer it.

After dialing the seventh and final number in the familiar sequence, she left her finger in the hole and watched it ride the wheel back to the starting point.

When someone outside tapped on the front window, she started in alarm because she had been so absorbed in that scenario of Vincent in their home. She really felt she was there—like she could reach over and touch the ringing phone herself.

Leni rapped on the glass again, harder this time, using the backs of two fingers. When she eventually had her friend's full attention, she shrugged as if to ask *When are you coming out of there?*

Isabelle could not see little Broximon from where she was but assumed he was somewhere nearby. *Her* Broximon—not the real one, but the imposter she had unconsciously created from memory and frantic need to help her out of this trouble.

Perhaps it was thinking about her false Broximon. Or the memory that followed of the multitude of Simon Hadens massed together to confuse Chaos when it arrived. It might even have been as simple as seeing the rotary dial on this telephone with its numbers and letters you could choose from and combine.

Whatever gave her the idea, like a cloud that crosses a brilliant morning sun and changes the light over the world completely for a few dramatic moments, Isabelle suddenly realized something and instantly she passed from doubt and confusion to crystal clarity. Without hesitating at all she closed her eyes and thought of Petras Urbsys. In her mind she re-created the best possible image of the man she had known so well and respected tremendously. She thought in particular about his joie de vivre combined with that polymath's knowledge and endless curiosity. . . .

Time passed while she thought of him, remembered him, and then she heard his voice very near: "Did I ever tell you about the Blue Morpho butterfly?"

Although her first reaction on hearing his familiar voice was to yelp with joy, Isabelle managed to keep her eyes closed and silently mouth no. She had never heard of the butterfly before. She hoped and prayed to the gods that Petras would speak again now and prove her inspiration correct.

"I had a framed specimen of a Blue Morpho up on the wall in here for years but then I sold it. A seven-inch wingspan, Isabelle. Can you imagine that? Amazing!"

Unable to wait any longer, she opened her eyes and saw Petras sitting on the floor facing her. His elbows were on his spread knees and he was smiling his missing-tooth smile at her. He was even wearing the tan construction boots she remembered he liked so much. "The top of the Blue Morpho's wings are a magnificent electric blue. A blue you cannot imagine until you have seen it. But that is only one of the reasons why it is a favorite of mine. The second reason will be helpful to you now, I believe."

• • •

Because he stood so low to the ground, when false Broximon looked into the store he had to look up. As a result, he was the first to see one of the three large blue butterflies fluttering around inside Petras

Urbsys's shop. Out of nowhere a second appeared and then a third. He stared at them for a while with a child's wonderment. The sight of those gorgeous butterflies flying around in there was eerie and out of kilter. Particularly because they kept appearing and disappearing. There they were, now they're gone—nope! Here they are again. How did they do that in plain sight?

When he brought it to Leni's attention she seemed unimpressed. There were other things on her mind. One minute she had peered into the store and seen Isabelle crouched alone in a corner fiddling with a telephone. The next time she looked in the window, Isabelle was in that same position talking to Petras Urbsys.

"Why are there blue butterflies inside that store?"

Leni was straining so hard to see what else was going on inside "that store" that she barely managed to answer "I dunno." About the only thing she did know was Isabelle and Petras were watching the butterflies with great concentration. The old man gestured toward them with both hands as if explaining something about them to her.

He was. Before the Blue Morphos flew into the room, Petras explained to her the difference between mimicry and camouflage in the animal kingdom. Isabelle began by thinking What does this have to do with what's going on now? but she remained quiet and just listened. Soon she was listening with interest that grew into genuine pleasure, as had usually happened during her visits with Petras. He was a natural teacher. His enthusiasm was contagious and made subjects intriguing that never in a million years would have appealed to her if he hadn't introduced and talked about them. When he found something fascinating he was eager and worked hard to make you think so too.

When the butterflies appeared out of nowhere they were as striking as Petras had said. Isabelle wanted to talk about them and ask questions, but he stopped her and said "Just watch them a while before saying anything more." She did that and noticed the same thing Broximon had observed—the butterflies seemed to appear and disappear as they flew in and out of the light around the room. It was not one specific place where it happened either. She could not figure out how it happened but found it very intriguing and mysterious.

Petras watched her watching the butterflies. He was hoping she would come to the right conclusions by herself but if not, he would tell her the necessary information anyway. Much better though if she discovered things for herself. The more of this she worked through on her own, the easier it would be for Isabelle to find and use her important reserves when it was necessary.

Once when she visited him in the store he had been eating a large piece of chocolate cake from the bakery across the street. It was gooey and in his enthusiasm to devour it, he had bits of chocolate and crumbs stuck to his mouth in several places. Without a word she reached into her purse, pulled out a paper tissue, and handed it to him. Petras took it but put it down until he had finished eating and in that eager process, gotten even more cake on his face. Only when he was done and had sighed contentedly did he use her tissue.

"That's the difference between us, Isabelle. You see a crumb and want to wipe it away. But I believe people should live like an old man eating cake. For him there is nothing else left in his life but that delicious sweetness in his mouth. So he enjoys it more than you ever could and doesn't worry about how the crumbs look."

Speaking to him now, she mentioned that cake incident and said she was trying to look at these butterflies the same way he ate his cake. Petras grinned but said nothing. She rose from the floor and walked over to the part of the room the butterflies had chosen, for the moment, to do their air dance.

Outside, Leni watched it happen through the front window but it left her even more confused about what to do next. Petras watched too, still not saying a thing. Indifferent, Broximon had turned away and was content watching the cars go by on the street.

The three butterflies didn't appear to mind Isabelle's presence, even when she moved up close and walked here and there to observe them from different angles.

"Their wings are schizophrenic."

Petras shifted his position. "What do you mean?"

"The tops are blue but the bottoms are black. At least they look black."

"Why do you think that is?"

She kept staring at the butterflies. "I don't know."

"Watch what happens to them when they fly in and out of the light. But it's better to sit down and watch from the floor."

In and out of the light they dipped and danced, spun and played tag with one another.

"They disappear. They disappear when they fly into the light."

"No, it just looks that way from where you are sitting. The truth is they are still there but you can't see them for some moments. It is their camouflage, Isabelle. Remember what I told you before about mimicry and camouflage. It is how these butterflies survive."

She glanced at Petras. "That's why the bottom of their wings is black? Anything below can't see them because they're so dark."

He corrected her. "But only for a moment—just enough time for them to escape. Remember though, only the *bottoms* of their wings are dark. The tops are blue; a great blue.

"Black to your enemies, blue to all others."

What Isabelle had realized while looking at the old telephone was that she could conjure a Petras in the same way she had earlier conjured false Broximon, but with one great difference. She had unconsciously reconstructed Broximon out of her fear, weakness, and need. In contrast, this Petras was a fully conscious creation, the deliberate product of love and a trust in her best memories of her friend. She had brought *that* man here now to help her.

In this singular world somewhere on the borderline between life and death, it was becoming clear that she had the power to do remarkable things. Even more so than Leni because Isabelle was alive in this world and Leni was not. At the same time, Isabelle now realized she must be extremely careful and precise about her choices. Here she could conjure "leprechauns" or summon the dead, but which versions and whether they would be of any help depended entirely on *her* foresight, perception, and will.

• • •

A little later as she was leaving, Petras said one last thing. "The heart and the mind rarely lie at the same time, Isabelle."

She stopped in the doorway and waited for him to continue but he didn't. "I don't understand that."

"Whatever you do now, listen to yourself carefully before acting. Try to recognize which part of you is telling the truth and which part is lying only because it's safe or easier."

"Know thyself?" she asked with a smile.

"Know thyselvessss" he answered, elongating the last syllable so that he sounded like a buzzing bee.

When she stepped outside and pulled the door shut behind her, both Leni and false Broximon were there with sour looks on their faces. They had been waiting a long time.

"Well?"

"I want a *Mohr im hemd.* I'm trying to think of a place around here we can go to get one."

Isabelle's response was so unexpected that without thinking, Leni automatically asked "*What* do you want?"

Isabelle repeated "A *Mohr im hemd.*"

Broximon looked at both women and asked anyone "What's a *Mohr im hemd?*"

Leni looked from Isabelle to Broximon and then back at Isabelle again, her face all confused. "Chocolate cake."

• • • • • •

Vincent Ettrich was thinking about food when the telephone rang. While he crossed the living room to answer it, a bowl of soup was in the middle of his thoughts. A large white bowl full of thick goulash soup and several pieces of fresh bread. Brown bread, brown soup, white bowl . . .

He picked up the phone and absentmindedly said "Hello?"

"Glass soup."

The wording was so close to what he'd been thinking that Ettrich had to pause a moment to separate the two. Then another moment to remember and realize the import of what he had just heard.

Glass soup.

"Who is this?"

"Someone who knows both Isabelle and what glass soup means."

Broximon came out of the guest room where Ettrich had put a child's sleeping bag on the couch in there for him to use. "What's going on?" He'd been taking a nap. His voice sounded yawny.

Ettrich pointed to the telephone receiver and signaled for Brox to wait. "What do you want?"

"It's not what I want, Mr. Ettrich, it's what *you* want."

Vincent surfed through his mind trying to place the voice. Had he heard it before? He didn't think so. "I don't know what you're talking about."

"Then it would be good for us to meet so that I can explain, if you have time."

Broximon mouthed *What's up?*

Ettrich took the receiver from his ear and silently, slowly mouthed *Glass soup.*

Understanding immediately, Broximon tensed.

"Are you also a friend of John Flannery? We don't need to meet."

The voice on the other end of the phone became coy. "You're wrong. What would you say if I told you she was here?"

"Isabelle?"

"Yes, she's in Vienna."

• • •

Outside of the apartment Broximon's presence was a real problem. This became obvious immediately after he moved in with Ettrich and often accompanied him on errands around the neighborhood. People didn't stop and stare at Broximon—they gasped and froze when they saw him. They covered their mouths with their hands at the sight of this perfectly formed, nattily dressed tiny man. He looked like something out of a fairy tale or a Fellini film. Broximon was slightly over nineteen inches tall. Bigger than when he had climbed out of an envelope in front of Simon Haden, he was nevertheless impossibly small in this environment. Despite his size, he had a man's face and the only clothes he'd brought here were showy, elegant, and problematic. Ettrich shook his head emphatically no when Broximon showed them to him the first time.

"What, you gotta problem with pinstripes?"

"Broximon, you saw how people react to you on the street. If you don't want to attract attention here, you cannot wear those clothes anymore."

"Why not?"

"Because in *this* world, nineteen-inch-tall people are children. But you do not look like a child. Do you understand how that can make things difficult? You're not even tall enough to qualify as a midget, or at least I don't think so. You said you don't want to attract attention and I agree. You should keep a low profile." Ettrich was sitting on the couch and Broximon was standing nearby. He was not even as high as Ettrich's knee.

"So what am I supposed to do?"

As if he'd been waiting for just that question, Ettrich reached for a red and black plastic bag next to him with the words *Sports Experts* written in white across it. "Here's your new wardrobe."

Inside the bag were two new stiff pairs of indigo children's jeans, two yellow sweatshirts, and a lilac-colored baseball cap that said across the brim HOME RUN BOY. Broximon's eyes first widened in outrage and then sunk down through dismay into resigned disgust. But he didn't say a word in protest because he knew that Vincent was right.

"Around the house you can wear whatever you want, but when we go out this should be your uniform."

"Anything else, Commander?"

"Yes." Ettrich picked up a sheaf of papers that had been under the bag of clothes. "When anyone asks why you're so small, tell them you have Hutchinson-Gilford Progeria Syndrome." He offered the papers to Brox who eyed them suspiciously. "I downloaded a couple of articles on the disease from the Internet. It's all in there."

"*What* am I supposed to have?"

"Progeria is a very rare genetic disease that ages a person seven times faster than normal. Kids who get it die of old age at thirteen. I know about it because my agency was hired to do an advertising campaign for one of their research foundations. When we are out on the street and anyone asks, tell them you're my son and that you have progeria."

Broximon looked at Ettrich like maybe this whole thing was a joke and he was about to hear the punch line. On realizing that Vincent was entirely serious, Brox exploded. "Get the fuck out of here! Are you out of your mind? Progeria. I thought you made that name up. Do you really think anyone is going to believe that I'm your son and I have a disease that sounds like a planet in a science fiction movie?"

"Well, Brox, no more than they believe seeing a two-foot-tall man dressed in a double-breasted suit and Gucci loafers."

Broximon looked down at his beautiful Gucci loafers, each the size of a large mouse. While he looked, his lips were all over the place with emotion. He knew Vincent was right about everything but that only made it worse.

He had come here to help save Isabelle but failed immediately. He couldn't go home to Haden's world, and there was nothing for him to do now but fret, watch Austrian TV, and take naps. Broximon had never slept so much in his entire life.

Worse was yet to come. The backpack was the last straw. Broximon was so bored staying inside the apartment that he went out with Ettrich every chance he got. Vincent didn't object because he felt sorry for the little guy, but sometimes he wished he could do certain things alone. Another real problem with going out together was Broximon was so small that he had a hard time keeping up, even when Vincent walked slowly. Crossing a wide busy street as quickly as he could, Broximon still moved at the speed of an old woman. Cars were impatient and unforgiving. Their horns followed him everywhere. Hurrying along, he would look up furious at their loud obnoxiousness but all he would see were the menacing silver smiles of car grilles.

Ettrich longed to say *Look, just let me pick you up and help you here. As soon as we get to the other side of the street I'll put you down again—it's no big deal.* But having lived with Brox for even this short amount of time, he knew that the little man was vain, argumentative, and not so secretly scared of this world.

But one day when they were crossing Schonbrunnerstrasse he was hit. By a bicycle, thank God, and only a glancing blow. Some bike messenger wearing silver sunglasses and dressed all in orange swerved between cars, didn't see Broximon in the hurly-burly, and hit him. The messenger felt only a slight bump when it happened but nothing more. He kept going.

Broximon, shocked and shaken, got up slowly off the pavement. He knew now for sure that he would have to accept drastic changes here or else this place would eat him up. He didn't leave the apartment or his room for two days after that, nor would he speak.

Ettrich knew what had to be done and did it. He came home one afternoon with another bag from Sports Experts but put this one in the hall closet. He waited for Broximon to reemerge and bring up the subject. Three days later he did in a most truculent way but Ettrich was ready. He went to the closet, got the bag and brought it into the living room. He put it down on the floor near Broximon without a word and left the room again.

Five minutes later while he was standing in the kitchen drinking a glass of cold grapefruit juice, Ettrich heard a wail followed by a long-drawn-out cry of "Noooooo!" come from the living room. He did not react. He waited to see if anything else came from in there. When it didn't, he drank some more juice and looked out the window at the small garden planted in the *Hof* downstairs.

More time passed until eventually someone cleared his throat behind him. Vincent turned and saw Broximon standing on the other side of the doorway holding the thing in both hands. It looked very much like he had been crying. Ettrich was so touched and embarrassed to see this that he averted his eyes.

"You cannot be serious with this thing."

"Do you have a better idea, Brox? You're the one who got run over. We have to do something."

"I wasn't run over. I was knocked down."

Ettrich drank the last of the juice and smacked his lips before replying. "Yeah well, so the next time you'll be run over, okay?"

It was a backpack. But one of those specially designed backpacks used to carry small children in. The kind you pop junior into so that the baby can come along and see the world when you're going out for a walk or a bike ride on a sunny day. The awfullest part was that before carrying the pack to the kitchen to confront Ettrich, Broximon actually tried it on and the damned thing fit. After making sure Vincent was nowhere about, he maneuvered the pack around so that he could climb in and see how it felt. It felt fine.

"I'm supposed to ride around in this contraption on your back every time we go out?"

"I didn't say that, Brox. What I'm going to do is take it along so in case we *do* need it out there, we'll be prepared."

"And by the way, did you happen to see the name of this thing? Did you see what it's called on the label here?"

Ettrich pretended there was more juice in the empty glass and tipped it up to his mouth again. Yes, he knew what it was called but it was the only pack of its kind he found that he thought would fit Broximon.

"Babby Basket. I assume they meant *baby* basket, but they misspelled it. I'm supposed to go out on the street wearing these ridiculous horrible clothes and ride around on your back in something called the Babby Basket?

"Look, I have an idea—why don't you just kill me now? Save us all the fuss. Your apartment is up high enough; throw me out that window. Us little progeria people fall just as fast as you big ones."

Ettrich rubbed his nose "Don't be melodramatic. Do you want some grapefruit juice?"

• • •

After that ominous phone call today, Broximon went to the hall closet and got out the Babby Basket without Ettrich having to say anything. Every time they returned home after using it, Broximon took the cursed thing and buried it as deep as he could in the back of the closet. That didn't change anything but it made him feel microscopically better.

Emerging from the dark land of coats with it in his hand, he was startled to hear Vincent's vexed voice right behind him.

"Know what else that fucker said? He asked in this very sweet, very docile voice if I knew that the word *anijo* was Eskimo for falling snow, and that *anjou* is both a kind of pear and a region of France. He knows what my son's name is and was riffing on it. The fucker taunted me with how much he knows."

Brox said hotly "Calm down! What the hell good is it going to do if you meet him all crazy and pissed off?"

"He knows my son's *name,* Broximon! He knows about Anjo and glass soup and that Isabelle is here. Chaos is here—it talked to me on the phone. I'm not pissed off—I'm scared for them."

"Well, don't be—it does no good. Let's go meet this guy and hear what he has to say."

"Know what he answered when I asked if I could bring you with me? He asked if progeria was anything like a profiterole. He wanted to know if he could eat you."

• • • • • •

Isabelle, Leni, and false Broximon sat together on a brown park bench and stared up at the high oddity looming in front of them.

"It's called a *flakturm.*"

"Say that word again."

"Flak-turm."

"Hmm." False Broximon had never heard that word before but that was not surprising because he didn't speak German.

"It's an antiaircraft tower. The German army built them during World War Two. They put big guns on top to shoot at American airplanes going by. It's made of pure concrete. After the war it was discovered they're so thick and indestructible that they couldn't demolish them by dynamiting them or whatever, without damaging every building in the neighborhood. So they just left them standing. I think there's something like five still left around town."

"What do they do with them now?"

"Nothing. There's not much you can do. An architect wanted to build a hotel on top of one, but the city refused. This is the only one that's actually used, as far as I know. They made it into an aquarium. There are exotic fish and reptiles inside. There are even sharks. That big glass canopy coming off the side is a tropical rain forest. Inside it really is like a jungle. There are monkeys and parrots."

"Sharks and monkeys living inside an antiaircraft tower? Now *that's* surreal."

After the failure at the café, the three of them had walked into this park with the *flakturm* in the center on their way to Isabelle's apartment. They were only about ten minutes away now.

They had gone to a café near Petras's store because Isabelle remembered they served *Mohr in hemd* there. More than that, she wanted some time to think over what she had learned with Petras just now before seeing Vincent again.

When they arrived the café was half-empty. They had their pick of tables. They chose a large one by a window that was filled with light. Isabelle looked for a waiter so they could order but none was about. She settled into the wide seat and looked around, smiling.

Leni started to say something to her. Sitting on the windowsill, false Broximon sensed what she was about to say. He shook his head at her and glared. *Let Isabelle find out for herself,* his eyes said. *Don't you say a word.* Leni looked away.

Isabelle's revelation came a few minutes later. At first she didn't mind or really notice that when the passing waiters finally *did* appear, none of them paid attention to her, although she kept raising a hand or her voice to beckon them over. Waiters in Viennese cafés are known for being testy and self-directed. They come and go as they please and if you don't like that, tough. Cafés are not hurried places. You don't go there to have a quick one and leave. You go there to chat or read or dream. The waiters know this and act accordingly.

In time though it became all too clear that these waiters weren't ignoring Isabelle—they couldn't see her.

"They don't see me." Her voice was quiet and composed. She was only stating a fact.

Leni nodded her head once in agreement, her eyes closed because she did not want to see her friend's face. False Broximon did nothing.

"Why didn't you tell me, Leni?"

"Don't you remember the guards at the border talking about that man on the bicycle that comes over here a few times a week to try and communicate with his mother? But he almost never succeeds. This is what it's like for any dead person who returns here."

"But I'm not dead!"

"You came here from Simon Haden's land. That's why Chaos tricked you into choosing to go there; because after you've *chosen* to experience that stage of death there's no returning."

"But I brought Vincent back from death. I brought us both back. I did it before."

To her dismay both of them shook their heads this time. "Vincent had just died. You came before he created his world, which is the second part of death. If that had happened before you reached him, you never would have been able to save him."

"Then where is *here*? Where exactly are we?" Isabelle made an exasperated gesture meant to take in everything around them, everything real, her world, the world that she knew intimately.

"This is the other side of the glass. Remember? You're on our side of it now."

• • •

They were sitting in this park instead of finishing the short walk to Isabelle's apartment because she was afraid of how she would react when she saw Vincent again. See him but not be able to touch him? Smell him but not kiss him? This was the worst part of being on the other side of the glass. She was back in her world, back to everything she knew so well. There it all was—right in front of her. She could see it, hear it . . . She was sure that if she *had* been able to order that *Mohr im hemd* she would have been able to smell its rich deliciousness. Everything from her life was here—except her in it.

• • • • • •

"Hello there, young fellow. What's your name?" A handsome old man wearing a gray Tyrolean hat asked in German, looking delighted to see Broximon perched high up on Ettrich's back in his Babby Basket.

Broximon tried to ignore him but it was difficult because the traffic light was red and they stood together on the curb waiting for it to change. There was nowhere else to go and the old man was clearly waiting for an answer.

"Vincent, what did he say?"

Ettrich leaned his head back and translated "He wants to know your name."

"Ah English! I speak English. Hallo, little man. What is your name?"

"Marvin Gaye" Broximon said in his deepest adult voice and turned away.

A red and white city bus passed close by, drowning out whatever the old man said next. Broximon didn't ask him to repeat it but he did anyway. His voice sounded completely different this time. He spoke with no accent at all. "I thought your name was Broximon."

The light changed to green but none of them moved. The old man smiled but the others didn't.

"Who are you?"

"Vincent, we just talked on the telephone. Don't you remember?"

"That was *you*?"

The old gentleman lifted his hat in the gallant/jaunty "how do you do?" manner.

"What are you doing here? I thought we were supposed to meet at Heldenplatz?"

"Change of plan. Would you like to see Isabelle? She's right nearby."

Ettrich was instantly torn between deep suspicion and desire. Isabelle was here? She was near? He had missed her so much. And the baby? How was their child?

"Where is she?"

"In a park a few minutes from here. I'll take you there right now if you'd like."

Broximon piped in over Ettrich's shoulder "Why should we trust you?"

The old man reached up and tickled Broximon under the chin. "Why shouldn't you? All I'm suggesting is that we walk over to a park."

Broximon leaned forward and whispered in Ettrich's ear farthest from the old man. Ettrich listened but said nothing and the expression on his face didn't change. Then he said "All right, we'll go with you."

"Excellent. Follow me."

He walked a few steps ahead of them and for the first minutes, Broximon continued whispering to Ettrich. Eventually Brox straightened up in his seat and asked "Did you take John Flannery's place?"

"Yes I did."

"You're Chaos?"

"Let's say I represent the firm."

"Aren't you a little old to be doing this?"

The old man wiggled a "naughty-naughty" finger at Broximon and winked. "Just because there's snow on the roof doesn't mean there isn't a fire in the fireplace.

"Anyway I don't do miracles, which really *is* a young man's game. So don't ask me for one of those. Besides, the last two fellows they sent here could work miracles but look at what Vincent did to them. I loved how you handed Flannery. Oh, I had a good laugh at that. Him and that big dog. You vaporized them both. That was a stroke of pure genius.

"Everyone underestimated you, Vincent. They didn't give you your due. I told them that; I said Ettrich is a clever man, he's wily. Send me this time and let me just talk to him. I know he'll listen." He patted his chest. "Because my one and only specialty is order; tidying things up. You should see my desk at home—it's always spotless. As a rule, old people are good at organizing things because we've had so much experience. Plus we don't have much else to do.

"Take a right at the corner—we're almost there.

"I like contracts. Treaties, ironclad agreements, and binding clauses. No loopholes allowed. No sly gaps in the fence where someone can slip through. I want things signed, sealed, and delivered. Then you know exactly where you stand. Surprises are my enemy."

Neither Ettrich nor Broximon knew what the old guy was getting at, nor were they really listening as he rattled on. Instead they watched him—his gestures, his gait, the way he frequently turned to smile at them.

"You didn't say what your name was."

"You can call me Putnam."

Down the street the *flakturm* came into view. Ettrich knew what it was but Broximon didn't. At the moment however, architecture wasn't much on his mind. When he saw the building he frowned at how strange and out of place it was. Then he went back to studying the garrulous old man in the hat.

"So I told them let me go and talk to Vincent Ettrich. Let me try to make a deal with him that we're all happy with. He's a reasonable man. I'm sure I can find a way. They said go ahead, give it a try."

"And part of your deal would be to eat Broximon like a profiterole?"

"That was a joke, Vincent! I was kidding. Come on, did you really think I was serious? I didn't have to bring you here now. I didn't have to show you Isabelle. That was my decision—a gift to you to prove my good intentions."

They walked up some stairs and entered the park. Immediately to the right at the top was a fenced-in soccer/basketball court. It was bustling with boys of all ages playing, running, shouting, their soccer and basketballs flying around everywhere. Sitting on benches right outside the cage were a whole other group of kids watching these games, or watching the girls that were among them, or showing off, smoking, being loud, singing, practicing bad karate moves, practicing the latest dance steps . . .

One of the girls sitting on a bench happened to look over and saw Broximon. She let out an ugly short high squeal and touched her face. Her girlfriends looked his way to see what she was squealing about. When they saw him they all reacted differently. One jumped up and walked quickly away into the park and never looked back. Two other girls started giggling and then punched each other to shut up.

The boys were even worse. When they saw Broximon they gaped at him or smiled either malevolently or stupidly, as if they were visiting a zoo and had happened upon the cage of some bizarre animal. Never having seen anything like this little freak in his Babby Basket, this child with the distinctive man's face, what else could they do but stare at him until they'd had their fill?

Ettrich saw the reactions and winced. He said "They're just being kids, Brox. They're all dummies."

Every time it had happened here, and this was certainly not the first time, it hurt and shamed Broximon deeply. How the citizens of this world reacted to him made Broximon want to disappear even more. But he never said a word about it. Why should he? There was nothing anyone could do and Ettrich had enough problems as it was.

"Do you want me to make them go away? I'll be happy to." Putnam had dropped back to walk beside Vincent, right up next to Broximon.

In spite of himself, the little man's curiosity got the best of him. He found himself asking "What can you do?"

"Oh, many things. For starters, I can bring the birds down. Fun stuff. That would be entertaining. We'd have our own Hitchcock film right here in the park. You just have to say the word and we'll have *The Birds*." Putnam pointed up toward a towering chestnut tree nearby. Looking attentively, they saw that it was chockfull of crows sitting on the branches. Big fat things, there must have been twenty-five of them up there scattered throughout the tree. Oddly, they were all silent which was not like that screechy breed. Caught up in the events of their own loud busy world below, the kids paid no attention to them.

"Or rats, if you prefer something more earthbound. There are a large number of rats in this park. You don't see them now because during the day they keep their own council. But they're there to help if I ask them." Putnam spoke in a sympathetic, concerned voice.

"Let's just get out of here" Broximon managed to say although his imagination delighted in images of all these young shitheads and their tight-jean queens fleeing screaming from waves of attacking rats and crows.

Ettrich hefted him higher onto his back and picked up the pace. "How much farther do we have to go?"

"We're almost there. Come on."

A few hundred feet farther on, Isabelle craned her head back to look once again at the stained gray *flakturm*. Leni saw Vincent first when he and the old man came into view. "Isabelle."

"Yeah?" She didn't move her head.

"Vincent's here."

"What? Where?"

Leni pointed "There. Right over there."

"Oh my God." When Isabelle first saw him, she unconsciously slid both hands around the bulge of her stomach, around their unborn child. Her hands told Anjo *Look, look, there he is. There's your father.* "Who is that with him? Who's that old guy?"

"I don't know."

False Broximon saw his real self in the carrier on Ettrich's back. He was fascinated but at the same time in turmoil about how he felt. That's him, he thought, that's me. That's who I'm supposed to be. He felt like a counterfeit bill.

Putnam led Ettrich to a group of picnic tables about twenty feet away from Isabelle and her companions. He gestured for Vincent to sit down, his back facing the *flakturm*. When he did, Putnam pointed to an empty bench nearby. "She's sitting over there, watching you. She's smiling and rubbing her stomach."

Vincent looked over but saw nothing. Neither did Broximon. "I don't see anyone."

"Yes, Isabelle's sitting there, along with Leni Salomon and a Broximon but a bad copy of this one. She must have made it herself."

Vincent and real Broximon listened to this but neither of them saw anything. "Prove it."

Putnam called out "Isabelle, would you come over here, please?"

She checked Leni who enthusiastically nodded for her to go. Isabelle walked over to the table and sat down facing Vincent. His features were drawn and thin. What had he been eating? That's the first thing that crossed her mind when she looked across the table at her great love—He hasn't been eating enough.

Putnam pointed directly at her and said to Vincent "She's here now. She's sitting directly across from you. Say whatever you want."

Vincent looked toward her but not at her. It reminded Isabelle of a blind person whose eyes appear normal. The disconcerting way they have of seeming to see you but not really.

"I'm still waiting for you to prove this."

Instead of responding, the old man looked at Isabelle and waited. In time he turned back to Vincent and spoke. "She says she wants you to put both of your hands on the table, palms down."

What was there to lose? Lifting his hands from his lap, he put them on the table. He wanted to turn and see how Broximon was reacting to all this. But Ettrich didn't want to miss any expression on Putnam's face that might indicate something important.

"Now look at the palm of your left hand. I'm only telling you what she's telling me."

Hesitantly Vincent lifted it and turning it over, peered at his palm. The word *celadon* was written across it in Isabelle's sloppy but distinctive handwriting in celadon-blue letters.

"Look at your right hand."

Written in the center of that palm was *anak* which Ettrich now knew was the Eskimo word for shit.

He remembered the incident at the cemetery when they both put their hands on Petras's gravestone. Vincent was instantly transported back to the time Isabelle learned from the old man how to enter death. And later that same day when they were sitting together on the tram, how they'd held hands and played the "unknown word" game together. Unknown words like *celadon* and *anak*. The game that was only possible because of the magic that happened now when they touched.

"What do you want, Mr. Putnam?"

"Do you believe me now, Vincent? Do you believe that she's here?"

"Yes. But why can't I see her?"

Broximon knew the answer to that but remained silent. He clamored to get out of the carrier but knew it was not the moment to ask Ettrich to put him down.

"You will never see Isabelle here again. She is too far into death, past the point of no return. She *chose* to do that, Vincent. It was her decision; she wasn't coerced. If someone chooses to go there, then they have to stay. Those are the rules, set in stone. We have no control over them."

Broximon knew this was true. But he also knew, because he had been there when it happened, that Isabelle had chosen to go over because she had been tricked by Chaos. She had done it to protect their child. Broximon did not need to see the writing on Vincent's hands to know that she existed in another dimension now and could never wholly return here again. It was finished. Disconsolate, he asked Putnam "If she's gone for good, then why are you even here? You've won. What more do you want?"

"To make Vincent an offer, as I said on the telephone. You see, he can still be together with Isabelle, but just not here."

On the other side of the table Isabelle slowly straightened, like a cat rising out of its sleeping spot in the sun. Alert but uncertain, she made sure her hands were still touching Ettrich's.

"Even if you're here alone, Vincent, you remain dangerous to us. You know too much about life and death and what goes on in between. I'll be honest with you and get right to the point.

"Here's our offer—we will make it possible for you and Isabelle to be together in *your* afterlife dreamworld. You already died once so you've been through the first stage. If you agree to this, we'll arrange to send you directly to the second stage, which is your dreamworld. I'm sure Broximon has explained it all to you by now.

"Isabelle and Anjo will meet you there and the three of you can be together forever. The best part is you will be able to create that world. Sculpt it as if it were a piece of clay, down to the smallest detail, so that everything there is exactly to your specifications. Your own personally designed heaven, Vincent. We'll even allow you to consult with Isabelle about what she wants so that you can include it and make her happy too. It really will be your own paradise."

Despite a million arguments against it, Ettrich chose to go in a different direction. "And Anjo? What would happen to him after he's born?"

Putnam rubbed his hands together slowly, as if they were arthritic and he was trying to warm and make them feel better. "Anjo would grow up happy and healthy in your heaven. That's not a bad place to be, eh? It would be your decision whether or not you wanted to tell him where he was."

"And what would it be like when he got older?"

The old man leaned back in his chair and put his hands behind his head. "You could give him the perfect girlfriend or wife, a job he enjoyed, a bright red Ferrari." He smiled at his little joke and looked up at an airplane crossing the sky. "Maybe give him some kids later if that's what he wanted, or a million-dollar house with an ocean view . . . things that made him content. It's all up to you. Give him whatever he wants, Vincent. You're the creator—it'll be your world."

"What's the catch?"

Putnam responded without any hesitation "The catch is you'll always know. Both you and Isabelle will always know where you are, what it really is, and how you got there. No matter how wonderful you make your world, you'll always know that it isn't here."

"Ha!" Broximon squawked from the Babby Basket, unable to contain his indignation.

Out on the street a car passed with all its windows rolled down. Its stereo was blasting an old AC/DC song.

Sitting on the park bench twenty feet away, Leni heard the song and smiled a little. She remembered teenage days and how she had so recently crossed a Highway to Hell in her own dreamworld.

Isabelle also heard the music but had a totally different reaction to it. At the moment the car passed, she was looking at Broximon in his basket. She asked herself When did I last hear an AC/DC song? That time I ate pizza with Simon Haden and told him some things about my past because he kept asking. She'd spoken a little about her childhood. She had told him about Brogsma, her imaginary childhood friend. How he was her constant companion back then because she was scared of so many things in life. The Brogsma she created was a fifty-fifty mix of a child her age and an adult. As a result, he always knew how to handle things because he possessed the best qualities of both a grown-up and a child. He gave her the best advice. He was funnier than anyone. No one else could see him but Isabelle so he was always at her side when she needed him. Always there to comfort her and make her feel safe when she was frightened.

Brogsma.

Broximon.

"Oh my God, he got the name wrong! He thought it was *Broximon*. That's so unbelievably sweet."

Putnam looked at her after this unexpected outburst and wondered what she was babbling about. But when she continued to stare at Broximon without saying anything more, Putnam returned to the conversation with Ettrich.

Isabelle had always known Simon Haden cared for her, but never grasped the full extent until this moment. Now she realized that Simon had taken his memories of her childhood stories with him into death and one of the people he had populated his dreamworld with was her Brogsma.

And because Simon was so snobby about what he wore, he gave the same characteristic to her Brogsma. Today he was dressed like a skateboarder for some reason, but in the past whenever she had encountered Broximon he had always been dressed exquisitely—like an English lord or an Italian millionaire. But that was only because Simon dressed that way too.

From the beginning, this beautifully attired Broximon had been there to help. He was the first one to speak to her in Haden's dreamworld. Later when she met him in real life at Leni's funeral he had tried to help her but failed.

She looked over at the bench where Leni was sitting next to the false Broximon. What an irony: Isabelle had created *him* from her memories of the real Broximon, thinking he could help her out of this mess. But now Isabelle understood both Broximons were flawed copies of a being *she* had invented when she was a girl.

Back then she had created Brogsma to protect and comfort her. Simon had created Broximon, and now Vincent was supposed to create a whole dreamworld where they would all live happily ever after . . . outside outside outside. Everyone kept feverishly creating outside things to save themselves. But the door opened inward, that she knew for sure.

Isabelle remembered a line she had read recently: "You must find yourself where you already are." She was thirty-two years old. There were so many different phases in life. So many different Isabelle Neukors had inhabited her days on earth. Why not turn to some of them now for help? Selves that had already lived and prevailed. Why not ask them for help? Why not ask herself for help?

Like sixteen-year-old Isabelle who had walked all night alone across Bombay back to her hotel because she had lost her wallet and had no money for a taxi. That brave, impulsive girl saw the walk as a fun adventure. Never once did it cross her mind that it was dangerous.

So—help me now, sixteen-year-old me. Take my place behind the wheel. Please drive this stretch of dark unknown road because I am too frightened and lost and out of control. The headlights stopped working a while ago and there is no map but that didn't bother you half my lifetime ago in Bombay.

Or help me, twenty-eight-year-old Isabelle, who had the strength to face the fact she was an alcoholic and then the courage to admit it to the right people who helped her to save herself. Help me now, twenty-eight-year-old me.

She was again looking at the antiaircraft tower while thinking these things. Her mind spinning like a kind of turbine, these thoughts about her different past selves fueling it. Which of them could best help me now? What do I have to do to find her? Can this idea really work?

She needed strength and courage now. She also needed a version of herself who was intimate with this situation, the players and the stakes involved. Her sixteen-year-old self did not know Vincent Ettrich or very much about how life worked, for that matter. How could anyone at sixteen when life is just beginning to show its hand?

Her twenty-eight-year-old self had not gone yet into death to rescue the love of her life. At twenty-eight she fucked too many men, it was a kind of cold sport back then, and love (whatever that was) lived on another planet—definitely not the one she inhabited. What she needed now was an Isabelle her age with her résumé and her scars. An Isabelle who knew most of what she knew but was undaunted by it.

While thinking this over, her eyes slid down one long stained side of the cement *flakturm,* to the tall trees in front of it waving in the wind, and then over to the enclosed children's playground nearby. The warm breeze had picked up. She felt it over her skin and in her hair. Perhaps it would rain later on. The sounds of rustling leaves and the occasional call of a bird were near.

Two days before her friend Leni Salomon died, Isabelle had gone for a long walk alone around the neighborhood. For no specific reason she had awakened that morning brimming with happiness and expectancy. Breakfast with Vincent was intimate and funny. He told stories she had never heard before that made her laugh, and he kept buttering pieces of toast for her with a jeweler's precision. Just that gesture alone, the care he took doing something so trivial but with such unmistakable love, swept her heart off its feet. When they had finished eating, he took her hand and brought it to his cool lips. He looked in her eyes for the longest time but said nothing and neither did she. Everything they needed for the rest of their lives together was there in that moment, that room, his gesture.

Afterward Vincent took the dog to the veterinary for a vaccination. The apartment felt too empty without him and the weather outside was so gorgeous that she decided to go for a walk. She ate fresh strawberry ice cream sitting outside at an Italian *eissalon* and then watched three black and white French bulldog puppies wrestling with each other in a pet store window on Neubaugasse. She wanted to amble around some more but suddenly felt overwhelmingly heavy and tired. This often happened to her now that the pregnancy was coming to term. Sometimes it made her feel frustrated, as if she wasn't in control of her body anymore. But it had been such a lovely walk that she only smiled at the inconvenience and considered where she could go sit down and continue enjoying this day without having to move anymore. She slowly walked over to Esterhazy Park and took a seat on a bench with a good view of the fenced-in children's playground.

In happy awe and a still-abiding feeling of disbelief, she watched the children. At that time of day most of them were infants brought out to play for a while in between naps. Isabelle thought Soon we'll have a baby exactly like them. Soon we'll be coming here or to some other park with a pram and a backpack full of extra diapers, a yellow plastic bottle with Anjo's favorite fruit juice inside, and a red bag of zwieback biscuits. While she thought these things, the baby turned inside her. Because he moved right then, she pretended Anjo was checking out the playground with her: sandbox, swings, slide . . . When he was big enough they would use each one. What fun they'd have. There was so much to look forward to!

Isabelle was experiencing a perfect moment and was fully aware of it. She knew she had missed too many other perfect moments in her life because she'd been greedy or distracted or blind to them, but not this one. She was fully conscious of the fact that sitting here looking at these children and dreaming of Anjo was one of those extraordinarily rare moments in life when all of her stars and dreams converged to make these minutes perfect. Nothing could be better than this, absolutely nothing at all.

"Hello."

She was so immersed in happiness and the serenity of the moment that she heard the voice only on the periphery of her consciousness.

"Is it okay if I sit here?"

With great calm she looked up and saw herself standing at the other end of the bench, dressed in different clothes from what she was wearing. She was surprised that she wasn't surprised. "Sure, of course. Sit down."

Isabelle sat down slowly and turned her legs to one side in a more comfortable position. "I need your help. I can't do this. I can't handle it but I know you can."

The one who had been sitting on the bench watching the children knew this was right: she felt like she could handle anything in the world at that moment. "What do you want me to do?"

"Take my place. You're still on that side of the glass and can do it. There are some things you don't know, but it doesn't matter. What's most important is you're strong and in control now and I'm not. Vincent won't recognize the difference between us if you don't tell him.

"I remember that day sitting in the park so well; I remember being *so* content and sure; just sure of everything. When was it, a month ago?

"I can't return because I chose to come over. But you live there now, so please, take the rest of my life. *Our* life; however long it's going to be. With all my being, I offer you my place in that world.

"Take the strength of how you feel right now, this minute. Take the happiness and expectation and hope . . ." she began to choke up ". . . and use it to live the rest of our life there. You're so much stronger now than I'll ever be—"

"You don't have to say anymore. All right." The expression on her face would have alarmed Putnam had he seen it. Because it was the look of a human being who does not doubt her purpose and is certain that it is good. A look that said *I know why I'm here, and I know what I must do. Don't try to stop me.*

On hearing her agree to do it, the other Isabelle slumped forward, all of the tension in her back and shoulders beginning to leave. She let out a big breath and then tried to breathe regularly, to bring it back to normal before she attempted to say anything else.

"How is it done? How does it work?"

"First I must tell you about butterflies. Blue Morpho butterflies. And camouflage. We'll have to fool them. We can't let Putnam see the real color of your wings. 'Black to your enemies, blue to all others.' "

"I don't know what you're talking about." For a few seconds her eyes slid from the face of the nervous distraught woman sitting on the other end of the bench, to the children playing in a sandbox ten feet away. She couldn't resist smiling again when she saw them.

Putnam had watched Isabelle get up and walk away from the table but didn't think anything about it. He only assumed that she was upset by what he had been telling her boyfriend. Putnam watched her walk away toward the other side of the park, then brought his eyes and attention back to Ettrich.

"When I was coming over here to meet you, Vincent, I saw the strangest thing. I must tell you about it. A man was walking down the street toward me; sort of a bum, but not too bad. You know the kind I'm talking about—just this side of shabby, just that side of respectable. I saw that first and was trying to decide how I felt about him. Then I noticed he had both hands up close to his mouth. When we got nearer I saw that he was holding a pigeon there and kissing it again and again."

Putnam stopped and waited for some reaction. Ettrich stared at his hands crossed on the table and didn't respond. Back in the Babby Basket, Broximon puckered his lips. He'd already crossed his arms over his chest minutes ago, skeptical of anything Putnam said.

"Disgusting, huh? Can you imagine kissing a city pigeon? Filthy, probably full of diseases . . . ugly stuff. But you know what happened, Vincent? My mind suddenly did this little flip and it dawned on me that the man loves the bird. I think what he's doing is revolting, but he doesn't. But who's right here? Maybe he knows something I don't."

Broximon couldn't take any more. "What are you talking about? What kind of drugs are you on?"

A naughty, teasing look lit the old man's face. "I'm saying that perhaps Vincent has to learn to love this pigeon I've just offered him."

When Isabelle realized that she had lost the other's attention to something behind her, she turned to see what it was. On the other side of a chest-high fence was a sandbox where three infants were busily playing together. They were sitting in a close circle because they didn't appear old enough to be able to stand on their own yet. Their mothers were nearby, smoking and chatting.

In companionable silence the Isabelles watched the children. Two were dressed in blue jean overalls, while the third wore shorts and a purple "Austria Memphis" soccer shirt. Their clothes were so small yet perfect. All of them wore white sneakers no larger than a cell phone. The Isabelle who was giving over her life thought Every one of those babies will live at least half a century longer than I will and probably more. Half a *century.* So will Anjo.

Thinking this, she once again caressed the big familiar curve of her stomach and with the greatest love thought of him in there. She remembered how he wriggled excitedly whenever she ate something sweet. Then about how he woke her some nights just moving around in her tummy. How glorious and mysterious it was to be awakened by your child moving inside of you. She had been comforted time and again during the pregnancy by the idea *I will never be alone again.*

She realized that if she thought about this anymore now it would crush her with grief and loss, so without allowing another moment to pass she slid down the bench. "After I do this, we must talk to those kids." One hand still on her stomach, she pointed with the other to the large rowdy group of teenagers that Ettrich had passed on entering the park.

"How *will* you do this?"

Isabelle was close enough so that instead of replying, she reached her free hand over and touched the other woman's bulging stomach. One hand on her own, one hand on the other's. Closing her eyes, she cleared her mind as best she could, which was very difficult. She remembered what Vincent had once said about talking to time. About how it understood if you did it the right way. Now she would try it.

With all the small strength she had left, from her side of the glass she willed everything she had, everything that she was, every hope, dream, and wish into the other's body and being. Like pushing a small boat out into the stream from shore, she gave her unborn child and the rest of her life a firm push forward into the other woman. Then she blessed both—the gesture and the life. With all of her soul she prayed that that would be enough.

She felt nothing different but when she opened her eyes again and instinctively looked down, Isabelle saw that her stomach was no longer round and full to bursting. No longer was that great joyous size and weight she had been carrying around for so long with her anymore. It was gone.

She stood and said "Come on, we have to hurry."

• • •

If the kids hadn't come when they did, Ettrich would have said yes to Putnam's proposition. He was that close; a few breaths away from agreeing to go into death again. *Anything, so long as we're together again. Just let me be with Isabelle and our baby and I don't give a damn where it is.* Broximon was horrified that that's exactly what he would say, but remained silent because it was not his place to disagree. Broximon only wished that he could get Ettrich alone for a few minutes so they could talk the whole thing over and he could try to reason with him a little.

In the time that they had lived together, Broximon had grown genuinely fond of Ettrich and worried about him constantly. Now here it was—the sum of all his fears. And it looked like he was about to fail again at protecting someone.

Good guy that he was, not for a minute did Brox think about his own welfare or what would happen to him if Vincent decided to go over. He only wanted his friend to think about everything calmly and with as much perspective as he could muster before choosing. He didn't trust anything Putnam had said although it made brilliant sense in its simplicity. Nevertheless he kept running the offer through his mind, looking for loopholes or tricks that would end up making Vincent even more miserable. But even Broximon had to reluctantly admit that Putnam's offer was so straightforward and shrewd that there probably was no need for hidden tricks. If Vincent wanted to rejoin his family he only had to voluntarily give up life and he would meet them in death where they were no threat to Chaos.

Intently watching Vincent, Putnam looked for any sign of a decision one way or the other. For his part, Broximon stared daggers at Putnam while trying to think up a plan, an idea, anything at all to stop his new friend from melting down into a yes. Ettrich still stared at his hands and thought I have to do this. I'm going to do this. Yes, I'm going to say yes.

Preoccupied, none of them really noticed the kids slowly moving toward them from every direction in the park. There were six boys approaching, but a much larger bunch stood back and watched. Every one of them—boys and girls, seven-year-olds up until nineteen—were grinning and waiting for the big moment that could come at any time now. Until a short while ago, their day in the park had been the same old–same old hanging around on a summer's day tedium. But then out of the blue this crazy thing had been dropped in their laps by a pretty pregnant stranger and now every one of them was lit up like sparklers.

After much arguing, the leaders of the group had carefully worked out who would do what. The two strongest boys were up front, followed by a second line of three others. Ten feet back the fastest runner in the group, a Turkish kid with the appropriate name Bulut, waited. There was nothing really for the girls to do but naturally all of the boys wanted them to witness everything that was about to happen. So the girls hung back, watching expectantly with wide eyes, chewed nails, and frayed nerves.

When the lead boys had closed to within a few feet of Putnam's picnic table, they looked for the signal. The leader, standing nearby, gave it. The two strongest raced over to the table, grabbed Broximon beneath the armpits, jerked him roughly out of the Babby Basket on Vincent's back and ran off with him. Bulut jumped from foot to foot like an adrenaline-cranked relay-race runner, waiting impatiently for the baton to arrive and be passed to him.

The whole time this was going on, Broximon was shouting "Lemme go. Lemme down. It's not funny! Let go!"

The boys ran with him dangling between them as if in some kind of strange three-legged race. On reaching Bulut, they handed Brox over. The bullet kid sped off across the park with the little man under his arm like they were both on fire.

It happened so quickly and unexpectedly that Putnam and Ettrich weren't even to their feet until Broximon had been passed to Bulut and they were racing away.

"Did you do this? What are you doing? Why?" Ettrich demanded of the old man.

For his part, Putnam was outraged. He was so livid that he couldn't even speak to defend himself. Moments before the snatch, he had recognized the look on Ettrich's face and knew that the man was going to cave in. Triumph was about to be his and then Putnam would truly be King of the Park having used only reason and cool. Why would he screw it up by pulling such a ridiculous useless prank? For some seconds after it happened he even thought Ettrich had done it to give himself more time. But how? How could he have pulled it off? They'd been together since entering the park. On the way in they had passed these kids but Ettrich didn't stop or even want him to sic the crows on them when they made fun of Broximon. Putnam was so mad and flustered by this nutty, totally unexpected turn of events that it never once crossed his mind that Isabelle might have caused it. Yes, he had seen her walk away minutes before, but she was safely doomed to remain where she was and consequently no matter for concern. It did not dawn on him that with whatever knowledge and power she'd gained as a living person who'd experienced both life and death, Isabelle might be a formidable opponent.

Ettrich took off running across the park after Broximon. The man was fast; he could move. Putnam could only stand still and watch, sizzling inside. Kids everywhere around them were hooting and hollering at what had just happened; they were calling out to each other, slapping five and dancing victory jigs. It was the craziest greatest thing to happen to them in a long time. A pregnant woman appearing out of nowhere and offering them one hundred euros to grab the little guy and run away with him? *Wahnsinn!* It was bliss. They would talk about it for years.

Way on the other side of the park, near the entrance they'd used before, Bulut slowed, stopped, and gently put Broximon down.

"Are you fuckin' *crazy*?" Brox asked in English.

The runner smiled at him, but was too out of breath to respond. A chubby teenage girl with big breasts held prisoner in a too tight T-shirt stepped forward and spoke to him in good but heavily accented English. "Isa-belle says you are to tell Vincent to say no. Do not go with Put-nam. She is here and she will come to you now." The girl didn't understand what she was saying but this was the message the woman had given her and she was determined to say it right.

Amazed, Broximon swallowed his fury at what had happened and asked her to repeat what she'd said. The girl did it slowly, proud of her English, carefully enunciating each word. Then she told him the other things the pregnant woman had told her to say. The girl knew the entire message was important. It had to be, because this woman had paid her boyfriend one hundred euros to kidnap the midget and once they were out of sight of the others, to tell him exactly this.

When she was finished Broximon took off back toward the picnic table. He was terrified he'd get there too late and Vincent would already be gone. But his gait was so slow and comical that when Bulut saw it, he bent over, half laughing hysterically. The girl smirked, adjusted one bra strap, and waited for her boyfriend to return from the mission.

Ettrich ended up almost trampling Broximon while running to save him. The truth was that he didn't see Brox because he was in such a panic to catch up. At the last moment he did see and was able to put on the brakes. Bending down, he scooped the little man up in one arm like a football. Both of them were breathless but Broximon started speaking the moment he was level with Ettrich's ear. He spoke as fast as he could while being carried upright back across the park, his arms wrapped tightly around Vincent's neck. He spoke until right before Ettrich sat down again at the table and stationed Brox on his lap as if he were a ventriloquist's doll.

Putnam had seen them coming and was already seated and waiting when they arrived. In a jovial voice he boomed out "Well, *that* was exciting. But what was it all about? Who were those kids?"

Vincent ignored the question. "I'm not going to go, Mr. Putnam. I'm staying here."

Instead of responding, Putnam put his chin in his hand and stared at Vincent awhile in silence.

Ettrich continued. "Isabelle will have to find a way to survive over there, like I will here. But I'm not going back. Not yet. Not till it's the right time."

"And what about Anjo, *Dad*?" The old man's voice was all acid and taunt.

Vincent didn't reply. He knew it was essential to do this carefully and with conviction.

"Aren't you at least a little concerned about the welfare of your son?"

"Yes, I'm very concerned, but Isabelle will have to handle it. And she will too. She's strong."

"So let me be sure I understand this, Vincent. You're going to abandon your great love and unborn child to an existence in some unthinkable netherworld just because you *believe* you should stay here?"

Vincent rubbed his mouth and said the truth. "Yes, stay here and fight you. I think that's exactly what she would want me to do. And even if not, that's what I am going to do."

"Should we call her back over here and ask if that's really what she wants you to do?"

Ettrich said "There's no need to call her. She's standing right behind you."

Putnam whipped around. Five feet away Isabelle was looking at him blankly, hands stuffed in her pockets. She wore different clothes from those she had on half an hour before. That more than anything was the tip-off as to what Ettrich had done. For a few seconds Putnam almost felt sorry for this chump and his pathetic ruse. But then the feeling passed of course. This was the same man who had so cleverly liquidated John Flannery? It was hard to believe.

Putnam sighed and turned back to face the fool. "Dignity, Vincent. I believe that is really the only admirable quality humans possess." He pointed a thumb over his shoulder at Isabelle who had not moved. "This is not dignified. Creating a false dream-girl Isabelle to fulfill your needs and assuage your guilt is not dignified. Shame on you, sir."

"Touch her if you think she's false."

Putnam shrugged dismissively. "Vincent, you're talking to me, remember? I know about these things. I don't need to touch her. I'm sure her flesh and bones are very convincing. Bravo—it's nice to see you using a few of the tricks you learned when you were dead.

"But that's not the point. She's *fake,* Vincent. You know it and I know it. She's a fabrication. The real Isabelle, the one you supposedly love so much, is waiting for you with your child on the other side of death. And *that* Isabelle you can't see. But your way of avoiding your responsibility to them is to create this . . . this blow-up fuck doll to take her place. You should be ashamed of yourself."

"I'm not going." Ettrich's voice was strong and resolute.

"You're just going to let her rot over there? Her and Anjo? You're really going to abandon them?"

Ettrich took a deep breath and let it all the way out before answering. "I'm not going over there."

Putnam looked at his watch because he couldn't think of anything else to do. There was nothing more he could say. Vincent Ettrich was not going to do it. Checkmate. He had defeated them. He had done something they had never expected: he was abandoning the love of his life and their child so that he could stay here and fight.

He stood up, looked at Vincent with that little creature Broximon sitting on his lap like some kind of odd pet. Putnam tried to snort and chuckle at the same time to show his derision. But it didn't come out right and only sounded like an old rheumy man clearing his throat. He strode out of the park without once looking back.

Only when he was gone from her sight did Isabelle walk the few steps over to their table.

Ettrich looked at her and had to ask "Is it really you? How did you come back here? How did you do it?"

It was a peculiar question coming from him but she answered it honestly. "I was never away, sweetheart. I've just been sitting in the park for a while."

• • • • • •

The real Isabelle, her dead friend Leni Salomon, and false Broximon watched the others talk and smile and touch before slowly making their way out of the park too, only via a different exit from the one Putnam had used. Broximon was sitting in the Babby Basket again. The expression on his face was relaxed and almost happy.

False Broximon watched them leave and then said to himself as much as to the two women nearby "I wish I had been able to talk to him. I would love to have asked a few questions."

Naturally they knew who he was talking about but didn't have any reply for that.

Leni took her friend's hand and held it tightly. "You just broke one of the biggest rules of all, Isabelle. So big that even Chaos couldn't see what you did because it's such a no-no. I don't know what's going to happen to them now. And I wonder if Vincent will ever realize that she's not really you. I hope your camouflage works."

"What's *really me,* Leni? I would rather the best of me be with him now rather than the worst. Anyway, the baby is real and that's all that matters." To Isabelle's surprise, a sob that had been hiding in her chest all this time leapt out and she had to fight hard to overcome it. When she was sure she had it under control, she said to Leni "I don't know what will happen either, but there was no alternative. I did the only thing I could."

Leni nodded and squeezed her hand. Unconsciously her eyes strayed to Isabelle's now-flat stomach. Leni could not imagine the pain her friend must be going through. She could not imagine what the magnitude of her loss must feel like.

"I want to go back now, Leni. I don't want to stay here any longer. Let's go back and try to find Simon. What do you think?"

Unexpectedly, one of the proverbs John Flannery had been so fond of spouting came to Leni's mind: whenever you take a mouthful of too-hot soup, the next thing you do will be wrong. She did *not* want to go back into death to try and find Simon Haden. But neither did she want to stay here and be reminded of all the things she had loved in life but were now beyond her grasp forever.

Hopefully some time in the future she would be permitted to return to her own afterlife dreamworld and work her way through it up to the next level. But what mattered most now was Isabelle. She had just done a remarkably selfless, brilliant thing. Leni knew she herself would never have been capable of doing it, dead or alive. For the first time she thought perhaps part of her afterlife experience was to accompany Isabelle Neukor here and learn from her. It was possible. Anything seemed possible here.

"I'll bet Simon would be overjoyed if we turned up on his doorstep again. Let's go find him."

The two women and the small man started walking. Leni said to Isabelle "You know what I was just thinking? That you and I had the same job. Only I had it in life and you had it in death."

Isabelle looked at her dubiously. "You made false teeth, Leni."

"And what do you think you just did for Vincent, hmm?"

It took time for Isabelle to understand the analogy, but when she got it she laughed and laughed.

Epilogue

Isabelle put the dish of still-steaming scrambled eggs and ham on the table. She scuffed back to the kitchen in her fuzzy red bedroom slippers followed closely by Hietzl the dog. It was an eternal optimist, forever thinking that there might be something for it in every one of their meals. She reemerged with a pot of green tea and a pitcher full of grapefruit juice. As she put them down on the table she called out "Breakfast is ready."

Hietzl bolted out of the room as usual when a meal was announced. It ran to the back of the long apartment to the bedroom where the television lived. Isabelle refused to allow it in the living room. The dog stood in the doorway waiting, its tail swishing frantically from side to side on the parquet floor. Hietzl loved family meals. It loved everyone sitting together at the table talking, laughing, the sound of voices, the sound of dishes, and the smell of food. At any moment someone might sneak Hietzl a little something to eat. And usually someone did.

"I *told* you not to go into that cave. Of course you were eaten."

"*What?* You told me elves were in that cave. Why else do you think I went in there? Unlike you, I know what I'm doing when I play that game."

Broximon came out of the TV room first, waving an arm in the air in protest. He was wearing a new gray sweat suit and bright white socks. Vincent followed holding the baby to his chest with one arm. The child had a wide face and large ears. Broximon secretly worried they might be too large and that when he grew older other kids would razz him about them. Anjo appeared to be following their argument but in truth he just liked the different loudnesses between the big man and the small one. Anjo also liked very much the bleeps and bloops of the video games they sometimes played together. That had become evident early on so now he always sat on his father's lap or in the Babby Basket next to Broximon on the couch whenever the two played.

Walking down the hall to the living room now, they accused each other of numerous incidents of lying, cheating, or just plain dumbness. But it was done quickly because all game talk had to stop when they got to the table. If for any reason they forgot and happened to continue, Isabelle gave them her Medusa look and neither wanted to see that one aimed their way.

So the parade entering the room that morning was led as usual by Hietzl, then came a glowering Broximon, followed by Vincent and Anjo.

Sitting at her place at the table, Isabelle looked up at them and nothing else was in her mind then but There they are—my men.